DEAD BITCH ARMY

Andre Duza

DEADITE PRESS
Tempe, Arizona

DEADITE PRESS

AN ERASERHEAD PRESS COMPANY
WWW.ERASERHEADPRESS.COM

Deadite Press
5929 S. Juniper St.
Tempe, AZ 85283

ISBN: 0-9762498-1-2

Thanks to:
Jerry Hickman,
Bob Harris, Mom, Nina, Babz,
Kristin Kennedy

Special thanks to:
Carlton Mellick III, Ed Carlson,
Darin Basile, Robert Shin MD,
Chris Perez, Tony Kern,
John Paul Allen, Geoff Baker
John Dunivant, Silverfish,
Bill Balzer, Rich Larson,
and James Ryman

In memory of:
Ishmeal Tony Miles
1969-1999

For Brenda....

I got a friend named Mary Jane and she makes me feel strange.

So I gotta call out her name....

I love you, Mary Jane....

Cypress Hill

Prologue

2004, Postwar Washington, DC

They were calling themselves the Revenant Clan now. They were free agents with a following large enough to qualify them as serious contenders to the new, toxic frontier and led by a queen with a point to prove to the Church that raised her as one of their own, then abandoned her.

The Ergeister Church had publically denounced what Bloody Mary and her army had been doing in the name of their religion and officially severed all ties with them earlier in the year. They felt that Mary had become mad with power and that she had forgotten the tenets of the religion that she and her army were supposed to represent. That was what they told the public. Most suspected that there were deeper reasons.

"The Queen... is she really... dead?" Brian's wide-eyed curiosity reminded Linda Ludlow of the way things were before the war.

Linda fumbled with her gas mask to stall for time. She excused herself from the discussion, sat down, took a deep breath, and sorted through the pile of papers on her desk in the front of the classroom. She couldn't stand to look any of the children in the eyes, especially Brian. She could see his eyes clearly through the semi-fogged visor of his gas mask. When she was brave enough to let her gaze travel around the crowded room, Linda saw twenty-six pairs of eyes looking out from behind a gas mask, locked on her.

Ethan Downing was the only exception. His father led a team who tried to infiltrate the Clan last week. Word came down from Queen Mary herself that they were to make an example of Ethan.

Principal Foster was happy to oblige. He was hoping that the Queen would reward him with a position in her Cabinet. The Revenant Clan was always looking for new recruits, as their turnover rate was prolific. Mary was a hard woman to please.

Principal Foster was flanked by two soldiers when he came into the classroom, snatched Ethan's gas mask off his face, and isolated him in the far corner of the classroom. He made Ethan sit right next to the window. He then opened it, exposing Ethan to the noxious fumes outside.

Reports were flooding the fledging airwaves, warning that botulinum toxin would be heavy in the air all week.

Ethan had already begun to cough.

Linda tried especially hard not to look at him... or to listen to the hollow, mechanized breathing of his classmates. It was bad enough that she could never escape the sound of her own breath behind the mask. That sound had become all too commonplace. The comedians had a field day with it. There were still a few. They performed in the street.

Today, of all days.... It was Linda's last day posing as a substitute teacher to gather information on Principal Foster. The government saw him as a threat.

Even with the disguise (a deep auburn wig, false teeth, and a dubious British accent), Linda worried that her hook-hand prosthesis would blow her cover. Not only was she infamous for her link to Tasha Armstrong, but she was also the founder of the New Philadelphia News Organization (NPNO), and a well-known enemy of the Clan. One thing in her favor was that people were having limbs amputated all the time to stop the spread of disease. Some were even performing the crude surgery themselves.

The war wiped out 60 percent of the planet's population. The suicide rate peaked in its aftermath. It was higher than it had ever been before the war.

Linda glanced peripherally at the huddled body that lay outside on the playground. It was Ronald Bedford, the history teacher. Principal Foster had him shot for threatening to do everything in his power to bring down the principal's operation. The children all watched from their windows when it happened. The principal called it a lesson.

ANDRE DUZA

Linda was too jaded to allow herself a heart to mourn. She had seen too much.

She pictured herself in Ronald Bedford's place. They'd do the same thing to her (or worse) if they figured out who she was.

Linda's eyes floated to the back wall of the classroom. Someone had vandalized the school over the weekend. They made their allegiance known in bright red paint. It was all over the place: **Death to the Dead Bitch Army!** Dead Bitch Army was what the Revenant Clan's enemies called them behind their backs.

Linda knew she had to say something before Brian asked her again. She continued to stall and hold out hope that some clever diversion would materialize in her mind. When nothing came to her, she became frustrated by the pressure. She felt like her standards were being compromised, which begin to ignite her sense of rebellion.

Just tell them the truth, Linda's inner voice told her. *It's your last day. By the time Principal Foster finds out what you've told these children, you'll be long gone.*

Brian opened his mouth to follow up on his question.

Linda interrupted him by clearing her throat. She stood and looked around the room.

"Okay, Brian. I'm going to answer your question with a story," she said.

"About the Queen?" Brian queried.

"That's right, Brian. But this story is a little different from the one that you've been taught in school, so I want you all to listen very carefully and save any questions that you might have until the end. Deal?"

"Deal." The class responded in unison.

Linda smiled and wet her tongue. She took a deep breath and began.

"Once upon a time…"

Chapter 1

There's Something About... Jane Doe
1969, Pennsylvania

"What did the little bitch do this time?" asked the helmet-haired, older woman with the take-no-prisoners type of face. The nametag on the breast pocket of her librarian cardigan read "Mrs. Ayres."

The youngish woman with the pretty name (Priya according to the name on her breast) only pretended to be startled away from her novel (The Thorn Birds) as she sat behind the desk in the cramped third-floor office. In fact, she had been picturing Mrs. Ayres' stiff, bobble-headed gait since the security doors at the bottom of the stairs banged shut and the intense click-clack of hard-soled shoes grew out of the residual echo. She knew that they could only belong to one person, the last person that she (or most of the other employees of the Lake Shore Foster Home) ever wanted to see. They nicknamed Mrs. Ayres, "Her Majestehhh," pronounced through the nose with a stuffy British accent.

Priya was a houseparent/nurse. Her shift began at 10:00 pm, after "lights out," when the place was "like a mausoleum," she would say. It was an old building, converted from a three-story house perched crookedly on an eight-acre plot. An addition built onto the right side of the building gave it a stately appearance. An outmoded playground covered with hard, unforgiving surfaces, sharp edges, and metal that conducted heat like a motherfucker in the summertime teased the younger children whose rooms looked down on it from on high. The play area was the top of the line... in 1962.

The old, wooden skeleton of the building screamed through the refined outer shell, but only at night, it seemed, when Priya was trying to concentrate on something else. The shifting wood chirped and bellowed, as if the place were conscious of its condition. Most of the time it was nothing—just an old building settling. Every once and a while, the other staff members would sneak up to the third floor and play tricks on Priya. She'd always hear them coming, but she'd end up replaying the settling old house anecdote and would attempt to block it out. Each time she'd scream, and they'd have a good laugh.

Including Priya, the third-shift staff consisted of two more houseparents—one male and one female. According to the schedule, it was Marion's turn to take the first dorm-watch, but he had already tucked the children in and disappeared downstairs by the time Priya arrived at 10:25. In return for keeping quite about her tardiness, Marion left Priya to languish in the third-floor office until someone relieved her at 3:00 am. In the meantime, Marion and the other houseparent were downstairs kicking back in front of the only television in the building.

Priya didn't expect Mrs. Ayres to drop what she was doing and drive the 22 miles from her home just because one of the children threw a tantrum. When it happened (about two hours ago), there were plenty of people on duty who were qualified to handle it. *Lonely old crow*, she thought to herself.

"She's sleeping now," Priya said to Mrs. Ayres. I gave her a sedative. We had a time trying to subdue her."

Mrs. Ayres looked away and seemed to ponder a grave decision.

"She needs help," Priya added. "I think it'd be wise to phone Dr. Wheeler in the morning."

"For a tantrum?" Mrs. Ayres spoke in a belittling manner. "Are you serious?"

"Sure, the guy was a criminal, but all that little girl in there knows is that we took someone she cares about away from her."

"We? I'm the one who fired him."

"She blames all of us, Mrs. Ayres. Not just you."

"Well, what do you propose I do? Give that child molester his job back just to keep her happy?"

Priya twisted her mouth.

"That wasn't necessary," she said. "And we don't know for

sure that he tried to molest her."

"The man was sitting on her bed, telling her stories about his church," Mrs. Ayres responded. "You tell me where in the groundskeeper handbook it suggests that such behavior is part of the job description."

"I understaaaaand. But like it or not, she bonded with him. She's been hurtin' since her best friend was adopted by the Armstrongs. You know that. We have to address those issues if we're going make any kind of progress with her. Otherwise, I think she's going to hurt somebody."

Mrs. Ayres simmered. She let her thumb slide across the tips of her short fingernails. It was Her Majestehhh's signature mannerism. She grabbed a large ring of keys from a hook on the wall, walked up to the door, and opened it.

"I know that you think you're going to save the world, but I've been doing this for 35 years, and I'm telling you that we can handle one six-year-old girl on our own. I'm not about to waste any more of the foundation's money on this child. Now, I don't want to hear any more about calling Dr. Wheeler. Is that understood?"

Priya looked at Mrs. Ayres in disbelief, offended by her patronizing tone. The young houseparent wasn't one to rock the boat or battle authority, so she resigned herself to Her Majestehhh's decision and looked away through narrowing eyelids.

"I understand."

Mrs. Ayres stopped before she reached the door to Room 19 and put on her game face. Jane Doe had a way about her that put people on the defensive. She spoke mostly with her eyes, which seemed to communicate with a wisdom that defied her precocious age.

"Those eyes! Looks like she's been through it," Marion commented when he first saw her.

Jane had been a ward of the foster home since the Lake Shore Foundation took guardianship of her when she was only six weeks old. The infant, wrapped in blankets and lacking identification, was left at the door of the Emergency Room; hence they named her Jane Doe. Her eyes seemed aware of the fact that she was all alone in the world, staring with indifference through the rounded opening of the swaddling fabric. Some of the nurses thought that the reason that Jane had not been adopted by the couples who had come shopping for babies was because of the lack of spark in those indifferent eyes because, aesthetically speaking, Jane fit the popular profile (healthy white baby) to a T.

As the years passed, the staff repeatedly attempted to help her develop some kind of personality—the "cute factor," they called it—to make her more appealing to parents looking to adopt a child. For a while, they treated her like a queen. The other children would make trouble as a result of their jealousy. It was during that period that Marion Forte took a special interest in Jane. She didn't understand why, but the attention made her feel uncomfortable. She could feel eyes on her whenever he was in the vicinity. She'd turn and catch him leering.

Aside from her dolls, Jane didn't have many friends. The few she'd made kept getting snatched up by desperate, fragile couples. Each time this happened, Jane retreated further into herself. There was one girl with whom she formed a special bond. She had been there almost as long as Jane until she, too, was finally adopted a few months ago. The girls called each other "blood sisters," a variation on what one of the older boys called his best friend: his "blood brother." The boy told them that to become blood brothers (or, as they thought of it, blood sisters), all it took was pricking a finger, drawing a few drops of blood, mixing them in a cup filled with water, and drinking the solution. There was an oath that went along with it too, the boy said, but he and his friend didn't know the words, so they just made something up.

Jane and her blood sister developed a bond that they both swore would be eternal: nothing or no one would ever come between them. The blood sisters were everything to each other, and other people didn't even factor in. The only exception was Joshua. Joshua Raye was the groundskeeper. He would tell Jane stories about his church and his experiences in Vietnam. He thought she looked like a "Mary Jane," so that's what he called her. "The name suits you," he told her. He said that he was really a priest and that he only took the job at Lake Shore to get closer to her after seeing her playing on the swings one day when he drove by.

Eventually, Mrs. Ayres decided that the friendship between the girls and Joshua was inappropriate. When Joshua didn't heed her warning to stay away from her, she had him fired.

That was when Jane's nightmares began. They always seemed to come when Marion Forte was working. He liked to come around and give the girls treats before bed. The treats varied depending on the age of the girls. In Jane's case, it was always something sweet to snack on: a donut or a Tastykake. He'd make them all promise not to tell: "Or else I'll get in trouble," he'd tell them. That was always the last thing Jane would remember before waking up so sore that she couldn't walk. She never remembered the actual nightmare, only a distinct feeling of suffocating and being pressed down into her bed. Sometimes she would wake up with the waistband of her underwear rolled and twisted. And then there was the blood that she would find in her underwear. It frightened her. She knew that grown women sometimes had blood "down there," but she didn't think it was right that this was happening to her at her age. None of the other girls had blood as far as she knew. But she thought that if she asked one of the houseparents about it, she'd get in trouble, so Jane would sneak off to the bathroom, still sore, and frantically try to wash the undergarments before anyone found out.

Mrs. Ayres was relieved to find Jane sleeping when she looked through the small, square window in the door to Room 19. She was ready to be all hard-ass, but instead, she looked upon Jane with pity, her eyes straining to cut through the darkness. She knew enough about child psychology to empathize with all the children in her care, but she refused to show any emotion. The hardline approach was her way of protecting herself from feeling vulnerable. Sometimes it worked against her, like when those allegations of racism were leveled against her and the staff at Lake Shore by a former employee.

Jane looked so peaceful lying on her side, knees bent, legs curled halfway. The wall beside her bed was covered with photographs of random families ripped from magazines. A framed photograph of Jane and her blood sister lay facedown on the windowsill above her head.

As she stood there, eyes adjusting to the darkness, Mrs. Ayres pondered the appropriate (and relatively inexpensive) plan of action for such a troubled soul. She was about to walk away when she caught… something: the glint of moisture from the overhead light in the hall shining through the small square window into Jane's room. She looked closer and saw that Jane wasn't sleeping at all. She was looking right at her with… those eyes. She could see that Jane was mouthing something to her as well.

"I H-A-T-E Y-O-U!"

*   *   *

As Jane came to consciousness, she felt a lovely sensation. It came in short, quick intervals, each one more thunderous than the last. There was lightheaded bewilderment and a twinge of a headache between each pleasurable surge. Her eyes fluttered open and saw demonic eyes looking back at her. The mouth and nose of the creature were buried between her legs. Its facial features were obscured by a ski mask. The eyes squinted when it noticed her horrified stare. It raised its head and watched her closely as if it didn't expect to see her awake. She might have blacked out for a moment from the shock.

Jane gasped awake. The pain was incredible.

"Shhhhhhh…," a hushed voice said, its breath leaping out in weird patterns. "Just go back to sleep. This is all just a wonderful dream."

Jane pretended to comply. She thought it best to play along until the demon was through with her.

The demon's darkened shape (like that of a beefy human male) climbed up from her legs and loomed over her. It was easily three or four times her size. It braced itself on one thick arm, its hand balled into a fist, pushing down into the soft mattress next to her head. Its other hand explored her squirming body, snaking along the quivering flesh beneath her hiked-up nightgown. Coarse fingertips circled her nipples and pinched and pulled. When the pain between her legs forced weird sounds from her larynx, it clamped its hand over her mouth and pressed down so hard that her teeth lacerated the inside of her lips. Jane thought this was the end, that the demon was going to kill her.

Jane assumed from the smoky breath that bathed her face that the demon breathed fire. She concluded that it must have been sent by God to punish her for all the trouble she had caused over the years. Lately, they had been learning about sin in their Bible-study meetings.

With each thrust, Jane felt as if she might burst. The long, fat snake-appendage reached up into her stomach and set fire to every-thing in its path. Friction had rubbed her raw and numb, but she could still feel her insides rupturing. She could hear her flesh ripping. She kept her eyes closed to keep from seeing anything that might sear the experience into her visual memory. The pain was reason enough. It was the worse she'd ever experienced. Radiating to all her recep-tors, it caused her body to scream, speaking through her legs, which kicked straight, and through her fingers, which clawed the sheets.

The demon lowered its body against Jane's. It had a warmth to it and a musty smell that she associated with old men. "Maybe it's the kind of soap they use," Jane thought, delirious from the agony.

A sweaty sheen caused its body to slide with each thrust. Its awkward rhythm indicated some kind of established routine as it changed from slow to fast, to incredibly fast, and back to slow at a moment's notice. Jane wondered if this was how babies were made, but instead of love and tenderness, all she could feel was sorrow, anger, and hatred.

"Such a goooood girl…" the demon panted into her ear, hot moisture dripping from each word.

Jane recognized the pattern of its sandpaper jawline when

their faces touched. That and the carefully trimmed beard made her think of Marion. She had read that a demon could take the form or shape of a person. Or maybe it wasn't a demon at all.

The demon lifted its torso off Jane. A breeze seeped in through the crooked gap between the old window and the sill, leveling on her sweat-covered form, and she felt cold instantly.

Jane's head was turned to the side, facing left. She waited for the demon's rhythm to slow down, then allowed her eyelids to part ever so slightly, eyeballs rolling right. She didn't know what she would see.

The demon didn't seem pleased to see her watching. Its eyelids shot open. There were only whites inside. It opened its mouth and let out an unintelligible sound—umph!—followed by a disoriented moan. Its head jerked forward as if to threaten her. A downward curving horn protruded from its forehead right between its eyes. Suddenly, a splash of liquid coated Jane's face. Some of it went in her nostrils and her mouth. She coughed. It smelled and tasted like blood.

The demon's torso slumped forward, arms falling limp. For a moment it looked like it hovered over Jane without support from its arms or legs.

The demon lurched and fell to the side. Blood speckled the wall. The snake-appendage silpped out of her with a pop, tweaking the pain to new limits. Through her daze, she noticed that there was another shape standing behind the demon. The second shape's arms were holding a long stick that had connected with the back of the demon's head. The demon hit the floor and did a rhythmless squirm-dance on its side. The second shape gave the demon a few swift kicks to the stomach and groin that provoked a series of flatulent noises.

"Oh, Mary… I'm so sorry, darlin'," the second shape said with a voice overwhelmed with grief. "I shoulda never left you."

Jane recognized the voice right away. It was Joshua.

Joshua grabbed a robe that hung from her closet door and sat down next to her on the bed. Sobbing, she sat up to meet him. He draped the robe over her shoulders, and they embraced.

"Don't worry, Mary. I'm gonna get you outta here."

Jane never said a word. She went limp in Joshua's arms. He scooped her up, stood, and carried her out the door.

One her way out, Jane looked down at the body on the floor. The light from the hall exposed its true identity. It was Marion Forte. He lay motionless with his pants down and a gardening tool planted in the back of his head, its pointed end sticking out the front.

The following is an excerpt from the novel
Bloody Mary by Linda Ludlow:

THE LEGEND OF MARY JANE

Since 1987, southeastern Pennsylvania has been plagued by a string
of grisly murders, each linked by the sighting of an ominous figure that
has since become an urban legend. The popular myth revolves around
the disappearance, in October 1987, of Mary Jane Mezerak, estranged wife of Philadelphia Rebels running back Carl Mezerak.

As with most legends, there are as many variations of the
story as there are people who claim to have actually seen her. Although some believe her to be nothing more than an apparition doomed
to haunt the lonely stretch of Ridley Creek Road where she was last
seen alive, others claim that she is an actual living corpse capable of
inflicting bodily harm.

The first recorded sighting, in November, was by a customer
of Odell's Surplus, who reported seeing a tall, thin woman in a flowing
dress exiting the store carrying a large burlap sack. In the man's own
words, "She looked like she was dead."

The woman ignored him as he pulled his truck into the parking lot, and she disappeared into the woods across the road from the
store. When the man entered the store, he found a body that had
been bludgeoned beyond recognition sprawled across the glass display counter. The gun cabinet had been pulverized. After the dust
had settled, a check of the inventory revealed some missing items: a
high-powered shotgun, a few hunting knives, some rope, and a gas
mask.

Thus began the legend of Bloody Mary.

The next sighting, in June 1988, was reported by a couple
hiking in Ridley Creek State Park. The young couple stumbled across
what appeared to be an abandoned house deep in the woods. Inside,
they found a makeshift bedroom and a kitchen stocked with half-

eaten animal carcasses and the body of a man who was later identified as Gerald York, a local mortician. The walls were covered with crude, indecipherable markings and old newspaper clippings about Carl Mezerak. Out back, they found what they described as an obstacle course rigged with lethal, handmade booby-traps. Terrified by what they found, the couple ran the three miles to their car and drove to the Ridley Township Police Station. The next day, the couple led the police to the old house.

A week later, the couple was returning from their 11-year-old daughter Rainah's dance recital when they were forced off the road by a pickup truck that had been reported stolen. The husband lost control and swerved into a tree just off of Kelly Drive in Philadelphia. When he came to, his wife was dead, and his daughter was gone. The devastated man said that the driver of the truck was a woman who appeared to be wearing a gas mask. To this day, there has been no sign of Rainah. Police speculate that she was thrown from the car and lost in the Schuylkill River. Her body was never found.

The incident gained national exposure and, since that time, the legend has grown into a phenomenon.

Police dismiss the legend as a hoax perpetuated by a woman named Natasha Armstrong. Evidence from the house in Ridley led police to her apartment in West Philadelphia, but Armstrong was nowhere to be found. Police believe that she is responsible for the murders.

Meanwhile, the murders continue....

Bloody Mary

Chapter 2

February 1999

IN THE NEWS TODAY… *In Yugoslavia, peacekeeping efforts continue in the shadow of tensions between NATO and Russian troops. When NATO forces arrived at the airport in Pristina yesterday, they were met by a contingent of Russian soldiers, who had flown in secretly a day earlier, blocking the entrance. Despite the Russians' warning that the road leading into the airport was heavily mined, a flow of retreating Serbian troops traveled the road without incident.*

As reports spread of targeted looting of Serbian homes and churches by returning Ethnic Albanians, a climate of unrest has overtaken Kosovo.

IN OTHER NEWS… *A manhunt is underway for Natasha Armstrong. Authorities from Pittsburgh, Philadelphia, and central Pennsylvania are on the lookout for the alleged serial killer. Armstrong, who first came to the attention of the police in her native West Philadelphia, was last seen in the Pittsburgh area.*

West Philly. So good to see you again, Tasha mused. She could see herself in the faces of the 'tweenaged girls playing hopscotch on a small side street. Further up the block, a group of slightly older girls giggled as they ran along the sidewalk. Tasha guessed that they had just rung the doorbell of the house in the middle of the block–the one with the red door. That was where the girls kept looking back to as they ran. Back in Tasha's day, they called it "Ding Dong Dixie." She would always be the one to ring the doorbell when her friends would chicken out at the last minute.

Tasha drove past a neighborhood corner store that reminded her of Park's Deli. She and her girlfriends would do step routines and play double Dutch in the street in front of Park's. When he was having a bad day, Mr. Park would come out and shoo them away with a broom. There was never any animosity behind it, though. Sometimes he would even crack a smile as he yelled at them. After all, Mr. Park donated a case of spring water to Tasha's neighborhood team the year they came in fourth place at the National Jumprope Tournament. He even cut out the article about them in the *Philadelphia Inquirer* and taped it to the register in his store.

The last memory Tasha had of that place was Mr. Park's wife carrying his dead body out into the street after he'd been shot in the head during a holdup. She was yelling hysterically in Korean and directing her anger and sorrow at everyone in sight, spitting and screaming, as if she blamed the entire community for producing the criminal that killed her husband. That was how Tasha understood her body language, at least.

A few people tried to help her, but Mrs. Park refused to let them touch her husband's body. Tasha remembered seeing smiles on some of the faces that lingered at the back of the crowd. Not everyone liked the Parks. They were hard on the people they viewed as troublemakers. And most of the people Tasha saw smiling or laughing were just that. The collective apathy and lack of empathy scared Tasha more than the blood that drained from Mr. Park's wound, or the way his body occasionally twitched and caused his wife to almost drop him several times.

Fights broke out as people began attacking the few troublemakers who found humor in the tragic event. Within an hour of the shooting, the commotion in front of Park's Deli had developed into a mini-riot.

"Those were the days," Tasha quipped sarcastically as she drove past.

There was a time when West Philly was all she. It might as

well have been its own planet, floating in a galaxy of racially segregated worlds that made up most of Philadelphia.

Tasha felt like an outsider now. In twelve years, this wasn't her first time back, but it was the first time that she understood what the flustered white folks who occasionally happened down her old block in the heart of the summer, when the ghettoblasters were blasting and fire hydrants were firing, must have felt like. Was she so different now that they, this new generation, would soak her too as she passed? Silly as it was, she smiled when they didn't.

Tasha's last time through was three years ago; it had been two years before that. The visits were always short. Back then, she would watch the night fade to day as she lay awake in the back seat of her old Honda Prelude. It seemed a lifetime since she slept in a bed. She knew it was bad when she found herself reminiscing about the motels she had stayed in before the money dried up. She started out with $3500, her entire savings. From time to time, she was able to find an odd job to sustain her for a bit, but ever since the incident in Doylestown, the police and the media had been connecting her with all the murders. Her face was everywhere, broadcast far and wide for a world waiting in judgment. At least the photograph that they were flashing was good, Tasha thought. Her big eyes glowed and mesmerized. Her eyes were probably her best feature, but she always felt that they made her look too weak, too "girlie-pretty." And no one would mistake Tasha for girlie or even pretty if she had her way.

The Doylestown incident was a careless mistake. It happened two years ago. Thinking that she was doing the right thing, she came out of hiding to help an elderly couple that Rainah had shot point blank just moments earlier, when an off-duty cop saw her standing over them.

Tasha's full lips pulled together to form a sardonic grin whenever she thought of her former life. She used to be a single mother with prospects and dreams of going back to school. She had studied psychology but dropped out because she simply couldn't afford it.

Her résumé said she had a bachelor's degree, though, because stretching the truth was the only way she knew how to get a real job.

She eventually landed a gig as a social worker. Although it didn't pay much, it made her feel like she was giving back to the community that raised her after her parents split up and started using her like a weapon to hurt each other. When the fighting turned violent, Tasha left home.

Somehow, sleeping in her car was easier back then, more acceptable. Tasha was young and full of dreams, putting it all on the line to find her way on her own. *I'll do anything,* she would muse, *anything not to end up bitter and complacent like mom.* Her father, to whom she had always been closer, didn't have time for her after the divorce. That hurt Tasha the most.

She blocked out that part of her life and filed the memories away in the back of her mind, right next to the blur that represented those five years she had spent in the hospital as a child. She didn't remember much about her parents anymore. Tasha only knew that she had been a difficult birth, and that she was a very sickly child. Her mother never let her forget that part.

Now, Tasha really meant it when she said, "I'll do *anything* to find my son." Anything came to mean squatting in abandoned buildings elbow to elbow with hardcore addicts, shell-shocked veterans, and runaways. They were her only family now. But she had to be careful. There was always the risk of trespassing on someone's territory. It happened to her more than once. That was how Tasha learned to kill with her bare hands. How easy it was to snap a person's neck! The first time was in Pittsburgh, in 1990. There had been a slew of Bloody Mary sightings in the area. Ninety-nine percent of the time, the sightings ended up being bogus, but Tasha couldn't sleep if she didn't investigate each one.

She awoke in an abandoned building to the sight of a huge brown penis dangling above her—it was ten inches long, at least. Turned out to be some crackhead looking for a piece. He managed to hike her skirt up without waking her. It was the last time she ever wore one. The next few minutes were fuzzy. She remembered being more angry than scared as he bent over to restrain her arms. The next thing she knew, she was straddling him from behind. She grabbed his head in both hands and twisted with all her strength. She was thinking of Bloody Mary when she did it. That night, Tasha fell asleep without fear or incident. She had wondered to herself if taking a life might change her, but she was already jaded by then. What she saw the previous year in Philly took care of that.

That memory was clear as day: a family of four (mother, father, and two small children) closing in on her. Though they were clearly dead, they mumbled and groaned through the garbage bags that melted to a shroud after Mary and her clan bound them, gagged them, and set them ablaze. Their charred remains inched after Tasha as she surveyed the scene, blaming her for what happened to them. Tasha was hot on Mary's trail at the time. She heard the neighbor's call to 911 on the police scanner that she kept in her car.

Tasha had come to learn that Griff was behind hallucinations like that one: vivid, crystal-clear visions that mimicked reality right down to the smell. Occasionally, some little details were off, but they were easy to miss. Especially when the hallucinations caught her off guard, which was almost always the case. She'd wake up naked, someplace crowded like a mall or a church on Sunday morning. Tasha stopped counting the times she wondered whether or not she'd been raped by the strange, often homeless men she'd wake to find herself curled up with. For a while, she lived in constant fear of Griff's mind games. Fear stuck to her every waking moment, like dark skin on an underachiever. But that was then.

Tasha eventually learned to spot Griff's tricks. Their hyper-realistic glow was easy to detect once she knew what to look for. Now she used the hallucinations as an early warning system, her own "spidey sense," she sometimes joked

Griff was Bloody Mary's right-hand man. He was famous for his skill with his hands and feet and infamous for clouding minds and moving large objects with his own. Griff called it "coaxing." That was all Tasha knew about him. She was ashamed to admit that there was a slight *thing* between them, even if it had never gone further than a look that passed between them.

Here she was… back in Philly, where she started. At her current speed (she was doing 40 miles per hour easily in a 25-mph zone), whole blocks passed in a blur by the passenger-side window like frames of celluloid racing from reel to reel. The neighborhoods blurred together and lost their individual identities.

Tasha had seen so much in the past twelve years. "Be careful what you wish for," her grandmother used to say when Tasha told her of her longing to escape West Philly's stranglehold.

Tasha's heavy eyes rolled hesitantly toward the rearview mirror. She flicked the menthol light through the hole in her cracked windshield and smiled. *Fucking Griff!*

The bus that chased her knocked cars, newsstands, and people alike out of the way. Its huge mouth and sharp, metallic teeth snapped shut just inches short of her rear bumper.

This was the second time in a week. And now *they* were chasing *her*. Usually, months would pass without any sign of them, and she'd be left to follow the trail of half-eaten corpses. They seemed to prefer lean twentysomethings, usually women. It was only a guess, but Tasha wondered if men weren't gamier than women, somehow harder to digest … or maybe it was an issue of homophobia with Griff. You know, eating cocks and sacks and all that.

It was just a thought.

When the trail of corpses dried up, she'd follow whispers on the tongues of people who claimed to see a dead woman walking.

As usual, they caught Tasha off guard. She figured it was just another bus until she saw that open mouth gobble up two elderly women crossing the street and then spit their remains some twenty feet in front of her. She had no choice but to run them over. She told herself that they were long dead by then. She tried to ignore the fact that they were still moving, that what was left of their mangled bodies motioned for her to stop.

BAM!

The bus rear-ended Tasha's car. The force thrust her forward, then back into the cracked vinyl cushion. She quickly regained control of the vehicle. Her swollen eyes checked the rearview mirror just as the jagged mouth of the bus took another bite, then another. Now that the bus was right up on her, Tasha could see that Mary was driving. She could tell by the way Mary's stiff body moved (like stop-motion) as she leaned back into the seat and hid her face behind the semi-walled booth in the driver's seat. Griff sat a few seats back. Tsun and Rainah took up the rear. They were leaning out the windows and taking shots at Tasha whenever she swayed into view.

Tasha could see that Griff was staring at her through his dreads. They sprouted from his head like thick, woven serpents and hung past his shoulders.

He flashed a sideways smile when their eyes met. Just then, the teeth snapped shut.

Twisted muthafucka! Tasha mouthed as she pressed her foot to the floor. She was planning to slalom the maze of stanchions that supported the elevated subway line to lose them. If she remembered correctly, they were under construction. *They always are,* she thought. *There's no way in hell that bus can follow me through.* She thought of the innocent people who would surely get caught up in the mix. It never failed. This *was* West Philly. So many of them would be dead in a year or two anyway.

Tasha spotted Mary in the rearview.

Bitch!

Mary stomped on the gas and rammed Tasha's car again. The impact sent the car tumbling out of control. Tasha closed her eyes and readily accepted that this was most likely the end of her life. She had reached this point many times in the last decade or so.

Each violent tumble seared itself into Tasha's memory. The windshield, like a cracked and dysfunctional television, flipped through the channels at top speed. Altogether, she tumbled seven times by her count.

"Whoa! Didju see that?" Tsun yelled with juvenile glee.

"Saw it," Rainah replied. "Kagen's gonna be upset that he missed that one."

"No doubt," Tsun chuckled.

"Sorry to spoil your fun," Griff said in his trademark, laid-back cadence. He was calm, cool, and deadly serious. Next to Mary, he was a bundle of joy. "But you might want to hold onto something. This is gonna be a big one."

All eyes shot to the front of the bus where Mary fought for control of the steering wheel. It was obvious that they were going to hit one of the El stanchions.

The bus folded and wrapped around the El stanchion just behind the driver's booth. The rear end swung around and into a second stanchion, jarring it from its mooring. The first crash sent them all to the floor. The second flung them up in the air. Rainah would've gone out the window if Griff hadn't coaxed them all frozen in midair as the bus warped and twisted around them.

The rusted stanchion shook the ground when it tumbled. It brought part of the track at the mouth of the subway tunnel down with it. The tunnel was set twenty-five feet above the street like a giant worm wrapped in concrete and decorated with graffiti tags. A ghostly horn echoed out from the darkness, then the piercing shriek of brakes biting down. But it was too late.

The train tumbled toward the street in a downward arc as it exited the tunnel. The cars buckled as they fell before toppling into a shifting, crumpled pile.

Tasha winced at the thunderous sound and squeezed her eyes shut at the flecks of debris that flew at her in the warm gust. The shockwaves caused her overturned car to bounce. Tasha was still belted in. She cried out when the car landed and again as the seatbelts tugged her sore body.

Nothing seemed to be broken except maybe her spirit. That and yet another stolen car.

Tasha looked up at the floor and thanked God. Frankly, it

was the first thing that came to mind. It didn't matter that she had her doubts about religion. She was lucky to be alive, and she knew it.

When the smoke cleared, Tasha heard wailing in the distance. The again, this *was* West Philly. She struggled for another inch and peeked out of the car window, which was now only about five or six inches high.

A pair of thin legs stepped drunkenly into view. Tsun squatted about twenty feet away and leaned his head down to get a look at her.

As the seconds marched on, it seemed more and more likely that Tasha would be there for a while. A few survivors from the train wreck banged and stomped on the windows to get out; inside, the lights flickered on and off. The effect was like a damned nightclub.

Tsun turned and glanced at the wreckage behind him, then crossed his legs and turned back to Tasha. When she finally locked eyes with him, he gave her a wave and a smile that made Tasha's blood pressure begin to climb.

She balled her fists as she considered what she might do to him. For a moment, Tasha let herself go. Surprisingly, it felt good to scream and flail, so she continued. She punctuated her feelings with a soothing expletive here and there.

A loud whistle interrupted Tasha's meltdown. When she looked back at Tsun, she saw a second set of legs behind him. Tsun's arrogant smirk disappeared as the second man slapped his head forward.

"Get off your ass!" Griff scolded. "We got *thinnngsss* to do."

Tasha immediately recognized the voice. Griff's tone (easygoing yet malevolent) was unmistakable.

Tasha did not hear a third set of footsteps that circled to the rear of her overturned car.

"Mary!" Griff yelled.

Tasha couldn't see her yet, but she knew that Mary was close. The pungent stench of rot and the sound of flies swarming gave her away.

Tasha tugged ferociously at the latch of her seat belt.

"You bitch," she roared at the filthy black skirt that flowed into her sights right outside the driver's side window. It caressed the ground and hid Mary's rotten legs and her old, thick-soled shoes. Tasha still remembered how they tasted. About a year ago, Mary used them to stomp her to sleep.

Frustration brought Tasha to tears. Claustrophobia crept up on her.

"What's the matter? You can't face me like a real woman?" she yelled.

Tasha paused and pounded her fist through what was left of the shattered windshield.

A slight wind lifted Mary's skirt to the left for a moment. It was her only response.

Tasha remembered the shotgun she found at Joe's. It was hidden under the driver's seat. In the time it took to realize that the floor was no longer below her, she noticed a shuffle in Mary's stance, as if she braced herself to catch something heavy.

Tasha closed her eyes and groaned at the thought of Mary's sawed-off shotgun (her favorite weapon) and how it could reshape her body in a bad way, like it did that security guard outside the Springfield Mall.

THUMP!

Tasha flinched at the pain in her hip. She waited but there was no blood, no fragmented bone or ripped clothing. Surely a blow from a sawed-off would have destroyed her leg completely. There was only a large bruise where she'd been hit. Her poor leg, though. With all the damage it had taken in the past few days, she wondered if it would have to be amputated.

THUMP!

The rusty axe bit clean through the door just short of Tasha's floating rib. She remembered the shotgun beneath her seat and strained her back reaching for it. She groaned and willed her shoulder socket loose to allow for more distance. She fingered the tip of the barrel forward until it peeked over the edge of the seat.

THUMP!

The shock from the third swing shook the entire car and knocked the shotgun right into her bobbling grasp.

THUMP!

The fourth one sent it flying out the window, where it landed just out of Tasha's reach.

She cursed it with her eyes as it lay there, mocking her plight. The hole from the axe had curved, metallic teeth that bit down on her leg. Strangely, there was no more pain, just a constant throbbing throughout her entire body and a dizzying static in her head.

Tasha closed her eyes and gave herself to the darkness that, for awhile, had been pleading to embrace her. The last thing she heard was the faint sound of sirens approaching.

Outside, an elderly, heavy-set woman crawled from the train wreckage. She rose to her feet and struggled to keep her balance. She lowered her hands from her face and instantly began to sway like a spring-mounted hood ornament. There was a dead woman staring back at her. The elderly woman collapsed into the arms of the second man to exit the train. Soon the street was crowded with survivors, shambling about semiconsciously, trying to make sense of what had happened and manage the shock.

Griff flagged down a passing car, snatched the driver from inside, and snapped his neck. It happened that quickly and right under the punch-drunk crowd's collective nose. He hopped in and pounded on the horn to signal for the others.

Chapter 3

August 14, 1999

IN THE NEWS TODAY... *In southeastern Kosovo, United States Marines faced attack and were forced to return fire, killing one gunman and injuring another. The surviving gunman was found to have ties to the Chinese military. China had already been under suspicion concerning military secrets that they allegedly pilfered from the US, secrets including information on the mass production of biological and chemical weapons. "China is still smarting from the Embassy bombing in Kosovo and is possibly looking to retaliate," said Secretary of Defense William Perry.*

Officials from Russia and China refused to comment on the rumors of secret talks between the two nations. The Russian Army's dubious actions in Pristina coupled with anti-US sentiment in China has NATO deeply concerned about the future of this tense situation.

IN OTHER NEWS... *A bipartisan group of politicians expressed concern that a majority of the American public underestimates the severity of the developing situation between the US, Russia, and China. Although the country's relationship with the two world powers continues to deteriorate, the average American is more interested in myths and rumors concerning the Y2K Bug and the exploits of a woman who is alleged to have murdered more than a dozen people.*

The group singles out the tabloid media, as well as organizations like Claymore Broadcasting Network (CBN), for their aggressive advertising campaign promoting legendary telejournalist/interviewer Linda Ludlow's interview with Natasha Armstrong, the woman at the center of the so-called Bloody Mary murder spree. The network is predicting record-breaking viewership numbers for the broadcast of the interview, which can be seen in its entirety at 9:00 this evening on CBN.

BANG!

The screen faded to black from the geometric CBN logo.

Synthesized voices decorated the heavy beat and the ominous metallic moan of the techno-serenade that scored the intro to tonight's top story. Apparently, a younger executive was behind the wheel on this one. Linda Ludlow grimaced her disapproval, which went unnoticed in the unlit background.

Self-indulgent crap, she thought.

Being the old veteran on the show, Linda was argumentative and demanding, as she thought she had to be to compete. To everyone else, she was just a bitch.

The hacks were working up a dramatization of Tasha Armstrong's "killing spree." The director was especially fond of one shot in particular. It was superimposed over Tasha's Photoshopped mugshot. The camera faced up from the floor as a stylized version of Bloody Mary arose from the shadows and posed amid deep red lighting. An artificial wind breathed life and lift into her full-length dress.

A Gothic organ climax grew as the camera zoomed in slowly on the gas mask that carefully shrouded Bloody Mary's face, then into a tight shot of Tasha's livid brown eyes....

Photographs of varying quality, dubious authenticity, and questionable provenance littered the media and sparked heated debates among friends and coworkers: was Bloody Mary real, or was Tasha Armstrong just another serial killer with a story? Of the lot, there were three pictures that stood out, which were taken by crime-scene photographer David Miller before his body was found lying next to his mud-caked camera in the woods at Ridley Creek State Park. The pictures, though grainy and blurred, were enough to validate Bloody Mary's existence to some.

Last photos taken by forensic photographer, David Miller.

The conspiracy theorists said that Miller was killed because of what he knew, although it was never determined exactly what that was. They said that Tasha Armstrong was just a patsy. Bloody Mary? She was definitely real. She was a product of the Government; a chemical warfare experiment that went horribly wrong. That's what *they* said.

No one had actually seen Bloody Mary and lived ... except for Tasha. But she couldn't prove it. What was certain was that legions of believers didn't include the courts or the police that beat the shit out of her after they dragged her barely conscious body from the overturned car on 46th street.

The legend of Bloody Mary had sparked widespread interest among teens and twentysomethings particularly. Rumors and stories were shared freely in the online community of weblogs and chatrooms. As the legend spread and the hype grew, groups and movements were formed in honor of Bloody Mary. Some had been derided as cults in the popular media, which had just begun to recognize what was already a reality to parents and teachers across the country. Small bands of youths who could be identified readily by their shirts, hair, accessories, and angst-ridden music had sprung up seemingly overnight....

American Murder: The Bloody Mary Murders
With Linda Ludlow

Linda sat at a round table. A 19-inch monitor faced her from across the table. Natasha Armstrong was on the screen. She was being filmed from prison. She wore an orange prison jumpsuit and a look of impatience.

LINDA: Good evening, and welcome to *American Murder*. Tonight, we'll be talking about the so-called Bloody Mary Murders. In the twelve years since the first murders, Natasha

Armstrong's face has graced the covers of countless tabloids and magazines. She has become a polarizing figure ever since. Is she a cold-blooded killer or an innocent victim?

According to the Pennsylvania State Police, Armstrong is responsible for a string of brutal and senseless murders including that of her own seven-year-old son, Dana. Armstrong ontends that Mary Jane Mezerak, estranged wife of profes sional football's most notorious bad boy, Carl Mezerak, is responsible for the crimes. Mary Jane Mezerak disappeared twelve years ago and is considered by police to be another one of Armstrong's victims. At the time of her disappearance, Mezerak was five months pregnant.

Armstrong argues that Ms. Mezerak is responsible for the murders. She also claims that Mary Jane is dead. Sound fantastic? Well, according to Armstrong, and a surprising 40% of those who participated in our viewers' poll, it's true. The fact that Armstrong has become a cult figure cannot be denied. References to Tasha Armstrong and the alleged walking corpse known as Bloody Mary have found their way into popular culture by way of television, alternative lifestyles, gang behavior, and youth-oriented music.

Just how popular is the Bloody Mary mythology? Two recent books—*Bloody Mary,* written by yours truly, and the provocatively titled *Dead Bitch Army,* a fictionalized account of Armstrong's story by shock-peddler Andre Duza—are currently numbers one and four, respectively, on the *New York Times* Bestseller List.

Armstrong was apprehended by police in February of this year at the scene of what has become known nationally as the El Tragedy, which claimed the lives of fourteen people. Witnesses at the scene claim that it was Armstrong who caused a municipal bus to swerve into the stanchions that supported the elevated train system. The impact severed the tracks and caused a crowded train to career down onto Market Street below. The car that Tasha was driving belonged to a local bar owner, Joe O'Brien. O'Brien, a fifty-four-year-old father of three, was later found dead at his establishment along with three others: thirty-six-year-old Sylvia Browning, thirty-nine-year-old Reinhart "Duff" Duffy, and nineteen-year-old Cedric Tony Moore, a teenager from West Philadelphia who had been reported missing weeks earlier. They were the victims of an apparent shootout.

Tonight, for the first time on live television, *American Murder* is proud to present a candid discussion with the woman who is at the center of the Bloody Mary controversy. Natasha Armstrong talks with me live… after these messages. We'll be right back.

* * *

CLICK...

Carl Mezerak limply tossed the remote aside and watched it bounce on the couch cushion. It was hopeless. Not even the television could keep his mind from returning again and again to all the things that had him feeling down. Like his legacy and how it was slipping away. Almost from the moment he entered the league more than a decade ago, his antics and volatility on and off the field made him one of the media's favorite targets. His record-setting rookie season was marred by the crucifixion he received in the press in the aftermath of his arrest for domestic abuse and the subsequent disappearance of his wife. After that, his every outburst, fine, and failure became front-page news. His exploits were exaggerated (or so Carl thought) to make him out to be public enemy number one. There were even implications that he had killed his beloved Mary Jane.

Over the course of his career, the exploits of Carl Mezerak were always big news. Most people in and out of the sports world believed that it was all over for Carl when he suffered a career-threatening injury in 1995, but Carl returned to the Philadelphia Rebels the following year. The good numbers were a surprise, but the bigger surprise was the change in attitude. He came to camp a changed man, winning over his teammates and coaches with a new-found maturity. His veteran leadership in a young locker room rallied the team; Carl made sure that the media spotlight stayed on the team's performance as they rose from last place to a respectable .500 finish. His monster seasons in 1997 and 1998 carried the Rebels to two consecutive Super Bowl appearances, and his redemption was complete.

But now, all this shit with Natasha Armstrong brought the worst of his past mistakes back down on him. His past troubles were national news again. In a flash, he had gone from Hall-of-Fame-contender-who-came-from-nothing to a rich nigger with a past who probably had something to do with his white wife's disappearance

When Natasha Armstrong was first taken in by the police, years ago, Carl felt sorry for her. Dark as she was, he knew the media would have a field day with her. He knew, and he wouldn't wish that on anyone. Then she started running her mouth. And Carl felt his world closing in.

When Carl was a rookie, the tabloids started to speculate about Mary's religious beliefs. The simple mountain folk who were splashed on the pages were mocked for their "backward Appalachian religion." The stories played up the "bizarre rituals" and "secret tent revivals." When the first stories came out, Carl's teammates would razz him about it, but he'd laugh it off. Spouses and girlfriends were fair game in the locker room.

Mary's father, who went by the name Mr. Joshua, was a high priest for the Church of 1000 Earthly Deities. He was a practioner of Ergeister, a neo-pagan religion with German roots that included spells and incantations as part of its rituals. The name Ergeister was derived from the German words for Earth (Erde) and spirit (geister). Mr. Joshua died long before Carl met Mary, but over time, he heard plenty of stories. Most of them revolved around Mr. Joshua's experiences in Vietnam—tales that conjured violent images that were hard to shake.

Carl theorized that the war had left Mr. Joshua a little fucked in the head, whether or not (not, he figured) he would have admitted it. Carl never had the nerve to ask Mary what she thought about his theory. He just assumed that she encouraged her father's denial. To hear her talk about the man, you'd think she even believed in his spirit-conjuring, hex-bestowing, end-of-the-world bullshit. But that was Mary's business. As long as it kept her occupied when he was away, Carl couldn't give a shit. He never had time for religion. So when he would come home to candles and weird talismans all over the place, he didn't think much of it. It was the same to him as crucifixes and Virgin Mother statues. If he was staying for more than a few weeks, he'd make Mary take them down or put them somewhere where he didn't have to look at them all the time. They'd argue about it, Mary would call her old church friend Griffen to vent, and that would be that.

Sometimes it bothered Carl that Mary was telling their business to another man, but she would insist that Griffen was like family to her. Still, Carl felt like he needed to address it at some point. First he had to figure out a way to broach the subject without coming off like a freak.

Carl had heard Griffen's voice a couple times. Sounded country. *What kind of brotha hangs out in the fuckin' mountains?* In his mind, Carl pictured a non-threatening black man like Sidney Poiter, but younger like Will Smith or Cuba Gooding Jr. Certainly not the type that he needed to fret over. It wasn't that he thought Mary was having an affair with this guy; it was just that Griffen was a man. As Carl saw it, *he* was the only man Mary needed in her life. Then he'd fly across the country for a game and forget all about it until the next time he spent more than a few weeks at home. That was how the cycle went.

The damage to Carl's legacy wasn't irreversible just yet, he thought. All he needed was one more good season to win them back.

One more fucking season….

It was too bad that the paparazzi didn't come with a remote. They were camped out in the woods across from his mansion. A court order kept them from coming any closer. They had come to see his reaction to the big interview. He told himself (and everyone else) that he didn't care enough to watch it. His subconscious half-suggested that Mary herself was behind the whole thing and that she had recruited this Natasha Armstrong to help carry out her elaborate plot.

Wouldn't that be some shit!

Carl walked into the bathroom and started to shave. The bathroom was located on the east wing, close to the wall that surrounded his estate. Something told Carl to look out the window. It was a feeling, like an itch. With his fingers, he parted the blinds and glanced out surreptitiously. He was careful not to let the razor in his other hand brush against the curtain. Shaving cream was a bitch to clean once it dried.

Before he could complete his next thought (something about vultures), Carl noticed the man with the camera who was crouching in his neighbor's tree.

SNAP!

Carl could make out what looked like a trampoline on the other side of the wall. He winced as a second man sprung up from the ground, legs spreading for balance as he reached the peak of his bounce.

SNAP!

A third photographer clung tenaciously to a rope as he swung back and forth outside the window.

SNAP!

Carl retreated. *Maybe they just get off on harassing me.* Carl was trying not to flip out as he would in the past. Yeah, that kind of thing made for great photographs. Great photographs were big money to those scum. *Persistent little fuckers.* Their persistence had a way of wearing Carl down. It made him contemplate raising a white flag and begging them to stop. Maybe if he just tried to explain himself, to tell them how bad it hurt when Mary up and left him. It wasn't like she didn't have reason to. By the time she did leave, they barely saw each other. Both of them had long ago lost the wild-eyed lust. Carl's insecurity conjured up a side-piece scenario: Mary wrapped in the arms of another man. But Carl was screwing everything under the sun and getting away with it like most of his teammates. Somewhere in the back of his mind, Carl figured that the cheating might eventually come back to bite him in the ass, but he was all about living for the moment back then. As long as he was discreet about it, he'd be fine, he figured. He remembered being fearful of Mary's reaction should she find out, but then he would move on to the next thought, which usually involved getting his dick wet. Given more time to consider the consequences, Carl might've decided against his numerous affairs.

Most of the women who went on to become football wives fell for their men because of their hypermasculinity; after years of neglect and infidelity, they stayed because of the money.
But Mary wasn't like most other women. First of all, she was good with a gun. She was raised in an environment where they killed and prepared their own food. Once she tried to teach Carl how to skin a rabbit, but he couldn't bear to touch the dead thing, let alone peel its pelt from its still-warm carcass.

Mary wasn't the girly type. The house housed no flowers or frilly patterns, no potpourri. The pillows on their bed didn't need their own closet. Mary wasn't the type to smile at the sight of an infant or go "awwww" when she felt touched or moved by something. In fact, Carl was certain that words like "touched" and "moved" didn't even exist in her vocabulary. There were no guilt games, no long sermons about her feelings. She didn't require that their bodies touch when they lounged together on the couch or layed next to each other in bed. He never saw her shed a tear.

That's not to say that she wasn't into her man. She just had a weird way of showing it: sort of a read-between-the-lines approach. Carl could dig it, at first. It was just the right prescription for a philanderer like himself.

Mary *did* have her secrets. The way her eyes surged whenever Carl tried to get at them hinted at something dark. He knew that she had had a difficult past; that she had been adopted; and that Mr. Joshua was a little on the nutty side. In the beginning, it seemed like Carl might eventually get through the barriers that hid Mary's inner self. He remembered an instance when she came right out and told him about how she was raped repeatedly at the foster home that she lived in until she was six. Her tone was so matter-of-fact that it made Carl uncomfortable. After describing the rapes in vivid detail, she told him that they were only the tip of the iceberg.

Mary's timing couldn't have been worse. Carl was in the middle of his rookie year when she decided to tell him about the rapes. It was his "all-about-me, Superman phase." You could've told him that his balls were on fire and he wouldn't have given a fuck. In retrospect, he probably came across that way more times than he'd like to admit.

After that time that he punched her, Mary retreated back into her shell. The way Carl figured it, without many friends to confide in, she withdrew into her religion. She developed a strange affect that was almost reptilian and started obsessing about the end of the world and all that it entailed. She would disappear for hours at a time, only to return with her clothing ripped, her hair disheveled. She would give him some hollow excuse about falling down the stairs or something to that effect. Sometimes Carl would find bloodstains on her clothing when he looked through the hamper. Next came her weird preoccupation with his fame and the affect it had on people. Mary saw that power as something that could be used as a weapon.

The last time Carl saw his wife, she was running up Ridley Creek Road. She had stormed from his car when he denied that the child she said she was pregnant with was his, what with all her disappearing acts and her bad excuses. Could've been anybody's, right? Carl had been waiting for the right moment to confront Mary with his suspicions of infidelity, and she had essentially picked it for him. Besides, he was always under the impression that Mary couldn't bear children, that the rapes had damaged her uterus. He didn't think she liked kids anyway.

Carl remembered when he first laid eyes on Mary. It was at the campus library. He had just transferred to Penn State. He had to leave Ohio State because of a fight that left another student in a coma. Witnesses saw the guy taunting Carl with racial epithets. That detail kept Carl from going to jail.

Carl was feigning studying when he noticed Mary. At first glance, her sinewy shape blended right into the H. R. Giger-style mural that hung from the wall behind her. Her smooth, creamy flesh was alabaster, soft as a whisper of brush against canvas. It was only a shade or two from being translucent except for the pattern of freckles on both sides of her nose. Her blond hair was flecked with red. It poured down her face and crested at her unusually broad shoulders.

Mary was so different from the type of white girl that Carl preferred. He liked dark hair, dark features, dark complexion. Her fair skin was the antithesis of Carl's rich, chocolate hue. He was black as night with its starry eyes shut, so dark that he gave other black people pause when they saw him coming down a dark street. It was something that he struggled with all his life, thanks in part to his childhood friends, even those who weren't much lighter skinned.

When he was a kid, they called him Jungle Boy, Smoke, Tar Baby…. Their insults always revolved around his complexion and his wide nose. The girls sang songs about how black he was and how they'd never touch him even if he was the last person on earth.

As a result, Carl only dated white girls. He made it a rule.

It took Carl a week of staking out the library every night just to get Mary's attention. It took even longer to get her to go out with him. She was so wrapped up in her occult books and in researching adoption records. Carl eventually gave up.

It was just a coincidence that they ran into each other four years later. Mary looked so out of place in that record store. It was the kind of store that sold R&B and Hip-Hop records in the front and guns, knives, and brass knuckles way in the back, which was where Mary was standing. She had a strange look in her eyes when Carl walked up on her, like she was fighting back something.

They got to talking. He offered her a ride home, and she accepted.

Carl was in the middle of a sentence when Mary climbed onto his lap. He remembered almost crashing his truck. He eventually pulled over behind a cemetery. They went at it like animals. It was the best sex he'd ever had.

Carl traced the outline of his jaw for any remaining stubble. He'd actually finished shaving about fifteen minutes ago, but he was lured back to the mirror by the brutal honesty of his reflection. Its reluctant glare saw through to the core, to whom he really was.

Frankly, he despised what he saw.

Carl gave his middle finger to the window.

Wouldn't be surprised if they could see me even now.

Carl eyed the quiet television with contempt. He had turned it slightly so that he could watch from the toilet.

He caressed the surface of his head. *It's about that time,* he thought, referring to his hair. Back in the day, they would have said he was "wolfing." He liked to keep his scalp clean-shaven. The last thing he needed was for it to nap up and reveal the African in him.

He pointed the remote at the television.

CLICK....

TASHA: First of all, Joe O'Brien murdered that kid because he was fu(beep)ing his daughter. I sat there and watched the whole thing. You know, it's not like I haven't already told you all this earlier. So why don't you stop actin' like you're hearing it for the first time?

LINDA: You already told me what?

TASHA: I just told you that I watched that bloated muther(beep)ker...

LINDA: You mean Joseph O'Brien?

TASHA: I watched him shoot that boy for nothing.

LINDA: Did you try to stop him?

TASHA: How could I? Look, I'm sure there are far more interesting people than me that you could be interviewing. What about all that sh(beep)t going on over in Kosovo? What about all the Bible-thump-ers, or the Nostradamus freaks that got everybody so crazy worrying about the millennium? Just turn on the television and you hear a new theory every five minutes.

LINDA: You'd be surprised by the number of people who would rather hear about you, Tasha.

TASHA: I guess that's why that bullsh(beep)t book you wrote last year made the bestseller list.

LINDA: People love a good story.

TASHA: Oh... so I should be flattered?

LINDA: I wouldn't go that far.

TASHA: Okay. You tell me how I should feel about that, since you seem to know so much about me.

LINDA: ...We were discussing the fact that you did nothing to help Cedric Moore when
it seems to me that you clearly could have.

TASHA: You make it sound so malicious. I had just gotten my ass kicked at the time. Rainah probably would have killed me if I hadn't gotten away. I needed somewhere to hide. What? You think I went to that hill-jack dive for a drink? I'd like to see what you would've done.

LINDA: First of all, I would never end up in a situation like that. But hypothetically speaking, I probably would have found a payphone and called for help.

TASHA: Not likely.

LINDA: ...All right, let me ask you this, then: If Cedric Moore was killed in the basement, as you've alleged, then why was his body found upstairs in the bar area?

TASHA: He got up and walked upstairs. That's how.

LINDA: Let me get this straight. You're saying that after he was shot in the head, he got up and walked up a flight of stairs?

TASHA: That's what I'm saying. It scared the sh(beep)t out of me when he came to. I couldn't really sleep, so I was sitting there just kinda looking at him when he made this burping sound. Then he just kinda coughed himself awake and started throwing up blood. From the look on his face, I'd say he was in shock. I don't even think he saw me.

LINDA: The coroner says he was probably dragged up the stairs.

TASHA: Well, good for him.

LINDA: So you're saying that the coroner lied?

TASHA: No matter what I say, you're not going to take my word over his.

LINDA: That's not true. You have every right to your side of the story.

TASHA: Well, I've told you my side, so why don't we just move on?

LINDA: Fair enough. Speaking of the dead rising, how do you explain Bloody Mary? Your version has her rising from the dead to kill twenty-one people.

TASHA: As far as *why* Mary is still alive?

LINDA: Yes.

TASHA: I really couldn't tell you. You'd have to ask her yourself. The only other person who might have a clue died twelve years ago.

LINDA: You mean Gerald York?

TASHA: That's right.

LINDA: Why don't we talk about your son Dana? In the *Time* magazine article, you say, and I quote: "My head was gushing blood. I climbed to my feet just as Bloody Mary crashed through the living room window. She took off in my car with my boy still inside and vanished into the night. That was the last time I saw him." Give me a detailed description of what happened that night. You say you were visiting with Mr. York?

TASHA: I was looking for him.

LINDA: Looking for Mr. York?

TASHA: ...I was in the man's house. Who else would I be looking for?

*   *   *

"Man, what a bitch," Carl mumbled and turned back to the mirror. To him, most of the black ones were.

With the tips of his fingers, Carl gave his bald head one last sweep to reaffirm the beginning of a good day or at least an adequate one. He checked the difficult spot on the back of his head and balked at the remaining stubble. Bad omen.

Carl glanced reluctantly at the screen.

Why is this bitch so obsessed with Mary? He labored to recall if he'd somehow met Tasha before. *Nice piece,* he thought, *black and all.*

He skimmed through his catalog of past conquests. Nothing.

*   *   *

LINDA: You strike me as a very angry woman.

TASHA: Wha'd you expect?

LINDA: Right. Back to the *Times* article. You say that you saw other people with this Bloody Mary. Were they abducted as well?

TASHA: How should I know? Could've been anybody: runaways, junkies. All 'cept Griffen and that big redhead—I think his name is Kagen. They were both older than the rest of 'em. It's because of Griff that I took the rap for 46th and Market.

LINDA: As I understood it, you were the one who caused the bus to swerve out of control, an accident that resulted in a commuter train crashing thirty-five feet to the street below. Fourteen people lost their lives that day. It is expected that the police will bring charges against you.... What about Paul Doherty, the motorist who stopped to help? Don't you remember snapping his neck when he got out of his car? There is a witness who says he saw you do it.

TASHA: For the hundredth time, *Mary* was driving the bus! It was *Griff* who killed that guy!

LINDA: Ah, yes, now I recall. Griffen convinced everyone, with his ESP, that you were driving the bus, right? According to you, it wasn't the first time he had done that. Is that why you were found lying in the street instead of in Joe O'Brien's car, where you claimed to be?

TASHA: Basically, yes. Only he... Griff... he calls it coaxing.

LINDA: Your son, Dana… if I'm correct, he would've been nineteen this year.

TASHA: Twenty. His birthday was two months ago, on the 6th. He *is* alive, you know.

LINDA: Well, let's say that your story is true. What would Bloody Mary's motive be? Why *your* son; why this Griffen character with his ESP?

TASHA: …Again; I honestly don't know.

LINDA: Okay. Well, we've all seen the artists' conceptions, or misconceptions, perhaps, of your description of Bloody Mary. I want you to describe her to me… in your own words.

TASHA: You know that still photo you guys always run? I think they were leaving a hotel; Mary and Carl, I mean. This was way before she died. Take a good look at her face: sweet-looking girl, nice and physically fit, could use a little sun, though, and maybe a personality to fix that blank-ass expression. If you look long enough, you get the sense that there's some freaky sh(beep)t goin' on behind that indifferent stare. Know what I mean? There's just something there.

Police artist's sketch of Mary Jane Mezerak aka
Blood Mary as described by Natasha Armstrong

LINDA: Now, let's get back to the first time you say you saw her. Tell me what happened.

TASHA: Well... you know that Gerry was a mortician?

LINDA: You mean Gerald York?

TASHA: Yeah. We had been broken up for awhile when he called me, out of the blue. He told me something had happened to a Joe. That's what he called the cadavers: Joes. It was a member of the Salmazo family. I forget her name. I think she was a niece of the Don or whatever. She was the one who had the pipe bomb explode in her face.

LINDA: You mean as in the Salmazo family that has been linked to organized crime?

TASHA: That's right. Gerry dealt with all types. Anyway, Floyd-tha-'ssistant forgot to put the girl's body in the freezer when he closed up for the night, and it rotted. When Gerry called me, he was hysterical. They were going to have a closed-casket funeral, but Gerry had fixed her body up so nice that he persuaded them to have a wake first. So, now he needed someone to take her place. Gerry was afraid he'd lose his license, or worse. Those Mafia guys don't fu(beep)k around, you know. ...He found that dead girl's—Mary's—body by acci-dent. At least that's what he told me. He said it looked like she got hit by a car or something. She was about the same height and size as the Salmazo girl. Gerry called her "a gift from God." A gift from God. Ain't that some sh(beep)t.

LINDA: ...You *are* aware that it's against the law to tamper with a corpse or to disturb a crime scene, aren't you? Wouldn't your knowl-edge of such an incident make you an accessory to the crime? Why would he put you in jeopardy like that? Why would you?

TASHA: I loved Gerry. At the time, I would've done just about anything for him. This was the Mafia we're talking about, and he was responsible for what happened to the girl's body. So I kept quiet.

*　　*　　*

Carl found himself deeply enthralled by what was playing out on the tube. He stroked his jaw line unconsciously, his fingers repeatedly gliding over his face, searching for stubble. Carl shook away the daze and tried to remember what he was supposed to do next.

*　　*　　*

LINDA: Okay, Tasha, you were giving us some history on Bloody Mary and how you came to meet her.
TASHA: I called him about a week later to see if everything was all right... and because I missed him. When he heard my voice he just hung up on me. I heard him mumble something into the phone, then CLICK. I called Gerry back, but this time the phone was dead. The next thing I know, my dumb ass is pulling up in front of his house. I left Dana in the car thinking I would only be a minute. I never liked him being around all those chemicals.

Mary was standing over Gerry's body. His neck was twisted all the way around, and it looked like he was still gasping for air. I guess it could have just been nerves, though. Mary's just standing there, like she was proud of what she'd done. I must've startled her because, when she saw me, she reacted like... like she'd... seen a ghost. Her eyes got real big—this was back before they dried up. They were just, sorta ... clouded over. She gets this weird look on her face and she says, "Yyyyooooouuuuuu!" in a real raspy voice. It was the only thing I've ever heard her say.

When I was done hyperventilating, I tried to run, but she was faster than I expected; stronger too.... Once I watched her pop her neck back into place after I clocked her with an aluminum baseball bat. She just reset it and kept coming... with that look. She can move her face enough for you to figure out what's on her mind, you know. I could see that she was angry.

Anyway, that's the last thing I remember. Mary must've clocked me something good. When I woke up, she was on her way out the window. The police found my car two days later at a rest stop on the turnpike. There was no sign of Mary or my son.

Two Nights and Two Days in ~~Hell~~ Joe's Tavern

One of the neighbors must've heard the gunshots. Tasha, who had been waiting behind a wall of bushes across the street, saw the whole thing. Out in the suburbs they liked to leave their blinds open. Tasha never could understand it.

Griff had coaxed a family man to kill his wife and teenaged daughter. They were shot in the face with a vintage European shotgun.

Griff let the family man live. He said he liked the guy's heart; something about honor among gladiators, blah, blah, blah. Griff liked to stand on his soapbox every now and then.

"You never had a family," Griff told the man repeatedly. The man was in a trance. Standing motionless, his wife and daughter destroyed and lifeless at his feet, the family man wept with a completely straight face. Griff was standing chest to shoulder with him, glaring at the side of his face. Griff's wide brown eyes radiated a light that had to be felt rather than seen.

"People will try to convince you otherwise, but you will always stand firm. You've never had a family. There is no one to miss, no one to weep, for because you've always been alone."

Rainah decided to go for a walk after they loaded the bodies into the van. It was a nice night, and she was feeling a little nostalgic for her life before Mary. She lived in a neighborhood similar to the family man's. She was a lot like the teenaged daughter that they just mopped up: blonde, attractive in a California-earthy kind of way, somewhere between athletic and girlie-girl. In some ways, Tasha and Rainah were alike, too. Both were awkward kids who developed into attractive women, and both had no qualms about resorting to violence when need be.

Tasha had become familiar with the habits of Mary's crew. They operated like a family. Mary was the wise old matriarch. Griff and Kagen were the uncles. Rainah, Derek, and Tsun were the children. There had been other children in the past, faces who came and went for whatever reason. Tasha had killed one of them—a big, bad motherfucker who called himself Dolph Ox. That was about five years ago. Griff, Rainah, and Dolph Ox were trolling for victims along the crowded boardwalk in Wildwood, New Jersey. Tasha had followed them from the rim of the beach about 75 feet away, the tide licking her feet. She carried a Winchester Model 70 in a long burlap sack over her left shoulder and her shoes in her right hand. It was late at night. Against the seamless black of the ocean-sky mural that framed her, she was invisible to the people up on the boardwalk.

Griff and the others stopped to harass a young couple. A few hours had gone by, and the crowd was thinning out. Tasha lay down on her stomach and took aim. She was gunning for Griff; without Griff's coaxing, things would be much easier for her. When she fired, she saw Dolph's head jerk forward and spit out a red mist. His big body crumpled to the ground. She thought that maybe she saw Griff smiling at her afterward, but with all the commotion that descended after her first shot, it was hard to pinpoint any one thing through the tiny scope.

They killed for two reasons: for practice and for food. Griff was big on practice. Tasha had seen some of the makeshift obstacle courses that they'd left behind: complicated things made from scrap metal, wood, wire, rope, body parts, stolen athletic equipment, whatever they could get their hands on. Sometimes they would kidnap their victims and set them loose inside. If the booby traps didn't get them, then one of the family surely would.

Tasha found it ironic that they were more functional than many real families; more functional than her own, at least. For one thing, they seemed to genuinely care for one another. Except for Mary, who spent most of her time hidden away. Generally, Mary only emerged to communicate with Griff; he was the only person she spoke to directly. Their relationship was symbiotic.

Her actions seemed to indicate that she was aware of her urban-legend status in the public eye. On occasion, she would go off on her own and nurture her image by "being seen." It was always at a distance. Mary reveled in the reactions she received, like it was all a game or maybe part of some bigger plan.

Tasha followed Rainah on her stroll. She took the low road, crouching from bush to bush, tree to tree, parked car to parked car. She had heard Griff mention to Rainah that they would meet her in the parking lot of an all-night market a couple blocks down the road before he drove off. She figured that Mary was with them in the van.

In retrospect, Tasha was overconfident when she approached Rainah, who was squatting to pee in an alley between two houses. She walked right out of the shadows and shoved the barrel of a .357 up Rainah's nose.

Before she could shoot, something inside her demanded that she look down at the puddle by her feet. In it, she saw Mary framed by the blue-black sky and the angry clouds, looking down from the roof of the house behind her. Then she saw the axe traveling end over end, coming right at her.

The blunt end of the axe whacked Tasha in the knee and dropped her. It hurt so badly that she let go of her gun. By the time she hit the ground, Rainah was already on her feet and approaching. She wiggled into her tight jeans and waited for Tasha to try to get up. When she did, Rainah kicked her in the ribs. Tasha hit the ground hard. She curled around the pain and began to cough uncontrollably.

"You just have the worst fucking luck, don't you girl?" Rainah said.

Tasha turned away from the spray of filthy water that leapt out of the puddle when Mary landed in it just inches away from her face. She turned back reluctantly and tracked her eyes up the long, tall silhouette that she knew so well.

Mary reached over her right shoulder and pulled her sawed-off from the holster on her back. Tasha closed her eyes. The next thing she heard was a car screech to a stop out in front of the house and a megaphone that instructed them all to freeze.

Mary and Rainah were long gone before the voice finished its sentence. From her back, Tasha looked up just as Rainah's leg disappeared over the edge of the roof.

Tasha took off running. She ran down the sidewalk at top speed. The police car made chase.

Another officer, on foot, climbed the fire escape after Rainah and Mary.

Poor guy doesn't know what he's getting himself into.

It seemed to Tasha that she had been running for hours. She stopped behind a dumpster to regain her strength when she noticed the open basement window. Joe's Tavern, a typical Upper Darby dive. It was just the break she needed.

She watched and listened from the safety of the darkness. She could see the spotlight pass by occasionally. She heard the police radios. She watched and listened and watched and listened and watched and... passed out.

Two Nights and Two Days Later

"That boy's got himself a set of balls, mouthin' off to you like that," Duff said, as he gave eyes to Keith, who then gave eyes to Crazy Jake, whose real name was Matthew.

Jake wasn't the type to involve himself in the typical barroom gossip unless he was put on the spot, as he was now. Duff liked to do shit like that just to bring Jake down from his high horse.

"Either that or he's stupid."

Jake glanced angrily at Duff's broken smile and saw Joe behind the bar, where he always stood with his fat arms crossed over his barrel chest. Like everyone else who drank here regularly, Jake was afraid of Joe. Some of the stories had to be true. Someone said that he once fought off seven state troopers before they finally shot him. Three times. Twice in the head. Joe claimed that his metal plate saved him. He said he got it when a mine blew up in his face in 'Nam. He had been dragging two of his friends out of a ditch at the time. Or was it three friends? Or was it a grenade instead of a mine? The story was a little different each time Jake heard it, but it was always badass. Especially when Joe himself told it.

Anything was better than the truth, which was that Joe O'Brien was a fat slob. He always had been. In his bar, he was God. It was a little place: the quintessential dive. It was hidden amidst a row of unoccupied storefronts on Marshall Road. It was the kind of place that you might pass a million times without realizing it was there. A cast of regulars was Joe's only real business, but he managed somehow. As long as the liquor sold, they were fine. And the liquor always sold.

"The kid's a punk, just like the rest of 'em," Joe grunted, wiping a spot on the bar that he'd already cleaned numerous times in the last five minutes. He slung the damp towel over his thick, rounded shoulder. "All that yellin' and arm-wavin' don't mean a damn thing to me."

"So what'd you do to him?" Duff's enthusiasm made Joe sick, but it was nice to have a fan. "Please tell me you busted him right in his big fat nose."

"He probably kissed his ass and gave him a drink," Sylvia's downtrodden voice snuck through the pinball noise and twangy guitar. She and Marcia had been trading insults about their significant others.

Joe lifted his gun from the shelf below the register and set it on top of the bar.

"I suggest you keep your BITCH quiet, Duff."

Duff rose from his seat and glared, but Joe had the kind of face that was well suited for staring matches and mugshots. Besides, Duff was a pussy. Everyone knew it.

"Give her a break, Joe. She was only kidding," Marcia said. She was always coming to Sylvia's rescue.

"Yeah, right," Sylvia whispered.

Duff walked up and leaned over her from behind.

"Come on, babe. I know ya hate 'em, but not tonight, please?"

"God, you're such a loser," Marcia said to Duff. Her expression read genuine contempt. "I don't know what in God's name Sylvia sees in you."

Duff gave his wife a peck on her cheek. Her skin was coarse and tight from too many years of too much sun. Her head begin to bob from alcohol's spell. Her normally bugged-out eyes were half shut. With his lips still attached to Sylvia's face, Duff glanced at Marcia.

"I don't believe I was speaking to you, ho-bag."

"That's real mature," Marcia said, as she grabbed her things and stood. "You two are made for each other."

Joe's tongue caressed his lips as he followed the bounce of Marcia's low, swollen ass. She passed him and hurried toward the door as if she knew that Joe was undressing her with his reddened eyes. Marcia was a little heftier than Joe liked his women—the ones he allowed himself to be seen with, that is. Behind closed doors, it was a different story. For a fat slob, Joe got his fair share of action. There were always the occasional groupies who found the fact that he owned a bar a prestigious enough feat to earn him a free ticket to "ride their legs to heaven," as he liked to say. Unfortunately, it always ended the same: he'd give them a job; they'd drink up his booze, pocket half the night's take; he'd fire them; they'd cry harassment and threaten to sue or attempt to blackmail him. He was broke to begin with, so none of them ever got a red cent.

Women. Fuck 'em.... Joe looked up and caught Marcia's malevolent glare. *She wants me,* he thought, as she opened the door and walked out into the light of day and the sound of cars zooming by.

A thump from the long dark hallway that led to the basement door spun Joe's head toward it. It couldn't have been the body beneath the noisy wooden steps. He made sure to lodge it in tight behind the old jukebox that liked to make its own selections based on whatever mood it was in. It was probably just a coincidence, some kind of short or mechanical flaw. The only lit room, which was off to the left, vomited the heavy stench of cigarettes, piss, and sometimes even sex—just like a good dive bathroom should. Most likely, it was only Paul. He had gone back there about ten minutes ago to do some lines and smoke a joint.

Joe turned back to the tables slowly. He knew that if he wasn't careful, his expression might unintentionally ignite suspicion and guide curious eyes right to his perfect hiding place.

"Hey Joe, turn up the tube," Duff yelled. He cupped his hands over his mouth to magnify his light, shaky voice. He leaned in closer to the wall-mounted set that peered down at him. "I think they're talking about that nigger on the news."

Joe fumbled through the side drawer for the remote, aimed, and gave sound to the nodding head whose concerned frown looked a little too forced, even for a bigshot news reporter.

"...EXTENSIVE SEARCH FOR CEDRIC MOORE. FAMILY AND FRIENDS SAY HE SEEMED TO SIMPLY VANISH IN FRONT OF THEM SOMETIME WEDNESDAY AFTERNOON...."

Joe hit the mute button and tossed the remote back into the drawer. Duff, Sylvia, Keith, and Crazy Jake turned simultaneously to face him.

"Maybe Holly knows where he is," Jake offered. "If I were you, I'd find out before he gets his hands all over her and you wind up with one-a-dem half-and-half grandkids."

Joe cringed and shook his head as if to escape a dizzy spell. "I don't even want to hear you *THINK* about that kinda shit in here!" He clenched his teeth to illustrate how he felt about the subject. "You hear me, Jake?"

Once again, Jake was on the spot. With Joe's swollen eyes bearing down from across the room, Jake opened his mouth, and, for an uncomfortable moment or two, he was robbed of all his thoughts.

"Hey, I'm on your side, man." Jake raised his hands and smiled to break Joe's glare. Jake stared at a star-shaped stain on Joe's belly to avoid looking him in the eyes. There were only three people left in the room besides Joe behind the bar and Paul riding the snake like he did every night in the bathroom stall, yet Jake felt as if every living thing down to the smallest microorganism silently awaited his next move.

Jake peered over his right shoulder and saw the TV. The same talking head from earlier leaned close to the screen and pointed his mic as if he too were waiting.

"All right! Enough already!" Joe flashed a smile and motioned with his open hand for everyone to relax. With his mind racing to the body and back, he began to think that maybe it wasn't such a good idea to let himself get too angry.

His daughter Holly was everything to him, from the time her blue-green eyes first rolled open and locked on him. He couldn't wash the image of that... boy writhing like an animal on top of her from his mind, soiling her porcelain skin, her Christian glow with his black....

Although he wore his hate like a cheerleader for the cause, that was about as deep as it went in Joe's mind. What really got under his skin was that in his vision, Holly was always enjoying it.

Joe gave his head a hard nod to express the intensity of his disgust. He looked up and caught Jake's head and flopping hair in mid-turn. Duff and Sylvia were too busy playing kissie-face to pay attention anymore.

Joe began to hum the familiar chorus to the Johnny Cash song that he must have programmed more than an hour ago on the jukebox. The corners of his mouth rose with his spirits as he tried his best to follow the lyrics, but they lost him repeatedly until the chorus returned and vindicated his effort.

"Because you're mine... I walk the line...."

Joe raised his bushy left eyebrow to the slow, shuffling footsteps that whispered from the mouth of the dark hallway. *Paul must be flyin' by now*, he thought. He could almost taste cocaine's numbing tingle in the back of his throat as he thought of Paul. Just then, a jarring image of the body downstairs flashed across his mind and woke him from it. It made him nervous that he couldn't see all the way down the hall.

Three days had passed since Joe put a bullet between Cedric's eyes. Each day ended with a quick check before closing to see if Cedric was really dead. Still. Of course he was.

Joe blew off the shuffling sound and turned back to the boys, the TV, and Johnny Cash still walking the line. It wasn't long before the nagging feeling to turn and take another look down the hall opened Joe's pores and brought beads of sweat to the surface, but he was determined to beat it. He tried to distance himself completely by thinking of Holly and her innocent smile. He knew that it would be some time before she got over Cedric's sudden disappearance. As long as Joe kept his mouth shut and played up the sympathetic father bit, he'd eventually come out on top.

"What the..." Duff's whiny voice cracked. Joe turned and immediately froze.

Cedric Moore followed the gasps, the chairs that slid away from the tables, and the rustling feet that headed instantly for the back of the bar. Although it was probably due to the dizzying remnants of a coma, his slow movement came across as confidence.

"I ti... told you that... that I wwww... would find some www... wayyyy to pay you back," Cedric said. He labored for every single breath. His face, for the most part, was still fixed in the petrified grimace that Joe remembered, twisted into a parody of itself as if a massive stroke had touched it. Tears of dried, dark blood marked narrow trails down to his chin. He lifted his hand and pointed to the bullet hole in the right side of his forehead. His voice sounded different, raspier than it did three days ago when he cried and begged Joe for his life.

Joe's eyes locked on Cedric's pale, sagging face. He had shot Cedric in the head, point-blank. How could he have possibly survived? Joe remembered the feeling, like satisfaction, as he watched Cedric try to comprehend what had happened after the first shot, his hands flailing wildly about his face and to the back of his head like Curly from the *Three Stooges*.

Cedric shuffled slowly to the bar, stumbling all the way. His eyes fluttered, his balance came and went. Joe didn't see the disregarded, full rocks glass that Cedric took from the bar and cupped in his palm.

"Llllook what yyyou did to meeeeeee," Cedric rasped.

Joe always hated the name Cedric. And he hated that Cedric was so dark and that Holly was hot for him. With her sallow Irish hue, Holly looked as if Joe had spit her right out. He was proud that everyone noticed enough to mention it whenever they were together.

Joe searched for excuses through the gibberish that crowded his head as Cedric took a few stumble-steps closer to the bar.

"Yyyyou just ccccc... ouldn't accept that ssshhhheee was happy, ccccould you?"

Joe backed away. His mind was still a blank. He couldn't pull himself from Cedric's eyes, which peered blankly from behind bloated eyelids.

The rocks glass caught Joe completely off guard when it shattered against his cheek. The double shot of bourbon inside immediately burned his eyes and stung the fresh laceration just beside his nose. Joe doubled over and met the bar with his forehead.

"YOU   FFFFFFFFFFUCKIN'   IGNORANT, RRREDNECK MMMMUTHAFFFFFF!"

Cedric grabbed for anything within reach to use as a weapon. He fell against the bar and hung on with his forearms.

"Jesus Christ!" Joe cried out. Intense heat soaked deeper into his eyes than he could rub. He fingered the shard of glass that was embedded in his face and yanked it out. His eyes fluttered open and shut as he dealt with the pain.

"It's not what you think!" Joe screamed. He signaled to Duff, who rose instantly from the huddle of trembling bodies behind the pool table and drew a .22 from his waist.

"Step away from him!" Duff commanded as he hid behind his gun, which was pointed at Cedric. He made a quick scan for Sylvia, who had just woken up from her drunken nod-off. Her limp neck caused her head to bob. Her tired eyes questioned her surroundings.

"Hey, wha's goin-aaahn?" she stammered, slurring and missing syllables.

While Cedric was distracted, Joe reached blindly for his gun. His right hand volleyed from his eyes to the top of his head to deflect the bottles that toppled from the shelves behind him.

For once, he drew it smoothly with an all-in-one motion that he had practiced repeatedly. Fastening his grip around the handle, Joe looked up just in time to see the beer bottle-shaped lamp that rested on the second shelf swing down at him in slow motion. Joe had always meant to tighten those shelf brackets. "Them things'r rustier'n shit," he would say. "Could fall anytime."

Joe gasped and let off three wild shots in Cedric's general direction before the lamp smacked him in the mouth, the light bulb bursting on impact with a hot pop. A spark from the light bulb set Joe's head on fire as it met his greasy, Brylcreemed pate.

Joe's first shot missed Cedric completely. It caused Duff to slide sideways out of its path, hands in the air like a ballerina offering her body to the arms of another.

The second shot shattered Sylvia's front teeth and continued out the back of her neck in a flash of red. Her head snapped backwards and bounced back onto the hardwood table, which cracked it open it like an egg.

"Noooo!" Duff cried out. He squeezed the trigger as fast as he could.

Tasha had followed Cedric up to the stairs and saw the whole thing unfold from behind the cellar door. Her friends used to joke about her knack for happening upon drama. She had a nose for it, they said. Tasha turned and headed back down the stairs. It was time to go.

Joe stumbled to and fro behind the bar, screaming and slapping at the flames that engulfed his head and shoulders. One of Duff's wild shots caught him in the shoulder, but with everything else that was going on, he didn't even feel it. The batting and rubbing spread the flames. The white-hot bite chased Joe's skin away in strips. He gasped, and the flames found his tongue and the inner lining of his mouth.

Tasha found it much harder to squeeze out of the basement window than it was to enter. She had a tough time getting her sprained leg through; she had to bend it in a way that made the pain scream.

Joe fell to his knees, his face hidden in his blistered hands. In his mind, an annoying jingle sounded over the flames' cackling voice.
STOP! DROP! AND ROLL! STOP! DROP! AND ROLL!
He knew that it was all over if he fainted. The flames were halfway down his back.
STOP! DROP! AND ROLL, YOU IDIOT!
His mind began to wander as it struggled to overcome the pain and fear, both of which worked together to bring him down. Joe tried his best to get a grip on the situation.
1. Need water.
2. The sink behind the bar is broken. You've been doing the dishes in the bathroom for the past week.
3. Gotta find something big enough to... God it hurts so bad... something like a toilet...
Joe broke from his daze and sprinted into the bathroom.

Good thing I didn't try to swallow it, Paul thought, pulling the crumpled paper from his mouth. The lump and the saliva stringing from it reminded him of the time he ate that hooker while she was on the rag, and he paused to keep himself from gagging. *Heroin,* he mused.

Paul massaged his thick, heavy face and considered the sheet of acid that he had shoved in his mouth some time ago. The sound of what he thought were gunshots stung his ears.

How long had he been there? *Half an hour, an hour at least,* Paul guessed.

He listened over the erratic buzzing undercurrent of his altered state for the rumble of hasty feet from the hallway outside the bathroom. He could easily visualize a scene to accompany the low guttural grunting that filled the hall. It was a familiar voice, yet it sounded completely foreign at the same time.

Probably just somebody running for the John. Paul pinched his dick in sympathy.

Now *he* had to piss. Paul sat in the only stall. He hoped that the approaching figure didn't have to puke.

"Always something," he groaned, hurrying to tie his shoes and straighten up his overall appearance. His eyes paused as he noticed his favorite scribbled message. He smiled and closed his eyes to adjust the double and triple images of sloppy cursive letters that danced before him: **JESUS** ~~**SAVES**~~ **SHITS JUST LIKE THE REST OF US.**

The charging footsteps continued to echo around the hall. Now they were right outside the door. The boom was deafening when the door burst open and something terribly kinetic spun in. Paul was so startled, he nearly fell off the toilet seat. Then he froze and listened to the deep, anguished groaning, the crackle of flames, the rapid-fire slapping, then a thud. Joe fumbled with the faucets, but they never worked. How could he have forgotten? The plumbing was shit to begin with, and it cost too much to fix.

Paul lowered his head to get a look under the stall door.

"Joe?" Paul said, curious. Paul recognized the worn boots and jeans that Joe wore every day.

Paul smelled charred meat. He was hiking his pants up, preparing to stand, when the stall door flew at him and found his teeth.

Tasha climbed to her feet and limped down the alley between Joe's Tavern and a hardware store. The bustling traffic out front swallowed any noise from inside the bar. She toggled the lock of the first parked car she saw: an '83 Cutlass with the keys still in the ignition. Tasha smiled when she saw the photo that dangled from the rearview. It was an old picture of Joe O'Brien smiling as he stood in front of his bar.

It was two days later when she found them again. She had been following a gut feeling, as she often did, and that led her right to them. It was all too convenient, but Tasha didn't bother to question it at the time. They were in the back of the old bus depot on 58th and Vine Streets. Surly banter competed with blaring funk music, engines coughing, and the sizzle-snap of sparks leaping from welders' torches coming from the immense, active garage. The lot behind it was dark and populated only by buses that had been pulled from rotation to be repaired. Rainah had lured one of the mechanics outside where Griff and Derek waited to ambush him. Mary was there too, hiding in the shadows. They had been casing the place since Mary first spied the well-muscled grease-monkey. She thought he'd make a great practice subject.

Reacting to the sight of them as if it held a grudge, Tasha's leg flexed straight and sent her foot down hard on the gas pedal. If it weren't for Griff, she would've ran them down. She sideswiped them, screeched to a hard stop, then threw the gearshift into reverse. Tasha flew past them again and wound up barreling toward a woman and her young daughter as they crossed the street a half a block away. She swerved to avoid them and spun out. She looked at the frightened woman in desperation. Their eyes locked in recognition.

A bus pulled from the lot behind the depot garage and turned toward them. The mother yanked her daughter by the arm and took off running as the charging bus telegraphed a path right toward them. A few of the mechanics were chasing it, yelling and hurling tools. Tasha shoved the gearshift to D and stepped on the gas.

Chapter 4

IN THE NEWS TODAY... *The Russian military, which has quietly observed NATO's attempts to restore peace in wartorn Kosovo, continues to increase its foothold at the Pristina airport as troops and supplies flow in from the east. "Sadly, I fear that the Russians have ulterior motives," said British Lt. Gen. Raymond McCarthy, head of NATO's humanitarian effort. "Russia has a long history with Yugoslavia, and I suspect that they harbor resentment for NATO's interference in the Balkans. They see this as their territory. We are the outsiders."*

IN OTHER NEWS...
(The scene opens on a long, empty corridor lined on both sides by rows of stacked lockers built into the wall. A bell rings, and within seconds, the hallway is flooded with teenagers racing to and from class. The camera zooms out to a wide shot and reveals a short, older gentleman in an expensive suit—a newscaster—submerged to his biceps in youths. He trades greetings with a few of the teens and lifts a microphone up to his mouth.)

REPORTER: *Gordon County High: a good school located in an affluent district. Hardly the place you'd expect the students to bring deadly weapons to class. But that's exactly what happened yesterday afternoon—just two days into the school year—when among other questionable items, axes like this one here (holds up 14" Tomahawk) were confiscated from a senior and two sophomores.*

CUT TO:
Previously shot footage of flustered students congregating outside the school. Police officers escort three handcuffed students with pixelated

faces (a boy and two girls) to a cluster of squad cars in the parking lot and guide them into separate cars. Along the way, the boy turns to the camera. His arms are cuffed behind him. Words jump out of the flash of full-frontal pink within the pixelated blur. "Gas-Mask Mafia bitchizzzzz," he says. The police officer behind him shoves him forward.

REPORTER (VOICEOVER): *The weapons were found after a member of the Gas-Mask Mafia consulted authorities in an attempt to break away from the group. A search of the teens' bags turned up the weapons, along with gas masks, rope, and duct tape. Classmates say that the teens consider themselves to be disciples of Bloody Mary, the shadowy figure at the heart of the rumors surrounding what have become known as the Bloody Mary Murders. This frightening trend is gaining popularity among troubled teens throughout the country. Although some followers of Bloody Mary have turned to crime, even murder, police claim that the Gordon County teens were likely "just kids looking for an outlet."*

CUT TO:
The hallway is empty again as students settle into their classes. The reporter is standing with a male student. A few of the student's friends linger in the background.

REPORTER: *Since Natasha Armstrong's capture in February, we've been hearing a lot about Bloody Mary and the Gas-Mask Mafia. I wanted to find out from the teens themselves their thoughts on this phenomenon, which most adults view as a cult of reckless behavior and violence. I'm standing here with Douglass Cloutowski...*

STUDENT: *Call me Clout.*

REPORTER: *...Douglass is a senior at Gordon County High.*

Douglass, I want you to help our viewers understand the appeal of this Bloody Mary business. Did you know the students who were taken into custody?

CLOUT: *First of all, like I said, call me Clout. Nobody calls me Douglass. But yeah, I knew them. They weren't friends of mine or anything. They ran with a... "different" crowd, know what I mean?*

REPORTER: *You're insinuating that they were outcasts of some sort?*

CLOUT: *You could say that. Nobody around here really takes that Gas-Mask Mafia stuff seriously. It's you guys who keep building them up into some big, like, worldwide epidemic or something. They seem like just a bunch of misfits cryin' out for attention, if you ask me. Next week, it'll be the chupacabra or the mothman or something. I hear the rave's going to be cool, though.*

REPORTER: *So, I take it you don't believe in Bloody Mary?*

CLOUT: *Nah. But my buddy Jim said he saw her up in the Pine Barrens. She was holding hands with the Jersey Devil.*

Clout's friends burst into laughter. The reporter is visibly annoyed. He snatches the microphone away from Clout's face. The camera whips to frame the embarrassed reporter.

REPORTER: *Sorry about that, folks. Clearly it doesn't look like I'm going to find any answers today.*

Fiendin'

After nearly a decade of reliability, Carl's coveted "weed system" was finally breaking down. He absolutely hated dealing with the dealers and their idiosyncratic behavior. It had been a while (his senior year in college to be exact) since he had to interact with any of them personally. He was advised to wash his hands of that shit once he signed with the pros. "If you absolutely must have it, you let your people get it for you," he was told.

Carl's "people" had been pulling sneaky shit lately. Information had been leaked to the tabloids on more than one occasion. He never found out who it was, so he fired everyone and changed everything up. *Fuck it.* At the time, he didn't think about what he'd do when he ran out of weed, or groceries, or toilet paper. Somehow the rest of that shit wasn't all that important to him at the moment. He wasn't especially hungry, and he didn't have to take a shit. But for the first time in years, Carl *was* down to less than an eighth of weed, and he was stressing something awful about scoring more. There were four main dealers that his people bought from: big dawgs in the hustle who only sold in bulk. Carl was good for a few pounds each visit. He'd break off a little for the delivery man, and the rest was his. It didn't take him long to go through it, especially in the off-season, when he was running from a problem, or when the steroids had him stuck on deck for a hulk-out. Three of the dealers he had known since his college days. Each had his own set of rules and rituals.

There was the Diggs Man (aka Riddick Diggs III) in Atlantic City. Diggs was the type who was well aware of the power he wielded as a dealer. He liked to hold court and lord over his customers with his vast knowledge of obscure subject matter that he had acquired during his extended jaunts of paranoia-induced loneliness. He'd offer a bong hit, pack it, then just hold it himself until he finished babbling, following wild tangents and turning what sometimes started out as a legitimate gripe/concern/observation into a long-winded rant filled with half-sentences and confusing metaphors. Back when he dealt with Diggs all the time, Carl knew just the right time to jump in, foil his thought process, and be up outta there.

Then there was Ralph "Chiba" Braithwaite in Center City. Chiba was raised by bonafide hippies, so, naturally, he hated them.

He came across as a right-wing asshole, but he knew everything there was to know about the cultivation of marijuana. To Chiba, selling weed was a legitimate business endeavor, and he was all about the money. He was absolutely terrified of being caught. The fear was so bad that he forbade his customers from saying "weed," "pot," or any other identifier. He used code words for everything and referred to the transaction with riddles. "How many touchdowns you gonna score against Notre Dame," he'd say. And Carl would answer with the number of pounds he needed. Chiba was convinced that the government or some other authority was using satellite-controlled spy cameras to watch the public. The cameras were placed in mundane household appliances, clothing, and accessories, such as glasses, rings, and watches. Needless to say, Chiba had a hard time holding on to any such items for long.

Nutter was the man to see in West Philly. His shtick was similar to Chiba's but with an ethnic slant. His means of expression weren't commensurate with his intellect, which led to malapropism-filled diatribes that tested Carl's patience. It reminded him of the guys who used to sit in the back of the bus when he was a kid, pontificating about the state of the black community. A typical conversation went something like, "You see, it's tha simple fact that you got-ta really appreciate the intricatory complexivities and constipulations of the stronglehold they have over us. The man... he don't wanna see tha *black man* gravitate to a point of excellence compository and comparative with his own positions of grandioseness in this racist power structure whereby we cohabituate and exist."

Last but not least was Len Sparks, a guy who Carl had never met. Len operated out of Upper Darby, and he had arguably the best weed in the area. Other than that, Carl didn't know much about him. Oh yeah... Len was biracial (half Jamaican & half German). His former buyer used to make a point of bringing that up every time Len's name was mentioned.

Carl felt silly in the disguise that he'd put together: a fake beard, wayfarer sunglasses, and one of those Chinese straw hats made popular by Wu Tang. He sat in the inconspicuous rental car (a Honda Civic) with his forearms resting on the steering wheel, his chin resting on his forearms, and stared out the windshield at the third-floor window of the apartment building a block and a half away from where he was parked. He was about seventy-percent certain that the window looked into Len Sparks's place. Sparks was the first person who returned Carl's phone call, so that's where he went. As a safety precaution, he told Sparks that he'd send one of his boys as usual. If Sparks was anything like the typical civilian (what Carl called non-celebrities), he would probably have his whole family there waiting to meet Carl had he told him that he was coming personally. Stranger things have happened.

Carl had never been in the Tuckerman Court, a five-story apartment building, so he could only speculate about the layout of the place. Sparks lived in apartment 316, which was probably on the right side of the building, where Carl faced. The window that he watched was three stories up and third from the corner. He only assumed it to be Spark's place because of the crowd. They were kids mostly, a diverse mix of black, white, and ambiguous brown twentysomethings from what Carl could see. The scene reminded him of those old college keggers that he sometimes missed. It could have been nothing, just an innocent party in a different apartment, but Carl had a sinking suspicion that they were there to see him. Carl called that feeling his "celebrity sixth sense." He had been stalling for the past twenty minutes, hoping that Chiba, Diggs, or Nutter would call. Carl felt more comfortable dealing with people he knew. *Fuck it,* he thought. *I'm going in.*

Carl used the rows of parked cars to shield him from the passing traffic as he walked down Shadelane Ave toward the Tuckerman. He passed a little black kid on a bike with a banana seat and nodded when the boy looked his way. The boy nodded back and kept on looking as he rolled slowly passed. Carl could feel the boy's eyes on his back. He could tell by the sound of the bike's rubber tires that they rolled more slowly until they finally stopped.

"Just go on about your business, kid. Nothing to see here,"

Carl mumbled to himself.

The kid jump-started his bike in motion. Carl could hear the boy coming toward him.

"Shit!" he hissed.

Carl ignored the boy as he came up on his left side and stared inquisitively. He circled Carl in a wide arc, then took off quickly down a side street. Carl was relieved until he heard the boy yell in the distance, "Yo, John! Yo, Malik!" His voice was filled with an enthusiasm that Carl recognized.

Maybe he was just being paranoid.

Carl continued on to the Tuckerman. He was approximately half a block away when he passed a sista talking loudly on a payphone. She stopped talking when she saw him. But Carl kept on walking. Maybe she was reacting to something or somebody else. Carl never looked her way, so he couldn't be sure it was because of him. But he had a feeling.

"Probably going to see some *white girl*," Carl heard the sista say. "That fool can't handle no real woman."

What were the chances that she was talking about him? Eighty-five, ninety percent? That's how Carl figured it. Rather than turn and confront her like he was compelled to do, Carl kept walking. There was still a slight chance that the sista was talking about someone else. Best to be optimistic in a situation like this, he thought. The people in the area most likely knew who Len Sparks was. Somebody was bound to make the connection when they saw Carl go into the Tuckerman. As long as he played it cool, he could deny any rumors that might arise. No one could prove that Carl Mezerak was behind the disguise.

So Carl kept walking.

He could see that some of the people beyond the third floor window were wearing Philadelphia Rebels jerseys, the vintage kind that sold for big money.

Carl stopped walking. *Fuck!*

"There he is!" A high-pitched voice ambushed Carl from behind. It was the kid on the bike. He was speeding toward Carl with six of his friends, all of them with bikes of their own. They were riding so fast that they threw their bikes from side to side with each peddle-thrust.

Carl was contemplating moves in both directions, unwilling to commit to either.

He felt a sting in his thigh. He flinched, but it was only his cellphone. He snatched it from his pocket and checked the caller ID. It was Chiba. There was a swell of optimism.

"What's the word?" Carl said, rushing the words out.

"I got that thang," Chiba responded.

That was all Carl needed to hear. He turned and walked quickly back to his car.

"Aye! Hold up!" the boy on the bike yelled. He and his friends were about two hundred feet away and approaching fast.

There was no way Carl would make it back to his car unless he ran. So he did.

*   *   *

Now the world (or 48 million households, according to the Nielsen Ratings) knew Tasha's story. The papers mocked her description of Bloody Mary and of Griff's coaxing in their headlines. The tabloid TV shows snipped, trimmed, and spliced together soundbites that made her look like a fucking lunatic and foisted them upon the public ad nauseam. Since being formally charged in the El Tragedy, Tasha had been held in solitary confinement at Eastern State Penitentiary.

Tasha guarded every moment she spent outside her cell. It was only for an hour a day, trapped in a caged-in basketball court in the main yard while guards posted at the door pretended not to watch her and guards posted on towers high above the yard pretended not to watch them. Most of the time, she just paced and tried to think ahead. The paparazzi had paid off some of the guards to provoke a response from her. A few guards were supplied with hidden cameras and were promised rewards based on the magnitude of her reaction. But Tasha was a rock.

But she was leaving all that behind today. She was being transferred from Eastern State to the Ries Clinic, a facility for the criminally insane, until her trial. Tasha felt a certain sense of relief that she would soon be among people who were crazier than she was. The strain of maintaining her composure throughout her stint at Eastern State left her mentally and emotionally weak. Something was brewing inside her, a weak tickle wrapped in prickly heat. She felt it from the moment she woke up this morning. She figured it was just nerves. Moving day was always a shock to the system, as she remembered.

They told her at the last minute that the press would be waiting in the parking lot outside the administration office. Tasha was in no condition to face the public. She had been sitting for hours on an uncomfortable wooden bench, her wrists and legs connected by shackles to her waist as she waited for her transfer papers to be processed. The side of her face was at crotch level with her escort, a big lummox of a man holding a shotgun at a slant across his body. The bulge in his pants dared acknowledgement. They always seemed to assign the largest guards to escort her, big strapping meat-eaters with arms like anacondas. Tasha made it a point to ask for their names. Today's escort was "Allen Dent... Officer Allen Dent." That's exactly how he said it, like laying it out that way somehow made it sound like a more important designation than it actually was.

That feeling Tasha woke up with had blossomed into full-blown anxiety. Unless she composed herself in the time it took to walk from the office to the elevator, travel down two floors, then walk from the elevator to the front doors (approximately four minutes), she was going to make a spectacle of herself. Those reporters knew how to push the right buttons. So far, she resisted the temptation to reach out and strangle one of them. The shackles left her with limited motion, which only served to frustrate her more. Things weren't looking good.

Tasha made it to the elevator. She festered in the awkward silence inside the 6' x 6' box, with Allen Dent's giant body warming her. An anguished gurgling sound erupted from her lungs without warning.

"C'mon, now. You were doing so good," Officer Dent said. "I had money ridin' on whether or not you'd make it to the car."

Tasha recognized the voice right away. Its monotone timbre was unmistakable. *Griff.* It made her temperature drop, her muscles tense. She turned her head slowly, in disbelief. Her mouth hung open. Her eyes threatened to leap from her face. Reaction superseded thought. Tasha yanked her arms, her wrists pulling her pelvis forward as she tried to lift them. She made strange sounds indicative of struggle. Her intention was to wrap her hands around Officer Dent/Griff's thick neck and wring Griff out of him, but the shackles were uncooperative. Their jingle-jangling seemed to mock her. She cursed him in incomplete sentences.

"You... fucking... motherfucker. Swear-ta-God I'm gonna..."

"You sure you want to continue down this road, Tasha? You know how you are when you get riled up. Those fuckin' vultures out there'll use it to make you look guilty. You'll lose whatever credibility you have left."

But she was already riled up by the shackles that restricted her movement and left her powerless. She screamed and tugged herself off-balance. She landed on her ass and bounced. She sat there motionless and began to sob. She was surprised at how good it felt to let go.

"Okay, you win. I can't do this anymore," Tasha wept.

Snaking his beefy fingers up under her armpit, Officer Dent/Griff lifted Tasha to her feet.

"I was just going to tell you how proud I was of your performance. I know how hard it must have been to keep from telling that bitch where to shove her fucking questions. You could teach a Rainah and Tsun a few things about self-control."

"Please, just gimme back my son."

"Can't do that. Sorry."

"You can't be totally ruthless. I mean, didn't you have a

mother? How would you feel if…"

"You're barking up the wrong tree, Tasha. I'm not the one with the grudge. I'm only the messenger."

"But you know Mary. You can talk to her… tell her to stop this madness."

"Now why the hell would I want to do that?"

"Then why did you come here? To torture me? Kill me? Or just to rub it in my face that I'm in custody for crimes that you and your people committed?"

"C'mon, Tasha… You've got me all wrong. I just wanted to express my… admiration. I've had the pleasure of seeing you in action over the years, and I have to say that you've always left me entertained. You have a fire inside you that most *men* can't even touch."

"You people stole my son—my only son. Why are you doing this to me? What the fuck is it that she wants? Because I'll do anything."

"Anything, huh?"

"Anything," Tasha reiterated. Though reluctant, she let her eyes roll down to Officer Dent/Griff's crotch. Waterlogged by emotion, her sexuality shined ugly, giving off a murky vibe that only fetishists would find attractive. "I… I've seen the way you look at me sometimes."

Officer Dent was at least a foot and a half taller than Tasha and twice her size. It seemed to take her eyes forever to travel up to his face. He was glaring down at her, Griff's expression manipulating Dent's features to suit his own. Their faces were vastly different. Together, they birthed a strange-looking mask.

"Is that what you think this is about? A piece-a-ass? Bitch, I'm a soldier! You understand me? I lay my life on the line every single day for what I believe. You think that because you see Tsun actin' a fool that this is all some kind of game? You think we live just to fuck with you and that muthafuckin' has-been Carl Mezerak? If it were up to me, we wouldn't waste another ounce of sweat on your insignificant asses. But Mary *has to have* her revenge. When the shit hits the fan, we'll still be ready, though. And when the dust clears, we'll be the ones standing on top like certified, motherfuckin' badasses. Fuck the Green Berets and the Navy SEALs. Fuck all-a-dem niggas. What about you, huh? Where you gonna be? I'll tell you where. You'll be fossil fuel for the next wave of evolution, just like all the other suckas who didn't see it coming."

Tasha countered, "Look, you have your way, and I have mine. I can respect that. You said that you wouldn't waste another ounce of sweat on me if you had your way. Well, I'd like to propose a deal, just between you and me. I'm appealing to whatever shred of humanity you have left in you as a man. As a black man. Please? I'm begging you. Please give me back my son? I give you my word that I won't go to the police, and once I'm gone, you'll never hear from me again."

"Let me clarify something for you, Tasha. Don't mistake my composure for some kind of affection. We *ain't* friends. You got that? I came here because I believe in honor among warriors, the code of the battlefield...."

Code of the battlefield?!? It was a clear thought, so Tasha knew that Griff probably intercepted it. If he did, he didn't acknowledge it.

"Aside from that, nothing changes."

"But I meant it when I said you'd never hear from me again. I could go someplace far away. Start a new life."

"You say that now, but I know you better than you know yourself, Tasha. Aggressive women like you and Mary... y'all seem to have a specialty for nurturing grudges and using them to inspire all kinds of devious shit."

"But she wouldn't have to know. And I swear I wouldn't..."

"Oh, she'll know. Besides, I've known Mary since she was a kid, when I used to do odd jobs for her father. We're like family. You expect me to ignore that kind of history just to help your sorry ass? I don't think so. And let's say I did help you: How long before your anger and contempt make you consider doing somethin' stupid? A month? A year? Two years? I've got more important things to worry about without having to constantly look over my shoulder. This way, I know just where you are and what you're up to. Mary gives the word, and I find you. I lead you to us."

Suddenly it all made sense, how Tasha was always able to locate them so easily.

"You didn't really think you were finding us on your own, did you?"

The elevator bucked to rest on the first floor. The row of numbers above the door flashed "one." The soft bell dinged. Tasha's shackles pulled taught against her wrists, ankles, and the small of her back as she adjusted her balance. It made her want to scream again. Obviously she had touched a

The elevator doors bounced apart and glided into the first-floor wall's outer lip at either side. Commotion greeted them from the opposite end of the corridor. Tasha's vision narrowed to follow the elongated hallway. The doors at the other end seemed to grow further away. She was overcome with a sense of urgency. It made her have to pee.

Officer Dent/Griff pushed her forward. Her toes became wedged in the space between the elevator and the first-floor wall, causing her to stumble to her knees.

"Get up," he demanded. This time he didn't help her.

Tasha resisted when Officer Dent/Griff tried to shove her again. She turned and held her ground. Tasha closed her eyes and counted down from ten. She was out of options. She took a deep breath, turned, and shuffled forward. Officer Dent/Griff followed closely behind.

Tasha scrunched her face and held it until the barreling sensation to let loose dwindled. The doors leading outside were less than ten feet away. The commotion made it hard for her to think, so she didn't. Most of the thoughts that begged for her attention revolved around self-pity. She took a deep breath and prepared herself to deal with a million questions at once. The prospect touched off a fight-or-flight response.

Tasha abbreviated the pace of her shuffle, shackles jangling. She waited until Officer Dent/Griff was right up on her back, close enough that she could feel his hot breath leaking down on her.

Tasha whipped around and lunged at him. Her face was distorted by hate. Brutish growl-tones leapt from her throat as she reached out with her shackled hands and tried to claw his face and neck. She didn't see exactly what he did, but before Tasha knew it, Dent/Griff had spun her around, clamped his massive hand around the back of her neck, and squeezed her into semi-submission.

Tasha cried out in deep emotional anguish; fuck pain.

"I-HATE-CHOOOWWWWW!" She screamed so loud that it strained her voice. "I-FUCKIN-HATE-CHOOOWWWW!"

Officer Dent/Griff continued to squeeze as he led her forward. Tasha shrieked.

"You might as well kill me now, motherfucker, 'cause if it takes me 'til my last breath, I'm going to hunt you fuckers down. YOU HEAR ME?!? You think you know suffering? You don't know SHIT! Just wait. I swear to God!"

Suddenly, there was no more commotion seeping through the doors, which meant that the reporters outside could probably hear her screaming.

"Careful, now. That's just the kind of talk that the press likes to hear," Griff quipped.

"I don't care anymore. It's not like I've got anything else to lose."

"In that case, do me a favor and hold that thought," Griff said.

The double doors swung open. Tasha's eyes were red and puffy from crying. Other than that, she maintained her composure. She squinted at the harsh daylight. There were reporters as far as she could see, brandishing microphones with call-letters of media outlets. They lined the steps on either side of the doors. The wave of über-silence that greeted her arrival was short-lived.

So many voices calling "Tasha," so many questions…. They all seemed to contain the same words in different sequences.

"Natasha, is it true that…"

"Ms. Armstrong, what do you have to say to…"

"Can you tell us why, Tasha?"

From the outer fringes of the crowd, passers-by lobbed insults and made threats.

"Murderer!" "Whore!" "I hope you rot in hell!"

"Give us some space, please," Griff barked at the swarm of bodies that pushed toward them. Palming the small of her back, Officer Dent/Griff guided Tasha forward through the writhing mass. With his other hand, he waved the hungry journalists back in a fashion that resembled Frankenstein waving at the flames. Tasha felt herself being led to the right. She recognized a familiar face. It was Griff. He wore a faded T-shirt, baggy cargo pants, and a vintage blazer that hugged his sturdy frame. His hair was pulled back into a high ponytail. He stood directly in front of her, blocking her path. She had no choice but to stop when she reached him.

Griff leaned at her and stuck a big, black microphone in her face. The soft tip of it brushed against her lips. Tasha turned and looked up at Officer Dent, who appeared confused and disoriented, as if waking from an intense dream. He was looking around and frowning. *Where am I?* his perplexed expression seemed to say.

The crowd went silent in anticipation of Tasha's first words. In her head, she heard Griff's voice.

"You were saying…?"

Three Weeks Later

"Yyyyooooouuuuuu!"

It was the fifth… no, sixth time that Tasha woke up to the chilling rasp of Mary's desiccated voice and the image of her standing over Gerald York's body, glaring back at Tasha like she knew her. It was a wonder that Tasha got to sleep at all with all the questions that flooded her mind: *What did the dream mean? What does she want from me? Why me? Will I ever see Dana again? How am I going to get myself out of this mess? Is she really alive... or am I just fucked in the head?*

From the outside, The Ries Clinic looked like madness made manifest. The old marble edifice looked as if a set of gargoyles could be found on each corner. When it sunk in that this was where she would spend the next couple months before her trial, she nearly lost it in the van.

Calm down, girl. Millions of people have been down this road and survived... and so will you.

They gave her the smallest room they had. It used to be a bathroom before it was converted to accommodate yet another lost soul. The brass told her that they saved it for wack-job killers like her.

She stared out the thin vertical window in her door long enough to imagine that she could fit her whole body through it. Then she could take Tarkington's gun (he was the late-shift guard) and use it to beat the shit out of him before she killed him. Even though he spent most of his watch right outside her door, he took his sweet ol' time acknowledging her when she was in the midst of one of her nightmare-tantrums. It made her blood boil that they wrote her off as some delusional menace to society. All she wanted was another human voice to interrupt her inner maniacal babbling. For now, her psychosis was her only luxury to escape from the paralyzing solitude of the four padded walls; six if you count the ceiling and the floor.

Tasha saw the lust in Tarkington's eyes when he looked at her. Guys like him were such easy reads. He wore his libido on his tattooed right forearm in the form of a naked blond woman, legs spread, puckered face-lips in place of a vagina. Tasha knew what she'd have to do to get on his good side. So she offered him a deal.

She couldn't even remember the last time she was with a man. For the record, Tarkington wasn't that ugly... for a white guy, although he could stand to lose a few pounds. And maybe use some deodorant.

Just as she expected, it was usually over pretty quickly when he took her. The whole time, Tarkington had this look of prepubescent oafishness that reminded her of the all the quick-cummers in high school who, until it came time to put up, bragged of their prowess in bed to anyone who would listen.

Before long, Tasha had access to the entire third floor when everyone else was asleep: the halls, the common area, and the small iron balcony out back that overlooked the parking lot and the woods beyond it. The only condition was that she couldn't wander out of Tarkington's sight. To make certain that she honored the agreement, he would keep his laser-scope locked on her. He told her that he was itching to see just how accurate it was. She wanted to shove that thing down his throat. He wanted to shove it somewhere else.

Tasha's only other option was to wait for the strange waking dreams that came sporadically, like a cold or a case of the shits. In them, she would find herself alone in the hallway outside her room, with no knowledge of how she got there. A chorus of snoring poked through the silence. The door to her room would be hanging wide open behind her. The guard station right outside of it would be empty. The floor of the hallway had a reflective sheen that popped at night when people walked across it. Whatever it was they used to clean it made the rubber soles of her slippers stick when she lifted her feet. It was one of those things about the place that, like the vague chemical odor and the nonsensical rantings of many of the other patients, generally went unnoticed by those who were accustomed to it. In the waking dreams, the sound made her more paranoid with each step. Once she realized that she was in control her actions, Tasha would make a break for the front door. To get there from the third floor, she had to travel down three flights of stairs, past two guard posts (which were always empty), and out the noisy stairwell door that opened onto the main lobby. She'd cover the final stretch in a mad dash, but no matter how fast she was, she could never reach the front door. Sometimes her fingertips would graze the metal handle. Sometimes the door would be open, in which case she chased the doorway and the scenery outside in the courtyard. Just when she thought she was making progress, that she was free, she'd wake up in her bed like nothing ever happened.

Tasha wanted to blame Griff from the start, but the waking dreams seemed like a more natural process than his coaxing. She called them waking dreams because they had a texture indicative of reality. Dreams were all Tasha had anymore. She became adept at distinguishing the punch-drunk aura of the dreams from the hyper-realistic glow of Griff's illusions and both from the crispness of real-world clarity, merciless as it was. Maybe Griff was just getting better.

One night after an especially messy fuck session, Tasha managed to swipe a utility knife from the storage room while Tarkington's wife kept him frazzled on the telephone. She hid the blade in her vagina. She knew they'd come looking when they realized it was missing from the storage room. They always blamed her for everything.

Tasha could hear the hollow whine of Mrs. Tarkington's voice from the end of the hall. They had been married for fifteen years, according to Tarkington. *It can't possibly be the sex that has kept them together for so long,* she thought to herself. First of all, he had one of the smallest dicks that Tasha had ever seen. It was only about three inches fully erect, and even that was more than he could control.

Tarkington was number one on Tasha's shitlist. The list was as follows:

1. Tarkington
2. Griff
3. Mary
4. Linda Ludlow
5. That reporter who called her "subhuman"

The list was arranged by opportunity, not by level of malice. If that were the case, Mary's name would occupy every number, with maybe a subcategory for Griff. His name filled Tasha with a sense of shame—groveling the way she had. And to a man!

Tasha couldn't wait to give Linda Ludlow a piece of her mind. Linda had this smug way of playing to the worst impulses of her audience or fronting like there was valor in interviewing a dangerous criminal live, via satellite. Tasha thought back the end of their interview together when Linda leaned in and said, "Nothing personal. I do have an audience to consider."

Today was hardly the first time suicide had crossed Tasha's mind. Death would surely be better than the daily fix of lamenting the disappearance of Dana or chatting with the unbearable silence that pressed her to speak. If it weren't for Dana, Tasha would have ended it all when they first caught her rather than deal with all this. If that wasn't bad enough, she had to deal with Doc Wilkinson's patronizing psychobabble for an hour every Monday, Wednesday, and Friday. He tried to tell her that something in her past was responsible for promoting her murderous inclinations. He didn't think she was evil like everyone else did, but he also didn't think that she was innocent. He certainly didn't buy her story about Mary. Tasha felt stupid for thinking that he might. He said that although he believed that *she* believed what she was saying, it was all fabricated by her mind to compensate for the feelings of guilt over her crimes.

Doc Wilkinson wasn't totally off the mark about her past. Tasha's anger toward her parents and how their relationship ended helped turn her into the survivor that she liked to think she was. But that was it. There were a few unanswered questions about her childhood, but they weren't the kinds of things that would turn someone into a murderer. Saving her son's life and defending her own were Tasha's only motives.

Doc Wilkinson suggested hypnotherapy to help bring the memories out. He said that facing them was the only way for her to excise her anger and start the healing process. *Whatever*, Tasha thought. But the doctor harped on it so much that she eventually conceded. It wasn't like she had other commitments lined up, and she was more than a little curious to know what exactly happened during those five years that she spent in the hospital. She never forgot how her parents (especially her mother) seemed preoccupied with telling her that she had been a sickly child. Tasha always felt that they were hiding something. When she asked them to elaborate, they would only say that it was a difficult birth. She figured it was their way of telling her that she didn't want to know the truth. It couldn't have been any worse than what she was currently going through.

ANDRE DUZA

Chapter 5

Carl was angry today, angrier than ever before, it seemed. The weed wasn't working anymore, so he walked around in perpetual 'roid-rage mode. He had already gone through one of the five pounds that he bought from Chiba trying to chase away his demons. In fact, the weed was making things worse. It caused him to overanalyze everything. This morning, for instance, he couldn't get it up for Kayla. His mind hadn't been straight since. He blamed it on the steroids. His subconscious mind kept telling him that he was losing his touch—on the field and off. He'd heard it all before, but lately, the voice seemed to be getting louder, its tone spiteful instead of simply matter-of-fact.

"Fuckin' Anadrol!" Carl grunted. Kayla straddled him impatiently, awaiting her cue to commence bucking like a cowgirl. He pounded the mattress with his fists to punctuate his frustration.

The rain was beginning to bother Carl even more than the crowd. *They are so goddamn fickle.* He remembered a time when he was the flavor of the month, when the sea of voices swelled as he trotted onto the field. He felt at one with them, this raging entity of shifting colors and raw passion. It was then that he was at his best. He felt so alive, so invincible.

Just last year, they were calling Carl "the comeback kid." Now they booed him at appearances and press conferences. They called him a "joke" and a "has-been" and spit down on him when he entered and left the tunnel, even at home. Between plays, he used to ham it up for the omnipresent cameras. Now the flashes stung him like bullets.

The shriek of the whistle brought the lights and the crowd back to him: 75,000 voices merged into one sonorous roar. It was game time, at home against the Bandits. Carl could barely think over all the noise. He studied the sideline as he hunched into position; still no Kayla.

Strangely, the Bandits had replaced McDowal, their run-stop-per, with Jefferies, who was much smaller and more docile. Carl had never known Jefferies to start on defense. He was a special teams guy all the way: small and fast, like a cheetah. Carl wasn't about to complain, though. He glared at the empty seat that he had reserved for Kayla. She probably had a legitimate reason. Traffic was always hell during the Monday night games, and she was like a mouse behind the wheel. Carl imagined her lips in full pout, her bronzed skin glowing as it always did when she was happy or horny. As much as he fought it, he couldn't help but give her a male companion in his jealousy-riddled imaginings. In Carl's visions, it was always some wimpy guy, not a chiseled warrior like himself. In his mind, Carl watched Kayla smile at the man in a way that he thought only he could inspire. The grin grew larger than he'd ever seen as the poindexter ignited her entire body in ways that he could barely comprehend.

"Blue 22! Blue 22! Hut! Hut!"

The call startled him away from his wandering thoughts and brought a chill that sprinted up his back and down his arms. He didn't have time to plant his cleats in as deep as he would've liked. *Ah, it's only that punk Jefferies*, he thought, as he took the ball and launched. Almost immediately, he slammed into what felt like a brick wall.

Carl woke to a warm, damp stream meeting his brow and rolling down his right cheek. He could tell right away that he was at the bottom of a pile of men. He opened his eyes and saw the tiny, animated Bandits mascot standing over him. It couldn't have been more than six inches tall. It stood over Carl's facemask and pissed on him.

"'ave a taste-a-this, you bloody monkey," it scoffed in a garbled Cockney accent.

Carl panicked and began to flail, but there was little room to move. He turned his head, squeezed his eyes shut, and let out a desperate groan.

"Git the FUCK offa me!" he roared, but the pile only shifted slightly.

When he forced himself to look again, there was only a dirty white helmet. The Bandits mascot, in full colonial regalia, one hand on its hip, the other pointing toward the heavens, was fixed in place. The stench of urine that assaulted his senses only seconds ago was replaced by that of pungent body odor.

God, not another concussion, Carl thought. It was the only reasonable explanation for his hallucination.

"I said GIT- THE-FUCK-OFFA-ME!" Carl could feel his lungs collapsing. He struggled for enough room to bend his elbow and shove as the pile finally began to lighten.

Jefferies couldn't possibly have hit him like that.

Carl wriggled like a snake held by its throat, but the bodies still pressed against him, restricting his movement. All he could do was close his eyes and wait.

Carl opened one eye as the pile lightened. Standing over him were Williams, Drexler, Rowdy, and... McDowal??? Confused, Carl climbed to his feet and brushed off his uniform.

How the fuck did that happen? Carl watched McDowal high-five his teammates on his way back to the line. *How could they have switched?* He was positive that it was Jefferies who lined up against him... positive.

Carl saw Jefferies languishing on the sideline. He had been there the entire time. Carl watched him wave his hand as if to direct someone toward him, his face suddenly aglow. It was Kayla.

Carl froze as his mind tried to process the scene: the way Kayla looked at that bastard; the way Jefferies cracked that sidewise smile (there was something sneaky about it, something lascivious, like he was going to lick her or something); the way Jefferies looked Kayla over with his squinted eyes. Carl's eyelids bulged with every seductive sway of Kayla's hips, every flash of her big white teeth. Those teeth. At times, they looked more like fangs; he loved how they made her appear untamed, especially when she was angry. Carl couldn't take his eyes off them.

Pussy was easy for him, even top-quality pussy. He could get that at the drop of a hat whenever he wanted. There was just something about Kayla.

Kayla moved her eyes from Jefferies over to Carl. She gave

Carl a sudden, sly wink that stole his breath.

Carl faced the ground to keep from exploding and making himself look like an ass. The Astroturf was a brighter shade of green than usual, almost fluorescent. He counted down slowly from ten and then looked up.

This time, Kayla was flirting with Gustav. *But he's nothing but an overgrown hick!* Somehow she had made it down to the sideline, among the players. Kayla placed her hands on her smooth, taut thighs and arched her delicate back as if to encourage Gustav to mount her. Gustav simply stared, dumbfounded. His mouth, which hid somewhere beneath his shaggy mess of a beard, hung open like a famished canine ogling a plate of scraps.

This was too much.

Kayla was bent over, and Gustav was using Kayla's back as a surface on which to write out his phone number. He was taking his sweet old time so that he could maintain the groin-to-ass contact as long as possible. *Maybe he don't know how to write his name.*

Kayla's brown eyes peeked coquettishly at Carl from the corners.

You fuckin' BITCH!!!!

As much as Carl didn't want to admit it, he felt like dropping to his knees and crying. Kayla was supposed to be different from the golddiggin' bitches that most players "dated." She was more like his mother.

Rage tempted Carl to explode toward Gustav in a mad charge, but the people, and the cameras.... And Gustav wasn't exactly a pushover. It took a moment for Carl to recognize the chant.

"STERRR-RRROIDS... STERRR-RRROIDS!"

"Aye, motherfucker, this ain't no place for drug addicts," McMahon sneered. "If you don't mind, some of us have a game to play!"

Robertson spoke up too, but he was Danish, and it was hard to understand him even when he wasn't angry and spitting all over the place.

Carl lingered only momentarily on his two angry teammates

before his head whipped back to the sideline.

Kayla was gone. A quick search turned up Jefferies, who was warming the bench. Gustav was there, too, looking dumb. "Oh God. I think I'm losing it," Carl whispered.

Carl wasn't exactly sure why he looked up at the Panavision screen. Maybe it was to see if they'd replay the hit he just took so he could find out what the hell happened. Instead, it showed only his face, all wrinkled and dumbstruck, his mouth open wide and threatening to swallow the smaller version of himself that stared up at it. The camera moved to a painted fan in the nosebleed seats who was holding a banner that read STEROIDS MAKE YOUR NUTS SHRIVEL UP.

While Carl stared at the image, he noticed a man in the background. Something about the man, a dark brotha (almost as dark as Carl) with dreads and a stare born of life in the gutter, begged Carl to look closer. His face was narrow in a way that made his large, brown eyes stand out and seem even bigger than they were.

A warm, sick feeling made Carl's hair stand on end. It felt like he was standing face to face with the dreadlocked brotha. Carl's mind started to make silly assumptions, like that the brotha had something to do with the hallucinations. It was more than suspicion; it was a distinct feeling. It started with a throbbing headache, then a dizzy spell, followed by the feeling that he was no longer in control. The feeling was on its way to smothering him. His breath became harder to catch. He felt a sensation of hands wrapping around his thick neck and beginning to squeeze. Just before the camera cut away, the dreadlocked brotha lifted his index finger to his temple and made small circles, as if to indicate that Carl was indeed crazy.

"STERRR-RRROIDS... STERRR-RRROIDS!"

"MEZERAK! GET YOUR ASS OUTTA THERE!" Coach Dudson hollered through his hands, his barrel chest heaving as it always did when he lost his temper. He shook a balled fist at Carl to accentuate his disgust. Under different circumstances, it might have been comical. Dudson was a character.

Carl stutter-stepped toward the bench and checked the Bandits' sideline one last time. Kayla was nowhere to be found. He let out a deep sigh, dropped his head, and slowly walked off the field.

*　　*　　*

Excerpt: Hypnotherapy Transcript
Q: Peter E. Wilkinson, MD, PhD
A: Natasha Evangeline Armstrong

Q: You are traveling down a time vortex that spins your body 'round and 'round and 'round. As you spin, I want you to focus on the light at the other end of the vortex. Do you see the light?

A: Yes.

Q: The light is moving closer to you and growing larger as it approaches. In a few seconds, the light will be close enough that you can reach out and touch it. When this happens, you are going to move forward into the light. When you come out the other end, you will be five years old.

(Tasha's voice takes on a childlike tone and quality.)

A: I hate it here.

Q: Can you start by telling me where here is?

A: I'm in my room.

Q: Your room at the hospital?

A: No, duh! At the home.

Q: Can you tell me the name of the place?

A: Um… I think it's L-a-k-e-s-h-o-r-e….

Q: Lake Shore Foster Home? Lake Shore Home for Children?

A: Yes. Lake Shore Foster Home.

Q: Okay. So, what is it about the foster home that you don't like?

A: I dunno. Everything.

Q: Could you be more specific, please?

A: The houseparents are always yelling at us. They don't let us have any fun. Mrs. Ayres said that we don't have the lucks-shuree of having fun. She said we have to be on our best behavior for when the families come looking for kids.

Q: Who is Mrs. Ayres?

A: Mrs. Ayres is the boss of the houseparents. She's really mean. I don't like her. The houseparents don't like her either. Sometimes I hear them call her naughty names.

Q: What about your friends? You must be friends with some of the other children there. Can you tell me about them?

A: I'm friends with Jane. She's my bestest friend. The other kids… they make fun of me, and they call me names. They're all older than me. Jane is older than me, too, but just a little bit.

Q: That's not very nice of them. What kinds of names do they call you?

A: I'm not aspossed-ta say. Mrs. Ayres says that they're bad words. Sometimes they make monkey noises… and they say that no family is gonna want me 'cause I'm black.

Q: I'm sorry to hear that, Tasha. Can you tell me a little about your friend Jane?

A: We're blood sisters….

Q: Is that so?

A: Yup. She's like… about my height; pretty hair. (She demonstrates by running her fingers down the sides of her face.) She doesn't talk a lot. The other kids make fun of her, too. They're always telling her to speak up. She hates it here, too.

Q: What else about the foster home makes you hate being there so much?

A: I dunno… the food. It's always cold.

Q: Anything else? I want you to think really hard now, Tasha.

A: (Tasha begins to sob and cry as she talks.) I just wish Jane and me could be with a real family.

Q: Okay, Tasha. When I count to three, you are going to be back in that time vortex, spinning 'round and 'round and 'round. The light at the end is moving closer. This time, when you move into the light, you will think of the last thing that you remember from the Lake Shore

Foster Home. One… two… three….

A: (sobbing)

Q: What's the matter, Tasha?

A: Jane hates me. She won't even look at me. I want to say goodbye to her, but she won't talk to me.

Q: Why does she hate you?

A: We said we would never leave each other… but I just wanna be in a family. I just wanna have a mommy and a daddy.

Q: You were adopted by a family? Well, congratulations. That's great news. I would think Jane would be happy for you.

A: Nooooo… you don't knowwwww…. We took the oath wh… when we started bein' blood sisters. Tommy said that you can't break the oath. He… he said that bad things will happen.Q: Is Tommy one of the other children in the foster home?

A: Yes. He's a lot older than me, though. He's the one who told us about blood brothers. He said that he did it with his best friend.

Q: I see. Where are you right now, Tasha?

A: I'm in my new mommy and daddy's car.

Q: With the Armstrongs?

A: Yes.

Q: Where are you going?

A: We just left the home. I can still see Jane. She's standing in the driveway. She won't even wave or nothing. She's just standing there, watching us drive away. She hates meeee….

Q: I'm sure it must be difficult losing a friend in a situation like that, but she doesn't hate you. She'll eventually move on and, one day, a nice family will come along and adopt *her,* too.

A: No. She told me. She said, "I hate-choo."

Q: I thought she wouldn't speak to you?

A: That's what she said when I told her I was leaving. Jane is different. She's been there so long. The families… they like her at first, but then… I don't know. They think she's weird or somethin'.

Q: I'd like to move on from Jane now, Tasha. I want you to tell me a little bit about the Armstro….

A: But she *hates* meeee….

Q: All right... all right.... Trust me, Tasha: she'll get over it.
A: Noooooo....
Q: ...So tell me, what are your mommy and daddy doing right now?
A: Daddy's driving. They keep lookin' back at me in the mirror, smilin' at me.
Q: Are they saying anything?
A: They're talkin' about somethin'. They're kinda whispering. They think I can't hear them.
Q: What are they talking about?
A: ...They're talkin' about me.... "They start young, don't they? Getcha so you feel as though you ain't worth..." (gasps) He said a bad word!
Q: That's okay, Tasha. What else are they saying?
A: "No child-a-mine is ever gonna think she's worthless."

*　　*　　*

What Psychic Patrice Ellerbee Saw

Mary Jane Mezerak died on impact, struck down by a van (a sky-blue Chevy, if her memory served her) on Ridley Creek Road, just outside of Philly. She was twenty-four and with child. She was wide awake when she died.

Her body landed in Fred Baker's yard. It was October 23rd, and with Halloween right around the corner, she fit right in with the elaborate decorations that made Fred an outcast in the community. The neighbors complained that his display disturbed the children. It was the same few whiners every year. The Lonely Housewives Brigade, Fred called them. They had nothing better to do with their time.

The word on Fred was that he worked in the movies back in the day, before the severe social anxiety set in. Now his time was spent in his basement with his sculpted animals and aliens and classic movie monsters.

This year, he kept it nice and simple: a full-sized coffin and some skeletons that Fred got at an auction when they closed down the medical college on Garrett Road. He dressed them in tuxedos and gave them cigars to hold. Recycled Christmas bulbs kept their eyes aglow.

Mary's body lay twisted in Fred's coffin. Her right leg dangled stiffly over one edge. Her arms, which were forced out in front of her when her body took flight, made it look as if she was beckoning to the heavily wooded embankment across the way.

Three days and nights passed before Fred decided to call someone. He didn't want to call the police and deal with their intrusions, so he called a friend of a friend who might be able to "help him out." A heavy downpour vomited a sleek car into view. "York's Funeral Home" was inscribed in cursive letters along the side. From inside emerged a dapper man. He was more of a silhouette in the rain, long and broad, like a cross between Humphrey Bogart and the Grim Reaper. He approached tentatively until he was close enough to size her up. He drew his cigarette down to the butt in one deep drag.

The shadow-man pulled a pair of gloves from his pocket, slipped them on, and crouched over the body.

Chapter 6

Stoned Is the Way of the Walk

Clout massaged the sore spot on the back of his head and struggled to find meaning in his last semiconscious thoughts, his mind afloat in a dizzying vortex of swaying, human-like shapes that stretched longer and thinner. *What's going on? Where am I?* Clout exhaled and cursed the ground, making sure to keep it low so as not to alert the undesirables to his location.

A trace of the last song he'd heard woke his mind, the same one that the long, thin bodies swayed to before he awoke here in this diverse, cross-section of white and black poverty. An ambiguous moment allowed the song to escape the confines of his throbbing head and echo off into the blue-black horizon of lifeless tenements and abandoned cars. *STONED IS THE WAY OF THE WALK.* Cypress Hill was one of his favorites.

Clout raised his hand. His fingers left ethereal trails, especially his middle finger, which was extended as if tossing out a "fuck you." He let it bounce, punctuating the beats of the music.

This was definitely not the place for a skinny white boy from Upper Darby to be walking all by himself. *Leave it to the niggers,* he thought. *Who else would keep a place so neat?* His father had taught him well. Like most people he knew, Clout was the kind of racist who'd act like a best friend to those he discriminated against (mainly blacks and Latinos), at least until they turned their back.

Little things jumped out at him, things that he had seen before: the huge malt liquor billboard for one, which featured an average-looking black man sandwiched between two smiling, Hollywood-black women in the backseat of a limo. The women were staring at the 40-ounce resting right between his legs, neck facing straight up, suds rising inside. Clout was standing right in front of it. It always put a cynical smile on his face when he saw it from the expressway that looked down over this part of the city. It stood about a mile from his girlfriend, Monica's exit on Ferguson Avenue. That was where he, Todd Fienrich, and Laura Singh were headed. That was the last thing that Clout remembered. The billboard's proximity to Monica's house gave him a slight sense of security. He wasn't all that far out of his way. But where were Todd and Laura?

Clout had seen the people who called this area home. Most of them were morbidly obese and penniless and steeped in unresolved anger and unrelenting envy. It was as if the billboard was there to deliberately mock them.

There was also a rumor about people disappearing in this six-block corridor of empty, dilapidated rowhomes the lead to the junkyard on Decatur and Claxton.

Where Clout was from, the general opinion was that the city was a filthy, dangerous place—"dangerous" being code for "overrun by blacks." Clout himself was looked down upon in school. He was hip-hop all the way, from his Timberland boots and baggy jeans to his close-cut, B-boy hairstyle. "I just like their music," he'd say. Really he envied their rich flavor and their grasp of the body's true language. Behind his back, they called him a wigger. When the insults finally reached him, Clout reacted by turning up the racist humor. Eventually, it became second nature.

Clout suddenly remembered the black van that had been following them and the blond chick (Rainah) back at the Raven's Den, a club up on Market. He had only stopped there to get away from the van. He thought it was a coincidence at first when the van kept turning onto the same streets that he did.

The memories began to fall into place. Clout remembered when his eyes met Rainah's. He remembered her slender, athletic build and how she moved like a divine serpent amidst the lusting bodies that gyrated and thrashed on the dance floor. Insecurity made him doubt initially whether she was looking at him. Although he didn't want to admit it, Rainah was out of his league. On top of that, he was standing next to Todd and Laura at the time. They surely brought him down a notch or two.

Todd and Laura were an odd couple to say the least. Todd was the epitome of starched, buttoned-up, white-bread America. Laura was Indian: "from the red-dot tribe," she'd say when people would ask what kind of Indian. Clout hated when Laura let her family name roll from her tongue the correct way, as if she was somehow better because her parents were born rich in India. Plus she talked too goddamned much.

Todd's father, a Vietnam veteran, was constantly bitching about "chinks" and "sand-niggers." He liked to hold court. "One of them bastards is going to be the death of us," he would say. "Just watch the evening news if you don't believe me."

As a result, Todd hid his relationship with Laura from him. Pops had big dreams for Todd to follow in his footsteps and enlist, but Todd proved too delicate for a career in the armed services. It was a sore spot that time hadn't managed to heal.

Clout couldn't take his eyes off Rainah as she danced up to him: the way that her subtle musculature moved in perfect synchronicity with the music. He ogled her as she writhed to the seismic beat under the strobe lights. In retrospect, he probably looked like a pervert. When he caught her eye for the third time, he mustered the courage to smile at her. To his surprise, she smiled back. The next thing he knew she was in his face, close enough that their noses briefly touched. It made him forget all about Todd and Laura.

"You lookin' for a party?" Rainah whispered in Clout's ear so softly that he was surprised he heard it over the music and the fragmented moan of a hundred voices chirping at once. "Because I know where there's one that you'll never forget."

Her words seemed to affect him physically as he watched her disappear into the crowd. Maybe it was the weed, though; he, Todd, and Laura had been smoking all afternoon.

The rest was a little foggy.

Clout stopped and shook his head. He plumbed his shallow masculinity to try to maintain a stone face and a semi-confident posture. He could see that there was nothing but empty buildings for blocks up ahead, so he turned right at the next corner. He looked up at the intersecting street signs: Decatur and Claxton.

Clout had a sinking feeling. He checked the signs again to make sure. Decatur and Claxton.

He could see a junkyard in the distance. It was the junkyard from all the stories he'd heard. There was a large house sitting on a raised mound of land in the middle of the place. Legions of scrapped automobiles lay crushed in piles at its feet. It was the only building in sight.

Rusted razor wire snarled from atop the fenced-in perimeter that stretched for more than a block on all sides of the junkyard. A crooked sign dangled from the opened gate, but Clout couldn't read it without his glasses. This place was different from the kinds of houses one might expect to find in the ghetto. It was an old, imposing building, like some badly aging Southern estate set deep in a steel and concrete bayou.

Clout squinted for a better look, as there were... *things* scattered here and there. They looked almost like men standing in various poses: not real men, but statues, probably made of old auto parts.

Then he saw it: *his* car, parked off to the side of the house, next to three others that appeared fairly new. *Is this the party?* Todd and Laura were probably inside right now wondering where he was.

Clout spent the next few minutes trying to figure out how the hell he wound up outside. Did Rainah bring him out here to get down and dirty? Was he so drunk that he passed out on her? Maybe she tried but just couldn't move him.

"Cl... Clou... tttt!"

A rasped male voice grabbed his attention and directed it toward the island of metal carcasses and living shadows in the junkyard. A moving shape grew larger before his eyes. A dash of white coalesced into a tattered shirt. A rhythmic bounce became a drastic limp. It took him a minute to realize that it was a person... someone he knew, in fact.

"Todd?"

Although he was unsure, Clout went with his first instinct. He hoped it was just a result of too many drinks that caused Todd (if that was in fact who it was) to hobble along as if he could barely walk. Clout wasn't ready to accept that it looked a lot like Todd's legs were bleeding from his shins down to the folded cuffs of his oversized pants. They dragged along the ground and left trails that paralleled the yellow lines painted in the street. Yes, it was Todd, the guy he'd known since first grade; the same guy who Clout always defended when the jocks gave him a hard time in school; the same one whose mother Clout had a serious crush on.

Todd stumbled to a halt and rested on the large stick that supported him under his armpit. His curly, black hair framed the margins of his face, matted by sweat and mud. He was at war with balance, fighting to keep from bearing weight on his feet. He labored to steady his wobbling knees and lift his legs one after the other. He was in obvious pain.

"T... Todd, are you okay? What the hell is going on? Where's Laura?"

Clout's baritone voice had climbed an octave. It was a nervous habit. He began to wonder if he really wanted to know what had happened. Maybe he should just turn tail and run. He could live with being a coward. It was better than being dead.

Todd grunted with every step. The loudest came when he almost lost his balance. He had to step down hard to catch himself. That was when Clout saw what all the moaning was about.

Todd's feet had been crudely amputated. The left one still dangled from the stump at his ankle. Clout wondered if Todd could feel the strand of flesh that kept it from falling off completely.

Clout swallowed the lump in his throat and, after a few tentative moments, walked forward to meet Todd halfway.

"No!" It was evident in Todd's heaving chest and stomach and his bouncing Adam's apple that the pain was too much for him to speak in complete sentences. He gave it his all, regardless. He fought against fatigue to raise his arm and wave Clout away. "I... I thought you were dead."

"What??? Why would you think that? Please tell me what's

going on."

"You shouldn't have come back. The girl... the one from the bar... she's crazy. They all are! We have to get outta here or they'll kill us both!"

It was hard to believe Todd's eyes could get any bigger than they already were. They were now about twice... no, three times as big. The look on his face was a mixture of pain, paranoia, and determination that kept his eyes from blinking or straying from Clout. His lips curled away from his teeth, his nostrils flared and dripped snot with each harrowing step.

"They? Who's they?" Clout cleared his throat and lifted his chin to move the bile along. "Where's Laura?"

"I didn't w... want to leave her, Clout, but I had to get away." Todd struggled with his words. He glanced at his wounds, his eyes welling up, his voice wavering. "Look what they did to me!"

A downward surge tickled Clout's stomach and left his scrawny legs trembling.

The thought of someone deliberately cutting off his feet, or even having the nerve to conjure up such a violent act, kept Clout's mouth agape and incapable of forming words.

A sudden CLICK-CLACK spun Clout in every possible direction as it bounced from building to building. He'd seen enough television to realize what would most likely come next.

POP!

From the corner of his eye, he saw Todd's legs buckle. He collapsed to the ground like a cripple waking from an optimistic dream to find himself standing.

Clout dropped to a crouch. That was the first time he'd ever seen someone get shot, and it was nothing like on TV. Not even close.

He rubbed his forearms to escape the chills that coursed through his body and inspected his trembling limbs. He knew that shock wasn't too far off. He wondered how Todd managed to evade it for so long.

Todd was in the throes of violent convulsions. He was lying

on his back; his large blue eyes were still fixed on Clout. A pool of blood began to form and grow beneath the small of Todd's back.

Without looking him in the eyes, Clout reached out, placed a comforting hand on Todd's cold arm, and tried to reassure him that everything would be all right. With each burst of movement, Todd's limbs became more flaccid, his speech less coherent. Soon, he was reduced to babbling and spitting through clenched teeth. He grabbed Clout's hand and squeezed as hard as he could.

Clout could feel the life flicker away from Todd's twitching body. He snatched his hand from Todd's frigid grip and crawled backwards until his arms gave out and dropped him on his ass.

"Stop looking at me," he quietly demanded, as Todd's glazed eyes seemed to follow him. "Please! There's nothing I can do. I'm sorry, man. Just... stop looking at me!"

From somewhere in the night, another sound stole Clout's attention. It was like a blade slicing through the air, or at least how he thought that might sound.

Clout rolled onto his stomach and hid his head beneath his arms. He peeked in time to see a steel arrow bite deep into Todd's abdomen. An attached wire extended off into the darkness. It torqued straight with a snap.

Clout watched Todd's body skid backward past the sign on the fence (he was close enough to read it now) and into the belly of the junkyard.

TORCHSONG SCRAPYARD, the sign read.

Clout wiped away the sweat that crept toward his eyes and tried to make sense of the situation. A spontaneous burst brought him to his feet. He turned to run and was met by a car door flung open to greet him.

Clout's wrist was broken. He knew it right away. He saw the way his hand bent backward before the glass in the driver's side door shattered into a million pieces and gouged a deep ridge in his forearm. Somehow that didn't hurt half as bad as the door hitting his knee and his groin.

Stay conscious. Clout's mind was pushing for sleep, and it was starting to win.

He woke to three men standing above him. The vision stretched and strained his recuperating senses. Clout massaged his head. The blow had created a delayed ripple that caused his vision to freeze up while his mind slowly processed the image. Blackened goggles stared down and reflected his sorry image.

The figures loomed over him like stone centennials, confident and stoic as they huddled around their frightened prey. They wore gas masks that muffled their breathing.

Were there three or four of them? Clout exercised his eyelids, squeezing them together and blinking, until he was sure. *Three.* Each looked like a cross between a ninja and a rogue SWAT paratrooper. The large one in the middle (Clout's scattered mind immediately dubbed him Big Burly) held some exotic-looking bladed weapon.

Big Burly inched his grip down the barrel of the metallic crossbow that rested against his wide back and lifted it over his head. He flipped the handle into his other hand, then aimed it at Clout. His finger caressed the trigger.

Clout burst to his feet, threw his arms up, and screamed. He ran toward the junkyard as fast as he could. As the sign, the stacked cars, and the sculptures quickly bounced toward him, Clout wondered how the hell he managed to do what he just did, but it was a fleeting thought. He was more concerned with the thought that the ninja-paratroopers would pick him off at any second. Clout turned and looked back, expecting to find them in close pursuit, but they simply stood there and watched him run away.

A loud winding sound gave Clout an extra burst of speed. He couldn't tell where the sound was coming from, and he didn't care. There was a brief sensation that his mind registered as pain when, in fact, it was more jarring than anything else. Before he knew it, his feet had left the ground. He looked up, with sullen eyes, at the thick wire that clotheslined him to the ground. It came from two sculptures that faced each other on either side of the dirt path. Their arms, twisted metal fingers spread like feathers at the apex of a large wing, were extended. He followed the wire that extended from hand to hand, forming a raised tripwire.

"Owww... Fuck!" Clout moaned, working his coarse tongue through the thick layer of blood and phlegm that his stomach belched up.

Clout grunted, jumped to his feet, and assumed a defensive stance. He coughed a few short breaths from his swollen, blood-flushed face and focused on his surroundings. He caressed his chest.

"I wouldn't stay in one place for too long, friend," a muffled, female voice muttered, jarring him out of semi-concentration.

Clout spun past her, then corrected his motion when his mind caught up to his reflexes. She was peeking out from behind a vestigial light post. The first thing he noticed was how closely the heavy fabric of her uniform pursued every beguiling contour of her tantalizing shape, recating to her movement enough to follow and compensate. He wondered if she looked as good beneath the suit and gas mask.

Clout was reluctant to trust his inner voice. It tried to convince him that she was just a girl, hence less of a threat than the others.

Rainah lifted her arm and flashed a large hunting knife. She slid it across her throat to taunt him and then exploded toward him without warning.

"Oh shit!" She was getting closer.

Clout considered standing his ground, but his legs had already decided otherwise.

She was fast, really fast. Even as he sprinted away at top speed, she was right on top of him. They raced through the labyrinth of metal monoliths.

Clout faked right, and then ran left down a smaller path. Huge columns of flattened cars hid all but the night.

Rainah's muffled giggles (like those of a mischievous school-girl) chilled his bones. He turned and found her doubled over, hands on both knees as she continued to crack up. Clout continued to the end of the row and broke left.

"Oh... my... God!" The words came out slowly as he took in the whole scene: two manmade angels side by side, as if in flight, carrying a third corpus. They hung from thick, iron posts that were buried deep in the dirt.

Their wings were made of canvas, metal, and barbed wire. Clout's mouth hung open in wonderment. He took a long look at the third body. It looked different than the other two, more like a real corpse. Its skin was shriveled and dry; its lips were thin and emaciated. The exposed ribcage jutted outward like surreal fangs from its decomposed chest as if they themselves had died trying to escape the flesh.

Clout caught the sublime glint of a large blade in his peripheral vision... or maybe it was in his mind. He rubbernecked for the girl. He knew it was foolish to think that she had given up chase. He knew that she was watching him right now.

Clout surveyed the walls of wreckage for any sign of her. Most of the cars were crushed to shit, but she was small—maybe five-foot two at the most.

TWANG!

Always from behind, he thought. Assuming that this was the end of his life, Clout rolled his eyes and awaited the pain that he knew would be more intense than anything he could imagine. At the last moment, he turned, like a man, to meet his fate. His courage surprised even him.

From above, there was a CLICK. Clout peered at the corpse in the arms of the angels. It rose up and was coming right at him.

Better that thing than a bullet... or a knife. It was all he had time to think before instinct caused him to shut his eyes tighter than ever before. He fell to his ass, his arms shielding his head. The shriveled corpse bounced to an abrupt stop just short of him. He opened his eyes in time to catch the last bob of its head.

"You fuckers!" Clout yelled in frustration. "What did I ever do to you?"

He crawled backward and immediately shrunk under the sudden downwind. Something told him to look up, but instead he looked down at the X carved into the ground just beneath his legs.

"Three... two... ONE!"

There was a loud noise, like an explosion. A Chevrolet swung down and landed on the X.

"Lan nao cung!" Tsun exclaimed as the rigged Chevy slammed to the ground. "I wish I seen the look on his face."

Griff and Derek, who were crouching behind a dirt mound, stood and looked down in search of the shaky white subtitles that inexplicably appeared whenever Tsun spoke in his native tongue. His English was awkward, and he could never seem to coordinate his mouth with the words that poured from it, which made him look like a character in a dubbed kung-fu flick.

Griff read the subtitles out loud: "Every time? Don't be so sure," he warned Tsun, his thick arm held out in front of him to convey his intention.

Tsun was already in mid-jog. "I gotta see this!" he yelled cheerfully in English.

Griff shared an annoyed glance with Derek, who then hoisted Todd's body over his left shoulder and shook his head.

"Maybe we should put a leash on him," Derek remarked. He was the most introverted of the lot and was gifted with a droll sense of humor. Griff found him seven years ago, hiding from the police in the basement of one of their old compounds.

Derek had just robbed the First Trust Bank on Main, killing two tellers and a cop in the process. Griff walked up on Derek in the hiding spot as he crouched in the corner behind some boxes of canned food and offered him help. Derek later revealed that he'd murdered his father and two older sisters in a fit of rage when he was only thirteen and had been on the run ever sense. They had all taken part in abusing him.

"Never a dull moment with that guy," Derek joked. He patted Todd (who was still alive) on the back, then he and Griff started toward the labyrinth.

Tsun's blond highlights, which made him look like an Asian pop star, came into view as they arrived.

Clout wriggled, still conscious, beneath Tsun. Clout had managed to dive out of the way of the booby-trapped Chevy at the last minute. His right ankle and foot were gravely injured, but his condition was not critical.

Three figures floated, wraith-like, out of the darkness and surrounded Clout and Tsun. Now that they had taken off their gas masks, Clout realized that the girl with the knife was the same one from the Raven's Den.

"What tha matta?" Tsun poked the boy. "You sceah-id or some-ting? I thought you not believe in us?"

Clout's eyes leaked a steady flow that left streaks of clean white skin behind on his dirt-laden mug. He was so frightened that Tsun's remark about him not believing went right over his head. He couldn't help thinking of Todd's father's war stories as he followed Tsun's unstable glare, his almond eyes slanted drastically.

Tsun walked over and yanked Todd's body from Derek's shoulder.

"Hey!" Derek danced to catch his balance and took a heavy step towards Tsun. "Watch it, you little fffff..."

"Careful, Derek," Griff scolded. He swayed his index finger like an upturned pendulum. "Remember what I told you about control."

Derek stepped back and balled his fists.

"You wanna see what we do to you friend?" Tsun groaned at Clout, who flinched at the antipathy in his voice and turned away. "Look at him! I wanna to see if I can make you believe."

Tsun waited for Clout's hesitant eyes to find him. When they did, he cocked his foot and commenced kicking and stomping on Todd's head and torso. "This look real enough for you?" He kicked. "What about this, huh?" He stomped. "Or this!"

"Tsun!" Griff reprimanded, to no avail.

"He's outta control," Derek whispered to Rainah.

"That's putting it lightly," Rainah replied.

For Tsun, this was the next best thing to sex.

"You see his face? That look real to you?"

Clout vomited.

"That's enough, Tsun!" Griff's voice sank, but Tsun continued nevertheless. He was in the zone.

"How 'bout now, huh?"

Considering his violent nature, it might come as a surprise that there was nothing abnormal about Tsun's childhood: no alcoholism, no neglect, no sexual abuse—nothing but strict Eastern values. If one were to ask him about his aggressive tendencies, he'd just say that he was wired wrong, and who was *he* to argue with nature.

Griff never really liked Tsun; neither did the rest of them, for that matter. Mary brought him in personally. She kidnapped him from a Pathmark parking lot a few years back, and until recently, he was her little pet. Recently, though, he had been getting on everyone's nerves because of his lack of restraint and his mistakes. They were all itching to take a shot at him.

"Have it your way, dumbass," Griff said, flashing his teeth in a primal display. He aimed his crossbow and pulled the trigger.

"Owwwww... thu chó chet (what the fuck)!" The pain chased Tsun in circles. He clutched his right inner thigh, knees buckling when the muscles surrounding the wound tensed. He grabbed his leg and fell on top of Todd.

Even in his next-to-lifeless state, Todd's swollen eyes flew open and bulged. The pain outside the bounds of human expression. A single tear seemed to anoint his soul's departure.

Griff, Rainah, and Derek looked down simultaneously and read the subtitles.

Tsun held his throbbing thigh in both hands and rocked back and forth. A sudden burst of thought made him reach for his gun.

"Tsun, don't!" Rainah's voice startled him.

Thanks to Griff, Tsun's arm had already locked up before he could reach his gun. Tsun turned slowly. Pulsating anger warmed his entire body.

Griff winked and pointed, thumb cocked.

Tsun sought the ground for comfort. He would have overlooked Clout entirely had he not seen a single blue eye peeking from the beaten lump that Clout had become.

"What the fuck you lookin' at?" Tsun's words caused Clout

DEAD BITCH ARMY   111

to curl into a tight ball. Tsun turned and directed his anger at Griff. "You get on my fucking nerves, man! You think you tough shit because of you mind games and because you the only one she talk to!"

"Tsun!" Rainah knew it was too late for him. She saw the look in Griff's eyes. It was the same look he gave Carl Mezerak whenever he happened to pop up on the tube in uniform or in various commercials.

Tsun squirmed on his ass. There was no way he was going out without a fight. He let out a deep groan as Griff grabbed the protruding arrow and dug it in with a twist.

"Owwwww! I'm sorry! I'm sorry!"

Griff pushed and pulled and twisted.

"There you go, talking your trash, Tsun," Griff grinned, his ambiguous mug like that of a naughty child who had been caught making mischief. "Has anyone here ever heard me say that I thought I was 'tough shit?'"

Rainah and Derek shook their heads.

"I didn't think so."

Griff continued to manipulate the arrow. He was enjoying every minute of it. "Hey, you!" He nudged Clout with his foot. "I asked you a question."

"Wh... what was the question?" Clout struggled to speak but tried not to sound as scared as he was. He'd always heard that people like this thrived on others' fear.

Griff paused, his eyebrows raised in disbelief.

Derek and Rainah gave little more than a shrug as Griff eyed each of them. They were afraid of him as well.

"Someone please finish this muthafucka." Although Griff was visibly angry, his mouth still managed a naughty grin.

Clout scanned the surrounding area, then Derek, then Rainah. He worried that Tsun and Griff stood close enough to reach out and punish him for staring, but he looked anyway and quickly found that he was right on the money... and that Griff hit a lot harder than Tsun.

"I guess that's my cue." Rainah let the words pour tentatively from her small mouth. She lifted her knife, flipped it across the back of her hand, and smiled. "Thought I'd be another notch in your belt, huh?"

Her hips swung with exaggerated movements as she approached. The least she could do was to give Clout a little show.

"You shoulda never came back after I clocked you on the head the first time. I was willing to consider you one that got away."

"Oh my God! Please!" Clout's feeble attempt to lift himself was thwarted by Griff's fist. It met his back with a hollow thump that gave his kidney a jolt. Clout slammed back to the ground, flesh and bone meeting it with a CLAP, kicking up dust.

Clout wretched and grabbed at his back. He struggled to catch his breath. His body raged with adrenaline; otherwise, the pain alone would have sent him into shock. At least he was still alive. He honestly thought it was all over when Tsun first ran up and threw his mask at him.

Clout placed his hands beneath him, palms pressed against the ground, and waited until Rainah was just about ready to lunge. Suddenly, he burst to his feet and darted through the gap between Derek and Griff. His shattered foot held the weight. He looked frantically for a way out.

"Hey, asshole!" Rainah took a step toward Clout but was halted by Griff's extended forearm.

"Where's he gonna go?" Griff remarked calmly.

Derek lowered his gun.

"Didn't you see that coming?" Rainah said to Griff.

Griff smirked. "I was too busy watching you shake your ass."

"If you let me finish, none of this happen," Tsun interjected.

"You again?" Griff grabbed the arrow and twisted. "I want us to see eye to eye on something. We are a family here, and as long as you are a part of this family, you *will* do exactly as I say. And you'll do it with a smile, like there's nowhere in the world you'd rather be. Now, I told you before to keep that hyper-ass, thrill-kill bullshit in check. We've got a war to prepare for. We can't afford any mistakes."

"Here we go again," Rainah whispered to herself. She was

careful to save her negative thoughts for times like these when Griff was preoccupied.

"Maybe you think it'll all be a piece of cake?" Griff continued.

"No.... I... I'm sorry." Tsun's voice shook as the pain snatched his breath away between syllables.

"What was that?" Griff leaned in closer and cupped his hand to his ear.

"AHHHHH! PLEASE, I SAID I WAS SORRY! I MEAN IT!"

"Much better. Now, either you understand me, or you don't." This time, Griff threw a little muscle into the downward thrust.

"OWWWW! PLEASE! I DO, I DO... I UNDASTAND!"

Griff traced the outline of his goatee with his thumb and index finger as he pondered.

Tsun had calmed a little. "I got yoh point, Griff.... I promise!"

Griff released his grip. "Now, that's more lik-," he began.

"Ahhh... Griff," Derek interrupted reluctantly.

Griff turned more quickly than Derek expected. His anger toward Tsun turned with him.

Derek recoiled.

"Sorry to interrupt, but our boy is making his break."

Clout ran as fast as he could toward the old house. It didn't seem like the greatest idea to him, but the only other option was to stay hidden behind the row of stacked cars, and he knew that they'd find him eventually. He prayed that there would be a phone inside the house so that he could call the police. As he ran, Clout tried not to think about Laura. She was probably dead.

Tsun tried to stand and fell back on his ass.

"Shit! Shit!" He indulged his anger with fantasies of retribution. *Fucking black mothahfuckah,* he thought. He snatched his gun from his waist and took aim at Griff's back.

"Ahhh man... don't go in *there,*" Rainah sang, as she watched Clout clear the steps to the front porch of the house.

"What should we do?" Derek said to Griff.

Rainah buried her face in Derek's shoulder and shook her head.

"This has been one fucked-up night," she said.

BLAM!

Rainah gasped and lifted her hand to her mouth.

Tsun raised up as tall as he could while still on his knees. His entire body stiffened, eyes rolling back, blood seeping from his nose. A thicker stream of blood leaked from the hole in his right temple. Jagged flaps of skin, bone, and brain matter curled outward on the left side of his head. He still held the gun in his hand. It was pointed at his own head. Tsun's chin dropped to his chest. He looked at his leg and noticed that there was no arrow.

Tsun probed his temple with his fingers in the unlikely chance that it too was a trick. The action, which took all his strength, would be his last.

Griff gave in to a boyish grin that ignited his entire face as Tsun traced the wound, then collapsed.

"Damn, Griff," Rainah said, more disappointed than upset. "We needed him. I know he was a pain in the ass but he would've come around eventually."

Griff looked at her without expression.

They turned in unison toward the sound of the screen door slamming shut and watched Clout disappear into the house.

Derek shook his head. "Shit, man. Mary's gonna be salty."

Griff coaxed a thought to Kagen, who was still inside.

"Kagen'll take care of him," Griff said. "You know how he gets when someone disturbs him while he's working."

Chapter 7

IN THE NEWS TODAY... *Waitress Kayla Shepherd, whose mutilated body was found dangling from the Benjamin Franklin Bridge in Philadelphia last Monday night, has been linked to Philadelphia Rebels' running back Carl Mezerak. Shepherd was dating Mezerak at the time of her murder. Police have not yet officially ruled out Mezerak as a suspect.*

Many fans and commentators are speculating that this is the end for Carl Mezerak. Since being ejected from Monday night's game against the Bandits and suspended indefinitely by the team, Mezerak has been keeping a low profile. Mezerak, whose estranged wife Mary Jane has been missing for twelve years, has reportedly locked himself in his mansion outside Philadelphia and has not been seen for days....

"So, what's it going to be tonight?" Carl mumbled. His tone was colored by anger.

He rifled through the dresser drawer, blaming his outdated clothing for his own indecisiveness. Sharlene liked her men smooth and dapper, which he was not. Grab some faded jeans and a large T-shirt (when he should have been wearing an XXL), and Carl was good to go. Confident women intimidated him, but he somehow managed to fake it all the way into Sharlene's pants. It was only his hand, but she was a headstrong bitch, so he considered it a victory. Had it been anyone else, Carl would have thrown her out on her ass at the first sign of defiance. Fame had granted him a great deal of power, more than he could have ever imagined back when daydreams occupied most of his time. Daydreaming was how he survived high school when he wasn't playing football.

Sharlene was a dominatrix—on the down-low, of course. Carl knew her before her failed quest for stardom left her jaded and sent her down a deviant path; in those days, she was just a kid, another aspiring model. He would have fucked her then, but she had this rule about married men.

Nothing was worse than leaving the game he loved so much. They called it a "suspension pending further action," but he knew what they really meant. That whole night was a drug-induced blur: the animated thing on Jefferies' helmet, Kayla, Gustav, everything. Now he was on an all-night binge that left him hallucinating at the Seacrest Diner in Jersey....

Carl moped in the locker room after Coach Dudson pulled him from the game against the Bandits. One of the equipment guys told him about Kayla. "Somebody left her hanging from the Ben Franklin Bridge," he said.

A restoration project kept the bridge closed until last week. Two construction workers found Kayla hogtied and swaying in the light breeze.

Someone leaked the coroner's report to the media. Kayla had been raped with a foreign object (something like a broom handle or a pool stick) and beaten to death. Carl had a rock-solid alibi, though. He was coming apart at the seams in front of 75,000 screaming football fans when it happened. Still, the media cast the familiar light of suspicion on him.

They would call him a bastard if they knew how he prioritized his grief, assigning the bulk of it to his tarnished legacy. He saved a little for Kayla, whom he genuinely liked. She was probably the nicest girl he had ever corrupted with his seven-figure salary and his insatiable libido. He usually liked them a little thinner than she was, but she was pretty enough in the face for him to overlook the extra pounds.

For once, the contemptuous flutter went over Carl's head as he sat alone in a booth at the Seacrest Diner. The place was packed with families and senior citizens and a few wayward twentysomethings in search of a caffeine fix. There was the waitress with the stank-attitude... and the green-eyed lady in the parking lot who stood naked in the rain, watching him through the window.

The Seacrest was the kind of place where the aroma of day-old coffee, bacon, and cheesesteaks infected the air. Moments of sobriety reminded Carl when it was time for another nip of Grey Goose from his paper cup or perhaps another blunt out back, but all that wasn't enough to soothe the anger of watching Kayla fawn over Jefferies and Gustav, even though he knew that it couldn't possibly have been her on the sidelines.

At some point, a half-empty bottle of vodka appeared on Carl's right shoulder and pestered him to keep drinking. Its vulgar language was in stark contrast to the childlike way it let its tiny legs dangle, its swinging feet bouncing off Carl's clavicle. It had suggested earlier that he drive into the oncoming traffic on I-95.

"Who's gonna miss your sorry ass?" it joked.

It was 2:00 AM. Carl had been drinking off and on since 10:00 the previous night and smoking weed since he couldn't get it up for Kayla several mornings ago.

If it weren't for that damn bottle on his shoulder, Carl never would have fucked the green-eyed lady. They did it on the hood of his Porsche. And he didn't even use a condom, which was usually rule number one. "Ain't no pussy good enough to get burnt while I'm up in it," he'd say, quoting Snoop Dogg. "The rest of 'em wanna have your baby so they can get some money." Except for those green eyes, Carl barely remembered what the woman in the parking lot looked like. There were only hints: the shape of her face; her hair; the way she looked at him when he thrust deep into her and rolled his hips from side to side. Come to think of it, he never even found out her name.

No matter how hard he tried to forget, Carl kept coming back to the condom. *What the hell was I thinking?* He wasn't sure if he came in her or not.

Each time the bell at the front gate rang, Carl expected to see Detectives Murphy and Lawrence at the end of his driveway again. It was only a matter of time before they came up with some way to connect him to what happened to Kayla. They had already paid him a visit shortly after the coroner's report was leaked to the media. At the time, Carl was still recovering from Monday night, and he was afraid they'd view his unkempt state with suspicion. He thought he was busted when he found Kayla's battered corpse slumped in his closet. She was naked. Her wrists and ankles were decorated with deep, lacerating rope burns. Her shoulders glowed pink from the bruises left by her weight pulling against the joints as she hung from the bridge. Her torso and legs were spotted with welts and dirty sweat and topped off with patches of caked blood. There was an especially large area of blood around her groin and inner thighs. Her head rested at an awkward angle, turned to the side and looking down. Her eyes were open and staring straight ahead. Burst blood vessels left her left iris swimming in dark red that drained out from the corner of her eye. Her mouth was clenched shut, as if she died staving off the worst kind of pain, and there her front teeth were missing; the rest were stained red.

Carl had opened the closet door to hang up a few articles of clothing that were draped over the back of the couch as Murphy and Lawrence followed him from room to room, firing off questions about the murder. Murphy, who had witnessed Carl's startled reaction, grabbed the door and yanked it away from him, hoping to find something incriminating. Luckily for Carl, it turned out to be just another hallucination. Carl didn't waste any time worrying about his mental state. The sight of Kayla's body kicked his adrenaline into high gear, and there it remained, even after he realized that the vision wasn't real. It certainly looked real enough.

Carl felt that Murphy, the black one, had it in for him. Maybe it was because they were so much alike. Carl could see it in the way Murphy carried himself: rigid and stoic, like the stereotypical white man. The first thing Carl noticed was that Murphy was darker and uglier than he was. That was one of the devices he used to judge other black men, the way the black girls did when he was a kid. *Fucking bitches.*

Carl saw the way he scoffed at the fruits of his excess when they thought he wasn't looking: the fountain in the living room, the wall of televisions right behind it, the pool out back, and the courtyard lined with twelve-foot stone columns. Roman sentinels made of marble stood guard at the entrance of the estate.

Lawrence, on the other hand, was nothing more than walking work ethic. If it was illegal, it was wrong; there were no two ways about it. Carl was just a lead to be followed.

Carl massaged his scalp and probed deeper into the dresser drawer. He grabbed a pair of khakis and a white T-shirt and headed for the stairs to turn off the television on the second floor.

RINGGG!

"Shit!" Carl spun around on the staircase ... and paused. He decided to screen the call.

RINGGG!

CLICK!

"You've reached the crib of Carl, The Mez." That was his nickname. "I'm not in right now, but if you leave your name and number after the tone, I'll try to get back to you."

"Hi Carrlll, this is Sharrrlene. I have to run out for an hour or so. Need to pick up some last-minute goodies. I should have everything ready by around nine-ish. And I do mean everythin', honey.... By the way, I've got a couple friends who want to meet you. I didn't think you'd mind."

BEEP!

Carl gave his crotch a foreboding glare and returned to the master bedroom. He considered masturbating to ease the pressure. He pinched his khakis, pulled them away from his penis, and gave his ass a good shake to allow his erection more room to bloom.

A couple friends, hunh? For a moment, the prospect intimidated him. But there was nothing like sex to ease his tension.

Carl shook his head at the length of his dry spell. Not since Kayla had he had a good piece of ass. Before he ran into Sharlene, he was beginning to consider going out and manhandling some anxious groupie. They were everywhere.

Carl plopped down on the edge of his bed, cupped his face,

and began to massage.

He reminded himself to check the downstairs closet again on the way out. He had been checking it occasionally since the hallucination. Carl glanced out the window and saw the mailman shove a manila envelope in the mailbox out front. It was most likely a photograph from a fan. His agent made sure that only the best and most raunchy ones were sent to the house.

Sometimes they were good for a quick date with his palm.

*   *   *

It smelled like meat cooking—something good, like sirloin steak. It was coming from the door on the left side of the hallway. The hallway opened onto a spacious living room. A small vestibule separated the front door from the rest of the room.

Clout stood with his back against the wall, stomach sucked in, behind the opened vestibule door.

He was shivering from the bum's rush of emotions. Tears marked his dirty cheeks. He didn't feel like he was crying anymore, though. He was too busy trying to figure out what his mind was telling him. He thought about something that the Asian guy had said. Something about believing. It was signifigant for some reason, but Clout couldn't quite put his finger on why.

It came with a rousing build-up, like an earthquake bubbling up from the core of the Earth.

The reporter. The one who interviewed him in school. His next thought made him gasp. *She's real? Bloody Mary is real?*

Clout tensed up.

The way he saw it, he had two options.

Option A: Look for a phone, then hide.

Option B: Look for another way out of here.

The furniture in the living room was sparse. Metal folding chairs were placed in a loose circle; an old, trash-picked chalkboard hung on the front wall. Eraser smears indicated recent use. Candles lined the floor panels except for where the old couch sat against the left wall. It had enough space beneath it for Clout to hide if he needed to. The walls were decorated with framed black-and-white photographs (most of them old and washed out) and strange, alphabet-like symbols made of wood or straw or palm that were covered with flowers and wrapped in chicken wire.

Clout heard voices outside. They were coming closer. Anxiety tickled him and put pressure on his bladder. He could visualize each of their faces. His mind considered countless possibilities. Though he was standing still, his heart was pumping full speed.

Closer.

Clout test-flexed his arms and legs to warm them up. Fear left them partially numb.

He heard a car door or trunk open and close four times.

The voices left suddenly and were replaced by crickets and distant barking and a song coming from an old radio in the kitchen— "Stroll," by The Diamonds.

An engine groaned awake. Muffled beats laced with guitar chords pulsed. The car drove off.

Clout couldn't believe it. He exhaled so deeply that he lost his breath. It took him a moment to catch it. He stood there until his heart settled to a semi-normal pace.

Clout slid out from behind the vestibule door. He went blank. *The front door*, he thought.

He hurried over to it, squeezed the doorknob, and turned.

Locked.

But it was open just a few minutes ago.

He contemplated smashing out one of the windows, but the thought of making noise scared him. What if someone was here? What if that someone was in the kitchen?

Clout chose Option B.

Clout walked lightly on his feet toward the next room. On the way, he perused the photographs on the walls of the living room. There were a number of photos of an old church set between thick stands of towering pine trees. There were people dressed in turn-of-the-century clothing. In one photo, they posed in four rows in front of the church. The folks in the bottom row were kneeling on one knee. Their bearing spoke of a harder yet simpler time. At the far left stood a crooked-eyed man. He had been circled with black marker, and the name "Mr. Joshua" was written underneath him. He was clean-shaven, with an elastic-mouthed smile that seemed to go on for days in both directions. He was wearing a ceremonial robe of some kind. There was a passion in his crooked eyes that could easily be mistaken for maniacal zeal.

In another photo, a group of (mostly male) parishioners stood in front of a field that was cordoned off by chicken-wire fencing. They were dressed in durable clothing with a vintage military feel and armed with shotguns and rifles and hunting bows and machetes. A closer look revealed even more weapons (knives, old revolvers, hatchets) partially concealed in sheaths and holsters and hidden pockets throughout their clothing. Life-sized dummies made of straw and rope decorated the field behind them. There was a freestanding wall made of wood and a row of pockmarked targets mounted on its face.

There were photographs of children playing in the grass in front of the church. There was a little blond girl in most of the photos. She looked remarkably like the daughter of Mr. Joshua, but without his outsized smile.

So many photographs: fields; trees; arrows sticking out of targets; straw dummies with chunks missing from their bulk; the same group of people in durable clothing standing behind the little blond girl. She was kneeling in front of a downed white-tailed deer with a shotgun obscuring her torso. A young black male stuck out from the group. He stood over the blond girl with his hand on her shoulder. Clout saw the same boy in a few other photos.

A collection of dark areolas jumped out at Clout from a photo near the bottom of the collage. There were naked people. He saw bellies, saggy tits, raised Caesarean scars, graying winter-bush, varicose veins, and tiny, shriveled penises. He recognized some of the people from the other photographs. These weren't the kinds of naked people Clout was used to seeing in magazines or on his computer. These were regular folks. Their bodies were bent in clumsy positions, arms raised above their heads, hair flopping wild. There was a hint of ceremony to the way they were positioned around a fairly large firepit lined with rocks. Flames reached up and licked the air.

Clout had seen enough. He tiptoed past the kitchen door to the doorway of the next room and peeked inside. On the left, there was a wall. On the right, there was a staircase leading up; a door, presumably to the basement, was set into the hallway beside the stairs. Clout remembered seeing cellar doors against the front porch on his way in.

He sneaked over to the door and tested the knob. It turned. He lifted and pushed it open slightly.

Inside, there was complete darkness. A dense odor wafted out at him. It was similar to subway air in the summertime. Clout winced at the gust of stank. He prohibited his thoughts from settling on some kind of morbid conclusion regarding the origin of the smell. If there was a door down there, he was going to find it.

Clout opened the door all the way. The first few steps could be seen before everything was devoured by the darkness. He looked behind him, then started down the steps. He stopped halfway between the pitch-black wall of darkness and the illuminated entrance. He breathed through his mouth to avoid the smell.

He heard a dry, desiccated voice.

"Help us…." Its affected pitch was genderless.

"Hello?" he called nervously.

He heard a series of gasps, as if a small group of people were just made aware of his presence. There were stirring sounds—weight shifting, metal tapping, curious grunts and whispers. Suddenly, sounds of movement were coming from every direction.

"Are you here to save us?" a male voice inquired.

"The police are here?" asked another.

"Oh God… it's finally over," a female voice whined. Her voice screeched with enthusiasm.

It was as if the dark had come alive.

"Ssssssh. They'll here you," said another voice.

"I don't think it's the police. I can't be sure."

"It looks like a man."

"Are you alone?" a male voice asked.

"Yes, I'm alone. I can't see a thing. What's going on down there?" Clout responded.

"Oh Christ… it's just a kid!"

"Bloody Mary is what's going on, kid. Just get down here and get us out of these cages."

Cages???? It sent a chill up his back.

"Please tell me that you have a gun."

"My friend Laura… is she down here?"

"I… I'm h… here, Ahll-out," Laura whimpered, in a strange voice.

"Oh my God, Laura! Are you all right?" Clout inquired.

"Mo," she sobbed. "…h-ey cu ouh my hh… ongue."

Clout pieced it together in his head. *C-u-t o-u-t m-y t-o-n-g-u-e.* He almost collapsed.

"…h-ears hodd?" Laura added.

Clout worked it out again. *W-h-e-r-e's T-o-d-d?*

"He's dead, Laura. They killed him. I watched him di…"

"We're *all* gonna die if you don't shut up and get us out of here," a desperate-sounding male voice scolded.

One of the women started to wail. "We're all gonna diiieeee."

A male voice joined her.

"Pleeeease beee QUIET," Clout rasped.

The wailing grew louder. Other voices yelled for quiet. The noise made Clout jump, paranoid. He turned and eyed the lit entrance at the top of the steps. He was tempted to run, but… the cellar door… and Laura….

"SHUT UP!" yelled a male voice swimming in hysterics. He wasn't trying to keep his voice down anymore. "EVERYBODY JUST SHUT UP!!!"

Clout turned and shot up the stairs. He thrust his hands at the door, pushed it open, and ran out. He closed it behind him and pressed his back against the wall, knowing full well that he couldn't just leave

Laura down there. He wouldn't be able to live with himself if he did.

He flinched at a sound from the hallway. It was the kitchen door closing. Heavy footsteps followed. Someone was coming this way; from the sound of the footsteps, it was someone big.

Clout's eyes darted. He peered up the staircase that led to the second floor. Right now, it was his only option.

There were voices coming from the first room Clout came to on the second floor, like children singing in goofy tones. He crept up to the open doorway and peered inside. Underneath the voices, a creaking sound bounced around the room. It seemed to stop once he stuck his head in.

Clout's eyes stared squarely at the middle of the room, where an old 13-inch black-and-white television sat on top of a much larger, floor-model TV. An old, front-loading VCR was sandwiched between them. The TV on the bottom was one of those old family deals built into a fake wooden cabinet. He didn't think they made that kind anymore. The 13-inch on top was oval-shaped, with clear, oscillating knobs and an improvised coat-hanger antenna that did next to nothing to improve the reception of the late local news, which flickered across the screen. Beneath it, the larger one flashed a distorted montage of *Ren and Stimpy.* Their kinetic lines cast a drab, ever-changing spectrum upon the room and Clout, who approached warily, entranced by the moving images that lit a path in the otherwise pitch-black void.

The stench of something rotten was strong. There were flies everywhere, so many that their buzzing chant seemed directionless. Clout swatted at the few that circled his head. Maybe this was where they kept the bodies. If so, he didn't want to see.

Clout walked on his tip-toes. When he reached the TVs, he planted a hand on either side of the 13-inch and attempted to turn it. Maybe he could use it as a light source to find an open window or something.

White letters caught his attention from the small screen. Clout backed away and watched. The letters were accompanied by a police artist's sketch that he'd seen many times before. **Artist's Ren-**

dering of Mary Jane Mezerak, aka Bloody Mary, it read. He heard the anchorman blithely mention Natasha Armstrong's name.

Clout fumbled with the volume. The old speaker coughed up louder static, which in turn gave his heart rate a boost. He quickly turned it down and listened over the flies. He thought he might have heard someone approaching. A distinct rise in the flies' insectoid chatter left Clout feeling as if he should turn around. It sounded as if they were converging on a certain spot directly behind him.

Clout led with his upturned ear as he turned toward the front wall. He cursed himself for overlooking it when he first entered.

Mary planted her feet and lowered her head to meet Clout's eyes directly as she rose slowly from her seat. Rage pushed her lower jaw forward, balled her fists, and soaked her body in an orgasmic flush. She was holding a baby in her arms. It wasn't quite fully formed, and it was dead, almost mummified.

Mary placed her stillborn son in an old crib that sat next to her rocking chair. There were candles everywhere. None of them were lit. Two small dinner plates rested at either end of a warped, wooden shelf on the wall above the rocking chair. There were pieces of jewelry and other personal effects scattered between the plates. A short, stubby candle sat in the center of each plate and served as a prop for what looked like photographs. Clout glimpsed a photo of Carl Mezerak (or someone who looked like him) in the left plate.

There were more of the alphabet-like symbols on the wall. A large part of the wall was covered with some kind of picture that was part mural, part map. Clout didn't have time to study it, although he saw a few things: flames, a city in ruins, a procession of bodies, and a mushroom cloud.

She stood before him in the flesh: Bloody Mary, the urban legend. She was angelic, but in a darker sense. She just stood there, silently, and watched Clout try to make sense of what he saw. Flies congregated in droves on the wall behind her. In the darkness, it looked as if the wall were pulsating. Smaller factions mingled in Mary's personal space like moons to some vast celestial body.

She was way too thin to be a person in a suit, as some people were saying. Climbing her visually, from the floor up, Clout found himself momentarily hypnotized by her trademark dress. Compared with the doctored image that he'd seen on TV, it was a hell of a lot filthier. Bone revealed itself in sections here and there. The most exposed area was around her right eye socket and the corner of her mouth.

Clout finally found the courage to move. He took a few steps backward and told himself that it was only the TV that obstructed his left foot. He followed blindly with his right and was stopped again.

Now just calm down, Clout. This could work to your advantage. Just turrrn around, pick up the TV, and throw it at her as hard as you can.

Clout looked down at his feet and saw a steel-tipped boot on either side of him. He followed the lattice pattern up to thick ankles that were wrapped in denim. It was Kagen.

Chapter 8

IN THE NEWS TODAY... *A confrontation erupted in Gnjilane, Yugoslavia, when US Marines from an outpost in southeastern Kosovo answered a distress call from a small faction of KLA soldiers and found themselves outmanned, outgunned, and face to face with 200 Russian troopers who refused repeated orders from superiors to stand down.*

Reports of Russian President Boris Yeltsin's failing health have raised fears of a new Russia and a return to Cold War-era policies and relations.

Although the general public continues to underestimate the implications of the escalating conflict with Russia and China, a growing number of politicians from both parties have expressed concern that President Jackson's lack of experience with foreign affairs could lead to a worsening of problems.

IN OTHER NEWS... *A convenience store in downtown Pittsburgh was robbed at gunpoint by two men wearing gas masks and sporting Gas-Mask Mafia T-shirts. No one was hurt in the holdup, but the thieves did manage to escape with two thousand dollars. Police speculate that the two men have no real connection with Mezerak/Armstrong murders....*

Tasha sat in utter silence, her head bobbing as she faded in and out of sleep. The northeast corner of Room 36 was her favorite spot, so that's where she sat, dug in as tight as she could manage, arms wrapped around her knees, fingers interlocked. At some point, the bottom fell out completely and sent her plummeting headlong into slumber.

Usually she awoke with a distinct jolt, like she was literally yanked out of sleep. This time, her eyelids simply parted. Her eyes rolled lazily to the corners. There was someone sitting next to her. It was a little girl: her blood sister Jane. Tasha got the feeling that Jane was sitting there for a while, waiting patiently for Tasha to turn around and acknowledge her.

"The loneliness… it hurts, doesn't it?" Her tiny voice was as endearing and as chillingly unemotional as Tasha had half-remembered it.

Tasha jolted awake, startled. Her fingers slid apart and allowed her legs to kick straight, which, in turn, pushed out an unintentional fart.

Tasha made a growling sound and walloped the floor with the butt of her fist.

Tasha had been surfing waves of mindfuck since the hypnotherapy session. The new memories beat her down like a man might—like many men would. She tried to make herself small to escape them: that way, she felt protected by the two walls that cornered her.

Finding out that her parents had lied to her made her feel naïve and somehow less than whole. It wreaked havoc on her mental fortitude.

Jane. Mary Jane. It all seemed so obvious. That Mary was dead yet not dead: it spooked her like never before. As their relationship deepened with each new memory that crawled up from her subconscious, Tasha grew more frightened. There was just something about ~~Jane~~ *Mary* Jane…. You just had to know her. Tasha wasn't ready to start analyzing this grudge of Mary's and what exactly it was all about, but she had an idea.

Dana was Dr. Wilkinson's next target. He had trouble with the fact that Tasha's memory of her own son's childhood was vague at best. What she could recall sounded like stock scenes from family-friendly sitcoms and sappy, manipulative commercials. Tasha attributed her lack of recall to a diminished mental state due to emotional stress. "This hasn't exactly been my year, if ya know what I'm saying," she told him.

Tasha heard keys sliding into a lock. She had learned to

detect the faintest hint of activity outside her door, and her hearing had sharpened considerably. Someone was coming in.

The heavy lock clanged. The padded door hissed open. Tarkington walked in and knew right where to look.

"Time to come up out of yer hole, Armstrong," he said while chewing garishly on a piece of gum. "You have yourself a visitor."

*　　*　　*

"In the end, Tasha, I'm going to do this with or without your help." Linda Ludlow leaned away from the thick Plexiglas barrier to let her words find their mark. She tried to look as tough as she wanted to sound.

Tasha stared back stoically at Linda's made-up face. They'd been talking for forty-five minutes so far, and Linda's eyes still hadn't adjusted completely to the blinding bleached light of the visitors' area. The antiseptic glow affected everyone who entered; it left nothing to the imagination. Linda felt the need to dig for her compact and check her make-up, but her purse was all the way down by her feet. People would see her lean over. They'd wait anxiously to see what she pulled out just so they could tell their friends that they saw Linda Ludlow do something normal.

The security guards didn't even attempt to make Linda feel comfortable when she first arrived. Other than the proverbial double takes when they realized who she was, they ignored her in favor of their guns, which they held firm by their sides. She noticed how fervidly they watched Tasha, each of them reacting to her slightest movement. Linda couldn't help but smile internally. Tasha was far from a large woman: she was all of about five and a half feet, give or take. Yet she was as imposing as any of those with guns and their robotic mannerisms. And these weren't small men. Tasha showed all the signs of a person on the verge of a massive breakdown. The guards could detect it. Linda could detect it. It was just a matter of time.

"Please, Tasha...." Linda gave it her most unassuming tone and slanted her head to elicit sympathy, as she had been taught. "I know it's going to take a while for me to gain your trust.... The last thing I want to do is waste your time."

"Why don't you just come out and tell me what you want, Linda? There're plenty of other things I could be doing right now."

"Like what?"

Tasha simply stared straight ahead. She had Linda directly in her sights, but she was clearly preoccupied.

Tasha suddenly snapped alert. "Let's see. I could count the pads on the ceiling of my room for the millionth time... or unbraid my hair and braid it again. I could stand in front of my door like the rest of these zombies, hoping that someone walks by and pities me enough to LET ME THE FUCK OUT!"

Tasha snapped back into blank-stare mode. Without moving her head, she looked at each of the guards. All of them were a step or two closer, guns at the ready.

Linda placed her hand over her bosom and took a deep breath, alarmed. "What I really want, Tasha, is your help," she said apprehensively, "...and your forgiveness."

Tasha milked the discomfort of the quiet moment.

"You do remember that I'm a serial murderer, right?"

"I know what you're accused of, yes."

"You know... I'm black, too, right?" She flashed the backs of her hands.

"Contrary to what you might believe, Tasha, I'm not a racist." Linda's voice trembled. "The fact is that I'm here to help you clear your name. I happen to know you're innocent."

Tasha felt a warm surge in her chest. She was careful not to get her hopes up.

"I'm listening."

"I want you to tell me what you know about the "family."

Tasha smiled.

"Oh, I see."

"No, really. I want to help you."

"What are you gonna do, huh? You gonna hunt them down and interview them on your show?"

132   ANDRE DUZA

"Well, not exactly. I *would* like to find them, though."

Linda studied Tasha's face. Her eyes were full of the same curiosity that kept Linda awake those long nights staring at Tasha's alluring mugshot and wondering what made her tick. Linda wondered how many times they raped her. Given Tasha's reputation, she expected to see a few injured guards limping about. Clearly, that was not the case.

Her cries for help must be trapped within these white walls, Linda pondered, *if she even made a sound.*

Linda had been raped, too. It happened when she was eight… or nine? She didn't remember exactly. It was so long ago.   She wondered if Tasha had flashbacks like she did, even after fifty years. Lately, they only came when Linda was stressed or horny enough to welcome the borderline fantasies of her deviant side.

"Why are you on my side all of a sudden?" Tasha's eyes darted to the clock and back. Only fifteen minutes left. *Good!*

"Remember Patrice Ellerbee? You know, 'Psychic to the Stars?'"

Tasha planted her hands and started to rise from her chair. "Thanks for nothing," she said, disappointed.

"So you know about that?"

"Some of the guards tell me things. Now, if you don't mind…"

"A lot of people believe her, Tasha; a lot of influential people."

"So where are they, then?"

"Well… I'm here, aren't I?"

"*You* believe her?" Tasha added.

"Yes…. But that's not the only reason I'm here." The way Linda's voice trailed off suggested that she had more to say.

"I'm listening." Tasha raised her eyebrows to punctuate.

"I was driving home from the studio last week when a black van forced me off the road. I narrowly missed hitting a tree head on. The van pulled up a few yards in front of me, and a man got out and started walking toward my car. Initially, I thought he was coming over to apologize and to see if I was all right. It was Griff, Tasha. Somehow I knew it as soon as I saw his face. I'm not sure how I knew, but

I did. I was so scared. I tried to drive away, but all of a sudden, I couldn't move. He tossed something into my car and told me to "keep up the good work." As the van drove away, I saw someone staring at me through the back window. It was *her*. It was Mary."

Tasha paused, as if awaiting a punchline. "This better not be some kind of ploy to get me to help you," she warned.

"I promise you, Tasha."

"No promises, especially not from you. So what did he… Griff… give you?"

"An envelope," Linda said. She reached down and pulled an 8" x 10" photograph from her purse. She hesitated before holding it up to the Plexiglas. Linda hid her face behind the photo.

"I'm sorry, Tasha," she sobbed. After all she had done to complicate Tasha's life, here she was ripping her heart out, just reaching right in and snatching the fucker while it was still beating.

Dana's battered corpse was crisscrossed in rope from his shoulders down to his feet, his hands tied behind his back. He hung from a street sign at the corner of Halliwell Way and 5th Street. His eyes were protruding from bloated lids, suggesting asphyxia. Someone had painted circles around them with black ink or paint.

What a handsome young man Dana had became. Tasha analyzed his sagging face in search of any sign of her own. Part of her wanted to smile, as it was easy to see the resemblance. He had her eyes, her mouth.

Tasha thrust herself backward in her chair and sprung to her feet. The guard on her right motioned toward her. Upon seeing the photo, he decided to let her have a moment.

Tasha glared through her welling tears and prayed that her only child died quickly. Images of sallow black bodies swaying from inconspicuous tree limbs tainted Tasha's thoughts. Billie Holiday's "Strange Fruit" rang through her mind. The wound in Dana's head was the hardest thing to look at. She knew right away that a .44 was likely responsible for a hole that size.

Linda wanted to lower the photo and end the torture, but she was afraid that Tasha might snap.

"I need to get outta here," Tasha whispered. Her solemn tone crept up on Linda from the other side of the photograph. "Can I count on you?"

"Like I said before, I'm on your side," Linda replied.

Tasha had her doubts, but she needed an ally on the outside if she was going to find a way out. She had to avenge Dana. She glanced at each of the guards then jerked her head and summoned Linda close to the speaker. Linda leaned in.

"I need you to get me some things!"

"What kinds of things?"

"Don't ask. Just come back tomorrow, and I'll give you a list."

Linda deliberated for a moment. A *list???* She had a pretty good idea what to expect. She welcomed the uneasy feeling for a change.

"But don't they check the packages you get?" Linda half-hoped that she wouldn't have to follow through on her offer of help if it was going to get her in trouble.

"I'll do what I have to make sure they don't. You just remember to be here tomorrow."

*   *   *

The photograph in the mail (an 8" x 10" glossy of Carl performing cunnilingus on green-eyes on the hood of his Porsche) had thrown Carl for a loop. *Probably some paparazzo asswipe hiding in a parked car,* he figured. The sick bastard even doctored the photo to make green-eyes look like that sketch of Bloody Mary that they were running on the news.

Carl tried in vain to recall the layout of the parking lot. Fucking green-eyes in the rain was the only real memory from that night, but the woman he remembered looked nothing like that *thing* in the photograph. Both of them were naked from the waist down. Carl was holding her rotten legs open. His head was buried between them. He almost vomited when he first saw it.

Carl was in the middle of a primal thrust when he felt like there were eyes upon him other than Sharlene's. Her face was buried in his neck, teeth grinding away. He was pretty sure she had broken the skin. Sharlene was a little on the wild side.

For starters, they were having sex in a homemade dungeon. Sharlene straddled Carl, who was standing, black leather straps intertwining their sweating bodies, up under their armpits and around their waists and legs to where it harnessed in the back. Sharlene's best friend Claudette had to fasten them in.

Claudette awaited her turn in the next room with four of her girlfriends whom Carl had yet to meet. Their muffled giggling brought Carl closer to climax... so close that he had to stop and count to ten... then again to twenty. He was right on the brink.

Carl stole a few additional seconds to enjoy the break from Sharlene's dramatic reactions to his sudden full-thrust-and-pause method and his slight shifts in rhythm and direction. *My trademark moves,* he thought.

"Oh, take me to heaven, my African warrior! Take me! Take me!" Sharlene squealed.

Carl rolled his eyes, embarrassed, but it felt too damn good to let that ruin it. If it wasn't her shrieking voice or her violent bucking, then it was the feeling that came over him whenever the perfectly rounded base of her ass grazed his scrotum. As a matter of fact, it happened every time her warm vagina slid back down upon him. It caused his head to lurch back, his eyes to shut, his fingers and toes to straighten.

Carl focused on a corner of the room, his eyes slowly adjusting to the shades of darkness that grew deeper by the inch. The candles that served as a focal point atop their gothic iron stands had burnt out at least ten minutes ago. He pressed Sharlene's face into his shoulder and gave the darkness a scrutinizing glare. Either he was seeing things or there was someone standing there. Maybe it was one of Sharlene's girlfriends, filming the whole thing to sell to the tabloids or some website. The picture from the parking lot of the Seacrest had him spooked.

Carl followed the movement in the darkness and saw something, possibly a camcorder, rising slowly to about eye level.

"What's wrong, huh?" Sharlene clutched both sides of his face and teased in a childlike tone. "Is poor baby all worn out?"

Carl didn't even hear her.

Sharlene followed his eyes. They, along with the rest of his attention, were still fixed on the dark corner.

"Who else is in here?"

There were two consecutive blasts. The first was the louder. Quick bursts of light from the tip of a shotgun revealed a gaunt shape... and hints of a familiar face. It was just like the one from the photograph.

First, he thought of Tasha... that maybe she had escaped and decided to come after him. That would explain the whole Bloody Mary get-up.

The second blast blew Sharlene's head apart. The bulk of it ended up all over Carl's face and in his mouth. The impact threw the remaining flap of Sharlene's head to the right, where it smacked her shoulder and bounced back. The whole thing happened so fast that poor Sharlene never knew what hit her.

Carl whipped his face away and reeled backward into the wall. He realized that he had some of Sharlene's brain in his mouth, so he started spitting wildly.

The darkness seemed to move with Mary as she stepped heavily toward Carl. She grabbed a match from the nightstand and lit a candle, which gave her form a cinematic glow: rolling light on the right side, total darkness on the left. Her chest (exposed ribs and all) heaved and sank, and she gnashed her teeth. The remnants of an upper lip were raised in a snarl on one side. She looked utterly savage.

Tightening her hand around the sawed-off, Mary watched in silent ecstasy as Carl bounced from wall to wall, bound to Sharlene's body, which twitched uncontrollably. His massive arms worked frantically against Sharlene's flailing limbs. Her fingers grabbed his face and forced their way in and out of his nose and mouth.

"Git her off me! Git her off-a me!" Carl kept his face turned as far as he could from Sharlene's and promised himself that he'd never take another breath, not if it meant tasting one more drop of her saline blood. He pretended not to hear the flatulent bursts that accompanied the blood that oozed from her cranium.

Sharlene's slender thighs constricted and released spasmodically. Her feet were still crisscrossed behind him, her heels pressed into the small of his back, forcing his penis to plunge deeper and deeper.

He let his weight sink and focused on the slender, half-lit figure that stood over him, studying his reaction. "Please let me wake up from this," he whispered before his head became too heavy for even his thick neck to hold up. Carl finally noticed the screams and the hysterical chatter coming from the next room.

Mary gave the sawed-off barrel a good squeeze to acknowledge the rush of vengeance. She slid the gas mask down over her face, turned, and kicked the door open.

She posed in the doorway, chin up, chest rising and falling, and looked at the five scantily clad women. She could see in their faces that these women knew who she was. Their fear energized her.

Mary lifted her sawed-off and waited a moment so that they could anticipate the pain of being shot at close range.   Two of the women fainted when they saw what was happening in the homemade dungeon behind Mary. Sharlene's body continued to buck and protest its fate. Her feet dug in and pressed Carl into the wall like a toy infant struggling to crawl forward against an immovable object.

"Helppp meee!" he moaned. He beckoned to the horrified women.

Mary leveled off six, seven, eight, nine shots in succession. Soon, four bodies lay in pieces on the floor.

Griff heard the shots as he ran from the building chasing after the girl who ran from Sharlene's apartment.

Donna struggled to keep her balance as she plunged down the stairs, running for her life.

"Donna, wait! You're going too fast!" Shelley's voice nipped at her back.

Donna forced herself to turn and look. A lumpy, red texture was exposed from several layers beneath where Shelley's face used to be. Donna recognized Shelley's hair and the shape of her head, but her eyes, nose, and mouth were gone.

Donna lost her footing and regained it quickly. She slammed her right shoulder into the wall to keep from falling.

"Donna, wait! Where are you going?" Shelley's voice made Donna's flesh crawl. "Why are you running from me?"

"Stop following me!!!" Donna cried.

There was a window at the next landing. She wondered what floor she was on now. She had to be relatively close to ground level.

"Donna, please! Stop! Don't worry, I forgive you...."

Donna covered her ears and screamed. "Somebody help meeee!"

Donna reached the window and made a quick decision. She folded her arms in front of her, tucked her chin to her chest, and launched herself through the glass.

Donna formed a clumsy silhouette against the red-orange sky. She expected it to hurt when she smashed through the window, but not nearly as bad as it did. That was probably because of the meshed security wire between the panes of glass. And how could she have misjudged the floors so badly? She had been running down the stairs for a cool minute at least. She should at least have made it down to the third or second.

The ground charged toward her. She realized that death was unavoidable. Directly below her was a dumpster full of wooden work-benches, chairs, and tables. She saw faces—people! They were cheering.

"Aw, man! You think she felt that?" Rainah's blue-green eyes swelled with curiosity.

"I hope so," Kagen murmured. He took a Polaroid photo of

Donna in the dumpster.

"Whatever man," Derek smirked. He whipped a cigarette from his jacket and lit it in one quick motion. "Y'all are some silly muthafuckas, straight up."

Kagen came to a full stand and let his camera fall back around his neck.

"Did *you* graduate from art school with honors? Do *you* have people lined up to buy your paintings?" Kagen took a few steps forward. He was pointing at the ground.

"Bullshit, man. What people want to buy your shit?"

There was a long awkward moment. Rainah stood silently. Kagen looked as though he was about to go postal. His sagging eyes seethed with anger. His massive girth and crooked, coffee-stained teeth made him appear untamed. A ponytail held back his unruly, damaged red hair. He looked older than his forty-two years.

"There've been people. Mainly when I was in my twenties... and more conservative."

Derek shook his head, smoke trailing from his nose and the corner of his mouth.

"Man, you're somethin' else...."

"HEY!" Griff yelled down from the seventh floor. "You think people can't see you? Stop fucking around, grab that bitch, and bring her back up here."

Kagen walked to the edge of the building and scanned the area. He saw a Bob Evans restaurant that was closed for renovations and a used car lot across from it.

"You heard the man. Let's GO, GO, GO!" Kagen was second to Griff in the informal chain of command.

On his way back to the dumpster, he stopped and snapped another picture of Donna's corpse as it lay entangled in a mess of splintered wood.

Chapter 9

IN THE NEWS TODAY... *Y2K mania has captured the attention of the world, with people taking all kinds of measures to prepare for what might happen—updating their computers; constructing bunkers and panic rooms; stockpiling weapons, supplies, and non-perishable food; and closing out accounts at financial institutions in favor of in-home safes.*

"But what exactly is supposed to happen?" That seems to be the question on most people's minds. Theories range from the Biblical Apocalypse to a world war started by computers.

The Y2K problem, also known as the Year 2000 Bug or Millennium Bug, was pointed out by an email sent by a computer programmer in Massachusetts that put forth a theory that computer programs might shut down or malfunction because they stored years with only two digits, not four. On January 1, 2000, the software could interpret the "00" that will represent the year 2000 as the year 1900. It is thought that this glitch could result in a worldwide shutdown of electrical, financial, and governmental systems, as well as sensitive equipment related to national defense and the military.

Revenge

I AM ALIVE!

Written diagonally, at an upward slant, it was the first thing Carl Mezerak saw when he opened his eyes. Then he saw Sharlene.

More than half of her head was missing. Dried blood left the hair that remained on her head matted and maniacal. Her arms, like two slabs of meat, flopped over Carl's shoulders. Her flesh was as cold as refrigerated meat; the coarse patch of her pubic hair that brushed against his own made him want to scream.

Some details were still clear in his mind, like the way Sharlene bucked and tightened even after she was dead. He inspected the leather harness that held them together and almost cried when he realized how hard it would be to get out of this predicament. Surely the police were on their way, and all the money in the world wouldn't get him out of this one. Not in a million years.

What would he tell them when they came looking? *My ex-wife did it. That's right, my DEAD ex-wife....* He wasn't sure he believed it himself.

2:00 PM

The clock above the door was the first thing Carl saw when he woke up on the floor of his upstairs bathroom. Sharlene's body lay tangled in straps beside him. A bloody steak knife lay between them, drooling onto the bathmat. Carl didn't remember cutting her loose, let alone how they ended up at his place. He thought of the scene at Sharlene's and quickly tried to block it out. Now wasn't the time for questions. Not if he wanted to keep his ass out of jail.

Carl used a cloth to pick up the steak knife by the handle, and he bent the blade in the sink until it broke. He used the blade to whittle the wooden handle down to get rid of his fingerprints, washed the blade, then hid the two pieces in a pair of shoes until he dispose of them secretly. Next, he snatched a towel from the hook outside the sliding glass shower doors, dampened it with soapy water, and held it over his face as he dragged Sharlene's body by the arm into the closet in the hall where he kept his luggage. Dark blue veins curved and crisscrossed her body.

Carl stuffed Sharlene way in the back of the closet, placed the larger bags on top of her, and closed the door. He feverishly cleaned the blood off the floor. When he was done, Carl climbed in the shower, turned on the water, and exhaled. He paid little attention to the stinging pain in his abdomen, thighs, and groin as the scalding water pounded him.

Carl lost himself in a daydream. The steam reached out through the cracked door and settled in the rest of the room like a heavy morning fog. Paranoia urged him not to close the sliding glass door all the way so that he wouldn't be caught by surprise by anything.

Carl lost track of time. He came back to reality with a shock and slid the door of the shower open. Sharlene stared up at him.

But... but I... Carl went limp and collapsed against the back wall of the shower. *How can this be? How the FUCK can she be there?*

Carl glanced at the spitting showerhead for an answer that would never come. Something told him to look down, so he did.

His chest and stomach wore a weird, pinkish hue. His legs, too. And his...

"FUCK! FUCK! FUCK!" Carl skittered-slipped sideways and out of the direct path of the stinging water. If it weren't for the rear wall bracing him, he would have have fallen on his ass.

Carl surveyed his wounds. He had severe burns down his chest, stomach, thighs, and groin. His flesh was loose and rising. His proud brown hue was now bright pink and raw. He attempted to flex his stomach and chest to test his damaged skin's elasticity... and cringed in pain.

There was a sound at the bathroom door, like a handle being jostled. Carl saw movement in the mist, a blurred shadow oozing forward. Someone was definitely out there.

The police. Carl froze. He held his breath and waited. He didn't know why. Maybe it was his body's way of trying to slow his speeding heart. His chest tightened. The pain interrupted his first few attempts. He felt a surge at the thought of Sharlene's body. He'd spent at least two hours cleaning up, and there she was, like he never moved her.

Thin fingers curled one by one around the edge of the glass door and began to slide it open all the way. Carl stared at them, momentarily transfixed by fear and fascination. He thought he could see bone protruding from the tips and from the back of the hand.

Bloody Mary slid the door open and climbed into the shower: right leg first, then her head and shoulders, then the left leg.

Carl's mouth hung open. He couldn't believe what he was seeing. There was no mistaking it this time. It was Mary, his wife. Even though her eyes were missing, he recognized that haunting gaze, which said everything and nothing at the same time. Once he regained his breath and his cognitive abilities, he realized that she was naked; that her curves were still feminine and alluring; that he instantly recognized her mannerisms despite the progressive rot; and that her movement was strangely halted, like some stop-motion, B-movie incarnation. Her still-round breasts (for a second, he honestly wondered how they felt) were attached by webbed finger-like strands of brittle flesh. The thick mist blurred her facial features, like the kind that softened the faces of fair-skinned actresses in photo spreads after they hit thirty.

Carl followed the crack that raced diagonally up the glass when Mary slammed the shower door shut. She held her left wrist at a bend, up and under her forearm, which suggested to Carl that she was trying to conceal something from him.

Mary got in Carl's face. He attempted to avoid her hollow-eyed stare. Her sly, skeletal grin seemed to mock him. Dry skin crackled under the stress of her frown. She jutted her chin forward in anger, her neck extending, teeth grinding. Her back was arched. Her breasts mashed against him. They were brittle, with sharp edges, like the skin he used to pick from his feet after it had a day or so to harden. Her buttocks, exposed tailbone and all, stuck out in the opposite direction. Water escaped through the hollow wound below her right breast.

Carl closed his eyes and turned away, but he could still feel Mary's closeness. Even worse, he could smell her fetid, wet odor.

Mary grabbed his chin and forced him to face her. Her bony fingers dug into his skin like talons until he opened his eyes. As he stared directly into her dark, hollow eye sockets, Carl's mouth bounced open and closed in search of something to say.

With her other hand, Mary manipulated Carl's scrotum. Despite the pain, Carl became physically aroused. It took some time, but his subconscious recalled the language of her touch. She held his sack with her index finger and thumb. Unbeknownst to Carl, her other three fingers held a straight razor.

Carl's eyes fluttered open and shut as Mary pursued the outline of his face with her pointed fingertip.

"Wh... what happened to you?" He tried a submissive tone to appeal to her sympathetic side. Then he remembered that she never really had one.

Mary wrapped her fingers around Carl's throat. She lunged at him and thrust her dry tongue deep into his mouth.

Carl squeezed his eyes shut and tensed his entire body. The pain from his burns had receded some.

As she kissed him, Mary slid her hand down from Carl's neck and laced her fingers through his stiff digits. She lifted his hand and attempted to guide it along the vertical terrain of her decaying body. She met his initial resistance by squeezing his scrotum with her other hand.

Carl groaned and tried to arch his ass away from her hand, but the wall kept him from going back any further. He conceded.

Mary circled her breast before planting Carl's hand on it. The water had softened it momentary, but still the dead flesh crackled.

She led his hand down to her stomach.

Carl yanked away from her, looked down at his hand... and backtracked to whatever it was that cut his finger and caused it to bleed.

Mary followed his eyes to the hole in her ribcage. Jagged bones like sharp teeth flashed him a sideways smile.

Carl panned over to the stitch-patterned scar in her abdomen and trailed it up to her sternum.

Mary palmed the back of Carl's head and snatched it forward for one last aggressive kiss. She teased his tongue with her own before withdrawing it and biting down hard on his bottom lip. She yanked her head from side to side like a feral dog, slowly tearing Carl's lip away.

Carl screamed. He grabbed his mouth and spun away from her.

Mary raised her left arm over her head and slashed him with the razor.

Carl screamed again. He spun again, this time turning to face her in an attempt to defend himself.

Mary shoved him backward. Carl's back arched as he hit the wall. His screaming climbed an octave as she slashed him again and again. He dove through the glass door, shattering it. His right elbow collapsed beneath his bulk with a pressurized pop. He cried out at the new sensation. He was laying on his side, face to meaty flap with Sharlene.

Carl rolled onto his stomach and crawled toward the door of the bathroom.

Mary stepped from the shower and reached Carl in two strides. She finished her third stride with a kick to his ribs. She followed with another... and another, grunting with each blow.

Carl curled into a ball and groaned.

"Why are you doing this?" he yelled. His mutilated bottom lip gave the words a whistle. "I gave you all the money in the world! I gave you everything!"

Mary took a pair of scissors from the cabinet, bent over Carl, and plunged them into his back. She twisted it deeper and opened the blades as she dragged him into the hallway. She planted her feet and leaned into every tug.

The upstairs living room was in disarray. There were candles everywhere, too many for Mary to have arranged by herself while Carl marinated in the shower. The swooning flames merged with one another as Carl swayed on the brink of consciousness.

Carl moaned and reached drunkenly for Mary's hand... arm... anything. He caught hold of her wrist and struggled to hold on.

Mary's long shadow loomed over the room. Carl could see that she was leading him to the love seat beneath the front window.

Furthermore, he could see that there was something small sitting there... waiting for him. An inscription carved crudely into the wall above it read YOUR SON.

"M... Mary, I'm sorry!" He gargled out his words in short, guttural blasts. "I... I didn't know! Please! I never would have let you go."

Mary yanked Carl forward as if his words enraged her. She grabbed his face in both hands and shoved it in the face of the infant corpse.

Carl's puffy eyelids parted slowly and watched as his three sons merged into one. The thing was in worse shape than Mary. Bleached bone highlighted the top of its slumped head and most of its face. Carl studied it carefully, his mouth hanging open, his face masked in blood from the large cut on his brow.

Mary shoved Carl to the ground and walked away as if to allow him a moment to ponder what he had just seen.

As much as he tried to seem remorseful, Carl felt little more than numb. There was no resemblance that he could see other than the skeletal grin that the thing shared with its mother.

Da-deee.... Carl imagined the gentle coo of its voice. He remembered his vow never to have children. Deep down, the desire for a son was always there, but back then, with Mary, he was afraid of what it might do to their relationship. It wasn't like their bond was all that great in the first place. And he was only in his young twenties at the time.

Carl turned toward the heavy footsteps that approached him from behind. It was Mary. She held something heavy and sharp enough to leave a groove as she dragged it along the wooden floor. Though it was dark and his mind was dancing in and out of consciousness, Carl was pretty sure that it was an axe.

Clutching his broken ribs, Carl climbed to his feet and tested his balance, but the axe was already on its way down.

Mary let out a raspy growl as she dug the axe in deep. She jostled the handle to bring home her point and retracted the blade.

Carl staggered backward and cried out in pain. His whole

right side throbbed with heat and chaotic muscular activity. He probed the gash in his clavicle with his fingers. The wound felt alien to him.

Carl turned to face Mary's second charge. He held his arm out in front of him. The weak limb bobbled in the air directly in the path of the downward-facing blade. He snatched it back when the blade sliced through his forearm. Another swing planted the blade's tip in his left, upper pectoral muscle.

Carl's knees buckled, and he fell into her.

Mary palmed Carl's face and stood him upright. She dug in with her fingertips and shoved him back, but Carl was able to connect with a furious punch that turned her head to the side.

Carl chased Mary backwards with each successive blow until she caught hold of his broken left arm and jerked it. He bellowed in pain and swung blindly with his right. The force ripped her head from its base. It dangled loosely to the side, then fell to the floor. The rest of her body convulsed in shock.

Carl fell to his knees and coughed violently.

Mary's arms flailed in search of him, her hands grasping into claws as she staggered back and forth and pulled everything in her path to the ground.

Carl scanned the vicinity for her head but couldn't find it. An overturned candle ignited the love seat.

Carl struggled to his feet and pressed his back against the wall. Suddenly he saw Mary approaching swiftly, framed by the growing flames. She held the axe in her right hand and her head in her left.

He spun toward the doorway and lifted his arms to block the swinging axe.

This time, the blade sliced cleanly through his wrist and landed with a sucking noise on the right side of his face. Mary pushed her foot into Carl's midsection to yank out the axe.

Carl fell to the floor and crawled away on his belly.

Mary stood over Carl and struck him repeatedly in the back and legs until he stopped moving. She had been dreaming of this moment for more than a decade.

Mary raised her weapon. A savage wail bellowed from her

severed head.

"Ahhhhhhhhhrggggghhhhhhhh!!!!!!! WhatthaFFFUCK!" A chaotic swell burst outward from his chest and sent Carl into a rotating, electroshock waltz. Guided by the lingering memories of painful sensations, his arms flailed and swatted at himself as if he were wiping away insects that lived on his skin. He kept it going until he was out of breath and dizzy.

Carl huffed and puffed and lifted his left arm in front of his face. It was as good as new. His eyes tracked down to his chest, stomach and legs. His skin was whole and unmarked. He lifted his chin over his shoulder and checked his upper back. Reaching around to his buttocks and lower back, he inspected the smooth, taught texture with the back of his hand. Nothing.

Melting down from the top, scenery began to materialize all around Carl like some virtual paint-by-numbers demonstration. His head jerked in pursuit of the moist whooshing sound that accompanied the traveling colors. He knew this place. It was Sharlene's living room.

To his right, the kitchen appeared. On the floor, Sharlene's body lay tangled in straps. An overturned silverware drawer kept her company as it lay sideways on a pile of forks, spoons, and knives. A serrated steak knife was sticking out of the ground where someone had left it. There was blood everywhere, melting out from bespeckled patterns into fully realized stains on the walls, the furniture, the TV, and the carpeted floor. Carl's feet sank into the thick carpet and squeezed out dark red suds between his toes.

He entered the next room. Half-naked bodies were twisted in anguished poses. They had all been shot at point-blank range by something that packed a serious punch. Some of them were missing limbs. The opened, splattered heads made him turn away. Sharlene's bobbing meat-flap was still too fresh a memory. Real or not, his memories of the drive, the shower with Mary, and his death were crystal clear. Other than the blackouts and the missing time, they were as real as the present moment, as he stood completely naked in the middle of Sharlene's living room. He had no answers as to why this was happening to him. Maybe he really had died, and this was Hell.

Wait a minute.

Had he been holding the sawed-off shotgun the entire time? It certainly seemed that way.

"Don't do it, Mezerak!"

The voice was coming from the front of the room where the open door melted into shape, colors dripping down over humanoid shapes: men standing firm and poised for action. When their features became more distinct, Carl could see nervous tension in their eyes. They were cops—five of them. They crowded the doorway with their guns pointed at him. Standing in the back, halfway in and halfway out of the doorway, a cameraman peeked over their heads and shoulders, his face hidden behind a video camera. A placard on the camera read "Boys in Blue." It was a TV show, a reality thingee in the tradition of "Cops."

"I said PUT THE GUN DOWN! You're in deep enough as it is, bro."

Bro?

"Listen to 'em, man. The only way outta here is through us. Just put the gun down and give it up."

As Carl stood there, shivering and considering the options that filed past his mind's eye, he began to realize just how bad things looked: he was standing there, naked, holding a sawed-off shotgun, surrounded by dead women. Dead white women. Little factors like that one could spell the difference between a clean arrest and a Rodney King-style beatdown, or worse.

Carl thought about trying to reason with them, but what the hell would he say? "It wasn't me. It was my dead ex-wife." That would go over really well.

"Okay… Okay… I'm cool," Carl said holding one hand up over his head in surrender as he knelt slowly to the floor and attempted to put the gun down with the other hand. He knew that the slightest wrong move would mean his ass… so he couldn't understand why or how he wound up cocking the barrel and turning the gun on them.

Carl felt the first bullet dig into his flesh before he heard the gun go off. It hit him in the ribs and inspired an "agghh!" sound from his lungs. He doubled over and spun away. The other officers fired.

He still held the sawed-off. He whipped his arm down and told his fingers to "release," but his hand seemed to have a mind of its own. The skittish police continued to fire.

Carl dropped like a lead weight and rolled onto his back. Here he was, at the brink of death… again..

His wind was coming in short bursts. It slipped further away with each gasp, yet Carl dug deep and managed to hold on for a while longer. He had to work for each breath. He closed his eyes and concentrated to stave off the loss of consciousness. The pain was beyond comprehension, but Carl was more concerned with not dying. His struggle produced strange, guttural "umphs" and wet, choking noises that usually ended with a hard "k" sound.

One of the officers hurried over and knelt beside him. It was the white prick who called him "bro" earlier. Carl found it ironic that one of the men who had just shot him now seemed concerned about his well being.

The officer pressed two fingers against Carl's neck and waited. Carl tried to communicate by shaking his head. His eyes were glazed over. As he focused on the officer's eyes, Carl saw someone entirely different looking back. He zoomed out to get the entire picture. There was something peculiar about the officer's face. His features and mannerisms were not his own. In fact, they resembled someone that he had seen before, a familiar-looking brotha with dreads.

The officer leaned over him and whispered, "Hope you enjoyed the ride, champ."

"W… wh… whoooo… arrrreeee… yoouuuuu?" Carl was forced to take a breath between each word.

"Name's Griffen, but most people call me Griff," Griff said, speaking through the officer.

"I knnn-oh youuuuu," Carl moaned, as recall attached a face to the name and to the voice over the phone that haunted him for years. His idea of Mary's "church friend" was a much more studious-looking black man than the guy whose face floated across his mind. It was the same face that stared back at him from the Panavision screen during his last football game; the same one that stared at him from the passenger seat of the black van that followed him on I-95.

"Small world, huh?"

"W… whyyyy?"

"Oh, I think you know why. And despite all the bullshit you've accomplished, *this* is how they're going to remember you."

*   *   *

"Whatever you did to that fella, it musta been somethin' else," Kagen remarked, as he sat in the driver's seat of the van and watched a fourth group of cops run into the dilapidated factory that housed Sharlene's condo.

The parking lot was crowded with municipal vehicles with flashing lights on top; a local news van with huge, smiling faces plastered across its side; and a sleek SUV marked "Boys in Blue." A larger gathering of spectators had formed at the perimeter; a group of cops lingered. A few others mingled with a group of construction workers who were standing around the dumpster where Donna had landed, discussing the large bloodstain in the middle of the pile of broken furniture.

Kagen was parked across the street from the lot in a staggered line of cars that appeared to have been there all night. He sipped from a cup of Dunkin Donuts coffee and snapped an old newspaper open in front of him to appear as if he was reading it as he watched the busy scene from the driver's side window.

Griff and Mary sat Indian-style on the floor in the back of the van. He had her fingertips cupped in his palm as he faced her, their knees slightly touching. His eyes were still heavy from coaxing, which sometimes affected him like sleep when he came out of it.

"What's-a-matter? You jealous?" Griff responded, yawning and cricking his neck.

"That you can screw-job people's heads like that? Shit yeah, I am."

"Where's Rainah and Derek?" Griff inquired, suddenly concerned. He seemed to be speaking for Mary, who had just whipped her head from side to side in a stiff, jerking motion and checked over each shoulder. She was sitting with her back to the front of the van.

Mary slid her hands away from Griff and used them to push herself to a crouch. She turned, crouch-walked to the front, and looked over Kagen's shoulder out the driver's side window. Her movements were audible, sounding off with an unnerving crackle-crunch. They were especially loud inside the van.

"Out there with the looky-loos," Kagen said and pointed with his thumb.

Mary squinted angrily and snatched the paper from Kagen's hands. She raised her arm, her bony finger crackle-crunching erect, and pointed out the windshield.

"Drive," Griff ordered.

"And just leave them there?"

There was no response.

Kagen tracked his eyes slowly right and up and ran right into Mary's hollow-eyed glare beaming down on him. He dropped the paper, turned the key in the ignition, and pulled out of the parking spot.

Rainah stood on her toes to see over the crowd. She was holding hands with Derek to come off like a couple that had just wandered by. Griff's voice hit them simultaneously.

"Sorry to interrupt you two, but you might want to turn around."

Startled by Griff's coaxing, Derek spun around as if he expected someone to be standing behind him.

"Shit," Rainah gasped. "C'mon."

Chapter 10

November 1999

<<COMMERCIAL>>

FADE IN:
The scene opens in the heavens, traveling forward through a landscape of plump, grey clouds with no land is sight. Worrisome music scores the journey. Flashes of lightning burst blue-white in random spots. Thunder mumbles softly. Sentences typed in a gothic red font materialize and fade out sliding diagonally away from their bulky, shadowed background. Voices (both male and female) accompany the words, sounding off on the heels of the previous one.

WORDS/VOICES (MALE AND FEMALE)
What is the meaning of life?
Where do we go when we die?
Is there life after death?
Why do bad things happen to good people?
Will I ever find true love/happiness?
Is there a God?
Which religion is "the right one?"
If God is all-powerful, then why is there evil?
How can I become a better person?
What is humanity's place in the cosmos?
How will the world end?
Where do I go from here?
Why can't I ever achieve financial success?
Will there ever be peace on Earth?
Is my life significant?

NARRATOR (MALE): In our neverending quest for enlightenment, we often find ourselves overwhelmed by unanswered questions and lost in a sense of spiritual ambiguity.

(The grey clouds shift to a soothing white fluffiness as the narrator speaks. They part allowing the sun and the tranquil, red-yellow sky to shine through. The worrisome music morphs angelic.)

NARRATOR (CONT'D): The Church of 1000 Earthly Deities offers an alternative to stodgy rules and doctrines. Come participate in a way of life that celebrates the untapped power that lives within us all, waiting to blossom and reconnect each of us with the spiritual oneness that inhabits every living thing. In these times of divisiveness and war-mongering, The Church of 1000 Earthly Deities stands as a beacon of hope for true salvation and inner peace.

(A deeper male voice speaks quickly as the scene fades.)

DEEPER VOICE: Paid for by the Church of 1000 Earthly Deities

"So tell me, Elliot: Do you think I'm a racist?"

Linda Ludlow had been counting down from twenty for the last half-hour. They were on their way back from Pittsburgh. Tasha had given Linda a lead on a guy named Jimmie Howser, a survivalist type who she had stayed with for a while when she was on the run. She said he might be willing to help Linda find Mary... for a price. "Just make sure you take somebody... 'non-white' along," Tasha warned.

House, as they called him, was a self-described "government-hatin' conspiracy theorist" who liked to compare white men with the Borg, even though he himself was white. As a rule, he only dealt with people of color.

Linda asked Elliot Woods, a black man, to come along and shoot for her. She had worked with him in the past, so they had a slight rapport. But Linda always felt on edge in his presence. Sometimes she wondered if she was being hypersensitive. Other than the way that he looked, Elliot was a nice guy and a decent cameraman. He had smooth caramel skin and nice eyes, but his features were arranged in a way that made him appear to be in perpetual glare-mode. He came off as one of those "angry black guys" to people who didn't *really* know him. People like Linda.

When they finally found the address that Tasha had provided (an old church in the middle of nowhere), an Asian man told them that Jimmie Howser had been missing for over a month and was presumed dead.

Elliot lowered his foot from the dash and sat up. He'd been trying to catch a quick nap, but Linda was determined not to let him succeed. She absolutely hated long drives.

Elliot caressed his bald head from back to front, his hand sliding down to his reddened eyes, index finger and thumb massaging the sleep from them. "Do we have to talk about this right now?"

"Why not?" Linda whined. "Is there something wrong with asking that question?" *Isn't that all you guys talk about?*

The engine's low hum distracted Elliot as he fished for a reply that wasn't too harsh. He was dying to tell her what he really thought. He knew it would be the genesis of a heated debate, though, and he just wasn't in the mood.

"So, how long 'til we get to Philly?" Still feeling a little groggy, Elliot faced the window and yawned the words out. "Man, this shit looks like straight Klan territory." That was what he said about anything that reminded him of the Midwest, where he spent two unhappy years in college.

"Last sign I saw said 100 miles," Linda said, her head bobbing as she checked the rearview for a more recent sign that she might have missed. "That was about twenty minutes ago."

Elliot pressed his soles against the floor and arched his back. "Man, I can't even feel my ass." He rubbed it ferociously.

"Don't worry, it's only four o'clock. I'll have you home in

time for the game...."

"Excuse me?"

Linda spun toward him and back, her face reading concern. Not too long ago she couldn't give a shit whom she offended; now, guilt ruled her.

Linda quietly dissected her last statement. She was only trying to break the ice. She had no real interest in basketball. She only knew of the game because she heard the guys at the station talking stats and debating the Sixers' chances. Most of them were black.

"What? What's the matter with what I said?"

Elliot allowed a few seconds to pass.

"Juss messin' with you, Ms. Ludlow. Don't go havin' a heart attack on me."

Linda waited for him to smile before she did as well.

"Hey... you never answered my question."

"Maaannn...!" Elliot let the syllable drag, as if the simple thought of discussing race drained him of his strength.

"What's the matter? It was just a simple question."

"Naw, unh-unh...." Elliot shook his head. He was ignorant of the sun's glare that rolled around the top of it. "It's never just a simple question with y'all."

Linda shuddered. She shrugged away her emotion.

"Now, what's that supposed to mean?"

Elliot reached down and adjusted the seat until it nudged at his back.

"Look, all I'm sayin' is that when a white person, such as yourself, starts acting like she's concerned about racial issues, there's usually an ulterior motive."

"That's not true."

"Maybe not on the planet you came from."

"I don't think I deserve that."

Elliot rolled his eyes.

"How long have I known you Ms. Ludlow? About five years? In all those years, this is the first time you've ever spoken to me about anything other than the weather, or some trivial crap like what I did over the weekend...."

"Granted.... But I don't see what's wrong with my curiosity."

"You're right, there's nothing wrong with it. But you have to understand the nature of these types of conversations. They always start off nice and friendly, but they hardly ever end that way."

"Don't you think you're being a tad oversensitive?"

"Sure. I'll admit it. I've got unresolved... issues with white people... some white people. And yes, I think the ability to openly discuss this subject with someone whom I know I'm probably going to disagree with without getting all emotional about it is something that I... something that *a lot of us* need to work on, but..."

"But what? How do you know you're going to disagree with me? Maybe I just want to know what it's like from your perspective, you know, to help me better understand where Tasha is coming from."

"Ohhhhh... I see. Since we're all alike and everthing...."

Linda sucked her tongue.

"C'mon. You know that's not what I meant." She stumbled over the first few syllables.

"I'm only messing with you again," Elliot grinned. "But look.... No disrespect. You're a legend and all, and I'm honored to be working with you, but I would rather not get into this with somebody whom I..."

"Go on...."

"...with somebody whom I... fuck it. You know you be exploitin' the hell out of the racial angle on your show, playin' on people's boneheaded preconceptions-an'-stuff."

"Oh, for Pete's sake." Linda threw her hands up. "Now I'm responsible for all the racism in the industry? Yes, it's a problem, but if you're going to try to make some kind of difference, you have to first learn how to play the game."

"And you've been playing the game for how long... 25 years?"

"If you're insinuating that I haven't made some kind of difference, then shame on you. And furthermore... who are you to cast judgment on my career? You're just a boy."

Turning repeatedly from the road to the passenger seat, Linda pressed Elliot to respond. Despite her anger, she was fairly impressed with his diction and slightly charmed by his wit. Her enlightened mindset had her wondering if "being impressed with his diction" was in some way racist. It was so much easier before, when she didn't take that kind of thing into account.

Elliot had a smug look on his face as he stared straight ahead. He was clearly milking the silence.

"See what I mean?" he said. "You're about ready to bite my head off and I was only being honest."

"What you were doing was trying to get a reaction from me."

"It worked, didn't it? I just wanted to prove my point."

Linda fumbled with the radio but found nothing to ease the tension. She welcomed the busy overhead signs that left elastic shadows on the windshield as the car passed beneath them. She scanned the metal monoliths that zoomed by on each side and the sheets of green flatlands beyond them. She glanced down at the speedometer and back to cars that zoomed by, her penciled eyebrows raised. She was doing well over sixty-five, and they were passing her with ease. Linda kept her mind busy with little things like that for a good twenty minutes. Finally, her stomach interjected with a rumble.

"You wanna get something to eat?" Linda asked. "The Shippensburg rest stop is coming up in two miles. My treat."

Elliot gave his flat stomach a pat. The thought of a good meal left him salivating and fighting off a slight case of nausea. He hadn't eaten since Pittsburgh.

"Sounds like a plan to me."

"God Is the Antidote"

"You see, the problem is that everyone is a little to blame, but no one wants to accept responsibility for whatever role he or she might play." Elliot was anxious to make Linda understand. "As far as white people are concerned, I think it's just that you guys have been at the top of the food chain, so to speak, for so long that you tend to think that everyone should act like you. Most of you fail to see that the way you got here was by first smiling in the faces of every culture you came across, and then turning on their asses and pillaging what they had when they turned their backs. The Spanish did it, the French did it, the English, the Romans... the list is long."

"'Top of the food chain?'" Linda mumbled through her rotisserie chicken. She wanted to say more, but she promised Elliot she'd listen.

"Just hear me out...."

Linda ran her fingers along her thin lips to indicate that she was zipping her mouth closed and nodded. Although she was genuinely intrigued, the urge to look up and take in the sights was powerful and constant.

She found the overall din somewhat intimidating. Televisions looked down from high corners, jingles blaring, pitchmen screaming. Sounds of mechanized voices, engines revving, and gunfire leapt out from the small arcade in the back. Cheerful folk of various ages hurried to and fro, otherwise unassuming underneath elaborate costumes. In one quick glance, Linda saw a few Ben Franklins, a Thomas Jefferson, and a bunch of Uncle Sams peppered throughout the anonymous travelers.

They came in two groups. Linda saw them drive up in the schoolbuses marked "Shippensburg High" and... all she could make out was "Church of" along the side of the other one. Red, white, and blue Mylar balloons and miniature flags on wooden sticks were everywhere; matching ribbons, bows and bunting borders decorated the walls and the floor-to-ceiling, wraparound windows of the rest area. The employees in their mini-franchise alcoves were required to dress for the occasion as well.

According to the banner that hung above the Starbucks triage, the town was celebrating "Forefathers' Day."

"Some kind-ah local warm-up for Thanksgiving, they tell me," the nice, young couple from Michigan who had approached Linda for an autograph told her.

The pamphlet that Linda read told a sappy story about a noble local politician who, four years ago, set out to convey to the community's youth the sense of brotherhood that the founding fathers possessed.

Elliot provided the low-down: that the holiday was initiated as a reminder to the Latino population, which had exploded in the last decade, of the sanctity and supremacy of red, white, and blue America, with an emphasis on the *white*. That's what Elliot told her.

This was just the kind of kitchy event that Linda would be covering if she didn't come through with her "big scoop." The network execs wanted her to do a comprehensive piece on the Armstrong/ Bloody Mary case when the police gunned down Carl Mezerak, but Linda told them no. She said she had a scoop that would blow the whole thing sky high, but she needed more time to put it together. She didn't tell them that her scoop was proof of Bloody Mary's existence. Half of the time, she wasn't even sure she believed it.

"So now, here we are, living in a world where yours is the predominant image that everyone strives to live up to, and not because it's the best looking, as most people have been fooled into believing, but because, like with religion, it's been beaten into our subconscious for centuries. The closer you look to that image, the better your chances are of making it in this fucked-up society. All the crying and bellyaching and protesting in the world won't do anything to further our cause because we're missing the point."

"Which is?"

"Which is that the only way for us to truly gain an equal footing would be to overthrow those in power the same way white people originally did, and that simply ain't going to happen. I mean, sure not all white people are racist, but when you plug cultural preservation into the equation, well… that's when people's minds start to close."

"Well, isn't that human nature?"

"Exactly my point. People too often limit their thinking to the surface when it comes to race. You guys seem to have a problem admitting that we live in a European-based society. Most of the things we celebrate—this mess here for instance…." Elliot surveyed the surroundings with a wide sweep of his hand. "This is all based on *your* heritage, and I'm talking European in general. Imagine that you, Linda Ludlow, lived in China, where only about 13 percent of the entire population looked like you. You and just about everyone else like you has a Chinese name, you speak Chinese, celebrate Chinese holidays, live your life according to the standards developed by the Chinese throughout history, and the whole time you're aware that you are not Chinese, and the reason you are there is because your ancestors were forcefully taken from the place where they originated and were enslaved. As a result, those same ancestors played a significant role in the development of China, but the whole time you're made to feel like you don't belong. For centuries, the majority of the population has joked at your expense, killed your people for fighting back against insurmountable oppression, and generally looked down upon you for being different. Now tell me, how would you feel?"

Linda took a moment to digest his point.

"I guess I never really looked at it that way...."

"Yeah, no one does. Not even black people. It's all about reaction these days. People think everything is balanced when, in fact, it's far from it. A black comedian tells a funny anecdote that comes from experiencing racism first hand and he's called a racist and lumped into the same category as, say, a white supremacist, whose humor comes from his belief that we're inferior beasts. That shit ain't fair, and it happens all the time. Sure, in a perfect world, there would be racist black people, but for the most part what, you hear is a reaction to being treated like shit simply because our skin is darker than yours."

Linda nodded between sentences and tried not to appear as though she was beginning to feel slighted by the fact that more people hadn't recognized her at the rest stop.

"As far as black people are concerned... well... I think racism has turned us into poorly educated, fat, insecure, overly sensitive, complacent, emotional zombies. Everything with us comes from the heart. It all starts in school. The history books tell us that we were slaves; we sang songs; blah, blah blah; Martin Luther King; blah, blah, blah; and here we are. There's never any real connection made to our roots in Africa. If you're Italian, you've got Italy. If you're Japanese, you've got Japan. And so forth. But *we* have no *real* cultural base, no home for our pride. Most of us consider Africans—and I mean off-the-boat Africans, ugly, ashy, nappy-headed 'other people' with poor fashion sense—to be like aliens. Now that's a *damn* shame."

"That *is* a shame. Most of the Africans that I've come across in this country seem... how can I say this..."

"Like good examples..."

"Well... I wasn't going to word it like that."

"Why not? I mean, we're both adults. In a sense, I agree. They come over here and work their asses off to make something of themselves. I mean, what they're doing, the Africans and Asians, are essentially gaining power the right way while we spend all our time and money on clothing and cars that we can't afford, trying not to look like our idea of a poor nigger, and making ridiculous distinctions between light-skinned, dark-skinned, good hair, bad hair, African, African American. It's all a waste of time and energy."

"Well, I wouldn't go that far."

"I would, and I grew up right up in it. We wonder why Africans look down on us when the answer is staring right back at us from some blinged-out hip-hop video, or that stank-ass crap that passes for R&B nowadays. Now, that's not to say that hip-hop is to blame. I, for one, can't get enough of the good shit, but you'd be hard pressed to find that stuff on the radio or TV. It seems to me that most people, regardless of race, respect those who respect themselves, which is why you're seeing this whole sort of move with my generation toward reclaiming our heritage. And I'm not talking about throwing on a kofi or a dashiki and basically acting the same as always. I'm talking about brothas and sistas going natural with their hair, or taking it upon themselves to find out about their history before slavery. A lot of times, that shit is scoffed at in the 'hood. People say, 'Oh he's tryin' to be all Afrocentric,' or some bullshit like that. Pisses me the fuck off."

Elliot's argument was conveyed with such passion that Linda couldn't help but look at him in a different light. She paused to find her voice.

"I think you'll find that as you get older, you tend to become less concerned with 'what's wrong' on a grand scale and more focused on how it directly affects you, and what measures you have to take to be the best you can be at whatever profession. It's like you were saying about gaining power the right way. Not to belittle your struggle, but if I, as a woman, wasted my time bitching and moaning about all the sexist bullshit that I had to endure—and I could tell you some stories that would make your head spin—I wouldn't be where I am today. The sad thing is that these days people, even women in the industry, whom I have paved the way for in my small way, seem to forget all that."

Elliot found himself strangely satisfied with their discussion. By this point in a conversation, he was usually at the peak of a heated debate and being made to defend his most controversial stances.

"I guess you can say the same thing about the black community. Nobody wants to hear about the civil rights struggles of the '60s and '70s. All that turn-the-other-cheek, Negro-spirituals business just turns people off, white and black. Nowadays, it's all about 'How can I get mine?' which, in itself, isn't necessarily a bad thing. But when you mix that desire with substandard education and lack of self-esteem, then you're just asking for trouble. And I hear you loud and clear on the whole 'wasted time' thing. On the one hand, I'm smart enough to know that the only real physical differences between the races were caused by geography as people migrated. In fact, I think if you broke it all the way down, I think it's people's overreliance on cultural distinctions that's the *real* root of the problem. Sure, it's good to celebrate and learn from our differences, but the minute you use culture to define people's worth, you limit them, whether it's by calling someone a Jew or Italian or Asian or when a black or Chinese or Indian parent makes a stink over the fact that their child's girlfriend or boyfriend doesn't belong to their respective group. I mean, isn't that, in a sense, racism? As much as it makes me cringe to say this, I think that underneath it all, we are all really just one race."

"Why on earth would that make you cringe?"

"Well, because most of the time when you hear that sort of thing, it's coming from somebody white who is completely ignorant of how hard it really is out there for the rest of us, so it comes across with a sort of 'sit down and shut up' kind of vibe. And as much as I agree with the 'one-race' statement, there's a part of me that just can't let go of the anger and resentment. The whole thing is pretty counterproductive, I know, but that's just how it is. I think we're all just doomed. Here we are, at the brink of a new century, and we're still letting names like 'spear chucker' and 'monkey' drive us to violence and other irrational behavior. So what if our ancestors carried spears? So did just about everyone's. Where's the real insult in that?"

Linda was beginning to drift. The crowd inside the rest stop had swelled by three times since they first sat down.

"Hellooo...?" Elliot's voice struck Linda like an electric current.

"I'm sorry," Linda said, sipping from her tea. "I guess I was lost in thought.... What do the kids call it? 'Zoning?'"

"Thinking about what?"

"Well... to be honest, I was wondering what you thought of all this. Does it bother you?"

"Well, that's where it gets tricky, you see. I'm sayin' that while I'm proud of who I am, I have also adapted, like we all learn to do."

"What exactly do you mean by 'adapt?'"

"Umm... like when I was little, right? My mom would always tell us that the best way to deal with racism is to just grin, bear it, and pray, and eventually our day will come, right?"

"Sounds to me like a woman who lived through the civil-rights era trying to protect her son," Linda said.

"Maybe so, but that shit never made sense to me, especially the stuff about prayer. You don't want to get me started on religion. I used to have this saying, 'God is the antidote for intelligence.'"

Linda was shocked. She always felt that if there was one thing that black people had going for them, it was their immutable faith. "You... don't believe in God?"

"Heeeelllllll no!" Linda could tell that Elliot was happy to say it.

"Well, why not?"

"Why should I?"

Linda reached for an answer.

"Were you raised to believe in God?"

"Of course. But I was also raised to believe in Santa Claus and the Easter Bunny and that Jesus was a white guy."

"So you *do* believe in Jesus?"

"I believe that there was a guy named Jesus who walked the Earth around 2000 years ago. I just don't believe he did anything extraordinary aside from convincing millions of people to take his word for his own greatness. I mean, he was probably just a well-intentioned, slightly nutty, charismatic dude with good leadership skills, but no different from Jim Jones, or David Koresh. You really wanna know what I think of religion?"

Elliot pointed across the cafeteria to a rotating magazine rack that stood outside the gift shop. On one of the shelves, the *National Enquirer* screamed for attention in bright colors. On the cover, there was a picture of Elvis Presley under the title ELVIS LIVES!

"To me, Jesus was basically the same as that dude. People loved him so much, for whatever reason, that they just couldn't accept the fact that he was dead."

Linda looked away, following a gut feeling that said "Someone is watching you." She expected… and hoped to encounter an awestruck stare, a sudden pause, then a verbal greeting that usually began with "Oh my God, it's…" or "Holy shit! Aren't you…?" What she found was a suburban father-type ogling her as he exited the men's bathroom.

Linda studied the man in rapid glances. He had a chubby face and tiny features that were deep-set and smothered in meat. Rose-colored cheeks gave him a clownish appearance. He continued to stare as he walked by her table. Linda felt naked, as though he was undressing her with his eyes, then peeling away her flesh to look even deeper. She shrunk as if to warm herself, her eyes following suspiciously, expecting the unexpected.

At this point, Elliot's voice was no more than a constant buzzing in Linda's ear. Mentally, she was miles away, but being the good listener that her years spent interviewing less interesting celebrities and politicians granted her, she managed a nod and an "um... hmm" at the appropriate moments. It was just enough to keep Elliot rambling.

The father-type was past her now and looking back as he walked across the open lobby, past the Starbucks kiosk and up to the front door of the place. He reached blindly for the door and flashed Linda a smile that rippled up from his mouth and rearranged his features for a brief moment. In that moment, Linda could've swore she saw the face of another man, one with dark, smoldering eyes and a marginally feminine mouth who looked as though he meant her harm. She lingered on the swinging door when the father-type walked out. Eventually, she dismissed the lingering feeling as her mind playing tricks.

Linda continued to show adequate interest in Elliot's heartfelt oration until she found a quiet moment to jump in.

"You'll have to excuse me, Elliot," she said. "Nature calls."

Linda left Elliot hang-jawed in the middle of a sentence as she stood, grabbed her purse, and headed for the ladies' room. Preoccupied, she accidentally walked into the men's room before apologizing and backtracking out the door. She was mortified by the smell inside. *How can they stand to live with themselves?*

When Linda came out of the ladies' room, Elliot's chair was empty. *Must be in the bathroom,* she figured, and took credit for inspiring him with a smile. She performed a quick sweep and...

There were bodies everywhere: on the floor, slumped in their chairs, lying on countertops, with arms and legs dangling over. Fresh blood poured from garish wounds and pooled around bodies sprawled in death-poses, decorating horrified expressions and staining the windows and the countrified wall murals with blotchy, red handprints. They looked like they had been shot multiple times, every last one of them. But how could that be? She was only in the bathroom for five, ten minutes tops, and she didn't hear a thing. Well... she did hear something, but she figured that it was just the mechanized voices and gunfire coming from the video game.

Elliot! Linda was startled by the sudden thought that he might be among the bodies. She had seen death many times in her career, but there was usually a camera crew and a few security personnel to help her maintain some feeling of detachment.

Linda pressed her back against the wall, palms flat, and inched along, searching the bodies on her way to the men's room door, ten feet away. She held her chin up and looked down over the edge of her eyelids. There were men, women, and children lying at her feet. One girl, not more than ten years old, was still holding her mother's hand as they lay side by side.

"Elliot! ELLIOT!" Linda yelled sideways into the men's room door. She aimed her voice down at the vent in the bottom. She paused, head tilted in anticipation, but there was no reply.

Linda rested the back of her head against the wall and closed her eyes. She took a deep breath and rolled her face toward the door again. "ELLIOT! Are you in the…"

Through the window, she saw a car pull out of its parking spot and fishtail wildly toward the exit of the parking lot. It was *her* car.

Elliot???

Clutching her purse, Linda worked her way through the maze of bodies and out the front door.

"ELLIOT! WAIT! STOP, FOR GOD'S SAKE! ELLIOT, WAIT!!"

By the time she reached the asphalt, her car was just pulling out onto the Pennsylvania Turnpike.

"HEY! WHAT THE HELL ARE YOU DOING? THAT'S MY CAR!" she screamed at the top of her lungs as she continued the hopeless chase.

She began to rethink her actions as she ran. What if it was the killer? She assumed it was Elliot driving, and that he was running because of fear. But she couldn't be sure. She didn't actually see him behind the wheel. Even if it were Elliot, what if he had something to do with the bodies inside?

Linda stopped at the edge of the parking lot, doubled over, and sucked wind like a vaccum cleaner. She caught her breath and dug into her purse for her cellphone.

Left it in the car. The memory backhanded her. "Shit!"

She turned back and started toward the rest stop.   She purposely blurred her vision as she made her way back in an attempt to mitigate the power of the scene that awaited her. She kept looking back at the turnpike, hoping that someone would drive into the parking lot. The cars kept on going.

Linda stopped when she reached the front door. Her hand was curled around the handle, ready to pull. The atmosphere inside would be more potent, the air more foul and acrid, now that she had a taste of fresh air. She held her breath and pulled.

One of the bodies coughed. Linda heard it as soon as she stepped inside. It came from her right, from a man. She wasn't sure which one until the fat man in the Danholt Trucking shirt with the bullet hole above his right eye sat up and looked at her. He lifted his arm and pointed.

"She did it," he said, bloody phlegm burbling beneath his words. "Barbara Walters did this to us."

Another one sat up and looked at Linda, then another, and another: Ben Franklins, Uncle Sams, and mothers and daughters still holding hands. Their faces melted from horrified to angry. They begin to bare teeth. Some of them tried to stand. Others were just waking up and finding Linda as if they knew right where to look.

Linda mumbled some gibberish about "being right back" as she stepped backward, turned, and ran out the door. She turned back in haste to see if anyone was following her.

It must have been twenty of them that poured out the door after her—men, women, and children, growling as they chased. Their eyes were swollen with hate, teeth clenched to the breaking point, mouths forfeiting spittle like feral dogs. In the front of the pack, a group of Uncle Sams ran with their arms out in front of them, fingers curled into claws.

Linda almost ran right into the side of her car when it skidded and bounced to a halt right in front of her.

There was a black man behind the wheel, but it wasn't Elliot. This one had long dreadlocks and a bulkier outline. When he turned to face her, Linda recognized his eyes and mouth. They made her think of the chubby-faced father-type who stared her up and down earlier.

Griff???

"In the flesh, baby," Griff said. "Now, get in!"

Linda turned back to the charging red, white, and blue mob. There were more of them now, so many that they began to fuse, distinctive facial features blurring into snarling masks, bodies trembling under the stress, losing and regaining form around the edges.

"Well????" Griff added.

Linda turned back to her car and hesitated. She already knew she had no choice. There was only one problem: Griff would probably kill her, too.

"You'd better hurry," Griff remarked, "I can't take care of all of 'em."

Linda closed her eyes, dove in headfirst, and pressed her face into the cushion. She lay motionless and waited to hear the roar of the engine and the tick-tick of gravel kicked up from beneath spinning tires. She heard neither. Seconds later, the engine coughed, then fell silent.

"What are you doing?" Linda yelled at the back of Griff's head. He seemed to be having trouble with the ignition.

"Something's wrong." Griff spun toward her, his dreadlocks following, and again when he spun to the window on the passenger's side. "Your piece-of-shit car won't start."

"What do you mean it won't start?" Linda's words lost cohesion as she tried to fight off the tears and the emotional uprising that knotted her stomach and shook her arms and legs. She could hear them coming over the stuttering engine.

From what she could tell, they were close, maybe only a couple yards away, but she was too afraid to look. She pressed her face deeper into the leather cushion.

"Oh God, they're gonna kill us." Her muffled voice was easily drowned by a hundred or more deep, guttural moans. She could feel their shadows engulf the car as if they were right outside, looking in. She opened her mouth to scream. Instead of her own voice, she heard the engine burst to life and the tires... they screamed for her.

Some of the crowd was close enough to pound and kick the rear fender and trunk as the car sped away. A few more seconds and they would've been holding the door handles.

Linda took a silent moment to celebrate their escape and then sat up quickly. The first thing she saw was Griff"'s smoldering eyes in the rearview mirror. They seemed to be smiling. She turned reluctantly and looked out the back window.

Nothing but parked cars and people walking to and from the rest stop met her gaze.

"Gotcha," Griff quipped.

Linda squinted and raised her field of vision to the wraparound window of the rest area. She saw nothing out of the ordinary: men, women, and children squeezed in booths and standing in line in front of fast-food alcove. Some were dressed in costumes. In the distance, she could still make out the decorations.

"So, I heard you were looking for us," Griff said.

Linda turned back to the eyes in the rearview. She sunk into the seat as if pushed by the impact of what was happening.

But how?

"I could try to explain it to you, Ms. Ludlow, but I doubt you'd understand," Griff said.

Linda took a moment to analyze her surroundings. She probably couldn't break the window with her hand, so the doors seemed to be her only way out. She looked down at the lock on her door... and watched it bend and snap off before her eyes. She tracked slowly to the other door and saw the same thing.

"Elliot! What did you do to him?"

"Your friend? He's in the trunk." Griff pointed with his thumb.

Linda contemplated asking whether he was dead or alive.

She even opened her mouth, but fear kept snatching away her words until she found silence even more unbearable.

"Is he... dead?"

Griff waited until Linda locked eyes with him in the rearview.

"You really wanna know? I can pull over and show you if you'd like."

Linda began to sob loudly. She took Griff's statement to mean that Elliot *was* dead and his frosty composure and indifference to her emotional state to mean that she was most likely next. She gave in to her emotions and wailed.

"Hey, hey, HEY!" Griff raised his voice. "That shit ain't gonna make a bit of difference."

Linda covered her face. She was too far gone to even think about calming down.

"I said SHUT... THE FUCK... UP!"

Linda froze. She held her breath for as long as she could. Eventually, the tears overwhelmed her again. There was nothing she could do about it.

She looked sheepishly at Griff to see if he understood that she just couldn't stop. The last thing she saw was the back of his fist approaching her face.

Chapter 11

Other than the disembodied feeling that made Linda doubt whether she was awake or not, something else was undeniable: the sound of flies buzzing and the smell of something rotten, like meat left out on a hot summer day. The fine hairs on her arms and face lifted, as if someone played at caressing her. She could only hope that she was dreaming.

Linda's eyes opened to a heavy blur. She blinked her vision clear and into focus.

Mary was standing right in front of her, so close that the heat from her post-mortem funk made Linda squint. Her skin was desiccated and brittle. Linda could hear it straining to accommodate the enraged expression on her face.

Mary clutched Linda's jaw and snatched her face to hers, eyes to empty, recessed sockets. Mary dug her sharp, pointed fingertips deep into Linda's flesh, eliciting a scream and wild squirming.

Linda eyes shot wide open, fully awake now.

Her arms… they were reaching up over her head, her wrists bound with nylon rope and tied to a broken light fixture that hung from the ceiling. Her bare feet dangled inches above the floor. Something hot was angling for Linda's attention. It radiated from her shoulders and wrists. It was pain.

Linda cried out, her voice trailing off as she faded out of consciousness.

When Linda woke up the second time, she thanked God that the nightmare was behind her. Her head was still jumbled, but in a good way, like the euphoric buzz that a good night's sleep might leave behind.

She opened her eyes. Her belly constricted.

Linda belched a sour wash of bile. The traveling spasm reached her shoulders and woke them to the weight tugging against the joints.

They were so tender that it felt as if her arms would tear from their sockets.

On the upside, daylight peeked in through the weathered cracks in the painted windows, so she could see where she was. She dangled from the light fixture, spinning slowly. At first, she thought that it was the room that was spinning, not her own body.

A large, cabinet-style television faced her. A front-loading VCR rested directly on top, with a small, 13-inch TV on top of it. In the front of the room, a thick-legged, high-backed rocking chair sat next to an old, beat-up crib that looked as if someone had gleaned it from the garbage. They were surrounded by hundreds of different-sized candles stacked on shelves and perched atop long, tall candleholders. Melted wax drooled over the edges and stretched into strands. Two small dinner plates lay at opposite ends of a warped, wooden shelf above the rocking chair. Random articles of jewelry, torn fabric, and kitschy trinkets littered the shelf all around them. A small box wrapped in crisscrossed string sat on the left plate. The plate on the right held a short, fat candle, a number of weathered black-and-white photographs stacked carelessly, and a doll made of brown fabric that had black yarn for hair.

Alphabet-like symbols made of wood or straw or palm covered with flowers and wrapped in chicken wire hung from the walls. A pictograph decorated the wall behind the rocking chair. The pictograph featured Bloody Mary... and something about an army. There were well-executed drawings of missiles flying side by side over a city and mushroom clouds.

There were old clothes everywhere. A jumble of shotguns and other firearms leaned, butts down, against the wall in the back corner. Overlapping newspaper clippings covered the back wall. There was a small door on the far left side of the wall—possibly a closet or another entrance.

Linda was staring at the doll when she suddenly stopped rotating. She would've never known that Griff was sitting in the folding chair directly across from her if she didn't look up. He appeared to have been there the whole time, sitting under another collage of newspaper clippings glued to the wall. He was wearing a T-shirt, cargo pants, and a dirty military jacket with a strange name stenciled above the breast pocket.

"Please," she begged. "Please let me down for a minute. Just one minute? My arms are so sore. Please?"

"Save it!" Griff raised his hand to silence her. "I've heard enough of your voice to last a fuckin' lifetime. So unless I ask you to speak, I don't want to hear a fuckin' word. Not a sound. You understand me?"

Linda nodded, her bottom lip quivering, her eyes leaking saline tears. Her shoulder joints were burning. It was difficult for her to keep her mouth shut when experience taught her that developing a rapport with a kidnapper was the best way to stay alive. To make things worse, she had to pee.

Griff squinted knowingly. He was in her thoughts with her, coaxing a vision of her bathroom. The tub and sink coughed out a continuous gush of water as if to tempt her bloated bladder.

"You can't hold it forever, you know," he teased.

Linda looked pitiful, weeping quietly, as she dangled from the ceiling with her arms above her head. Her face was red from all the blood that had rushed to it. She took in air with deep, Lamaze-type breaths. Each time that her inflating lungs made her ribcage expand, she felt a sharp pain shoot down both sides of her body. It hurt so bad that she kept falling in an out of consciousness, sometimes for only a few seconds at a time.

"May I say something, please?" she inquired sheepishly.

Griff nodded.

"I… I was thinking that… you know, maybe we can help each other," Linda said. "You see… I… I was looking for you, too."

"I watched your show; that interview you did with Tasha? You seemed so convinced that we were nothing more than figments of her psychotic imagination."

"But that was before… before I found out the truth."

"And now that you know, you're feeling guilty for all the bullshit you put her through."

"I… I was hoping we could work out some sort of compromise."

"Compromise, huh?" Griff pondered. "Well, it just so happens that we had something similar in mind."

Hope made Linda hiccup. Her body bounced and brought the pain. She faded.

"But first I want… HEY!"

"Huh?" Linda jerked back to consciousness and screamed at the pain that started at her wrists and shot down to her feet.

"I could always come back tomorrow if you're having trouble staying awake," Griff remarked.

"No! I'm sorry," Linda cried. "But it h… hurts suh-ohhhh baaad."

"I'm sure it does," Griff responded, stone-faced. " But you're just going to have to deal with it. Now, I was saying that I want to make sure we understand each other completely."

"I do. I do understand…."

"You didn't let me finish."

"I'm sorry."

"I have something I want you to see. Nothing major—just a little thing we put together for you. I think you'll get a kick out of it."

Linda's body spun toward the televisions and stopped. The sudden movement startled her. Pain followed. Linda bit her bottom lip and dealt with it. The small television on top flickered on.

On the screen was an overhead view of what looked like a junkyard. A black-and-white figure scrambled to his feet.

Linda recognized the man immediately as Elliot.

Her heart thumped like a jackhammer in her chest. She thought he was dead back in the car. As she watched, she wondered where he was right this minute. *Is he still alive? Is he as scared as I am?*

Elliot was running from someone. His legs were spread unusually wide, like a child mimicking a cowboy. Linda could tell by the way he held it against his side that his left arm was probably broken. Still, he reached feverishly for his crotch with both hands.

Behind him, three figures stepped into the frame and followed slowly. They were dressed in paramilitary gear and gas masks. Linda felt the kind of chill that she got when she saw clowns or those enormous Mardi Gras masks.

Linda grimaced and waited for the spasm to reach her shoulders. She knew the pain would be unbearable.

Elliot shook his left leg as if something had just crawled up his pants. Before he could shake his right, there was a brief flash. A puff of reddened smoke emanated from his crotch. It forced his legs out from under him. He fell into a full split, then backward.

Despite the absence of sound (the tape appeared as if it were taken from a surveillance camera), Linda could hear Elliot's agonizing cries in her mind. She could see it in his eyes as well, even though only the whites of them stood out from where the camera rested a small distance away.

With his hands, Elliot pushed against the ground and lifted himself slightly. His back was arched, his mouth wide open.

Linda could see dark liquid pool between his legs.

Elliot grabbed his legs in both hands—first the right, then the left—and tried desperately to put his thighs back into their sockets.

A flash of static passed, revealing another sight. Elliot was on his knees this time, a masked figure on either side of him. The masked figure on the right held a gun to his head in one hand; he held Elliot's discombobulated, helpless body upright with the other. Elliot was mumbling something and trying to lift his head to speak directly to them, but he didn't have the strength. Linda couldn't make out what he was saying. The figure on the left palmed Elliot's bald head and forced him to look up into the camera. The figure on the right waited for him to look into the lens and then pulled the trigger.

Elliot slumped immediately. His head bounced when his chin hit his chest. Linda watched his nerves' futile attempts to jolt him alive. His mouth was opening and closing as if he were trying to form a word, but only drool cascaded out.

The next picture that appeared on the TV in front of her was crisp, and now there was sound.

Linda matched each of the faces before her to Tasha's descriptions of Mary's accomplices. She strained to make sense of the laughter and the fragmented conversations. She zeroed in on the large man with the red ponytail who hunched over a kitchen sink, his back to the camera.

That must be...

"Hey!" Kagen barked as Derek snatched Elliot's head from the sink and tossed it to Rainah, who bobbled it before and dropping it to the floor.

Kagen slammed the disposable razor down on the countertop and stormed off. The camera followed him out the door, then tracked down shakily and focused on the dark brown blur that rolled to a stop on the floor, facing up.

Elliot's eyelids were half-open, showing white with horizontal brown crescents where the bottoms of his eyeballs peeked out. He wore a beard of shaving cream that had been scraped clean on one side.

Rainah picked Elliot's head up off the floor and held it out in front of her.

"P... Please don't do this. I don't want to die." She mocked Elliot's last words in a high-pitched voice, bouncing his head as she spoke.

Static filled the screen.

"I want you to understand that we ain't just fuckin' around here," Griff leaned forward and said. "This ain't no Hollywood script. This is real-fucking-life. We ain't crazy, we ain't delusional... and we *ain't* a bunch of burnouts trippin' on psychedelic lyrics. We are *soldiers*. And we are willing to lay down our lives for what we believe in. You tell your friends that. Tell 'em to stay the fuck out of our way, or I'll personally melt each and every last one of their fuckin' brains. Then I'll snatch up their seeds, and we'll have a big ol' feast."

Linda had wet herself right after they killed Elliot on the television screen. She began yanking her weight down under the cover of a coughing episode. Her arms and shoulders were so tender. The pain in her sides was intense, but she was becoming desensitized. Maybe if she yanked hard enough, she could rip her arms free and bleed to death. It was a stretch, but after seeing what they did to Elliot, she was now convinced it was the best option.

"You know… that really isn't necessary," Griff said in response to Linda's suicide attempt. "I understand that you're scared. You're wondering if you're going to die... or *how* you're going to die. Could it possibly hurt any worse than it does right now? Will anyone even care?"

Griff twirled a single finger against the side of his head and smiled.

"It's enough to drive a person crazy, isn't it?"

Linda wasn't sure if he Griff was looking for an actual response, but she gave him a nod and an "umm hmmm," just to be safe.

"As long as you listen and do what I tell you, then you just might survive this," Griff said. "Won't that be nice?"

"Just t… tell me what you want me to do," Linda whimpered. Her voice was but a whisper, yet it still hurt her throat on the way out. "I'll do anyth... thing."

Griff lingered on her last sentence... his eyes and mouth registered doubt.

"You believe that shit about as much as you believe in God," he said.

But Linda *did* believe in God... sometimes. At the moment, she *was* honestly willing to do anything to get her hands free.

Griff maintained his doubtful stare.

"All right," he said.

That was all Linda needed to hear. Welling optimism made her frantic. Her arms and shoulders protested. The pain came back worse than before. Linda thought she was too relieved to care; she was wrong.

Linda screamed with pure emotion. It was her first real scream, ever. It seemed kind of strange when she thought about it. Television and movies had taught her that screaming was fairly normal when, in fact, most women she knew had never screamed. Not like that, anyway. Linda was stuck somewhere between relief and pulse-pounding terror. Her eyes glistened.

"The plan is simple," Griff began. "We make it look like you escaped. You play the victim for a while, work the sympathy of the people. You set up an exclusive interview on Oprah or some other bitch-pulpit. They'll advertise the hell out of it, like those leeches like to do, and when the time comes, everyone will be watching when you tell them the truth about us."

"But they'll just think I'm crazy."

"Maybe so, but they'll still listen. After all, you're Linda Ludlow, the respected journalist. Your job is simply to set the wheels in motion. Your friends in the media, with their polls and their experts, will take it from there. Look at what they've already done. Thanks to you muthafuckas tryin' to outdo each other, Bloody Mary is a certified fuckin' phenomenon. To be honest, you guys saved us a lot of legwork. When that day comes and the world goes to shit, and people are looking for a familiar face to show them the way—that's where we come in."

Linda wanted to ask him if he was flippin' crazy with that plan of his.

"It's all right," Griff said. "If I were in your shoes, I'd probably think that I was crazy, too. But this whole thing is waaay bigger than me… bigger than Mary, too. The church… they've been preparing for it way before either of us came along. Ol' Mary… she's just one of many. And if you think she's bad, just wait. You'll see."

"Church?" Linda queried.

"The Church of 1000 Earthly Deities," Griff responded proudly. "Haven't you seen the commercial? They've been airing it late at night with all the infomercials."

Linda shook her head no.

"It's where me and Mary met. You see… I used go to this place called Wright Farms, which was a boarding school for, um, troubled youths from the inner city. I was 13 when my grandmother signed me up. The actual campus was way out near Huntingdon, out in the boonies of Pennsylvania. It was the kind of place where we had to do chores all the time when we weren't in class. You know: develop a sense of responsibility, tough love, and all that bullshit. The guards all had their own little side operations going on. They'd take us out on "supply runs" and secretly hire us out to some of the local businesses for landscaping or construction work. Then they'd pocket our money. If we said anything about it, they'd make life hell for us. I met Mr. Joshua, Mary's father, on a job, haulin' trash to the landfill for him. He was a high priest at the church. Now, you have to understand: coming from the 'hood, this place seemed like it was straight outta *Deliverance* or something. It turned out that the church played a significant role in the abolitionist movement during the slave trade. Who would've thought, right? Anyway… a couple of us would go out to the church from time to time and do odd jobs an' shit. That's when I met Mary. She was just a kid then, maybe eight or nine years old. Once Mr. Joshua caught me fucking around with a toy airplane I had found when I shoulda been workin'. I was just sitting there, coaxing it to chase this bird around. I had no idea he was watching. He sort of took a special interest in me after that. When my grandmother died, he took me in. Raised me like one of his own children."

"Wh… what kind of religion would endorse murdering innocent people?" Linda whined.

"The prophecy teaches us that society has to burn before the Great Awakening can happen. Many, many people will die… people that you care about. It ain't gonna be pretty. You could look at it like we're doing our victims a favor by taking them out early."

"If they do believe me," Linda said, "they're bound to come looking for all of you."

"Let them come. In a few months, most of them will be dead."

Linda thought about it for a moment. There were no options but one if she valued her life, so it didn't take her long to decide.

"What exactly is it that you want me to say?" she asked. "I don't really know anything about your… plans."

"Like I said, you'll find out soon enough."

"What about Tasha? How does she fit into all this?"

"Tasha???? We've been puttin' it to that bitch since Mary found her ass twelve years ago. If you ask me, she's just a distraction. Carl Mezerak, too. *Fuck* them. But Mary doesn't see it that way."

Linda remained silent.

"I'll let you in on a little secret," he added. "Tasha's son, Dana? He never really existed. The kid in the picture was just some punk we waxed."

Linda found that hard to believe. She had seen the way Tasha's eye lit up when she spoke of her son, the way her voice became softer, her overall manner less guarded. Maternal love wasn't something a person could fake.

"Okay. I'll do it," she whimpered. "I'll do whatever you want. Now can you *please* get me down from here? I'm begging you."

"Not so fast," Griff said, as he stood and walked toward her. He held a VHS tape in his right hand. He pointed with it as he spoke and let it bounce to emphasize his words. "You see, we've got to make it look like you've been through hell: dirty you up, give you a couple nice bruises. Then you'll be good to go."

Linda was too worked up to be any more afraid. Besides, how could "a couple nice bruises" compare with what she had already been through?

Griff ejected the surveillance tape marked "Elliot" from the VCR, inserted the tape in his hand, and pushed "play."

"A little something to keep you entertained until I get back. The first clip is from the Thom Montgomery Show. You remember him, right?"

"Who?" Linda whimpered.

"That seems to be the reaction I get from most people. Montgomery did an interview with Mary's father back in the seventies. It never aired, but Mary held onto the comp copy. The second clip is an old animated thing that we used to watch when we were kids. One of the traveling priests would bring it with him whenever he spoke at the church. The animation's kinda crude by today's standards, but it still gets the point across."

Linda passed out while Griff was talking. She woke up unaware of the time that had passed. Griff didn't seem to notice, as he was still rambling.

"Not sure who actually made the thing, or where the old priest got it from. Whoever it was, he was way ahead of his time. Anyway… we're gonna get them to show it at the rave. The kiddies'll love it."

Griff left the room.

Linda tilted her head and listened to the voices that the open door let in along with the light and the smell of cooked meat.

Video Clip 1
The Thom Montgomery Show

Excerpt from: **Unaired interview with Joshua Raye, High Priest of the Church of 1000 Earthly Deities, Huntingdon, Pennsylvania**

Thom Montgomery: How would you address the criticism that Ergeister is more of a cult than a legitimate religion?

Joshua Raye: Ergeister would not have survived as long as it has if we concerned ourselves with opinions based on ignorance and misinformation.

Thom Montgomery: Well, then, by all means: please educate us.

Joshua Raye: To put it in the simplest terms… Ergeister teaches that the world as we know it is separated into five elemental planes: wood, water, fire, wind, and earth. Each of these planes is governed by a guardian spirit, or geister, that allocates the flow of spirit energy to all living things.

Thom Montgomery: Interesting…. Is it true that you reject the dominant Christian notion of one God?

Joshua Raye: "Reject" is such a harsh word. But yes, we do not subscribe to the belief that there is one almighty God whose son died for the sins of man.

Thom Montgomery: And what about the reports of, ahem, candle-light incantations, spells, and curses?

Joshua Raye: What about them?

Thom Montgomery: Are they part of Ergeister's practices?

Joshua Raye: Some rituals are involved, yes.

Thom Montgomery: There have also been reports about cannibal-ism being practiced in Ergeister churches.

Joshua Raye: Ergeister is a very old religion. There have been instances of ritualistic cannibalism associated with the church in the past, but such archaic practices have been phased out long ago. I might add that those rituals took place during a time when we were forced to fight to defend our beliefs. They were performed out of a sense of honor toward our deceased. To... ingest the body of a fallen comrade was seen as a way of allowing them to live on through us. Soldiers for the church would also ingest the bodies of their enemies as a way of gaining their strength. Our detractors like to stigmatize it as some kind of barbarism, but among the believers, it was treated with a great deal of respect; much like the Catholics and their Holy Communion. Doesn't eating and drinking the body and blood of Christ smack of cannibalism?

Thom Montgomery: I guess you could say that, in a figurative sense. There seems to be a strong emphasis on apocalyptic prophecies in the Ergeister religion. Can you comment on this?

Joshua Raye: Yes. We are often guided by prophetic visions. And some...

Thom Montgomery: And how exactly do you... receive these vi-sions?

Joshua Raye: We hold our traditions sacred, Mr. Montgomery. They are not for you to dissect and scrutinize with your bias. I might add that you're more than welcome to pay a visit to the church and find out for yourself what goes on there.

Thom Montgomery: Thank you, but I think I'll pass.

Joshua Raye: I was saying before that some of our visions *do* relate to the end of the world. But I think you'd have a hard time finding a religion that doesn't cover that topic in some way. Of course, it's perfectly acceptable when we're talking about Christianity and the Book of Revelations, right? Because we don't follow the popular path; because our members live together on the church grounds; and because we actively train for the "Great Awakening," outsiders often come away with the wrong impression of what we're all about. We've been called everything: doomsday zealots, heathens, savages.... What the people out there need to understand is that Ergeister is more than a religion. Ergeister is a way of life. All of our members are with us because they want to be, not out of guilt or obligation.

<u>Video Clip 2</u>
Atrophy: An Animated Film

A barren, mid-afternoon sky is captured in crude, watercolor strokes painted over live action. A distant rumbling sends innocent eyes skyward to investigate. Voices stir with dubious curiosity. The demographic favors no specific type. The scene dissolves from one end of the spectrum to the other: from corporate wannabes to graduates of inner-city life moving about in entry-level, cubical dementia, to skateboarding rebels with deep pockets and no true cause, to harried single-mothers with children in tow.

Today, unity comes by way of a thousand eyes seduced by four billowing trails of smoke that approach from the east over the manmade horizon. Soon the missiles are close enough to see, close enough to serve as catalysts for countless interpretations of an impending apocalypse in quick review.

Widespread panic quickly ensues. From the tip of a charging missile, a watercolored grimace stretches to a snarling cackle and races right at the viewer.

There is a flash of white heat....

Legions of green suits and gas masks march beneath a blood-red sky, so many that they lull the mind into a semihypnotic state. They are shot from a low angle, the heavy rhythm in complete synchronicity with the thunder of hundreds of thousands of feet meeting the ground in unison. Flashes of brutality and warfare are intercut within the parade of bodies in unified motion. Men, women, and children alike fall in the path of the juggernaut. Voracious flames bring metal, wood, and human flesh to anguished, crackling song as they devour the infrastructures of entire cities.

A chronological montage portrays the fate of the few who survive the initial attack as they stumble and lurch to and fro in various stages of affliction: botulism, Ebola, anthrax.

A mother staggers, then falls dead in her tracks, leaving her young daughter alone in a landscape overrun by desperate survivors in search of food, water, and shelter. The child watches as her mother vomits deep yellow bile, her frail body thrashing furiously.

The soldiers march on.

In the heart of the army, a modified rig with an extended flatbed creeps along. Strapped across the front, Carl Mezerak's rotten corpse models his trademark "83" jersey. A large throne occupies the rear of the flatbed. On either side, soldiers stand at attention.

The camera zooms in on Mary as she stands....

Freedom

All Linda Ludlow could do was duck and pray they were gone, so that's what she did. She prayed that the pain in her arms and her sides would finally leave her alone and that the brisk autumn wind would find somewhere else to play instead of in the stalks of corn that swayed under its spell. Each gust threatened to part them and reveal her hiding place to the passing cars.

It had been at least an hour since Griff shoved Linda out of the black van while it was still moving. He certainly picked a desolate-enough area. The least he could have done was leave her in front of a hospital... or in a town that had one.

Linda glanced up past the plumber and the satisfied housewife that smiled down at her from a billboard across the country road. She stared at the full, looming moon as if it would help her estimate the time.

She looked down at her wrists. Her knees buckled at the sight. The magnitude of her injuries gave her a taste of the sensations to come. At the moment, the pain was bearable. She knew it would be a different story when her adrenaline subsided.

Folding her arms over her chest, Linda placed her wrists beneath her biceps and applied pressure.

A pair of headlights appeared on the horizon.

Linda stood and, with both arms, parted the stalks of corn that stood between her and the blacktop. She stomped and flattened them to the ground. She staggered to the center of the road, took a deep breath, and faced down the approaching car. It started to rain.

The halted flash of an interior light ignited spasms in Linda's weary limbs. An older man wearing glasses and a tie was driving.

The car slowed to a crawl fifteen feet away. The man inside squinted through the windshield to give definition to the human shape in the center of the road.

"What are you waiting for?" Linda screamed, black eyeshadow oozing down her cheek. She could hardly hear her own voice over the rain that pummeled the blacktop.

Ten feet and closing...

Linda lifted her arms above her head and waved them.

It reminded her of so many bad movies that she'd seen, the way the man's eyes bulged when he noticed Linda's wrists. Where her hands should have been, there were only charred, cauterized stumps. Her hair was soaked, and it clutched the sides of her face. Waterlogged tentacles fondled her face and neck. The rain's damp touch braided strands of smoke into wispy flight from her charred stumps. She held her arms high above her head and waved again. Her back, ribs, and shoulders were so sore that even the raindrops hurt.

The older man stomped on the gas and approached her at high speed. He swerved around her and kept going.

Linda leaned to his eye level as he passed with tires shrieking, rear fishtailing slightly. She could see that he was trying at all costs to avoid looking at her, but Linda was determined to get his attention. "IT'S ME! LINDA LUDLOW!" The back tire kicked muddy water and burnt rubber fumes up at her as she yelled.

Wiping her face with her forearm, Linda thought of how arrogant that would have sounded in most circumstances. It was raining so hard that the older man probably couldn't hear her anyway.

Linda lurched forward and curled her fingers into a fi...

She looked down at her arms, emotion welling in her throat... *the rest of my life this way....* The shock was starting to break her.

Linda was on the edge of a nervous breakdown. Already the rhythm of the falling rain had evolved to a more malevolent sound, like metal pipes bending and sneaking by each other in a tight space. Friction brought them to a high-pitched whine. Up ahead, the older man's taillights seemed to wink. All that was left were two pinheads of light against the deepest black she'd ever seen.

Someone tapped Linda on her shoulder. She whipped around, arms instinctively up to defend. Her heart felt like it was going to explode.

Linda plainly saw a cartoon bleeding real blood. Oddly, it was the first thing that struck her, not the fact the plumber and the satisfied housewife were alive and real and that they were at least twenty feet away.

Linda looked up at the billboard... and back. She struggled to make sense of what she saw. The plumber single-stepped toward her, dragging the satisfied housewife in tow. The woman's head dangled back and bobbed at the end of her limp neck, eyes rolled back. Her long, flowing hair painted the ground in abstract style as her lacerated brow provided a continuous stream of color. With his other hand, he rested his wrench on his shoulder, blood dripping from the tip.

"Tell the world!" the plumber said, pointing his wrench at Linda with authority. His hollow voice sounded a lot like Griff's.

Linda balled her lips up under her chattering teeth and scanned the cornstalks in search of Griff. Nothing.

Linda collapsed to her knees. Her muscles began to spasm as a mixture of fear and hypothermia claimed her.

"God, please let me die…."

Practice Makes Perfect

"Please tell me this is some kind of joke," the middle-aged soccer mom said to the square-jawed hero-type.

Only four of them remained on the lone El car: Urban Thug, Hero-Type, Pencil-Necked Corporate Slave, and Soccer Mom. Out of the four, Hero-Type was the one who, based on appearance alone, Soccer Mom trusted most to keep her ass alive.

"For the last time, would you please leave me alone so I can think?" Hero-Type responded as he paced back and forth, his hand massaging his stubbled chin.

Soccer Mom was far from what one would call informed, having gained all of her knowledge from "intelligently written" sitcoms, tabloid TV shows, and politically charged Saturday Night Live parodies and skits that ran way too long. She saw everything in stereotypes.

If she hadn't spoken with her best friend Stella for so long before leaving for work, she probably wouldn't be in this mess: stuck on a train in some forgotten part of the tunnel with three people she knew nothing about. These were people she figured she'd never see again, and now their faces were etched in her mind for good. There were seven of them when the train left the last stop, seven anonymous faces that bounced with every bump in the track and ignored the occasional blackout in the overhead lights. The blackouts came unannounced every five to seven minutes on the El. They only lasted about 5 to 15 seconds, and they were often preceded by a brief stutter in the lights.

The regulars most likely caught the 8:15 AM train; Soccer Mom barely made the 8:45. In fact, she had to run top speed to catch the last car by sticking her hand in the closing doors. On other days, she was the first one to snicker under her breath at people in the same position, especially when the doors closed and the train lurched forward, leaving them behind.

Soccer Mom had fallen asleep during the ride (they all had) and had woken up to confusion and raised voices. Somehow the car she was on had separated from the rest of the train and was abandoned in what seemed like an unusually dark, barren section of the subway. The grease-stained walls cast an eerie, comic-book glow upon the interior of the train car, as strange, spray-painted characters and urban glyphs peered in the windows.

Soccer Mom did everything to keep from dwelling on the three passengers that had already vanished since the train stopped 45 minutes ago. The alpha-males in the group tried opening the doors and windows. They were all locked. It left Soccer Mom questioning not so much *where* the three passengers went, but *who* had taken them, and *how*, within the span of 5 to 15 seconds, they had managed to walk in under the cover of darkness and abduct them without even the slightest sound. She was beginning to freak out.

The first one to go was Sassy Black Woman. Soccer Mom was fixated on her ass, pondering how it could be so fucking big in proportion to her relatively thin upper body. She mused to herself that maybe she ate through her anus instead of her mouth. The woman was in the middle of a detailed flow of colorful (albeit malapropism-laden) metaphors to illustrate her frustration at the fact that her cellphone wasn't working. Then it went dark. When the light came back, she was gone.

Urban Thug was the first to speak up when the lights came back on. Soccer Mom initially mistook him and Sassy Ass for a couple. Maybe it was the "don't fuck with me" glare that they both had down cold.

"Did I miss something?" Urban Thug said, "Or did that sista just up and disappear?"

"I saw it, too," replied Punk-Rock Girl. She was the second to go.

"I think we all fucking saw it," quipped Surly Union Man. He would be third.

"Hey! No need to curse at the lady," Hero-Type remarked in defense of Punk-Rock Girl's nonexistent honor.

"And who the fuck are you, the language police?" Surly Union Man shot back.

Soccer Mom rolled her eyes when the two men stood and squared off. She was sure that they were going to come to blows until the darkness returned and claimed Punk Pussy.

At that point, Soccer Ditz was still under the impression that it was some kind of elaborate joke. *Probably something for TV.* She even began to fix her hair for the big revelation.

The rest of the crowd hadn't yet noticed that Punk-Rock Girl was gone. They were too preoccupied with the adolescent chest-puffing between Teamster Man and Big Hero. It started off as a battle of words. Hero-Type held the clear advantage in the battle of insults and threats; judging by his body language, he was equally confident with the threat of physical confrontation. Surly Union Man was larger, but after a few moments, it was obvious that his aggression was born of insecurity, whereas Hero-Type was calm and cool under pressure. The television had taught her that was a sign of confidence. She figured he probably knew karate or Tae Bo or something.

Surly charged at Hero when he realized that he was outgunned intellectually. Before he could reach him, the darkness came again.

When the light returned, Hero-Type was bracing for a collision of bodies that never happened. His first reaction was to whip around in case Surly had somehow managed to get behind him. But he was gone, snatched away just like the others.

"Oh God, we're fucked," Pencil-Necked Corporate Slave whined and jumped out of his seat. "What are we gonna do now?"

"Your silly ass havin' a breakdown is the last thing we need right now," Urban Thug replied. He was still trying to force the latch on the door, but it wouldn't give.

"Man's got a point," Hero-Type added after giving up on the door at the other end and kicking it to broadcast his disappointment.

Soccer Mom, who had been playing the Helpless Female card, was the only one still in her seat. Though her good judgment urged her to, she just wasn't ready to abandon her "elaborate joke" idea just yet. That would mean admitting to herself that they were all in deep shit.

"Did you see it?" Pencil-Necked Corporate Slave addressed the entire group, his eyes threatening to jump out of his angular, loose-jawed visage. "The wall outside... it moved. I swear it did."

"Please sit down and let us handle this," Hero-Type replied angrily after whipping around to all the windows and finding nothing save for the same looming characters and balloon lettering in bright colors that screamed "LOOK AT US" from the walls.

"And how exactly are you going to *handle* this?" Pencil-Dick queried.

"Look, we're all a little scared here, but it would serve us all better if you'd learn to use that fear constructively."

"Well, excuse me, O Exalted One, if I don't share your optimism."

"So what do you suggest we do? Sit here and bitch about it? Realistically, the police are probably working on getting us out of here as we speak."

"I don't know about that," Urban Thug smirked.

"See?" Pencil-Man pointed at Urban Black Menace, his body alive with a childlike sense of validation. "At least he's honest."

Hero-Type glared at Urban Thug. "You're not helping matters any," he grumbled.

Urban Thug surrendered his hands to the air, shrugged an unspoken apology, and turned back to the emergency exit sign next to the window. This would be the fifth time that he followed the instructions to the letter, yet the window refused to budge.

"Okay, maybe he's right. Maybe you're both right and the police aren't coming," Hero-Type said. "Either way, there has to be a logical explanation, and…"

"Logical explanation??? Logical explanation???? Okay, I want you to logically explain to me how three people who were on this train when I got on just fucking disappeared through two locked doors and a shitload of windows that we still can't open or break. Better yet, explain to me how our car got separated from the rest of the train without any of our knowledge. Or how we were all conveniently sleeping when it happened. And why don't any of our cellphones work? Yeah, I know: the tunnel, right? Well, I've ridden this God-awful train every damned morning for the past fifteen years, and I don't know how many times I've placed or received a call in this tunnel. Sure, there's usually some interference down here, but now, I've got nothing—not even a 'No Service' message, or a low-battery light."

"You're missing my point," Hero-Type said.

"No. *You're* missing the point that we are stuck in this God-forsaken train in the middle of a part of the tunnel I have never seen in fifteen years, and to top it all off, none of us knows what is what because we all somehow managed to fall asleep at the same damned time. Now, does that sound logical to you?"

"Look, I'm not saying that I don't share your…"

"Haven't you been reading the papers, buddy?" Pencil-Dick interrupted. "It's Y2K. I know it."

"But that's not supposed to happen until New Year's," Urban Attitude said. "And how would computers make us all fall asleep?"

"I don't know. Maybe they accidentally released some kind of gas into the subway or something."

"What about New Year's?" Urban Thug added.

"New Year's…. That's what they say on the news, but they don't know. The whole God-darned country is run by computers. You think this subway system is any different? Oh God. They probably don't even know we're down here."

"Can I talk now?" Self-Important Hero asked.

"What? So you can tell me that I'm wrong?"

Hero-Type shook his head.

"Look, I understand where you're coming from. But, don't you think we'd have a better chance of getting out of here if we all worked together and focused on one thing at a time instead of listening to you provide negative commentary from the peanut gallery, so to speak?"

"Please stop fighting." Soccer Mom's voice was too soft to breach the male-dominated atmosphere.

"Hey, I'm only stating the obvious," said Pencil.

Hero balled his fists at his sides and took a deep breath to keep from lashing out.

"I'm obviously wasting my breath here, so I'll put it to you like this," he said. "Because you're so adamant that we're fucked, why don't you sit your stiff ass down, shut the hell up, and let the rest of us try to figure a way out of this mess. Got it?"

"That's what I'm sayin'," Urban said.

Pencil stared off into space, searching for a smart-ass response that would trump Hero's brute-strength approach while not baiting him into a physical altercation.

"I said GOT IT?"

"PLEASE STOP FIGHTING!" Soccer yelled. She sat hunched over, her hands covering her ears.

For the first time since the darkness last attacked, there was complete silence.

In a huff, Pencil plopped back into his seat and crossed his arms in front of him.

Hero watched him like a hawk. He eventually turned to Soccer and allowed his tense visage to relax into a concerned smile.

"I'm sorry, ma'am, but…"

"Wait a minute," Pencil interrupted. "Do you hear that?"

Hero tensed up immediately.

"Just a second," he said to Soccer and turned angrily to Pencil.

This time they all heard it. It sounded like feet, hundreds of them, skittering along the walls just outside the window behind Soccer.

Their eyes crawled tentatively to the window, then to Soccer, who had already jumped out of her seat and ran to the middle of the car behind Hero.

Pencil followed suit and joined them.

Hero glanced over at Urban. They had an unspoken bond that only guys of their rugged, no-nonsense ilk shared.

Together they followed the sounds down from the sides, to the ground below the car, where they scurried playfully back and forth, occasionally bumping into the bottom of the car.

"Should we call out?" Soccer whispered to Hero. "Maybe it's the police."

"Or maybe it's not," he responded. "Besides, whoever it is could easily see us in here from half a mile away. They're obviously playing with us."

His statement sent a chill down her spine.

"Hey! Who's out there?" Urban blurted out.

Hero reached out, grabbed his arm, and reprimanded him with a frown.

Urban yanked his arm away and opened his mouth to let Hero know just

where things stood between them, unspoken bond or not. He was cut off by the sound of giggling beneath the car.

"WHAT THE FUCK IS GOING ON?" Urban barked.

Pencil stepped further away from the window and fell into the seat behind him.

"How exactly do you explain that one, Mr. Logical?" he snapped.

"Oh my God. They're gonna kill us!" Soccer yelled as she clutched onto Hero.

"Okay, everyone just calm down," Hero demanded. "Whoever it is, they're just trying to mess with us. Let's not give them the satisfaction."

"Fuck that shit!" Urban growled as he retrieved his backpack from his seat and began to riffle through it. "I was willing to do things your way at first, but I damn sure ain't goin' out like no punk on this train. No fucking way!"

"Please! We *need* to stay calm if we're going to get out of this."

"No thanks. I'm through being calm. It's about time I showed these muthafuckas how an angry nigga deals with this kind of shit."

What, like hold a march that does nothing but tie up traffic and nurture false hope? Pencil wanted to say, but it wasn't the time or place.

Soccer found herself wondering which was worse: an angry black man or whoever it was running around outside. She had all kinds of exaggerated ideas about what Urban might pull from his backpack. They all did. Hers, however, was the closest to the truth, so she wasn't as surprised as the others when Urban pulled out a large black handgun.

Soccer had seen enough TV to know that guns were to angry blacks what revisionist history and a glamorized sense of cultural identity was to the rest of them. If not for Urban's mild-mannered demeanor up to this point, Soccer would've screamed when she saw it.

Hero saw it as an opportunity.

Pencil saw it as the same gun he stared down the barrel of last year when he was mugged. He eventually came to his senses and joined in Hero's enthusiasm.

"Now, let's see how funny they think this shit is," Urban spat out as he held the gun in both hands up by his shoulder. "C'mon! I don't hear you laughing now muthafu…"

Suddenly, darkness.

When the light returned, Soccer found herself clinging for dear life to Urban. She didn't mean to shove him away as hard as she did. The fact that just a few seconds ago she was clutching Hero and, to a lesser degree, that she was aligned pelvis to pelvis with a black man made her uncomfortable.

Urban interpreted her contact as repulsion, or attraction masked as repulsion.

Of the four of them, she expected Pencil to go next, but there he was, hiding on the floor between his seat and the one in front of it. Although Urban was cut from the same cloth as Hero, he was a minority. These days, they sometimes survived until the credits rolled, but it was typically their job to reach their limit, then fight back with a ferocity all their own. It usually meant sacrificing themselves for the greater good. That's what always happened on TV.

"I told him. I told him that we were fucked," Pencil said.

"Not now!" Urban replied.

"You were standing right next to him. Why didn't you use your gun?"

"I said shut up! And don't be tryin' to pin that shit on me. What about her?" He pointed at Soccer. "She was holding onto him."

"Wha...? Me????"

"Yeah... then she was holding onto you. One of you *must've* felt something."

"How dare you try to find fault with one of us," Soccer whimpered. "I don't know what happened. I was holding onto his arm, and the next thing I know..."

"Well, you must've felt him let go or something."

"NO, I DIDN'T! I DIDN'T FEEL ANYTHING, GODDAMMIT!"

Urban reached out to console her.

"Oh my God!" Pencil sprung to his feet and ran up next to Urban and Soccer.

"Someone just tapped me on the shoulder."

Their eyes darted simultaneously to the window above Pencil's seat, where the clownish devil-thing in fluorescent yellow grinned at them from the wall outside. It was holding its long, pointed index finger against its lips as if to say, "Ssssh!"

Funny that they never noticed that before.

Urban aimed his gun at the window and squeezed the trigger.

The gun clicked empty. From the end of the barrel, a thin, foot-long stick popped out. At the end of the stick, a rectangular cloth unraveled to reveal a flag with the word "BANG!" printed on it.

Pencil gasped.

Soccer fell to her knees and began to cry.

Urban threw the gun down and looked at the window. The yellow-faced devil-thing with the shit-eating grin was now frozen in a different pose. This time, it flipped them off. The sight gave Urban's heart a terrible stutter.

Beneath the train, they heard giggling. Then there was darkness.

When the lights came back on, Soccer didn't even bother to look out from behind her hands, which covered her face. When she finally parted her fingers, she saw Pencil standing alone with his mouth agape, patting himself down to make sure that he was actually still there. Afterward, he faced the ceiling and mouthed a silent "thank you" to God.

Soccer sank lower to the floor and continued to cry.

"Hey," Pencil whispered loudly, but Soccer was too distraught to respond whether or not she heard him.

"HEY!" This time he gave it a little volume.

"OH, FOR PETE'S SAKE, WHAT DO YOU WANT?" Soccer screamed. "You think I don't know that we're fucked, hunh? You want to criticize something I did or didn't do? Well, what about you? You were standing right next to him this time. Why didn't you do something?"

"I... I didn't... I couldn't see any..."

"Oh, please. Why don't you just come out and say it?"

"Say what? I don't follow."

"That you're a FUCKING COWARD. Out of all the people on this train, I ended up with the fucking coward. Oh GOD, I'm never going to see my kids agai..."

Interrupted by the now familiar skittering feet, Soccer and Pencil froze. They followed the footsteps from front to back, where Pencil was standing, to even further back at the end of the car. They sounded as if they were right outside the door.

Soccer and Pencil watched in silence as the doorknob began to jiggle, and then, as if it were never completely shut, the door slowly opened with a metallic creaking that affected them both physically.

Pencil half-turned to Soccer and, without a moment's hesitation, bolted toward the doorway. The ever-intrusive darkness made sure he never made it.

When the light returned, Soccer was all alone. At this point, she was beyond fear, beyond sorrow, beyond self-pity. The open door had ignited a surge of hope within her that was quickly snatched away, along with Pencil. Still, she saw the open door as her only hope.

Soccer wiped the tears from her eyes and inched her way toward the door. The murky darkness beyond it was both inviting and discouraging; it called to her. As she drew closer, she could smell the nauseating stench of fermented piss, soot, and the smoldering odor of darkness itself. Her glazed eyes focused on the doorway to the point of tunnel vision. With each step, her adrenaline pulsed, energizing her. On either side of her, the gauntlet of spray-painted buffoons peered in the windows and tried to break her concentration.

A flicker in the overhead light stopped her cold. This was it, her turn. And she was so close.

Soccer held her eyes shut and waited for the darkness to come and sweep her away to some Oz-like place, or perhaps to the other side of the looking glass. In these last moments, she chose to think of it that way. She waited and waited for the light that shone through the vascular wall of her closed eyelids to suddenly dim, but the flickering gradually settled back into a consistent glow.

She opened her eyes one at a time. Before her mind could persuade her not to do anything rash, Soccer ran as fast as she could until the floor of the car was no longer beneath her feet.

The floor of the tunnel was harder and colder than she expected. Judging by the way she landed on her ankle, she was certain that she had sprained it if not broken it, but the pain was strangely manageable. Soccer was a pussy when it came to pain, so she knew that her mind was trying to tell her something when it didn't hurt nearly as bad as it should have. She ripped a section from her skirt and tied it to her ankle without making a sound.

Soccer gave the knot one last check, then hobbled to her feet. She made it a point to stop concerning herself with the little things (*who* or *what* was doing *what*, and *why*) in favor of devising a mental plan to get her ass out of the tunnel in one piece. Hell, she had made it off the train, so someone must be watching out for her. Why else would she be the only survivor?

She felt her way through absolute black, which was blacker than the darkness that took her riding mates one by one. She guessed that she'd been staggering along for about fifteen minutes without looking back. So far, she had been successful in her attempt to ignore the fact that she couldn't see shit. She occupied her mind with the faint echo of screeching metal, the amplified drip-drip of toxic condensation falling from rusted pipes, and something... like a cicada's call on a hot summer day. The atmosphere that they, in concert, created was much like the dense vibe of gothic urban dread that crept through her house whenever her oldest son felt the need to crank up his stereo. It was usually some outfit named RZA or some gentleman called Mr. Len.

Somewhere behind her, Soccer heard giggling.

She spun around, half-expecting to see a cameraman and a stuffed shirt with a microphone and fake-ass enthusiasm, ready to let her off the hook.

In the distance, the light from the open door of the train car was but a rectangular sliver, and the illuminated outlines of the windows that ran along both sides decorated the walls that pressed them.

At first, she thought she was looking in the wrong place, but they were indeed the same walls upon which the colorful buffoons and clownish devil-things were projected. Only now, the walls were completely bare, save for a dozen or so layers of grease and dirt. In the shadows below, there was movement, a mass migration of shapes that oozed alongside the train toward her. She saw silhouetted heads and shoulders of various heights and proportions.

Soccer fought her instinct to run. The oozing darkness reached the end of the train and moved out into the light cast down by the open door.

What she saw stopped her heart completely.

Ending B

In the shadows below, there was movement, a mass migration of darkness that oozed alongside the train toward her; silhouetted heads and shoulders of various heights and proportions poked forth.

Soccer resisted her instinct to run. The oozing darkness reached the end of the train and moved out into the light cast down by the open door. She watched the overhead lights flicker out once again.

What she saw when the light returned made her legs turn to rubber. She could only describe it as a feeding frenzy. She mostly saw legs and feet. There were at least thirty pair, all rendered in blotchy watercolor. Some were clothed; some naked. One had hooves that stuck out from the cuffs of its dress slacks. A few of the more outrageous ones took on the look of famous cartoon characters (like Mickey Mouse or Bugs Bunny), after grotesque makeovers: sharp teeth and claws and big, red eyes filled with malice. They ripped huge pieces of flesh from her former riding mates, who had been reduced to partial torsos and limbs that barely resembled their former whole selves. Some of the *things* fought each other to get their share of the bounty.

Soccer ran until her heart threatened to explode out of her chest. Eventually, she was forced to stop and catch her breath. As she stood, hunched over, trying to will her lungs to inflate, she didn't notice the giant mouth that slowly closed some ten feet behind her. She didn't notice the hot, rancid smell or the low rumbling that surrounded her on all sides. It sounded like something bigger than she could comprehend breathing in and out, but in all honesty, it could have been the muffled sound of the traffic above.

When she planted her feet to run again, they sank into softness, causing her to lose her balance.

Soccer reached down, touched the floor with her hand, and rolled the sticky string that stretched up from it into a ball. The floor itself had a strange-yet-familiar fleshy consistency. She looked behind her and saw a wall of teeth that stretched from one side of the tunnel to the other. As absurd a sight as it was, those were undeniably teeth, which meant...

Before she knew it, she was knocked from her feet by a rush of knee-deep viscous liquid and carried toward an even darker tunnel up ahead.

Soccer reached out blindly for something to grasp to keep from being digested by whatever it was that was about to swallow her whole. She thought of all the Discovery Channel documentaries she'd watched, wondering what it must be like to be eaten alive.

As she approached the ledge that dropped off into the darker tunnel, Soccer let out one last desperate scream.

*   *   *

"I'm not even going to ask what you did to her," Rainah joked, as she watched Soccer Mom crumble to the ground.

"Maybe I gave her a look at your ugly ass," Griff replied.

"Fuck off," she scolded.

Rainah followed Griff, bouncing evil-eyes off the back of his head as he dragged Soccer's limp body up to where the other hostages were all bound and gagged. They sat next to each other in a dark passage to nowhere that branched off from the main track and traveled up an incline that ran parallel to it. It led to the underground shopping center that the city had abandoned back in the early '80s before the project was completed. They were going to call it Suburban Plaza.

Kagen turned them on to the place. He used to take his

victims there when he was a simple killer. It was like a subterranean ghost town, complete with a supermarket, nightclub, endless storefronts, and a restaurant decorated with defunct, smiley-faced corporate mascots set in welcoming poses that were supposed to welcome families and their dollars. The local politicians peddled their usual bullshit about a much-needed boost to the economy and all the jobs it would create, but the project went outrageously over budget.

The city never got around to digging out sections of the street for entrances and exits. As a result, the subway tunnel was the only way in. To get there, they had to trek nearly a mile through the tunnel from their improvised entrance at the back of the Torchsong Scrapyard.

"A present for you," Griff spoke to Hero-Type specifically. "Feel free to go to town on her if you'd like. I think she was into you."

Griff expected some form of defiance or rage out of him, but instead, Hero simply faced the ground.

Surly Union Man was feeling especially disappointed in himself over being duped. This menace that he had built up in his imagination was nothing but two human beings. Who gave a fuck *how* they did it or *why* they did it? He just wanted some good, old-fashioned retribution.

He managed to untie himself while they weren't paying attention. He had coordinated a plan with Punk-Rock Girl, Urban Thug, and Hero that relied on whispering, facial gestures, and head nods. Sassy Black Woman didn't want any part of it, and Pencil-Necked Corporate Slave had been unconscious since they snatched him from the train.

The plan called for Punk, Urban, and Hero to somehow distract Rainah and Griff while Surly tried to get his feet underneath him to launch an attack.

Sitting on his ass with the soles of his feet planted, Hero fell into a coughing fit. He slid down the wall and laid on his side. He started to convulse. Urban and Punk grunted through their gags and motioned with their heads down at Hero to indicate that he needed help.

"Are you fucking kidding me?" Rainah complained as she

walked over to Hero. "I expected this from her (pointing to Punk) or him (pointing at Pencil), but not from a strong specimen like you."

Hero continued to cough.

Rainah stood over him, looking down. She nudged him with her foot a few times.

"You'd better get that shit under control before somebody hears you."

"That's the point," Griff stated. "Well, partly. In about 7.2 seconds, this fuckin' idiot right here (pointing at Surly) is going to try to rush me from behind. Can you believe that shit?"

Hero was suddenly cured of his coughing attack.

"Uhwha... uhwha-arh-ewe-tahking-amout?" Surly mumbled through the gag, raising his hands in a questioning pose. "I-uhwas-jus-shhitting-ere."

Surly forgot that he was supposed to be tied up. His face drooped when he realized. His eyes were suddenly darting to his fellow hostages, looking for support. There was none to be found.

"Mut... uhwait! I uhwasn't twying to..."

Without warning, Surly launched himself at Griff. He was just out of arm's reach when Rainah landed on his back, wrapped her legs around his waist, and squeezed. He gasped and lurched as she forced the air from his body and spun in circles trying to get her off. Rainah held on tight. She pulled a box cutter from her sock and retracted the blade cover with her thumb. She reached around and slit Surly's throat.

He grabbed his neck with both hands and danced around a little before he fell down.

Rainah fell on top of him and groaned at the pain when her knees hit the ground. Everything below her knees was pinned beneath Surly's bulk, but she continued to squeeze until she heard his last breath escape with a "pppuuuhhhh" sound.

"Let that be a lesson for the rest of you muthatfuckas," Griff warned.

Rainah climbed to her feet and hurried over Hero. She brandished the box cutter with malice.

"Got something for you, too," she said.

She raised her hand and froze.

"Chill out girl. I want that one for the obstacle course," Griff coaxed to Rainah.

"Let go of me, Griff," she thought back.

"You promise to calm down?"

"I said, L-e-t GO of me!"

Rainah's forward motion sent her off balance when Griff released her. She righted herself and hurled the box cutter to the ground next to Hero, who cowered from the tiny explosion. She snatched her head toward Griff and glared at him.

Griff knew how Rainah felt about being coaxed like that. Projecting thoughts were one thing, but manipulating her will constituted rape in her mind. She had warned him about it repeatedly.

Griff raised his hands and shrugged.

"Sorry man, but you didn't leave me much choice," he said.

"Don't even fucking talk to me," Rainah replied. She walked a few feet away, leaned against the wall with her arms folded across her chest, and pouted.

Griff rolled his eyes and let them settle on Urban, who was trying to maintain some sense of bravado as he looked up at him.

"Women," Griff said under his breath.

He glanced over at Hero, who was sitting with his back to the wall like he never moved.

There was a large rusted vent recessed into the wall through which the main track was visible. Hero sat right next to it. Looking down diagonally, he peered through the vent on the sly and saw the train that they were just on sitting idle seventy-five feet away. Instead of one car, there were five or six, maybe more, but Hero's view was obstructed by the vent's wrought-iron border. Except for one of them, the cars that he could see were packed with morning commuters.

Rainah was still angry when she came back over and perused the line of hostages sitting against the wall. She wore an aggressive posture and had an unruly glint in her eyes. She spied Sassy staring at her, who quickly turned to look away.

"Something wrong, girlfriend?" Rainah leaned in and said. "'Cause I'm sensing that you've got something you want to say to me."

Sassy shook her head no while trying her best not to look Rainah in the eyes.

"You were all mouth up on that damn train. What's the matter now? Fat got your tongue?"

"Griff, you there?" Kagen's gravely voice jumped at them from Griff's waist. Griff reached down and grabbed his walkie-talkie.

"Whazzup, K?"

"Rainah with you?"

"She's right here. Why?"

"Mary's lookin' for you two. She wants to run the course a few more times for the rave."

"Tell her we're on our way with some new meat."

Genesis Game

ANDRE DUZA

Chapter 12

IN THE NEWS TODAY… *The Chinese military began what is being called a "campaign of mass genocide" in Tibet after the infamous Chinese General Lam Chin Man was killed in a riot led by a group of Chinese and American human-rights protesters. The riot began after 400 monks refused orders by gongzuo dui (Chinese work team) officials to denounce the Dalai Lama and walked out of a "patriotic reeducation" class. The Chinese military, which tried to block the monks from leaving, were attacked with stones and bottles by the human-rights protesters, and a riot ensued.*

In response to President Jackson's warning to call off the troops in Tibet or else face dire consequences, China issued an official statement reprimanding the US for interfering in their domestic matters.

"China will not back down to pressure from the United States," the statement read, "and we are prepared to take whatever measures necessary to keep the US out of our affairs."

President Jackson gave the Chinese military until the first of the year to withdraw its troops.

December 31, 1999, 8:24 PM

Tasha only had to endure Tarkington's undulating mass for about thirty seconds before orgasmic convulsions took hold of him. She seized the opportunity to snap his neck.

Jesus! Lay off the fucking snacks, why don't you, she thought as she dragged him, by his feet, into the storage room and shut the door. The bed in her room was light compared with his fat ass. She had used the mattress and frame to bench press (she'd lay beneath it on her back and push) until Tarkington had it bolted to the floor to spite her for declining his advances that day because she was on the rag.

Tasha kept her fingers crossed when she promised Linda Ludlow that she wouldn't hurt anyone during her escape. It was the only way Linda would agree to help her. Linda told Tasha that, despite her hatred, she had to consider Tarkington's family.

"Don't make them suffer because of what he did to you," Linda told her. "Certainly someone like *you* should understand what it's like to lose a loved one. I want you to keep that in mind when you make your... getaway... er, whatever you call it."

"When I fly the coop?" Tasha remarked, her tone floating somewhere between sarcasm and bitchery.

Tasha might've felt guilty if Tarkington wasn't such a pig about the way he fucked her. He liked to call her names while he did all the things that he couldn't do with his wife. She wondered how his wife would take the news when she found out that he was dead....

Bitch should thank me.

Tasha had three and a half hours until the next shift change. That would give her plenty of time to get out of here and make it to the rave. Although her access to the television was limited, it was next to impossible to miss the advertisements for Bloody Mary's Ball. Distressing chords set a dark, scary mood, energized by a thumping beat with hints of Christmas bells jingling in the background. Tasha knew they'd be there, hiding in the shadows. Somehow she could feel it.

Tasha hunched over, lifted the loose vent at the base of the wall, and reached in. She used it to hide the black clothing (thermal underwear, gloves, Kevlar vest, sweatshirt, durable pants, and boots) that she had instructed Linda Ludlow to send her. She grabbed them and tiptoed back to her room.

Maybe it was the mood that she was in, but Tasha couldn't help feeling that there was something ceremonial about the way she suited up. She almost expected to hear a military drum beat when she latched her belt buckle, taped the utility knife to the underside of her wrist, and slid Tarkington's precious chrome-plated .44, laser scope and all, against the nape of her back. With each accessory, a flash of memory stirred her hot anger. Not a single day passed since she saw the picture that she didn't envision Dana dangling helplessly from the street sign. She remembered the terror that his eyes conveyed so clearly.

Was he thinking of me at the time? Have I let him down? Could I have tried harder?

Tasha rifled through Tarkington's key ring for the one that would open the gun cabinet. She had her mind set on a shotgun. It had been so long since she held one that she felt a surge of giddy anticipation.

Tasha peeked out into the hallway.

Christmas lights flashed. Cardboard cut-out Santas smiled at her from the walls. Otherwise, the hallway was empty.

Tasha grasped the keys in her fist and sprinted out toward the empty guard station. She opened the gate, hurried over to the gun cabinet, and grabbed two shotguns and a nightstick. The only thing left now to do was getting to the parking lot. She wondered if it would go smoothly or if she'd have to take another life... or three... just to get out of here.

At this point, she really didn't give a fuck. In fact, she thought that she could use the practice.

Tasha soaked in the view as she cruised east along Market Street and watched the numbered streets count down: 23rd, 22nd. She was locked in a strange there-but-not-there state. City Hall stood, like a battle-worn titan, at the center of the giant grid of streets. On weekday mornings and afternoons, old power brokers and their sleek, ambitious protégés whizzed past each other, shoulder to shoulder, on all sides of the archaic structure. Tall buildings faced each other across the six-laned boulevard, creating a corridor that spanned for five blocks from 15th to 20th Streets. The immense structures blocked out the sun during the day and amplified the wind that wound up trapped in the tunnel-like grooves that extended beyond Market Street in every direction. The hard edges and flat, reflective faces of the skyscrapers never seemed to jell with the random Christmas decorations put up by the city, especially during years, like this one, when it didn't snow.

Market Street at night, after the workday gridlock let up, was an entirely different animal. In fact, Tasha's car was nearly alone on the road. In light of the Y2K paranoia, she wasn't surprised that many people had chosen to celebrate the new year far from home this year. Cities across the country took special measures to prepare for unrest in the event that something did happen when the clock struck midnight. There were hints and predictions of scaled-down celebrations. Small groups of barhoppers stumbled drunkenly down the street. The temperature was somewhere in the high forties, so people were dressed relatively lightly for wintertime. A red-faced brunette flashed her breasts at passing cars. Police patrolled the streets in teams of two. Tasha felt compelled to slouch down in her seat when she passed them.

It was only 9:30. They wouldn't realize that she was gone until the shift change, most likely. Besides, if they had somehow found out that she was gone, they would be looking for Tarkington's car, which she ditched about a half an hour ago at the corner of 34th and Spruce in University City; she continued on in a '96 Toyota Camry. The Camry was still warm from the happy young couple who had just parked it when Tasha broke in, plopped down her duffel bag full of weapons, which contained two Remington 870s and a nightstick, and drove off. She kept Tarkington's chrome-plated .44 in her lap, just in case.

Tasha spent the next half hour cruising by her old haunts: her apartment above the Chinese restaurant on 20th and Chestnut; the laundromat around the corner on Sansom with the troll-like attendant; Rittenhouse Square and Schuylkill River Park, where she'd sit and smoke a joint at the end of one of her evening walks; and the various buildings she had worked in back in her old life.

In a way, Tasha felt like she was saying goodbye. She had been tripping on bloodthirsty vibes since she snapped Tarkington's neck. She wasn't sure what would happen when she found Mary and the gang, but she was willing to go as far as she needed to claim her vengeance, even if it meant losing her own life. She wasn't afraid to die anymore; she was just a little sad that it had to be this way. If anything, death would reunite her with Dana. She had no idea what she'd say to him. She worried that she might not be able to look him in the eye. What if he held what they did to him against *her*? What if she died without avenging him?

Tasha wondered how Linda was doing. It had been six weeks since they found her on Worcester road, way out in Bucks County, with her hands cut off. The last Tasha had heard, Linda was due to be released from the hospital in a week. They had fitted her with prosthetic hands and were putting her through some rigorous physical therapy to learn how to use them.

Tasha actually felt bad for all the hateful things she wished would happen to Linda before their relationship had blossomed. Aside from the guards and Dr. Wilkinson, Linda was Tasha's only link to the outside world. After a while, she even began to look forward to her visits. At least she'd have someone to talk to who wasn't trying to dissect her brain… or get into her pants.

Now they had something other than their gender in common. Linda had seen Mary up close and personal and lived to talk about it. It established a bond that Tasha felt she should honor by paying Linda a visit. Linda never came out and said it was Mary and the gang that kidnapped her, but Tasha knew. She was interested to know where Linda's head was at as a result. But that would be counterproductive. She kept on driving.

The rave was being held in Ridley Creek State Park. Tasha planned to take Market Street to Route 1 to get there, but she was going the wrong way. And Market Street became one way (headed east) after 20th Street She was daydreaming when she passed it and didn't even realize. She would have to turn right on one of the side streets, take Walnut back to 20th, and head back up to Market. So that's what she did.

Bloody Mary's Ball

Tasha parked the Camry on the shoulder of Route 1, half a mile from the main entrance to Ridley Creek State Park. She grabbed her duffel bag and hiked through the woods to Picnic Area #5, where the rave was being held.

As part of the Pennsylvania State Park System, Ridley Creek State Park's 2600 acres of woodland offered recreational activities such as hiking, biking, fishing, picnicking, and several under-the-radar activities known mostly to unfaithful spouses and underaged kids looking to get drunk or high out in the open. There were hoity-toity formal gardens and colonial plantations that attempted to recreate the past.

Fourteen picnic areas were formed by immense, circular clearings in the woodland. Within each circle, there were green grassy fields sprinkled with picnic tables, charcoal grills, and restrooms. A smaller circle of blacktop sitting dead center served as the parking lot. A road jutted out from the right side and traveled down an incline to the entrance and the main road of the park.

Picnic Area #5 was where the information office, a two-story log cabin with wall maps, restrooms, refreshments, and an information kiosk, was located in the middle of the parking lot. It served as the broadcast hub for the DJs from WKDP, a popular, local college radio station. They were set up next to DJ Arachnoid (who claimed he could spin like he had eight arms) in the mezzanine area that overlooked the lobby. Part of the lobby was blocked out for the costume contest that WKDP was holding later that night.

Outside, the field was littered with hundreds of intoxicated young people in colorful get-ups, exhaling mist and wriggling like invertebrates caught in a violent rip current. Thunder-thump footsteps rumbled understated beneath a liquid melody, growing louder, like something large was approaching. Shockwaves rippled down and affected every living thing. Glowsticks whipped and whirled, and multicolored lightshows temporarily cast people in funny shades. Wisps of heat wafted up off their bodies and out of unbuttoned jackets and puffy coats, settling into a hazy layer of evaporated sweat.

Four large screens cycled through different silent images—kaleidoscope swirls of colors; shots of the crowd; clips from obscure cult films (Altered States, Spiral, Lair of the White Worm, etc); and dramatic reenactments of Bloody Mary sightings and general footage from various news and tabloid TV shows. The screens lay flat against scaffolding that rose twenty-five feet from the ground, built to house speakers and light fixtures that moved and projected green, blue, red, and purple lights. The scaffolds were placed about fifty feet apart from each other at the outer edge of the circular field. Between them, relocated picnic tables huddled in small groups. Vendors representing the local businesses that sponsored the event sold coffee, hot chocolate, power drinks, posters, novelty items, glow accessories, jackets, and T-shirts. A sign posted on the front of the clothing vendor stated that they were sold out of the popular Bloody Mary's Ball tee. The design on the front featured a skillfully painted picture of Mary looming over the tree-lined horizon of Ridley Creek Park.

They hired local bouncers for security. They were the guys in the bulky black sweatshirts with STAFF stamped across the back in bright white letters. They patrolled the crowd and stood at the top of the hill that opened out onto the picnic area, checking for weapons with a quick sweep of a handheld wand. As a precautionary measure, the event's organizers prohibited the use of video cameras. They were worried that someone might take footage of illegal drug use or some other kind of lascivious or prurient activity involving teenagers (which they knew couldn't be prevented) and use it to bring a case against one or all of the organizers or sponsors. It was up to the bouncers to confiscate the cameras from people as they entered. They tagged them and stored them in a van until the rave was over.

Ridley Township police beefed up their roving patrol of the main road and the various entrances to four cars instead of one. They crept along slowly, shining flashlights into the parked cars that lined both sides of the main road all the way down to the main gate, and on the latecomers who occasionally wandered by on their way to Area #5.

Technically, Ridley Creek Park closed at sundown, which happened before 6:00 PM this time of year. Picnic Area #5 was the only one permitted to remain open, but there were a number of revelers trying to sneak into the other areas.

The police were scolding a couple that had just been caught dry-humping in the grass inside Area #2 when Tasha happened by. She was deep in the belly of the woods, far enough back that she could walk casually by and watch if she wanted, but she was on a mission, so she kept going.

Tasha could hear the music whispering through the trees, beckoning to her as if DJ Arachnoid knew that she was coming. Aggressive tones spoke to her thirst for vengeance and inspired a synergistic swell that anesthetized her from the chill in the air. Gliding on a hunter's high, Tasha melted from tree to tree. She held Tarkington's chrome-plated .44 down by her side, ready to come out blasting at first sight of Mary, Griff, Rainah, Derek, or Kagen. The duffel bag hung over her shoulder.

The music was almost deafening when she reached the woods just outside of Area #5. There were people eating, urinating, and lounging around comatose. There were couples fucking in the undergrowth; E-tards rolling in small groups; and others passing lit bowls or blunts from one to another.

Tasha snatched her arm behind her back to conceal the gun.

"Oh shit, cops!" somebody said.

Tasha turned and shushed him with her finger. "Relax, kid. I'm not a cop."

"Then what *are* you supposed to be?"

Tasha looked down at her outfit. She looked like a SWAT officer gone native.

"Stupid," another voice scolded. "She's supposed to be Natasha Armstrong—right?"

Tasha felt a sting. Her eyes widened.

"Yeah, that's right," she said.

"Cool costume. I'll look for you in the contest."

Tasha turned and sunk into a crouch.

"One for the road?" inquired one young man who offered her a hit from a lit blunt.

Tasha ignored him and disappeared into the darkness.

The exchange worried Tasha that she stood out from the crowd. Plus, the wriggling bodies that danced in the field were packed so tight that she couldn't see more than a few feet into the kinetic swarm. She came upon a tree that bent and twisted in a way that seemed to say "Climb me." She tucked the .44 into her pants at the nape of her back and climbed.

Once she was high enough, she stood on a bulging knuckle and pressed the front of her body against the trunk to stabilize herself. The tree grew at a drastic slant that left Tasha facing the ground.

Tasha winced at the warm, syrupy atmosphere that floated above the crowd and took in the sight.

"Jeee-Zus Christ," she whispered.

Heads and shoulders bobbed and thrashed, creating a pulsating mass with thousands of parts moving independently. They filled the circular field like a giant pixelated donut.

Tasha's trigger-finger twitched each time her eyes fell upon one of the various depictions of Bloody Mary interposed in the crowd. It was strange to see the kids wearing fashionable outerwear over their costumes, as if zombie-chic had suddenly become a legitimate trend. They were heading toward the information center in the middle of the parking lot, attempting to maneuver through the crowd without damaging their costumes. A few of them weren't so successful.

A smaller, less cohesive crowd of mostly girls in halter tops and cargo pants, or miniskirts and leather boots with chunky soles, or knee-high, rainbow-colored socks congregated outside the information center, trying to get noticed while trying not to look like they were freezing their asses off. More Bloody Mary wannabes stood in a single-file line leading up to the front door of the building where the contest was being judged. They were each allowed to have one friend go in with them and help if necessary. A large barrel-chested man wearing a black bandana and shades stood with his arms folded in front of the door. Occasionally, he'd let one go in.

The longer Tasha stared, the more real some of the costumes began to look. The music, the lights, the warm, sticky atmosphere, and the hypnotic movement of the crowd all seemed to work together to pound the point into her head. There was one in particular that piqued her interest. Hovering lazily through the crowd, she (if indeed it was a girl) seemed uninterested in the contest. She was wearing a gas mask, so Tasha couldn't see her face, but she had the height and size down. Maybe she was a little thick around the waist and arms, and she didn't move with Mary's trademark stop-motion gait, but that could've been part of the disguise. Tasha wanted to investigate, but she needed to change into something less conspicuous if she wanted blend in with the crowd.

Tasha slid down from the tree and searched. She came to a small pocket of bushes that seemed to be shaking. She walked up on it and found a skinny white guy wearing a bright red bomber jacket, a red-and-black four-point jester hat, and a blank white mask on the back of his head. That white mask was the first thing she saw. It might have scared her had she been in a different frame of mind. The boy was getting his rocks off with a girl that he probably didn't know as she lay unconscious on her back.

Tasha pulled the .44 from her waist and trained it on the boy. "Get offa her... now!"

"Whoooaaaa…. This ain't what it looks like, man," the boy said as he turned and stood with his hands in the air. He was sporting a huge erection that pushed against the zipper of his baggy pants. A dollop of wetness marked the spot where the tip of his penis pushed forth.

Tasha flipped the .44 in her hand and cracked the boy over the head with the butt. He crumpled to the ground, unconscious. She took off his red bomber jacket and put it on over her sweatshirt. She slid the four-point jester hat over her head. She put the blank white mask on her face and fastened the Velcro chinstrap of the hat around it.

The energy was intense in the belly of the crowd. The ground literally shook beneath Tasha's feet. The air was thick and filled with strange odors that made her cough and threatened to suffocate her. She found it hard to comprehend why anyone would want to be packed so tightly together. The independently moving parts painted her clothing with sweat as she muscled her way through. At only 5'4", she couldn't see over the heads and shoulders that surrounded her, so she used their reactions to gauge the position of the Dead Bitch costume. She held the trigger of the .44 inside the duffel bag, which she carried low with her exposed thumb pressed against her fingers and the heel of her palm, which were inside the bag through an opening in the zipper.

Tasha told herself that she would kill the next person who shoved her, unintentional or not. Then it happened again... and again. The most she did was shove back, violently in some cases. No one seemed to mind, so she continued to shove until she found herself just two bodies behind the figure in the costume. The sight of those skeletal curves and that long, gaunt shape gave her a shot of adrenaline. Her hand tightened around the .44. Her arm flexed, ready to respond. Her pores opened and covered her body with a tingling sensation.

Tasha crouched and lowered the duffel bag to the ground between her feet and pulled the .44 from it.

DJ Arachnoid's voice leapt out of the speakers.

"It's about that time, boys and girls," he said enthusiastically, speaking over the music. "The new millennium is coming in about thirty seconds. I want you all to stop what you're doing and count down with me."

Most of the crowd stopped dancing and turned their attention to the screens, where shots from New Year's parties from across the globe played out. The seconds counted down. People had strange looks on their faces that seemed to indicate that they had just woken up from some kind of trance. Others were chatting up the people closest to them like they'd just met.

Someone said "hi" to Tasha.

She immediately crouched and tossed the .44 into the duffel bag. She stood and looked for the costume (it was moving farther away) before engaging the pretty young man who had stopped to admire her costume.

"Love the costume. My buddy Rob has got one just like it."

Tasha nodded, kicked the duffel bag up into her hands, and started after the Dead Bitch.

The crowd began counting in unison.

"Ten. Nine. Eight. Seven. Six. Five. Four. Three. Two. One."

Tasha noticed that the DJ Arachnoid seemed to stammer and choke one his last words, as if something had happened to him while he was talking. But then the crowd rejoiced. They indulged at once in party favors and raised glowsticks over their heads. The screens flashed red, white, and blue colors. Mortars placed on the roof of the information center shot fireworks into the air.

The music stopped. The screens suddenly went blank. The speakers spit out a series of crackles and pops. A test pattern filled the screen and counted down from three. A single word appeared against a black screen: ATROPHY.

Tasha's eyes crept up to the screen and watched the watercolor nightmare unfold. An eerie silence came over the crowd as they watched, confused, and gasped at the shocking imagery.

When it was over, a voice that Tasha immediately recognized came over the speakers. It was Griff.

"WHAT I'M ABOUT TO SAY MAY SCARE SOME OF YOU, SO I URGE YOU TO LEAVE NOW IF YOU FEEL THAT YOU CAN'T HANDLE THE TRUTH. THE FILM YOU HAVE JUST SEEN... *WILL* HAPPEN IN YOUR LIFETIME. THE FINAL WORLD WAR IS NEAR, AS THOSE OF YOU WHO WATCH THE NIGHTLY NEWS MAY ALREADY KNOW. EVERYTHING THAT YOU HOLD DEAR WILL PERISH IN THE GREAT ORGY OF FIRE AND DISEASE THAT THESE SO-CALLED WEAPONS OF MASS DESTRUCTION WILL LEAVE IN THEIR WAKE. GONE WILL BE YOUR COMFORTABLE SUBURBAN HOMES; YOUR DYSFUNCTIONAL FAMILIES; YOUR SCHOOLS, CHURCHES, AND SYNAGOGUES.

FATE HAS SEEN TO IT. THERE ARE THOSE WHO BELIEVE THAT JESUS CHRIST, AN EFFEMINATE, BLOND, BLUE-EYED, WHITE MAN FROM ISRAEL, WILL SAVE THOSE WITH FAITH WHO HAVE ACCEPTED HIM AS LORD AND SAVIOR. WELL, I'M HERE TO TELL YOU THAT IT AIN'T GONNA HAPPEN."

Tasha froze and uttered an unintelligible sound accompanied by a stuttered breath. In an instant, she completely forgot about the crowd. She was standing alone, surrounded by Griff's voice. Her blood ran cold, then scorching hot. She turned toward the information center. The scene glowed red in her sights.

Griff read from a sheet of paper as he stood in front of the microphone. It was attached to an arm that reached up and over the turntable setup. Mary was standing behind him. Her face was covered by her gas mask. She looked like just another contestant for the costume contest. DJ Arachnoid lay unconscious on the floor at their feet, while Derek stood over the DJs from WKDP, whom they had instructed to lie face down on the floor behind their booth, which consisted of a table lined with promotional goodies and wraparound skirting with the station's call sign plastered across it. Rainah stood at the bottom of the stairs that led up to the mezzanine. She appeared to be hanging all over the bouncer as a line of contestants dressed like Mary waited impatiently to be sent up and judged. No one could see the gun that she had pressed against the bouncer's side.

"THERE IS ONLY ONE PATH TO TRUE SALVATION IN THE NEW WORLD ORDER," Griff continued. "CHOOSE THAT PATH AND I GUARANTEE YOU THAT YOU *WILL* REAP GREAT REWARDS. IF NOT, WELL, I'LL LEAVE THAT TO YOUR IMAGINATION."

The contestants started making a fuss about what was taking so long.

"What the hell is this?" one said with regard to Griff's speech.

"What gives?" whined another. "Some of us have been standing in line for like a half-an-hour."

"Just tell them to patient," Rainah whispered to the bouncer, who complied.

"THE TIME IS NOW TO DECIDE WHETHER YOU WANT TO LIVE OR DIE." There was a sudden commotion from the stairs. Griff was caught up in the grandeur of the moment as he continued to read. He and Mary were standing too far from the steps to notice the disturbance anyway.

"Don't even *think* above moving," Derek warned the DJs, as he walked backward over to the steps. There was shit going on all around them, so he figured it was probably nothing important: maybe a fight among the restless contestants. When he reached the steps, he turned around and...

"FOR THOSE OF YOU WHO WISH TO JOIN US, WE WILL BE PROVIDING YOU WITH MORE INFORMATION IN THE VERY NEAR FU...."

Griff turned and saw a jester with a blank white face standing over Derek's unconscious body. The jester was pointing a .44 at him. A shotgun hung from its shoulder.

"Didn't see me coming this time, didju?" Tasha said as she squeezed the trigger repeatedly. Her voice was slightly muffled by the mask.

The first shot smacked Griff in the right shoulder and sent him reeling back into Mary. They fell into a pile of equipment cases.

A couple of stray bullets hit the turntable console and sent sparks flying. Smoke rose from the table and made it hard to see beyond it.

Tasha stepped over Derek and hurried closer. With her free hand, she waved the smoke away.

Griff rolled onto his back and thrust his palm at her.

An invisible gust lifted Tasha off her feet and shoved her backward. She managed to fire off a wild shot before the gun flew out of her hand. Her legs hit the railing of the mezzanine on her way over it.

Tasha landed hard on the floor of the lobby.

People screamed and scattered.

Despite the pain in her back and neck, Tasha got up as fast as she could. She pulled the mask and hat off of her head and took a deep breath. She was about to head for the steps when a long, gaunt shape appeared on the ledge above her.

Mary snatched off her gas mask and flashed a toothy grin and hollow-eyed glare down at Tasha. Rage inflated her body. She had a fire axe in her hand.

"SIS-TERRRRR!!!!!!!!!" Mary rasped passionately and leapt over the railing. She raised the axe up over her head as she came down.

Tasha rolled out of the way just in time. The axe bit through the clavicle of a teenaged boy who was running past her. His body spasmed before going limp.

Tasha planted her feet and launched toward the front door.

"GET OUTTA THE WAY!" she yelled, shoving people out of the way as she ran. On her way to the door, she glimpsed Rainah waking from her forced nap. She was rubbing the spot on her head where Tasha clocked her with the butt of the .44. She had a groggy, dumbfounded look on her face that gave Tasha satisfaction. If she hadn't been in such a hurry, Tasha would've found her gun and pumped a few bullets into her. She intended to do exactly that when she was done with Mary.

Outside, the majority of the crowd was screaming and stampeding toward the entrance of Picnic Area #5. Random bodies were trampled and shoved aside.

Tasha ran until she came to a clearing in the stampede. In one motion, she whipped around, slid the shotgun from her shoulder and... the shotgun overshot her hands and landed in the dirt between her and Mary, who had stopped about ten feet away. She was holding the fire axe in both hands.

Curiosity persuaded some of the crowd to stay behind to see what was going on. Standing at a safe distance, they begin to gather around the two women.

Mary glanced over at them, then down at the shotgun. She smiled and gave Tasha a look that said, "I DARE you!"

Tasha charged. She ran past the shotgun and caught Mary

around the waist as she was lifting the axe. Her forward motion sent them both to the ground. Tasha wrinkled her nose at the smell of rot and musty cloth that almost made her puke. Before Tasha knew it, she was on the bottom.

Mary straddled her and raised the axe in one hand. The other hand was clamped around Tasha's throat.

Tasha thrust her pelvis upward and sent Mary tumbling off.

Both women sprung to a stand.

The crowd of spectators was beginning to grow as the news reached the people who had scampered off initially.

Mary swung the axe, and it grazed Tasha's arm. She cried out and grasped the deep laceration. Mary swung again and again, but Tasha managed to spin awkwardly out of the blade's path each time.

Mary held the axe in a slanted, doubled-handed grasp across her body. She sunk into a half-crouch and traced the perimeter around Tasha in a sideways stumble, leg over leg. With her lead leg, she feigned to entice Tasha's hands down away from her face, then swung the axe.

Tasha leaned away from the initial swing, but the side of the blade struck her in the face on its return. She heard the bones in her jaw crunch. The pain sent shockwaves that threatened to turn her legs to rubber. But Tasha was determined to finish the fight. She inhaled to channel her remaining strength.

"YOUUU *BITCH!* YOU KILLED MY SON!!!!" Tasha exploded forward, swinging wildly.

Mary sidestepped Tasha's flurry. She reached out, caught Tasha's fist, and twisted, snapping her arm at the elbow. She swung the axe low with her other hand and took Tasha's feet out from under her.

"NOOOO!" Tasha cried out as she fell to the ground. She cradled her arm against her chest and pressed the loose mud with the left side of her face. There was a lesser pain in her shin, probably from an open wound.

Tasha dug her knees in and pushed herself in a directionless crawl. She spied her shotgun half-buried in the mud five feet away. She could hear Mary's feet slap the ground behind her as she crept forward. She kept thinking of Dana and how she promised herself that she'd avenge his death. She also thought of Mary's axe. She didn't want to feel that blade again.

Tasha barked out a deep, angry moan and lunged. She grabbed the shotgun, rolled to one knee, and took aim. The pain had her zooted on endorphins.

Suddenly, there were thousands of them, mirror images of Mary as far as she could see.

Tasha shut her eyes, as she thought initially that the army of clones was a manifestation of the pain, or adrenaline, or rage fucking with her vision. When she opened her eyes, they were still there... every last one.

"GRIFF! YOU FUCKING COWARD!" Tasha groaned in frustration.

Griff was standing outside the doorway of the information center with Rainah, who gave Tasha the finger when she spotted them. He was breathing heavily and holding his hand over the wound in his right shoulder.

Derek stumbled out soon after. His nose and mouth were bloody.

There was no way that the slugs from Tasha's shotgun would reach them from where she stood.

Tasha's eyes swelled maniacally. Rolling angrily from side to side, they perused the gallery of Dead Bitch clones. She trained her gun on the closest one and fired. She didn't bother to watch it fall before moving on to the next one. She cocked the barrel again and fired. She repeated this process until the gun clicked empty.

The gunshots prompted a second screaming exodus of young people toward the entrance of Area #5.

Tasha rifled through her pockets for more shells. She found a couple in her hip pocket.
She loaded them, cocked the barrel, and aimed indiscriminately, chasing the crowd in every direction.

"WHERE ARE YOU, YOU BITCH? SHOW YOUR-SELF!" Tasha roared.

Something hit Tasha from behind and stole her breath. She staggered forward and reached for the sharp pain in her back. She knew right away that she had been shot. A quick thought reminded her of the Kevlar vest that she was wearing.

Another round pounded her in the gut and sent her lurching backward to the ground. She hit her head when she landed and awoke seconds later to the sound of impact and the sight of blurred, kinetic shapes looming over her. It took her a moment to realize that the police were stomping and kicking her.

When they were satisfied that she was under control, the cops grabbed Tasha under the armpits and lifted her to her feet. She was dazed and swaying drunkenly. The handled her roughly as they slapped the cuffs on her and prepared to escort her to the nearest squad car.

Tasha suddenly snapped to her senses. She began to thrash. She got away from the cops for a moment and ran with her hands cuffed behind her back. One of them tackled her from behind and sat on top of her.

"NOOO!" Tasha screamed and spit like a savage. "YOU'RE LETTING THEM GET AWAY! THEY KILLED MY SON AND YOU'RE LETTING THEM GET AWAY! NOOOOO AAARRRGHHH!!!"

"I don't wanna hear another word outta your mouth, bitch!" said the cop who sat on top of her. Her grabbed Tasha by the hair and yanked her head up off the ground. He used it to steer her face in different directions. "You see all that? You see those bodies? Those were all kids that you shot. KIDS! If there weren't so many people around, I'd cap your ass right here and now. I swear I would."

Tasha's eyes crawled reluctantly from body to body. She knew that she would never be able to make the families of these victims understand. She began to cry.

Chapter 13

IN THE NEWS TODAY... *Partygoers returning from the Bloody Mary Rave in Ridley Creek State Park rioted along both West Chester and Baltimore Pikes and into Philadelphia this morning. The rampaging teens smashed out storefronts, set cars ablaze, and assaulted innocent passersby. Police estimate they caused more than one million dollars in damage.*

According to eyewitnesses at the rave, the riot started when Natasha Armstrong, who escaped from the Ries Clinic earlier in the evening, pulled out a gun and opened fire on contestants who were waiting to be judged in a Bloody Mary costume contest. Six people were killed: five from gunshot wounds delivered at close range, and one who was killed by a fire axe wielded by Armstrong. A security guard from the Ries Clinic was also killed during Armstrong's escape.

Ridley Township police speculate that Armstrong, who was described as "crazed," broke out of the Ries Clinic for the specific reason of coming to the rave. They theorize that she saw the contestants, who were dressed like the popular image of Bloody Mary, as real-life manifestations of her fictitious nemesis.

The police were finally able to subdue Armstrong, who was heard yelling that they (the police) were "letting the real killers get away," as they took her into custody.

There are, however, a few people who have come forward in support of Armstrong's claim that Bloody Mary does exist and that she had been at the rave. Most recently, one of two local DJs from WDKP who attended the rave suggested that what he saw was indeed "a living, breathing corpse."

The Ridley Township police dismiss these stories as drug-induced fantasies.

It would seem that the Y2K hype that swept the planet into a whirlwind of paranoid speculation over the past year was much ado about nothing. Aside from the riot and a few unrelated incidents of vandalism, the dawn of the new millennium passed without incident.

IN OTHER NEWS... *The deadline for China's troop withdrawal has passed, and President Jackson is meeting with his Cabinet today to discuss the nation's response to China's inaction. In an address to the nation, the President neither confirmed nor denied whether the use of military force has been considered in this matter.*

January 3, 2000

The nightmares.... They were visiting Linda twice, sometimes three nights a week—scattered vignettes of Mary and Griff pointing and laughing at her, their faces stretched and distorted as if cast by a funhouse mirror. It always ended with Linda holding her arms out in front of her face and screaming at the charred stumps where her hands used to be.

Linda's friends and colleagues bombarded her with cards, flowers, and videotaped well-wishes in the beginning. Her room at the hospital looked like a Technicolor forest, there were so many different floral arrangements. They came to visit by her bedside and filmed her while she read random support letters from fans on the local news. The executives at the network handled her with kid gloves until she was ready to talk about her ordeal.

Everything changed when she told them that Bloody Mary was real and that she and Griff were responsible for what had happened to her. The Ridley Township Police Department had just held a press conference where they attributed the violence to one person—Tasha Armstrong, whom they had in custody. After that, the news stopped covering the eyewitness accounts from people who had attended the rave. Most of the stories came from kids with multiple piercings, tattoos, and the kind of fashion sense that made them suspect in the eyes of the general viewing public. Some of them had probably taken part in the riot.

Linda was dying to know how Tasha was doing. She had been worrying about her ever since the nurse told her about what happened at the rave. She wished that she could have been there with her to help in some way. Linda didn't have it in her to actually kill a person, not even Griff. But she could damn-sure stand by and cheer while someone else (like Tasha) did it for her.

People looked at Linda… differently once she opened her big mouth. She expected it to some degree, but this was a whole *other* thing, like she was some kind of walking contagion.

I didn't ask for this, she wanted to tell them, while brandishing her hook-hands like fists balled in anger. But then they would call her crazy.

Conventional wisdom held that she was suffering from post-traumatic stress disorder and that her mention of Bloody Mary and Griff was just a result of her mind trying to avoid facing reality. In their opinion, she was probably attacked by a group of overzealous fanatics looking to give credence to the mythos. It was happening all over the country, they said.

"I must've missed all those reports about people having their hands amputated when I was investigating the case," Linda yelled sarcastically into the phone when she had her nurse call in to a cable talk show that was discussing her story on live TV.

After a while, the old pros in the industry began to distance themselves from her. The ambitious young go-getters, for whom she had paved the way, brought up her age and how it might have contributed to her inability to recover fully from such a traumatic event to expedite their corporate climb. Linda couldn't even give them the finger.

What had become of her reputation? Linda had worked so hard to get where she was. She had stepped on a few people in the process. Whether or not she was aware of it, Tasha was helping to enlighten Linda regarding her lack of consideration for other people's feelings. The years of navigating through a male-dominated environment had hardened her to the point where she saw the people she interviewed as a means to an end. That attitude eventually bled into her real life. Linda had to work twice as hard to put together a good story. She didn't have time to worry about feelings or else she'd still be doing weather in Toledo.

Linda remembered how good it felt to throw her weight around. *The New York Times* called her a prima donna back in 1975 and it stuck with her ever since. It used to bother her when some of her colleagues would whisper to each other when she walked past. They called her a hag, a bitch, a cunt. She would hide in the ladies room and cry.

Linda couldn't imagine what they were saying now. Well... she could, but it hurt too much to think about. Words like "crazy cripple" and "gimpy nutjob" came to mind.

She couldn't even look in the mirror without welling up. She saw herself as incomplete, damaged goods. Linda used to worry that she was too old to find another job should the network execs suddenly decide to drop her. She'd seen it happen before. Now she had these... *things* that were certain to hold her back, regardless of her thirty-plus years of broadcasting experience. Never mind the gender barriers that she had helped to topple. All people would hear would be her fanaticism; all they would see would be hooks for hands.

The doctors told her that, in time, she'd most likely be able to hold a glass or open a door, but she should not count on succeeding with more complicated tasks, like tying her shoes or buttoning a shirt. Linda tried her best to remain optimistic, like some of the people with similar conditions that she had interviewed over the years. She couldn't count the number of times she smiled in their faces and told them that everything was going to be all right. They probably wanted to deck her. That's what she wanted to do when the network execs met with her to discuss the direction of her career in light of her "situation." They tried to convince her to tone down "this Bloody Mary nonsense" and focus more on her recovery: "You know... to help inspire folks," one of them said.

More like to help rally folks behind the network, Linda mused. Essentially, they wanted a soft-news, survivor-story piece on working back from tragedy. They would run interviews with her "friends" and peers. They would call her a hero and an "inspiration to us all." Then they would kick her to the curb.

Linda swatted the prostheses to the floor and cried when the doctors first showed them to her. They were such horrible-looking things: hooks with blunt tips that could open and close extremely slowly. *Hooks for hands! HOOKS FOR HANDS!!!!!!* Linda just couldn't wrap her head around it. She wasn't ready to accept that she would never experience touch the way she used to. She would never again wrap her fingers around a glass of wine, or run them through her hair, or shake someone's hand—things she had taken for granted for so long.

So far, her relationship with the prostheses was in an awkward, getting-to-know-each-other phase.

"I'm not going to lie to you," one of the doctors warned. "The first few months will be the toughest of your life. No matter how frustrated they might make you, I'd advise using your prostheses as much as possible to acclimate your body to their weight and range of motion."

Subtle inconveniences woke Linda to her new reality from moment to moment: the frigid sting of metal against her skin when she had an itch; the inability to wipe herself. The first time she tried, she cut herself pretty badly. She broke down and cried on the toilet.

Gone was the fleeting satisfaction of masturbating to Charlie Rose or Stone Phillips (both of whom had worked under her at some point), the gentle pressure of her two fingers grasping her clitoris and tickling it to climax with the tip of her thumb.

Linda had begun a dialogue with her compassionate side, discussing things that she never would've wasted a moment on before her accident. A common topic was finding someone to enjoy her later years with. The desire for companionship had always been there, striving for acknowledgement, but Linda was all about her career. In some ways, she regretted it now.

One Week Later

Linda Ludlow felt like she was stealing someone's thunder when she showed up at the Ridley Township Police Station unannounced. Reporters skittered about like cockroaches in front of the building, waiting impatiently for news about Tasha. Her arraignment was scheduled for later in the morning. They shifted in unison like a school of fish when they saw Linda approaching.

What was it... the hook-hands that gave me away?

The crowd jogged toward her. Some of the reporters were holding their microphones out in front of them. The questions came so fast and from so many angles that they overlapped and eventually cancelled each other out. Linda remained calm. She gave them vague, one-word answers all the way to the front door of the station house.

Once inside, Linda walked right up to Lieutenant Marshall and demanded to see Tasha. She pulled a videocassette from her bag when he refused and held it pinched between the blunt tips of her hook-hand.

"What if I told you that I've got a piece of footage here that will blow your case against Tasha Armstrong out of the water?" Linda said.

Linda was so eager for them to see the tape that she ordered the chauffeur to drive her directly to the station when she was released from the hospital. The tape was delivered to her hospital room in a box marked "urgent." It had been languishing in a pile with various cards and gifts that she had yet to open for a few days before she found it. She didn't know what to expect when she popped it into the VCR in the nurses' lounge.

It was difficult to make out anything through the shaky footage of mostly legs and plump female asses. It appeared that someone had sneaked a camera into the rave to catch hidden video footage for one of those smarmy upskirt websites that Linda did a story about once.

Music bled through the scene. The bass was thumping. There were sounds of laughter, tribal calls, and hundreds of conversations.

The scene abruptly switched from the crowd to a blurry shot of the information center as Tasha came bolting out the front door. The music had stopped. Someone who looked like Mary ran out after her. The way she moved was unnatural, yet with its own grace. Linda could tell right away that it really was her, although she figured that most people would think it was doctored by a Hollywood special-effects team.

Without the music, the night amplified the screaming and mass panic. The camera shook and wobbled violently. People darted past the lens, pulling their friends in tow. The camera finally came to rest on Tasha as she turned and prepared to fire her shotgun. The gun slipped from her hands and landed in the grass between her and Mary.

The camera zoomed in to a tight shot of Mary's face. Her dead glare dominated the frame. Rotten skin wrinkled into a hollow-eyed frown. She snarled with the good corner of her mouth. A voice whispered from behind the camera, "Hoooo-leeee sheeyit. I think… I think it's really her!"

The footage continued until Tasha started shooting.

They watched the tape three times before Lieutenant Marshall was willing to accept that the thing they saw fighting with Tasha was more than just a person in a costume. He called more men into the room with each subsequent viewing. The officers who were at the rave that night saw it too. They couldn't confirm or deny the footage as being authentic because they had arrived moments later, after Tasha had opened fire. They all agreed that the footage was consistent with the eyewitness accounts, but it wasn't enough to exonerate Tasha. Until Linda could prove that Tasha was reacting in self-defense to what she thought she saw (thanks to Griff), she was still going to be charged with multiple homicides.

Linda attempted to explain it to them. They didn't buy it.

The basement was eerily silent, save for the rectangular lights that buzzed overhead; a few of them were threatening to flicker out.

Linda hurried through the earth-toned corridors on her way to the guard station at the entrance of "Holding." She hoped that, for once, Tasha would be happy to see her.

She offered a tentative smile to the officer at the metal detector, which he didn't return. She emptied her purse onto the metal tray, lifted her arms above her head, and stepped through. They both ignored the buzz and the red light that flashed at the top. At the risk of insulting his intelligence, Linda considered flashing her hook-hands in case he suspected her of hiding something.

"Armstrong is in Cell Two," he said. His voice was as indifferent as his stare. "Stay to the right of the yellow line at all times. You'll get your things back when you leave."

Linda nodded and entered through the large steel door.

"Good news, Tasha." Linda's voice was full of girlish enthusiasm as it was magnified by the muted gun-metal walls. It wasn't the news she was hoping to deliver, but it was a start. Hopefully, Tasha would see it that way, too.

"I'm Sasha," said an emaciated-looking man who approached the door of Cell One and engaged Linda with the worst smile she'd ever seen.

"Hey! Put a sock in it, O'Hara!" The officer's rigid voice bounced down the hallway from the guard station.

Linda followed the echo back to the door, smiled, and nodded "thank you" to the officer. As she continued walking, she could feel O'Hara staring at her.

"You might want to sit down for this one, Tasha...."

Linda choked. The next thing she knew, she was tracing her steps backwards to catch her fleeting balance. She closed her eyes and braced herself with short, controlled breaths. She was reluctant to open them again.

She started with the right eye... and followed Tasha's dangling feet up. She was wearing only panties. There was a large yellow stain at her crotch and dried urine on her inner thigh. There was a puddle on the floor a foot below her feet. It was apparent that they'd been beating her regularly—probably had raped her as well—

as she was laden with bruises and deep, ugly lacerations from head to toe.

Linda lingered on Tasha's face. It didn't look anything like her. Her bronze skin had faded to a pasty, ashen hue. She searched for some sign of peace in the concave left side, then the swollen right. It was so inflamed that Linda almost fooled herself into thinking it belonged to someone else.

Tasha's head was forced sideways at the point where her neck bore the brunt of her weight. The braided sheet that looped around her neck dug up into her jawbone all the way to her ears.

"OFFICER! PLEASE! HURRY!" Linda tried to relay everything in a single breath.

She pounded the bars and made a CLANK-CLANK sound. She leaned in, pressed her face between them, and started to cry.

"TASHA! TASHA! CAN YOU HEAR ME? TASHA!"

The officer rushed in, shoved Linda aside, and fumbled hastily with his keys. He radioed for back up, then snatched the rusted door open and ran in.

"Rudolph, Dietz, Perez.... You guys better get down to holding. We got a mess in Two."

Linda helped Officer Reynolds lower Tasha's limp body. She batted his arms away, held her body close, and cried loudly. She pondered Tasha's state of mind just before she leapt from the edge of the bed—if that was what really happened.

At that moment, Linda wanted to join her. She struggled to rationalize the whole thing as she rocked Tasha in her arms.

January 5

The tape from the rave was made public the night Tasha died. It ran at the end of a pieced-together segment about the last twelve years of her life on the evening news. More and more people came forward with eyewitness accounts in the hours after it aired. People who had heard how badly the police beat Tasha when they apprehended her starting crying foul. The bandwagon-jumpers flocked by the dozens. The sheer volume of the eyewitness accounts forced the police to consider that they might be true. And then...

A thirty-nine-year-old tax accountant named Harold Kikinger (Pencil-Necked Corporate Slave) was found wandering the street naked and badly beaten yesterday morning. He was barely alive by the time he reached the hospital. The police came and questioned him at his bedside. He told them that he had been kidnapped along with three other people and tortured in a house in the middle of the Torchsong Scrapyard on Decatur and Claxton Streets. The captives had been kept in cages in the basement of the house.

By the time he managed to escape, there was only one other victim left: a girl named Sarah (Punk-Rock Girl). He seemed to hesitate when they asked him what happened to her. His posture collapsed. His face twisted ugly.

"I left her," he wept. "She was so scared. I... I was trying to unlock her cage, but I couldn't stop shaking. I couldn't.... I didn't know what else to do. I left her...."

The others were taken from their cages one by one a few days apart. That was the last he saw of them. When asked who "they" were, Harold Kikinger looked around the room as if to make sure "they" weren't within earshot. He was sitting up, wrapped in blankets and shivering.

"Bloody Mary," he whispered. He had a ghastly look on his face, like something had rocked his world. He kept nodding his head. "She's real.... She's real.... She's real...."

*   *   *

Seventeen minutes had passed since Freemont led SWAT Team One to the Decatur Street entrance, and they still weren't responding. Dorien and his team awaited the word just outside the Claxton Street entrance, which was the only other way in.

"I'm not so sure this was a good idea," Captain Braugher

grumbled to Reynolds, who leaned on the hood of his car fifty feet from the gate that surrounded the Torchsong Scrapyard. He was holding a bullhorn.

"Want me to try again, Cap'n?" Reynolds guided Braugher's eyes to the bullhorn with his own. "Maybe they're ready to negotiate."

"Just sit tight, Reynolds," Braugher snapped. He patted him on the shoulder to acknowledge their allegiance despite the fact that his preoccupation with Freemont and Team One gave his words a hurried sting. "I get the feeling these crazy fucks aren't coming out until we go in and drag out their bodies."

"Fine with me," Reynolds replied.

Braugher eyed him up.

"I never look forward to killing another human being, son. And neither should you. It'll only get *you* killed."

The air was so thick that Alvarez felt he might choke on it if he took a deep breath. It was the prospect of days like this that seduced him away from his foundering marriage to the bottle and prompted him to join the academy. Back then, he would watch TV for days at a time; as a result, his image of the police was one of anything-goes, shotgun-toting valor. It was the furthest thing from reality, where all the real glory work was left to the SWAT boys. Freemont's guys were probably in the thick of it right now.

None of the police was happy with the way Captain Braugher and his precious SWAT teams came on the scene and stole the show from Lieutenant Marshall. Alvarez wore his disapproval on his sleeve as he knelt impatiently behind the passenger-side door of his squad car.

Cleeves, who took the other side, babbled an incoherent string of empowering religious axioms under his breath before making the sign of the cross with his fingers.

Fucking pansy! Alvarez mused. He had little patience for cowards and less for religion, probably because he, too, was afraid.... But he was too much of a man to come clean. Too much of a man.... That pretty much summed up Alvarez.

A wall of inconspicuous men, four bodies draped in black, approached the first row of stacked cars just beyond the Claxton Street entrance, their guns cocked, looking for the slightest movement. The man second from the left turned and motioned the others down into a crouched position. They continued forward.

"Dorien! It's been twenty minutes. If I don't hear anything from Freemont in five, I'm pulling your team out." Braugher's static-ridden voice attacked them from their headsets. "I don't like the way this place feels."

Dorien raised his hand, and the three other men froze in mid-step. He was clearly pissed. It was the first time he didn't look as if he were having the time of his life.

"What... and negotiate?" Dorien growled. "No thanks. Freemont's probably got his guys keeping quiet, that's all. You know how he is. Besides, these headsets suck to high heaven. Mine goes out on me all the time. Doesn't mean a thing."

Dorien scanned the labyrinth of steel and metal and glass. In the distance, he noticed a sculpture that he missed previously. It was sitting behind the wheel of a ford Taurus about nine feet up. It would have scared the shit out of him had it not looked so flimsy.

"I'll mind my Ps and Qs just the same," he said.

"Dorien! Listen!" Braugher's urgency startled him. "I'm picking up something to your far right. Looks like a girl at about... four o'clock."

Dorien slid his headset binoculars down from his brow.

"Got her."

"Okay. Watch your ass."

Back at the squad cars, Alvarez raised his binoculars and followed the pointing fingers. It really was a girl. She ran as fast as she could with her arms bound to her sides. She bit down on the rag that forced her mouth open and screamed.

Aside from her matted hair, filthy clothing, and the smeared mud on her face, she was hot. Alvarez couldn't help the fact that sex was the first thing that came to mind. He hadn't had any since his wife left him two months ago.

Alvarez watched Dorien wave the girl in. Once she was within reach, he yanked her down into a crouch and guided her welling eyes to the herd of squad cars. Instead of running, she clung to him and let out a defiant shriek when he tried to pull her free. She was shaking wildly and was most likely in shock.

Dorien bent over her and brushed a matted lock of blond hair away from her eyes. "Now you listen to me. If you stay here with us, then we're liable to get ourselves shot trying to protect you. I'm going to count to three... and when I do, I want you to haul ass over to those squad cars. You hear me?"

She didn't respond.

"DO YOU HEAR ME, I said?"

She nodded.

"One... two... THREE!"

Dorien sent her off with a shove, as gun barrels waved to cover her.

Captain Braugher ran out to meet her halfway.

Alvarez, who had braced himself for gunplay, grunted impatiently. This business of waiting around had them all on edge. Perhaps the SWAT team was above all that, with their Ninja threads, high-tech headsets, and their fancy-shmancy hand signals.

Alvarez seethed with envy. No amount of titillation would make up for his disappointment. Nevertheless, he continued to size up the girl.

Nice.

Braugher already had her draped in a blanket and sipping from the flask of Jim Beam he kept in his glove compartment. Rumor was that he just about lived in his car. Lately, he too had been having marital problems.

Alvarez caught himself wandering and readjusted his aim. He reflected on the promise he made to himself to fire the fatal shot when Bloody Mary showed her face. *Yeah, baby. Right between the eyes. We'll see just how dead you are then.*

"So, whaddya say, Cleeves?" Alvarez remarked. "You're

not gonna freeze up on me, are you?"

Fear spoke clearly through Cleeves's labored frown, tensed shoulders, and trembling hands. He gripped his .38 so tight that he couldn't feel his fingers. Cleeves was at home behind a desk. He was definitely not the kind of guy to wind up on anyone's list of preferred back-up in a firefight.

"Just grin and bear it, like everybody else," Lieutenant Marshall joked to Alvarez this morning when he assigned Cleeves to ride with him in Thibodaux's place. Thibodaux had been suspended for firing on a rape suspect. He shot him fifteen times. The man was unarmed.

"Freeze up on this, Chico," Cleeves replied, unfurling his middle finger.

Alvarez recoiled, as if reacting to a slap in the face.

"You know, you might want to direct your anger that way." Alvarez pointed his index finger at the old house in the junkyard and concealed any further anger beneath a steady grin.

It made no difference to Cleeves. He had already turned away.

Alvarez was livid.

"And you'd better watch it with that Chico shit."

Again with the race shit. It wasn't until Alvarez was in college that he first felt the sting of ignorance. He'd spent eighteen years as a suburban white kid with a nice tan. For a time, he denied his Cuban heritage. Both his mother and father were refugees. Contempt for their country started the ball of self-loathing rolling until it was their son's turn to pick it up and run with it.

Alvarez glared at Cleeves, who was busy with his own issues. He wanted to turn his gun on him and pull the trigger. The feeling grew the more he analyzed Cleeves's Anglo features.

Cleeves turned suddenly and faced him. He pointed toward Braugher who was trying to get Alvarez' attention.

"Hey, what are you waiting for?" Cleeves whined.

Alvarez locked eyes with Braugher, who then motioned him over. He sprung from behind the door, jogged up to Braugher, and eased the girl's arm from Braugher's shoulder to his own.

"Officer Alvarez, this is Darlene. Darlene... Officer Alvarez. We call him Chico."

Alvarez grinded his teeth. He was aware that, to them, it was just a harmless joke, which only made it worse.

Braugher lowered his face to Darlene's level and urged her with an accommodating wink. "Officer Alvarez is going to take you over to his car and ask you a few questions. Is that okay? Are you sure you don't want to go to the emergency room?"

Darlene was all eyes. She glanced up at him and nodded.

"Alvarez, see that she's taken care of."

Alvarez looked down and was immediately lost in her eyes. He just as quickly surmised that she was hiding something.

"TRIPWIRE!" Dorien dove forward and rolled to his knees. He motioned for his team to take cover. Even with all of his training, his tough exterior began to wither as he counted the seconds.... He expected to see at least one of his men come sailing by on the crest of a typhoon of orange-yellow flame.

Guilt was a difficult foe to shake. Dorien had triggered the tripwire himself and had almost got his whole team blown to pieces. Dorien would rather die than go through that... again.

The old wounds, never too far below the surface, rose up to taunt Dorien when he least expected it. The altered memories had been visiting him for the past thirty years, ever since he was plucked from Saigon with a seven-inch chunk of shrapnel buried in his gut. Body parts rained from the sky, severed limbs twitched, disembodied hands clawed at air. Sometimes they pointed at him or gave him the finger. A naked, headless Vietnamese woman danced stripper-style. Corpses upon corpses were stacked in a large mound, yelling out to the Viet Cong that Dorien was hiding at the bottom of the pile.

That is what tripwires do: they explode, right? Close to a minute had passed without an explosion.

He felt so ashamed. Twenty-one years on the force, and he was still making rookie mistakes.

"Dorien! Wake up!" Braugher's Jersey accent sent Dorien's

reflexes into action.

He spun to meet the metallic wail that approached from the east. He pressed his cheek against his rifle, teased the trigger with his index finger, and waited intently.

Deforrest was the first to see it. He was the closest. He had just enough time to cue up a reaction before the cackle of steady gunfire snatched away his attention.

"EVERYBODY DOWN!" Dorien ordered from the ground. They were way ahead of him.

"The shooter... Dorien, can you see him?" Braugher's voice sifted through the noise.

Dorien rolled to his back. He directed his focus on the echo and carefully traced it back to its source.

"That's a negative, Cap'n," he said.

"Well, look harder, dammit!"

"There is no shooter, sir. It's a recording... I repeat, it's a recording. They've got a PA system running into the house. There's a speaker in an old Chevy to my right. The cocksuckers are playing with us."

"You're kidding me!"

"DEFORREST!" Dorien roared. "WHADDYA GOT?"

"I've got two men, armed, coming fast. Looks like they're on some kind of rig. I can see the tracks in the dirt. I... I think it's Freemont and Yates."

Dorien exploded to his feet.

"Tony, Weeks, look sharp," he said as he jogged to Deforrest's side, crouched, and lifted his rifle.

The rig slammed to a stop at the tracks' end and hurled Freemont and Yates right at them. It was clear that both men were already dead.

Freemont's limp arms dragged gracefully in tow of his forward-leaning head and torso. Yates's body approached like a bull. He was doubled over, almost upside down.

Dorien noticed that there was something taped to Yates's back.

Deforrest fell back, and his eyes rolled back into his head.

He was nursing a mild case of shock. He could feel it deep in his gut. It was such an intangible feeling, like inertia's touch while descending on an elevator. He lifted his gun and fired at the approaching bodies.

"HOLD YOUR FIRE!" Dorien reached out to swat Deforrest's gun and push him out of the way, but Yates's body was too close. He recoiled, then dove to safety, and watched Freemont pass over him.

It must have been instinct that made Deforrest spread his arms to catch Yates.

Dorien looked away when he saw the first sign of pain in Deforrest's eyes. Yates's new spiked armor couldn't have been more perfectly aligned with Deforrest's chest and stomach.

Initially the sound of impact was like that of an axe biting into fresh pine; then it was given a voice, one that uttered a medley of raging grunts and convoluted obscenities as Deforrest plummeted to the ground. He fired his rifle into the air.

Dorien heard Weeks scream behind him, but he was already on his way over to Deforrest, whom he figured was dead or gravely injured. He couldn't live with himself if he didn't at least try to help him.

Dorien counted to three, grabbed Yates by the shoulders, and tried his best to pry his limp body from Deforrest, who cried out in pain. He cried out again when Dorien dropped him. He didn't mean to. It was just a reaction.

Something... a spark of motion caught Dorien's eye. He looked down at Yates's back, or the map of entry and exit wounds that had replaced it. There was a small digital display bordered in black tape. It was counting backwards from seven... six... five... four....

Shit! A timer!

Three... two... one....

"SHIT!" Dorien fell to his ass and immediately turned and planted his feet to launch himself forward.

Dorien was sliding from the hood of a car when he came to.

He panicked when he didn't feel anything beneath his feet, then again when he looked over the side to see that he was fifteen feet atop a stack of crushed automobiles. He scrambled back onto the hood and collapsed.

By the time Tony convinced his legs to stop moving, he had emptied his gun. As he ran, he managed to cover every angle. His mind replayed the image of Dorien flying through the air and the expression on Deforrest's face when the flash of noise and blinding light made a mess of him.

Tony made the mistake of looking. The desperate whine in Weeks's voice echoed in his mind. Weeks was begging Tony not to leave when the bomb exploded. Braugher had warned him never to get too attached to his comrades, but Tony was such an extrovert that he couldn't help it.

Tony threw his rifle to the ground and drew his sidearm, looking for someone—anyone—to hold accountable. He trained his gun on the old wooden door of the house. He stood only five feet from it. He was sure that he heard a sound from inside, like heavy furniture sliding across a wooden floor.

Tony burst forward, kicked open the door, and recoiled into a practiced half-kneel. He remembered seeing a metallic blur swing down from the ceiling. It staggered the moving shadow that charged at him. He remembered three bright flashes before his stomach and throat began to burn.

Tony fell onto his back. He just now realized that he had been shot. He reached for his throat and coughed up a flow of blood. He struggled to raise his gun, but it was only Higgins (one of Freemont's guys) crawling out of the darkness, unaware that the booby-trapped front door had sliced him in two at the waist.

"Run!" Higgins gurgled. "There's a bomb in the kitchen!"

Tony could feel his body growing colder as he tried in vain to catch his breath and keep from choking on his own blood. He was still holding his gun in his other hand. He closed his eyes, pressed the barrel up under his chin, and pulled the trigger.

The old house exploded and shook the ground for blocks.

It was like a bad dream, the worst Dorien ever had. He needed a moment to recuperate from his fall to the ground. The explosion had knocked him from the hood of the car and singed the back of his neck. He was aware that his left arm, a few ribs, and possibly his pelvis were broken. It could have been much worse though, especially considering the magnitude of the explosion, which leveled the entire house.

Dorien lowered his head and offered a silent prayer in memory of his fallen soldiers.

The heat from the burning house was intense, almost as intense as the pain in Dorien's groin. All that was left was a partial staircase and a portion of the living room.

Dorien cupped his groin in his hand, climbed to his feet, and scanned for survivors. He skipped over the general area where he guessed that the remains of Deforrest and Weeks might have wound up. And Tony…. Dorien found his body engulfed in flames beneath a pile of splintered wood and metal pipes. The flames seemed to cackle as they devoured him.

Dorien reached for his walkie-talkie, but it was gone.

That would explain why I haven't heard any chatter.

Dorien stumbled toward the main gate, out onto the street, and up to the crowd of squad cars. When he couldn't find any of his colleagues, he initially thought that they'd abandoned him. He spotted Darlene cowering behind the front tire of Alvarez' car, her knees huddled to her chest. She appeared to be in shock.

There were bodies everywhere. He saw Captain Braugher's first. He had been shot in the head at close range.

Dorien pondered how this could have happened. They had underestimated this Bloody Mary. He kept his field of vision high and away from the crowded street so as not to stir up his burgeoning panic. He certainly believed in Bloody Mary now.

Dorien staggered under Darlene's forward thrust as she hurried to embrace him.

"OH GOD! Thank you! Thank you! Thank you!" she cried

into his shoulder. "I thought I was going to die."

Dorien attempted to pry her free, but she wouldn't budge. He gave her a minute and tried again.

"You have to tell me what happened here!" He grasped her shoulders and held her out in front of him. He hoped that he wasn't being too hard on the poor girl, but he knew that they were still in immediate danger.

"No, please! Please don't make me remember!" Darlene was hysterical. "I just want to get as far away from here as possible. Please?"

Dorien hesitated. Darlene was rambling too fast for him to think, which meant it probably wasn't likely that he'd get anything useful out of her.

"Okay, okay. All right.... Calm down, ma'am. I'll getchu outta here, I promise."

"You promise?" Her tone was almost patronizing.

Dorien was lost in the flames' magnificent roar. The fire was bigger than the last time he looked. Dorien swooned at the beguiling glow. It was like staring into the sun. Only this thing was angry. Thank God he couldn't see the ground beyond the first row of cars from where he stood. He was already counseling himself about how he'd remember today, back in the junkyard. He knew that it would be impossible to forget this terrible day for years to come.

"Hey officer, wanna know what really happened?" Darlene was behind him now. She sounded different... almost playful.

"In a minute," he responded without looking at her. "I've got to radio for back-up." Dorien turned to ease her mind with a sympathetic nod... and found himself face to face with the barrel of a standard-issue .38 revolver.

Behind it, Darlene's large, blue eyes swirled with delight as she held the gun to his forehead.

"Okay…. But if I tell you, I'm gonna have to kill you," she chuckled.

"Wha...? Who are you?"

"I'm the bitch who took out all your little friends."

She squeezed the trigger.

"The name's Rainah. Not that it matters where you're going."

Rainah liked to watch her victims work toward some kind of understanding of their own deaths. Instantaneous deaths left her feeling cheated. Dorien's was incredibly satisfying. Shock led to terror. Terror led to anger. His eyes projected an intense desire to stay alive.

Reaching for her like zombie-pantomime, Dorien took two stagger-steps forward, balancing on noodle-limbs. His teeth slid from behind his lips like a great white shark and clenched to marshal his waning strength. He motioned for a third step, but his leg wouldn't budge. His face expressed pure terror. He looked up at Rainah, as if to beg her to make it all better again. His eyes rolled up. His body fell limp and crumbled to the ground.

Rainah tossed the .38 onto the hood of the squad car.

"Men," she quipped with a loose smirk to no one in particular.

She dug into her pocket for a rubber band and fixed her hair into a ponytail. She reached into the squad car, rapped three times on the horn, and started walking toward the scrapyard. Way in the back of the place, there was a trap door built into the trunk of an old, gutted Buick Skylark. It led down into the subway.

Rainah made sure to strut as she walked.

Chapter 14

"Stay away from the windows, girls."

"We will, dad," Rebecca McCreery huffed, her upturned mouth sporting a pout.

It was 2:00 PM, and Dr. McCreery's office was empty. He was an obstetrician. Today was the office's informal "take your child to work" day, and Rebecca thanked God it was almost over. Her father's last appointment was at 12:45, and since about 1:15, he'd been running around the office, "cleaning and working on the books," he said. He had the radio up so loud that the she and her friend, Christina, could hardly hear each other. It was some old '80s station blaring *One Thing Leads to Another* by the Fixx.

It was quietest in the bathroom. Rebecca's father hadn't gotten around to installing speakers in there yet—although he was planning to. That's where the girls decided to move their activities.

Inviting Christina turned out to be a good idea after all. Rebecca was apprehensive at first. She was afraid that Christina would find it boring and that she wouldn't like her anymore as a result. Next to Rhonda Dixon at school, Christina was her best friend.

When Rebecca had to go to her father's office, she usually would spend the day moping around. Sometimes she'd chat with her father's patients--the ones who didn't pretend to ignore her.

"Keep in mind that some people just don't want to be bothered," he told her. "Not all pregnancies are planned, while others cause problems that the expectant parents might not have foreseen. It can be a touchy subject for some people."

But isn't having a baby supposed to be a good thing? You know... like a gift from God? That's what her mother said.

"When I grow up, I'm gonna be rich," Rebecca sang to Christina.

"Not me." Christina batted her eyes in the bathroom mirror. She tossed her long braids over her shoulder. "I'm gonna be a supermodel, like Tyra Banks."

"Supermodels *are* rich, you dork." She jumped at the chance to correct Christina, who was slightly prettier than she was. "It's supposed to be harder for black girls, you know. That's what Tyra Banks said."

"Nanh-anh."

"Yanh-hanh! I saw her on *Access Hollywood*."

"Yeah, but that's only because of racism."

Rebecca didn't respond.

After a short pause, the girls turned and faced the bathroom mirror. They smiled at each other's reflections.

"Are you scared?" Rebecca nudged Christina with her elbow.

"Kinda. Are you?"

"Nope. You sure you still want to do it?"

The plan was to repeat the name "Bloody Mary" thirteen times while staring in the mirror. Everyone in the fifth grade was doing it.

Christina glanced nervously at Rebecca, who was just as afraid as she was.

"I'll do it if you will," Christina replied.

"Okay. Let's do it."

"Oh yeah…. Why did your dad tell us to stay away from the windows?"

Rebecca looked up at the skylight. She remembered hearing strained voices and blaring horns coming from the street before her father turned on the stereo, but there was nothing unusual about that on South Broad Street.

"I dunno. I guess the police have Broad Street blocked off. Didn't you hear the sirens?"

"Musta been when I went down to the basement. They got a cool aquarium down there."

Rebecca laughed.

"That's been down there since I was little." They were both only ten years old. "Where have you been?"

*   *   *

Walter Reilly was late for work again. He checked his watch reluctantly.

It was 2:15, and here he was, stuck at Broad and Chestnut Streets.

"GOD DAMMIT!" He pounded the steering wheel and eyed the gridlocked traffic up to where the jam ended at Locust Street. "Oh, c'mon! Four-friggin'-blocks! Give me a break!"

He promised his boss just last week that he'd be in at 2:00 PM sharp from now on. That was when his shift began. Granted, he had a good excuse this time, but he was notorious for laying it on thick. Why would this one be any different in the minds of his boss and the office busybodies who never let him get away with anything?

Lately, he had been doing so well. He thought today would be a good day: he was dressed and out the door by 1:00. Anything earlier than 1:20, and he was making good time.

Where is Eyewitness News when you need them? He wondered if maybe he could talk his way on camera. It was a long shot, but his job was on the line. He smirked as he envisioned himself amongst the urban riffraff that often lurked behind the reporters, waiting for the right moment to steal some face time.

He lowered his window to flag down the two cops that hurried by and stopped about a foot from the front of his car. The woman in the car in front of him (some old fat lady) beat him to it. Her approach was to draw their attention by cranking the volume on her stereo and moving about restlessly on her seat.

When Walter heard the ire in the older officer's voice as he spoke to his partner, he decided instead to eavesdrop.

"Crazy fuckers!!!!! Dispatch says the boys from the 13th precinct flushed 'em out-a-the subway tunnels somewhere around Walnut," the first officer grumbled.

"This Bloody Mary…" said the second officer to the first, his elastic face stirring with anxious curiosity. "You buyin' it? I mean, you don't think she's really…"

"You'll fare much better in this job if you learn not to ask so many questions, son. All I know is that these lunatics just wiped out seven cops and two SWAT units."

Seven cops... and two SWAT units.... Walter felt a rise in his chest. He forgot all about work.

Walter leaned out the window.

"Excuse me, officers?" Walter called out. "I don't mean to bother you, but is it safe for me to be sitting here? I mean I don't want to get shot or anyth…"

"Just sit tight, sir," the first officer said with a robotic tone. With his fingers spread, he pressed the air as he spoke. "We've got everything under control."

"Ahhh, but..." Walter wanted to tell him that he'd heard their whole conversation, and it didn't sound to him like they had everything under control. He wanted to, but he knew he would never be able to get it out. Not after the way the first officer stared him down.

"Never mind," he said.

Maybe he was overreacting. *They probably caught the guys already.*

Walter tried to relax and think of something else.

A woman approached in Walter's rearview. She looked a little rough around the edges. She was about an eight on his scale of one to ten of thirtysomething divorcées.

"Thousand bucks says she'll play up the helpless-woman act," he told himself.

Walter caught her eye and then glanced over at the two cops. They hadn't seen her yet. They hadn't seen the gun that she held behind her back, either. Walter sure as hell saw it, though. It was an enormous thing, like something Arnold Schwarzenegger might cradle in his bicep.

Half a block away, Griff leaned against a light post and watched the armed woman through his mirror-shades. He had his arms folded across his chest, right hand tucked beneath the lapel of his leather jacket and resting on the handle of a Glock 9mm.

He was slightly intimidated by the task at hand. His migraines had picked the perfect time to come back. They usually hit him every couple of months. His mind would play tricks on him—blurring his vision, making him forget things, and generally handing him a taste of his own mindfuck medicine in heavy, nauseating doses. Sometimes it would affect his ability to coax, which was what worried him now.

The doctor told Griff that the bullet in his brain would always cause him some occasional discomfort. He was twelve years old when, in a drunken rage, his father shot his mother to death and left Griff with a .38 caliber bullet lodged in his brain.

His next memory was waking up in the hospital two weeks later. At first, the images hit him like a freight train running off the tracks—vignettes of anonymous premonitions, memories, and deep, nasty fantasies. Thoughts that were not his own unraveled in the form of endless voices chattering away. The nosebleeds, pounding migraines, and nausea eventually drove Griff to take a dive off the Ben Franklin Bridge.

He never hit the water, though. When he stood on the edge of the bridge and looked down, he figured it would take about ten or twentty seconds to plunge from the tip of the highest arch to the Delaware River two hundred feet below. He closed his eyes and jumped, and when he finally opened them (five minutes later), he was floating, unassisted, ten feet above the water. It took him a while to realize that he had done it himself. It was just a fleeting thought during a moment of panic that caused him to come to a complete stop in midair.

The first thing Griff did when he learned to control his "gift" was to find his father and thank him for the abuse. What Griff did to him was legendary.

But that was then.

The migraines were usually a good indicator of an impending hallucination. The worst one involved a hooker they killed a few months ago. She ran around like a decapitated chicken after he shot her in the face. He had to blow her leg off to make her stop. And even that didn't kill her.

Something about her will to live pierced his thick skin and spoke to his vulnerable core. He remembered thinking that she was someone's daughter... or mother—an unassuming thirtysomething by day.

She looked a lot like the woman who stood in front of Walter Reilly's car. He had coaxed the officers to see this woman instead of Mary and her gun.

"Staaaayyy right where you are!" the voice behind Griff demanded.

With his concentration shattered, Griff took his eyes off Mary, Walter Reilly, and the two cops, and turned to confront the voice.

It was another cop. He was shaking like a leaf.

Griff couldn't help smiling.

Mary did a double take upon seeing the funny-looking man in the red Honda (Walter Reilly). His rotund face was flushed, as if he'd seen a ghost.

Mary checked her distorted reflection in his fender.

They could see her....

She whipped around and spotted Griff. He had just tossed a cop against a brick wall without touching him. Three more cops ran toward him.

Walter panicked at the sight of Mary. He stomped on the gas and rammed into the car behind him. Luckily, the old couple had already gotten out of their car to get a closer look at Mary. The old woman fainted after she slid her glasses up her nose and looked through them.

Mary charged the two cops just as they turned to see what it was that everyone was staring at. She swung her shotgun so hard that when the butt of it hit the second cop, he fell into a convulsive fit. She palmed the first cop's face and twisted. The initial SMACK from her palm sent the bridge of his nose into his brain. She flung him into Walter's car and climbed onto the hood.

Mary sunk into a stance and let her gun (an M-16) rip. Her upper body oscillated from side to side at her waist as she fired indiscriminately. She started at the three cops who had crept up on Griff a block away, then to the barricade two blocks down at Broad and Locust Streets.

Kagen and Derek picked off the scattered officers who lay in wait of a clear shot. Kagen was on the fifth floor of the bank at Broad and Walnut; Derek crouched on the roof of an adjacent building.

Rainah was a few blocks away, looking for a getaway vehicle. She could hear the ruckus coming from South Broad. The stampede of stuffed suits, designer markdowns, and slacker underachievers was moving her way fast.

Back on South Broad, the gunplay sent most of the bystanders scurrying. People were knocked to the ground and trampled. With all of the people in the line of fire, it was next to impossible for any of the cops to get a lock on Mary as she stood on the hood of Walter Reilly's red Honda and continued to blast away. Some of the more impatient cops returned fire with the same imprudence that Mary displayed.

Walter Reilly was curled into a tight ball behind his steering wheel as Mary's gun spit hot fire. He heard it click empty.

Mary tossed the gun down and leapt from the hood and onto the car beside Walter's. She leapt from that car to another, and another. She was headed toward a fire escape between two buildings.

People screamed and pointed. Helicopter blades chopped air as they darted in and out of the slivers of sky between highrise rooftops. Doomsday noises echoed down into the corridors of office buildings.

Griff hid behind a delivery truck and watched Mary scale the fire escape up to the first tier of a delinquent church that had become an office building across the street. A statue of the Virgin Mary on the roof of the building gave him an idea.

"Griff... you there?" Rainah's voice poured from Griff's walkie-talkie.

He snatched it from the inside pocket of his jacket.

"I'm here...."

"I'm on my way," Rainah said. "Look for a..."

"Brown minivan. I know."

"I'm three blocks away, on 17th and Sansom. But you probably knew that, too."

"Just wait for us there," Griff ordered. "There's too much heat on Broad."

"Watch your asses," Rainah replied. "I got two cops over here, snooping around. Looks like they're headed your way. Want me to take them out?"

"Are they onto you?"

"That's a negative."

"I wouldn't worry about it then. Griff out."

"Gotcha. Rainah out."

Griff coaxed to Mary, Derek, and Kagen simultaneously.

"*MJ... run to the skylight and be as still as you can. The rest of you get to 17ʰ and Sansom... brown minivan. I'll meet you there.*"

A manmade fog had begun to settle from the numerous engine blocks that had been battered by bullets. Some of them were on fire. Car doors were left wide open. From inside, stereos broadcasted "breaking news" reports of what was happening. Curious heads bobbed up from their hiding places to look around. The scene was one of mass panic.

"WHERE THE FUCK IS SHE? WHERE'D SHE GO?" a plainclothed detective yelled at Walter Reilly. He probably didn't mean to point his gun right at him, but knowing that didn't make Walter feel any better.

"Who?" Walter choked on his response. It wasn't what he meant to say.

Walter could see that the detective was running on rage. His eyes gave him away as they bullied Walter deeper into his seat, uncomfortable as it was.

Walter pointed to the fire escape.

The detective followed Walter's finger and traced the fire escape's zigzagging pattern up to the first tier of the building.

There was a statue—the Virgin Mary with her arms spread, hands upturned and beckoning.

The detective frowned. He turned to Walter and said, "Where?"

Walter shook his head without looking away from the statue. He couldn't shake the feeling that something was off.

"L... look! There!" Walter pointed at the church. "The statue.... Something's not right.... There's two of them."

The detective's gaze trailed Walter's finger. He noticed it right away, but it was the kind of realization that made him doubt what he saw. He took a second look... and that's when it registered.

One of the statues began to move. The image of the Virgin Mary melted away. In its place, Bloody Mary stood, looking down at the mayhem that she had caused. She could see the looks on people's faces as they tried to understand what they were witnessing. Their stupefaction was empowering.

The detective aimed his gun and fired. The sound startled Walter and hurt his ears.

Mary snatched a large handgun from the back of her waist and trained it on the detective. She felt the metal frame of the skylight balk under her weight.

*   *   *

Rebecca and Christina huddled closer under the bathroom sink, stirring with fear and guilt. They were under the impression that they had caused the havoc outside. Coming from West Philly, Christina had been through this type of thing before--the gunplay at least. Her mother had drilled her so often that she hit the floor after the first shot, Rebecca firmly in her grasp.

A long shadow evolved before their eyes, cast down on the linoleum floor by whomever it was that stood on the skylight above them and partially blocked out the sun. They had an idea who it was. According to the rumors at school, Bloody Mary would kill whoever was foolish enough to summon her in the mirror. Christina *used t*o think it was just a legend.

Mary's shaky balance rattled the skylight frame.

Rebecca and Christina were convinced she was coming for them.

The last time Rebecca saw her father, he was heading down to the first floor to drop off an overnight package. She closed her eyes and wished him back.

Mary came crashing down. She landed in a crouch, treated glass raining down on top of her. She whipped her head around and immediately saw the girls.

Rebecca refused to open her own eyes, but she could feel someone else's bearing down on her. She clutched Christina's hand as hard as she could.

Mary stood quickly, though it seemed to last forever to Christina, who saw the whole thing. She was breathing so fast. She didn't want to die.

"Is it her? Is she there?" Rebecca cried, tugging on Christina's arm.

Christina was too frightened to respond. She didn't even hear the question.

Mary returned Christina's scrutinizing gaze, then lunged forward, as if to say "What *the fuck* are you looking at?"

Christina flinched and hit her head on the sink.

"Christinaaaa! What's happening? I'm too scared to look!"

Mary reached down and snapped her kneecap back into place. It was twisted around completely as a result of the fall. Christina was reminded of a grasshopper.

Mary wiped the tiny shards of glass from her chest and shoulders and inadvertently spied the scribbled writing on the mirror.

Bloody Mary, it read.

Mary knew the game. She played it herself when she was a girl.

Rebecca forced her eyes open and lurched back, as if stunned by a massive electric current.

Mary bent over to meet the girls face to face.

Rebecca covered her eyes and screamed when Mary smiled at them.

Christina turned away and cringed at the sound of Mary's brittle flesh fighting to expand. No matter how hard she tried, she just couldn't scream. Her voice was gone, lodged somewhere in her chest.

The door to Dr. McCreery's office was in splintered chunks on the floor when the police finally arrived. Rebecca and Christina kept screaming about Bloody Mary. Dr. McCreery was able to calm them down when he returned from the lobby. Rebecca told him that Mary came through the skylight and smiled at them. "I thought we were gonna die," she said. "I closed my eyes and when I opened them, she was gone."

*　　*　　*

The crowd was localized in front of the building with the skylight on Broad Street. Derek and Kagen slipped in and out of sight on their way to the brown minivan parked on 17th and Sansom. Griff had ducked into an alley on 15th Street. He was concentrating with his eyes closed.

His mind's eye watched Mary running down a dark stairwell. He skipped ahead, down three flights and into the lobby of the building she was in. There were people everywhere rushing to get through the two revolving doors.

Griff moved up through the ceiling and onto the first floor. It was an open space littered with empty cubicles. Animated banners flashed from computer screens. Colorful webpages advertising designer clothing, celebrity gossip, and porn were left open for everyone to see. It appeared that people had left this place in a hurry. He traveled across the open room, looking out all the windows. There was one over by the drinking fountain that looked out onto the first level of a stacked parking garage across the way. Mary could hide in there and wait for them.

Griff coaxed a thought to Mary. *The lobby's hot. There's a window on the first floor. It's on the right, next to the water fountain. You should be able to get to the parking garage across the way. I'll guide you to us from there.*

Rainah was waiting behind the wheel when they arrived—first Derek, then Kagen, and finally Griff. They each climbed into the minivan and closed the door. Griff sat in the passenger seat. Derek and Kagen were in the back.

"Where's Mary?" Rainah inquired.

"Give me a minute," Griff responded.

Derek leaned toward Kagen and whispered. "Didju ever think... I mean, wonder if it's all bullshit?"

"No!" Griff responded before Kagen was able to. "And if you're seriously having thoughts like that, then you need to get the fuck outta this car!"

An immediate tension put them all on edge, unsure. Derek didn't know how to respond. He was waiting for Griff to smile and let him off the hook, but it wasn't happening. He was starting to get nervous.

Griff pulled the Glock from his jacket, turned, and pointed it over the back of the seat at Derek. The latch on the minivan door clacked, and the sliding door flew open by itself.

"Aw shit, man," Kagen said, squirming in his seat.

Rainah gasped and reached out to Griff. "Griff, don't! C'mon, man. He was only kidding."

"He wasn't kidding. Were you, Derek?" Griff said. "He's been having doubts for a while now. I gave him the benefit of the doubt because I thought he'd work that shit out. I guess I was wrong."

Derek looked genuinely confused. This was the last place that he expected to find himself. He thought they had a special bond... being that they were both black and all. He fished for an ally in Rainah or Kagen.

"Griff, this is *Derek* we're talking about," Rainah pleaded. "C'mon. He's *family*."

Derek lifted his hands as if to indicate surrender.

"It was just a thought, man," he said. "I'm sorry. I didn't grow up in it like you and Mary did. It... it can be a little overwhelming sometimes. That's all it was. I swear."

Griff stared. Derek was reluctant to keep looking him in the eyes, knowing what he could do. At the same time, he didn't want to look away and suggest disrespect.

"It won't happen again, Griff," Derek added. "I promise."

Griff waited a while longer before lowering his gun. The sliding door closed. The latch clacked in place. Griff turned around and faced forward.

"Make sure that it doesn't," he said to Derek.

Looking out the passenger-side window, Griff closed his eyes and guided Mary safely to the minivan. Because of all the activity on Broad, there was hardly anyone around where they were. The police were still combing through the building with the skylight and a few others on either side of it. The helicopters (two of them) were flying all around, looking down through the buildings. Griff had to carefully time Mary's movements.

"There she is!" Kagen yelled and pointed out the back window to the alley at the end of the block. Mary darted out of the alley and slid underneath a parked delivery truck.

"Let's go!" Griff ordered.

Rainah threw the truck in reverse and drove backwards to the end of the block. She pulled up next to the delivery truck. The sliding door opened. Mary climbed out from under the truck and jumped in. The door closed behind her.

"The subway entrance on 19th and Market," Griff said. "We've gotta get underground."

Rainah switched the gearshift to drive and stepped on the gas.

"Is it time?" she asked, nervous, but excited.

"Just about," Griff responded.

Derek peered out the back window as they drove. He was feeling contemplative, and a little emasculated. When the minivan turned onto Market, he could see the fringes of activity way down on 15th Street.

The minivan pulled up next to the subway entrance at 19th and Market. They sat still for a moment after Rainah shut off the engine. People were still heading toward 15th, but the crowd was sparse.

Griff ordered Derek to check the subway.

Derek got out and ran down the steps. The 19th Street platform was empty. He was halfway up the steps when air-raid sirens screamed. He stopped on the top step and looked up at the sky.

In the minutes that followed, buildings all around vomited out harried bodies faster than they could fit through the doorways. The revolving doors were already clogged with victims, yet some still tried to push... and push. People everywhere were looking up and pointing. Some of them were already starting to panic.

It both frightened and reassured Derek. He glanced over at the minivan. They were looking up through the windows. He could see tears in Rainah's eyes. Zeal shined through in the trembling smile on her face. He wished that one day he could be as certain as she was.

War

The first wave came from Russia and China, followed by nine straight months of bombing from both sides. As a result, entire cities lay in ruin.

Martial law was on its last legs, as the military no longer had the manpower to enforce it. Panic spread out from the larger cities. Growing factions of looters and roving thugs adopted a primal code of ethics as they chased the less capable survivors inland in search of food and shelter.

As a result, the Midwest became the flashpoint of a civil war.

Faced with imminent collapse, the United States launched a final assault on the heels of unsuccessful peace talks in Virginia. This time, the missiles carried chemical and biological warheads. The politicians claimed that Russia and China would eventually do it if we didn't.

Botulism toxin, Ebola, and smallpox laid most of Eastern Europe and Asia to waste.

It only took a year and a half.

Military scientists underestimated the scope of the residual effects, and eventually the toxic clouds covered the world, infecting every corner.

Epilogue

2004, Postwar Philadelphia

Linda Ludlow hustled down the hall and into her office in the old Philadelphia City Hall. What was left of the federal government made their Northeast headquarters there. With the different factions fighting for space, she knew it wouldn't be long before somebody else tried to take control of the historic building.

Linda slammed the door of her office shut and closed her eyes to remove herself mentally from the chaotic environment on the other side: anxious bodies scurrying to and fro with little regard for each other's personal space. She tapped the pointed tip of her prosthesis against the manila envelope that she held by her side. She was eager to see the photographs inside. An ambitious young reporter gave them to her in the ladies room. He walked right in while she was on the toilet and slid them under her stall. He told her that his friend (who worked as a cop in one of the federal communities) had traveled undercover with the Revenant Clan for two weeks... and that he sacrificed his life to get the pictures.

For your friend's sake, kid, I hope they're worth it, she thought.

Linda was momentarily startled by a woman screaming outside her door. It sounded as if she fell or was pushed. Gas masks were scarce these days, and some people weren't above stealing one from a friend or a family member. Reports were coming in that they'd be mandatory again by week's end. Linda kept her mask hidden above a panel in the drop ceiling in her office until she needed it.

On her desk lay a recently printed poster for the New Philadelphia News Organization (NPNO). The courier must have dropped it off while Linda was on undercover assignment in Washington. It took her a month and a half to wipe the images of those children's eyes staring at her through their gas masks from her mind. She felt guilty for leaving them in such a hopeless situation. After that experience, Linda swore that she would never do anything like that again. Her strength was in relaying information second- and third-hand. No more of this hero nonsense.

Linda held the poster up in front of her and smiled. The NPNO was her baby. She credited Tasha with giving her the strength to get it up and running.

"No time to celebrate, Linda," she remarked as she placed it back on her desk and gave it a tap.

She walked over to the window and reached into the folder.

The first photo was an overhead shot of the Revenant Clan's current base, an old military compound somewhere in Maryland.

The second photo was of the Clan in procession. It was an eerie sight, as it resembled the old animated film that Griff made her watch before the war. At the bottom of the photo, there was a figure circled in red ink.

Mary had people line up on either side to motivate her soldiers whenever the Clan passed through a town. The figure in question was leaning out of the crowd on the right side.

Linda lifted the photo up to her face and squinted. She felt an instant lump in her throat that was warm and heavy and threatening to cut off the oxygen to her brain.

She looked again to make sure she wasn't seeing things... that she really saw Tasha hiding in the crowd, draped in a wool blanket that she held over her head like a poor man's bonnet.

Linda could see in Tasha's face and neck that she had been rotting for some time.

Chemical/Biological Agents

• **Botulism toxin:** When inhaled, usually causes respiratory failure. Victim
  may seem fine up to 72 hours after initial contact with toxin. Toxin causes suffocation by
impairing nerves that control muscles needed for respiration. Can currently be produced in
large quantities.
  Fatal amount: One billionth of a gram
  Symptoms: Dizziness/euphoria, blurred vision, dry throat

• **Mustard gas:** A colorless, odorless liquid that, when inhaled, causes painful
  yellow blisters all over the body. Known to cause cancer of the skin, mouth, throat, and
  respiratory tract. Can currently be produced in large quantities.
  Fatal amount: One hundred milligrams
  Symptoms: Burning sensation in lungs, chest pain, watery eyes, itchy skin

• **Anthrax:** A bacteria that produces extremely resistant spores. When contracted
  either by touch or inhalation, spores produce a fatal toxin. Victim may not show signs for as
  long as six weeks after initial contact with spore (when inhaled.) Can currently be produced   in large quantities.
  Fatal amount: One billionth of a gram
  Symptoms: Flu-like symptoms, high fever, cough, fatigue, dizziness, nausea

The B Sides

Girl in the Cement Shoes

First of all, Arissa was high, high as a fucking kite, high as the invisible man in the sky who gave false hope to all the perpetual sleepers who settled for less and less until the once intangible notion of their own mortality crept up and ambushed them with the kind of doubts that always loomed in the background, like maybe that heaven and hell were a load of shit, and death was the absolute end.

Arissa wasn't that stupid. She was, however, a stoner. She knew it would color their opinion of her when she told the police what she had just seen. The only thing she knew for sure was that a dead woman killed her boyfriend Paul. Walked right up and planted an axe deep into that pretty face of his. He'd probably joke that it was an improvement. He was quite the fisherman, the kind who knew he was attractive yet still needed to hear it spoken aloud. It rubbed some people the wrong way, but then so did Arissa, with her manu-factured, wigger/granola/altrock-hybrid attitude, the dated tribal bands around her wrists, the Celtic charm dangling from her hemp necklace, and the nosering that everyone knew was fake. Arissa managed to get away with it, though. It worked for her. It was because she was so fucking beautiful.

Arissa saw the dead woman coming as they stood outside Paul's car. He was fumbling through his pockets for his keys (which were dangling from the ignition inside the locked car) and generally talking her ear off. Paul was a pretty deep guy, even if he was a little self-righteous. After three years, Arissa was pretty good at feigning interest, which was what she was doing when she looked up from the newspaper on the ground. The front page of the newspaper read **Natasha Armstrong Named as Suspect in Two More Murders.**

Arissa noticed the woman walking purposefully up Grays Ferry Avenue. She was a little on the thin side, but otherwise normal look-ing from about two hundred feet. There was something in her right hand.

Arissa squinted to see what it was while continuing to nod reflexively at Paul.

At one hundred and fifty feet, a few things were looking suspect to her. The woman's complexion was unlike anything in the usual spectrum, and she was so fucking thin, too thin to be standing on her own, or walking so deliberately, or carrying that huge fucking axe. And the way she moved: it was sensual, with its confident, stop-motion swagger. She wore a dress that hugged her torso down to the waist. The rest of it flowed and snapped in an artificial breeze that apparently only affected her, like some waterlogged, Spielbergian apparition given a comic-book makeover.

It was dark as hell on Grays Ferry Avenue at 11:17 PM that Tuesday, so what Arissa *could* see was vague at best.

The woman passed through a triangular area of light cast down by a street lamp.

What the... She looked like an irate corpse with hollow eyes, not quite skeletal, but certainly on her way there. Her brow was wrinkled in a distinct frown, teeth clenched. *Was she wearing a mask, or... or some kind of prosthetics?*

Arissa only managed a quick look before the shadows reclaimed the woman.

Was this some kind of hidden-camera stunt, another goddamned reality show? For a split second, she felt both violated and intrigued by the idea. Arissa dismissed all the Bloody Mary rumors at the watercooler, but in private, she derived guilty pleasure in the spooky vibe and the absurdity of it all. She didn't believe it for a second, though.

Bloody Mary was the first person Arissa thought of when she saw the woman in the light. And because it was simply not possible for what amounted to a zombie to exist, it had to be some kind of trick.

There was something very real about this, though. Something angry and intense worked with the menacing beat that energized the night as it poured from some anonymous car that was probably parked around the corner on Bainbridge.

There were two other people a block and a half away: a couple arguing over... it sounded like something mundane. Judging by their body language, Arissa guessed that they were married.

Paul babbled on, and Arissa watched as Mary (Arissa rolled her mind's eye every time the name arose) approached the married couple. When they saw her, the woman laughed. It was a nervous reaction, bursting from her lungs with the rush of breath that gave her shoulders a bounce, her opened hand finding her bosom. Backing away with cautious steps, the wife then threatened to use her purse as a weapon. She held it cocked behind her shoulder in a way that suggested a serious lack of coordination.

Mary didn't even break stride.

The woman shrieked out something that Arissa couldn't decipher and turned to her husband, but he had already taken off running.

Even though she was dead, Mary could still taste; right now, she was so close that she could savor the moment to come.

From where she stood some one hundred feet away, Arissa caught the lean of Mary's bony shoulder (back and to the right) and understood it to mean that she was about to lift the axe. The doomed woman fainted.

Mary stopped long enough to look down and back up, her attention redirected at Arissa and Paul. They were standing on the far north corner, where Grays Ferry and Bainbridge Streets met in a cock-eyed manner.

Arissa could see that Mary was livid, rage melting away from her rotten hue in rippled waves of heat distortion.

Not sure if she should flash a knowing smile and play it cool for the "cameras" or run for her life, Arissa froze. On the inside, she was all over the place, so distracted by the vast possibilities that she eventually panicked without making a sound.

To Paul, who was still digging in his pockets and prattling on from his soapbox, Arissa's silence simply meant that she was beguiled by his brilliance, as was usually the case in his mind. He hadn't even looked up at her or taken a breath in more than a minute. He liked to cast his gaze down as he ranted. When he did look up, he turned curiously to see what Arissa was looking at over his shoulder, and why her eyes had grown so big. It looked like it hurt her to keep them open that wide.

What Paul saw was the silhouette of a tall, thin, dead woman in mid-swing.

Arissa had no idea how many blocks she had run or how long she'd been hiding in the dumpster next to a bucket of stale coleslaw and what looked like a fetus in a clear plastic bag marked "BIOHAZARD." Her mind was busy rehashing the axe biting into Paul's skull, the sound of his body hitting the pavement, and Mary turning and walking nonchalantly away until Arissa called her a bitch (fucking bitch, to be exact). That stopped Mary dead in her tracks.

Mary whipped around, head and shoulders first. She was opening and closing her fist, as if trying to stifle something primal and destructive deep inside her. She threw down the axe and started coming after Arissa.

Arissa tried to get a good look at Mary's face before she ran so she'd at least have an idea of what she was dealing with. She wasn't ready to accept the truth. If only she could've seen her face, maybe she could try to reason with her... woman to woman... maybe something about sisterhood, and being givers of life, blah, blah, blah....

Arissa woke slowly, smiling, as if she'd forgotten everything. Her eyes crawled open to welcome the new...

Arissa shot up, hit her head on the dumpster lid, and fell right back on her ass. She sat still for a moment and listened. She heard an engine running and voices—two men, it sounded like. They were talking about pussy or... wait a minute... something about large bodies of water and shoes made of cement. Arissa was deathly afraid of large bodies of water.

Arissa slithered out of the dumpster and inched along the wall until she reached the mouth of the alley.

She peeked around the edge of the wall and saw two men

standing across the street, looking at her the way men usually did. There was an angry-looking black man with long dreadlocks, and a burly, middle-aged, whacked-out artist type with red hair pulled into a ponytail.

Arissa tossed the two men a polite smile. They were standing outside of an old piece-of-shit van—the kind with the bubble windows. Its sliding door was open halfway, but she couldn't see through the wall of darkness inside. Something about that just didn't sit right with her, so she decided not to ask them for help.

Startled by a noise from the building next to her, Arissa swung around and looked up at the sign on the front—Basile's Video.

She tried the door. Locked.

Well, of course it's locked, she thought. *It's almost midnight.*

There was a large window that looked into the place. Inside, a wall of television sets ran clips from recent home-video releases. Standing further back, cardboard cutouts of mass murderers, real and fictitious, were organized in a tight group. One of them held a sign promoting a documentary about serial killers and their effect on popular American culture.

Arissa could see a light on in the back. She stood on her toes to see over the shelves of DVDs that were in the way. Could've been nothing.

Across the street, bony fingers curled around the edge of the piece-of-shit van's sliding door and shoved it all the way open. Out of its black belly, two long legs covered in whisping fabric preceded Mary's dawning from the darkness. She stepped down and walked slowly up to Arissa, who was hypnotized by the rapid images and the hope that maybe someone was inside the video store.

Arissa didn't see Mary right away. Her reflection was right there in front of her, but Arissa was looking past it. The movement of her chest and shoulders as she took deep, furious breaths gradually gave Mary away.

Mary lunged as soon as Arissa spun around, and, clutching her by the throat, slammed her back against the window of the video store.

"Wait!" the man with the red ponytail called out to her. Mary stopped... and half-turned. She was clearly annoyed. "Sorry, MJ. Don't mean to interrupt, but maybe you could let us handle this one. I mean, you've already made your point with the boyfriend. No use wasting your time with this kid."

Without saying a word, Mary turned back to Arissa, who was trying to wriggle free from her grasp.

"Griff got me thinking about this phobia of hers," red ponytail commented. "Gave me an idea."

*   *   *

If there was one thing that petrified Arissa, it was large bodies of water. And here she was, at the bottom of the Delaware River, naked, save for some goggles, an oxygen tank, and her cumbersome new shoes. They were unlike any she'd ever owned: knee-high and made of cement, one solid block representing a pair.

"If it's any consolation, you'll be contributing to a work of art," red ponytail joked, as he shoved Arissa off the side of the pier, hands cuffed behind her. The rusted oxygen tank strapped to her back had fifteen minutes of air left in it. A waterproof light was taped across her chest. "Now make me proud."

She heard him remark to the black guy to "make it interesting" as she fell the fifteen feet into the river. "I wanna see real fear in those baby blues."

The water was freezing. Arissa hit the murky water and started sinking fast.

Red ponytail dove in and followed her down, snapping pictures along the way with the SL515 Reefmaster RC Underwater Camera that he swiped from the camera shop on 13th and Walnut, along with a shitload of professional photographic equipment.

Anchored down, yet floating, her hair lashing out, up, and to the sides in slow motion like tentacles, Arissa languished at the bottom. She was way past physical pain from the freezing water, from trying to force her hands through the cuffs, and from her new shoes. She was way past any sort of fear that she had ever known during her short life or even thought possible and was counting down the minutes (there were only seven left) until her inevitable end. Her mind played tricks on her as she faded in and out of shock. It conjured up vague monstrosities that darted in and out of the drab light's triangular reach, while larger ones remained just beyond it, suggesting what horrors might lie waiting in the darkness to devour her soon-to-be-lifeless body.

Right then, red ponytail snapped the last picture—an extreme close-up.

It was his favorite one, for now....

Mama's Boy-Toy…and the Nigga Inside His Head

"Yeah, there it is," Officer Frank Antonio de Mira smiled crookedly, half attempting to stifle it as he always did. The nightstick to which he referred slid gracefully across his palm, tickling the soft skin he was told was the sign of a lazy man, or a rich one. Squeezing his free hand shut, he made a fist and disregarded his momentary swim in the sea of self-pity. He continued the circular motion of his stick, which served as a sort of exclamation to the new authority issued along with his starched blues.

Was this the hunch they spoke of? Was it intuition? Or was it simply a dose of the usual paranoia that forced his eyes to the left, right, and, finally, to the kinetic giants above. Deep reds and yellows provided a rich backdrop for whatever it was the clouds were trying to convey. Like scrolling hieroglyphics, they suggested violent things—human-like shapes posing in positions that communicated horrible pain and anguish. They seemed almost deliberate, especially the eye he thought he saw blink at him.

Underneath the busy clouds, the air was still. De Mira labored to move in it. It was nothing so drastic as to call attention to itself, just a lag in real-time that affected every single thing but him.

On top of all that, de Mira felt like he was being watched. Usually, that feeling came with the territory, especially in the black neighborhoods. This feeling was different, though—more cerebral. There were no goose bumps as with the physical variant, no hairs standing on end. Yet it was strangely intrusive.

Mother???

Adjusting his gun like he always did when he was nervous, de Mira continued. He was certain he had already evacuated everyone in the area, but he wasn't about to hike back down the street and around the corner to the morgue just yet—not when he could clearly hear the echo of gunfire. Being the careful man that he was (his colleagues called it cowardice), de Mira convinced himself that the guys had the situation under control. He was usually lucky enough to find a similar loophole to exploit that kept him out of harm's way, and in Mother's good graces. Despite the effort he put into disguising his relationship with dear old mom, everyone knew that de Mira's balls rested snug in the gaudy, old, leather purse that never seemed to leave her wrist.

Maybe things would've been different had he been a she. Mother told him that she prayed throughout her entire pregnancy for God to give her a daughter. That was one of the weapons she used to get under his skin.

Perhaps things wouldn't have been so hard for him if his father hadn't committed suicide when he was eight years old. Mother blamed herself, and she blamed her child for putting too much strain on their relationship. She never told him that, but as a kid, de Mira could sense it. He never let on that he knew, just like with her habit.

Mother started taking pills after the suicide. At the time, de Mira thought it was a good thing. His uncle explained to him that the pills took her pain away. Her favorites were Vicodin and Percocet.

What they did was turn her into an addict. Deep down, de Mira resented Mother for what she'd become, and he resented her for bringing him down with her.

Intent on keeping him by her side as her health deteriorated, she used guilt to control every aspect of his life.

"Without me, you'd have nothing but the results of your bad decisions," she'd say to him. "If there's one thing you got from your father, it's the inability to do anything right."

Most of all, de Mira resented himself for falling into her trap time and time again.

If he didn't look so much like his father, Mother never would've talked him into sleeping with her. That was de Mira's biggest mistake. She held that over his head whenever she wanted something from him—which was just about every day. She would twist it to make it seem like he seduced her against her will.

As a result of all this, Frank Antonio de Mira was Mother's bitch, a thirty-three-year-old mama's boy through and through.

De Mira always wondered how he would have turned out had there been a male presence aside from the surrogate fathers who influenced what little masculinity he had from the other side of the 19" screen in his mother's bedroom. And there was God, who parented in absentia, or sometimes via his mother. She was good for barking scripture to excuse her questionable behavior—making him strip down to his undies and climb into bed with her whenever he wanted to watch TV, for instance. Hers was the only television in the house.

De Mira was thirteen years old when the idea of rebellion became more than just an idea. He was seventeen years old when his balls were finally big enough to inspire some action. He began acting out and using curse words like a sailor. He would stay out late without calling. Little shit like that.

He was twenty years old when he got into drugs. It started with weed. From there, he moved on to blow. He tried to hide it from Mother at first. One night, she got him so worked up that he told her. He said that she had driven him to it.

The next thing de Mira knew, Mother was coming right at him. She scratched and flailed at his face. She was crying and talking at the same time, warning him not to leave her like his father did.

De Mira shoved her to the ground. He didn't think he pushed her that hard.

Mother broke her hip in the fall. It was just his luck. She threatened to tell the police that he pushed her if he didn't lay off the drugs. And if he tried to leave, she'd tell them about the drugs.

After God, the police were the pinnacle of Mother's hierarchy of respect. She never passed up an opportunity to let de Mira know it.

Good ol' mom.

De Mira saw it as his destiny to become a cop. Now that his

authority exceeded Mother's, she couldn't tell him what to do. If she threatened to pull one of her trump cards, all he had to do was point to his gun and remind her of his access to a network of criminals and thugs who could make her body disappear without a trace. Not that he would ever entertain that line of thinking. Well, maybe.

So here he was, Frank Antonio de Mira, skirting his duty "to protect and serve." Again.

This time, it was something about people stealing cadavers. Dispatch said there were five of them. They were wearing gas masks to conceal their identities. All were heavily armed.

- 2 females (one 5'10" to 6'; the other about 5'5")
- 3 males (two 5'7" to 5'9"; the other around 6')

The thieves opened fire on the first unit that responded to the 911 call placed by a security guard at the morgue.

De Mira's unit was the fifth to arrive on the scene. The initial round of gunplay had died down by then, and there was some confusion about whether or not the suspects were still inside. Nevertheless, the police had the building surrounded. There was no way out.

De Mira's job was to evacuate the area. His partner, Officer Jack P. Davis, was assigned to keep traffic from turning onto the street.

De Mira was minding his own business, peering into cars that he had already checked, when he was suddenly overcome by a familiar scent. This scent reached beyond smell and worked its way deep into his subconscious mind.

He heard a voice in his head. *"Go on, say it. Who else could it be?"*

De Mira stopped in his tracks. Voices were nothing new to him. In fact, they were always there, usually some variant of Mother's tone reprimanding or berating him for something. But this was different. It was as if someone had switched inner narrators on him.

This voice belonged to a man whose laid-back, ethnically spiced cadence didn't fit any of the cast of usual suspects who populated de Mira's crowded mind.

"What's tha matter? You know I'm right," the voice added.

De Mira's head whipped back and forth, his eyes darting. He dropped his nightstick and drew his gun. Then he just stood there, holding the gun in both hands up against his clavicle. That was the way they used to do it on TV.

"If only you hadn't lost your temper, then maybe she'd be here to rescue you from all this. That's what you really want, isn't it?"

De Mira didn't know what to make of it. Was he losing it? Was it Mother somehow reaching out to him from hell... or wherever she was? But why would she sound like a black guy from the islands? Maybe he was a friend of hers, some poor soul suffering alongside her in hell. Had she finally overcome her prejudices in the afterlife?

De Mira stopped himself. He was getting carried away. He had an imagination on him that, when let loose, could run with the big dogs.

His partner, Officer Davis, was probably starting to wonder why he was taking so long. Their men were inside the morgue now. Word of it just came over his walkie-talkie.

There was sporadic gunfire, muffled by the old marble building. De Mira picked up as much as he could from his walkie-talkie. Between the shots, he could hear Sarge barking orders at someone.

"FREEZE! PUT YOUR HANDS WHERE I CAN SEE THEM! DOWN ON THE FLOOR NOW! I SAID 'GET DOWN!'"

There was brief commotion. And then, via their walkie-talkies, they described the scene to the men outside.

"Cadavers.... We shot at cadavers." *pssshhht...*

"Jeeeesus Christ! Jeeeesus fucking Christ!" *pssshhht...*

Then quiet.

"The suspects... whoever they were, they got away." *pssshhht...* "They got away right under our fucking noses!"

From the back: "That's impossible." *pssshhht...* "Unless they slipped out the front somehow." *pssshhht...*

From the front: "Not likely, asshole...."

From inside: "Knock that shit off right now and listen! The doctor here says they kidnapped one of his assistants—Hispanic female, about 5'6", one hundred and fifteen pounds, dark hair with blond highlights—along with the cadavers." *pssshhht...*

De Mira did the math and acknowledged the sum of her parts with a nod of approval.

From the back: "Come again? You say they have a hostage? How can that be? We had the place surrounded!" *pssshhht...*

From inside: "Just wait.... That's not all...." *pssshhht...* The voice spoke in short bursts as its owner tried to fit what he was seeing into some kind of rational box. But it just wasn't working. You could hear it in his voice. "Crazy fuckers arranged some of the cadavers to look like they're... doing shit." *pssshhht...* "I got a guy on all fours, bent backwards, his palms and feet planted on the floor; a woman straddling his stomach, leather belt for a bridle; she's holding on with one hand; the other is above her head, frozen, made to look like she's a bull rider. We got an obese woman. Jesus, she's huge." *pssshhht...* "She's slumped against the wall, her legs spread, an arm reaching out from her twat. Looks like it was cut off of another corpse and shoved inside her." *pssshhht...* "Holy Christ, this is all fucked up." *pssshhht...* "Bodies all over the place." *pssshhht...*

De Mira shuddered at the image that materialized in his head.

There was a sudden blast of music. It seemed deliberate, as if someone had cranked up the volume on a car stereo to get his attention.

De Mira spun toward the music. It was coming from the red Chrysler at the corner. The car was rocking back and forth. Its windows were completely fogged. He could've sworn he saw movement inside.

De Mira rested his hand on the butt of his holstered gun. He swallowed hard and approached the car. The Chrysler was hastily parked on the corner of Chestnut Street. De Mira stood on Walnut, a block away. Between them was Ionic Street, a tiny little dead-end block lined with dumpsters and ramshackle, cardboard domiciles. There was also a mural that covered the walls on both sides of the block colored in deep, psychedelic shades. The murals were popping up all over the place as part of the city's attempt to claim its own uniqueness and distance itself from its image as New York's envious younger stepsibling. The mural on Ionic Street was hands-down the best, with its surreal images and its overstated message that spoke of subversion and counterculture ideology. Although he didn't necessarily agree with the overall liberal tone of the piece, de Mira couldn't deny the artist's ability to get his or her point across through whacked-out visuals. It was a strange place to say the least, and he never passed without a quick inspection for the occasional new addition.

Walking at a snail's pace, de Mira began to close the distance. The heel of his sweaty palm pressed down on the gun-handle, fingers curled tightly around it and resting in their respective grooves. He reverted to his training to squelch the urge to turn and run the other way. It was his only link to anything resembling bravado.

Calm and cool. Ready for anything. Ready for anything. Ready for...

Anything but the muffled scream that came from inside the red Chrysler, as it continued to rock back and forth. Now that he recognized the song ("Dazed and Confused" by Led Zeppelin), de Mira told himself that it was probably just Robert Plant's wailing, even though the voice he just heard was distinctly (more) female.

The image in his mind (thanks to the scream, the rocking car, the fog-coated windows, and the overall atmosphere, which owed a good deal to the song) was that of gross sexual imposition. Maybe it started out consensual, or maybe... maybe it was the assistant from the morgue, the one who was kidnapped. In a few short moments, he was going to find out.

If de Mira had his way, he would be kicking back in a comfortable chair, reflecting on his college years, tame as they were. That's where the song tried to take him—to the days of youthful uncertainty, and marijuana. He never smoked it himself. Well, he took a hit but never inhaled. That was what he told Mother-dear when she confronted him, at least.

De Mira was about five feet away when the Chrysler stopped

rocking. There was no gradual slowing, no lingering bounce. It looked like an awkward freeze frame.

De Mira drew his gun in reaction and held it down by his side. He didn't want to make whomever it was feel threatened just yet, especially if they were armed. He always assumed the worst.

The music leapt out at him when the front and back doors swung open. The stench of sex followed closely behind it.

De Mira caught himself turning to flee and vetoed that action when he noticed that there was no one inside the car. It both frightened and relieved him. As he watched, the car seemed to celebrate a weight lifted from its bulk with a bounce. At first he thought it was the doors, but they were already wide open.

A sudden wind rushed by him. With it came the scent of cigarettes and body odor and the sound of muffled whimpering... and that voice....

"You shoulda just went about your way, mama's boy. Now you're gonna wish you never woke up this morning."

The voice was so obtrusive, so disruptive to his senses, that de Mira's reaction was to swat at it as if it were a fly diving in and out of his personal space. Then he raised his gun and tried to pinpoint the direction of the voice.

"Who are you?" De Mira said out loud.

"I'm the nigga who lives inside your head."

"Are you me? Am I crazy?"

"...No. And no. It's never as much fun when they think they're crazy. You're fine."

"Are you... God?"

"There is no God. Never was."

"Then who the hell ARE YOU??? What do you want?"

"I told you once already. I'm the nigga inside your head. And you brought this on yourself by interrupting me."

Standing there with his gun in his hand, de Mira felt incredibly vulnerable. His roving eyes spotted a reflection in the rear fender of the Chrysler. It looked like a dark brown man with long dreadlocks. He was holding a caramel-colored woman against her will. The woman was dressed in business-casual attire. The brown man held his hand over her mouth as she kicked and flailed. Heat-like ripples melted away from their bodies.

The assistant from the morgue, de Mira presumed.

He spun around and lifted his gun. His finger snaked around the trigger. He closed one eye to improve his aim. His heart was pounding in his chest.

There was no one there.

De Mira's eyes rolled back to the fender of the car. The reflection was gone.

"What's the matter, Frank? Scared? Well, you should be, because I know what you did to your mother. And I'm going to tell everyone."

De Mira gagged and began to cough. Suddenly, he had to pee. It had taken him an entire year to wash his mind of that image of mother gasping for air and reaching for the bubbling wound in her chest.

They'd put him away for good if they knew, maybe even give him the chair.

Good ol' mom. She was still affecting his life from beyond the grave.

The assistant screamed. It was coming from Ionic Street this time. De Mira was so focused on the car, and the voice, that he'd passed it moments ago without even noticing.

There it was again.

De Mira planted his feet and prepared himself to face it when a second voice emanated from the same area. It sounded like a person speaking through an electro-larynx. A third voice chimed in with its own artificial tone. One after the other, the second and third voices began to climb higher, repeating the assistant's despondent cry, until they reached a pitch closer to her own in what appeared to be an attempt to mimic it.

De Mira's first thought was to run. This was just too fucking weird and too much to deal with all at once. But that's exactly what

Mother would have him do, so he resisted.

De Mira gave his gun a reassuring glance, ran over to the wall of the old magazine shop at the entrance to Ionic Street, and planted his back firmly against it.

What would Ah-nuld do? Schwartzenegger was his favorite.

De Mira searched for a one-liner worthy of his hero. He closed his eyes and began to count, but then decided to go for broke, leaping out and pointing his gun....

"Don't mm... move, fff... ffuckers!" He stuttered when he was nervous.

What he saw reached down his throat and snatched his breath away.

There were two of them. They were huge, menacing. De Mira's eyes shot to the right, to where the larger one stood hunched, his arms down in front of him. The dreadlocked thing reminded him of the man he saw in the reflection.

Naked breasts and an abdomen peeked through the man's sturdy legs as he tried to subdue the assistant's flailing body. The handle of an oversized butcher's knife stuck out of his back pocket.

The other one looked like a Nazi mad scientist crossed with an emaciated, pallid form that looked like Nosferatu. A touch of a youthful Frank Gorsham gave him a comedic edge. He wore a white lab coat draped over bony joints. His bulging eyes changed colors as they spun. Minuscule round-rimmed glasses served no purpose perched atop his angular nose that pointed down to a shaky, spastic grin.

De Mira noticed puncture wounds on the assistant's upper torso and fresh bruises about her inner thighs and face. He also saw the look in her eyes as she stared up at the dreadlocked thing that held her.

And she saw de Mira, too. Judging from the look on her face, she seemed to measured him up and draw little faith in his ability to rescue her.

De Mira lifted his gun and struggled to control his trembling hands when he saw the oversized syringe that Sy-Fi (the name he gave the mad-scientist figure) lifted into view just before he thrust it into the assistant's belly.

The acoustics trapped the assistant's scream. It was much harder to bear at this distance. It surrounded de Mira and caused the narrow street to shrink, his muscles to fail.

A painful gulp to accommodate his chafed throat gave away his position.

Their eyes quickly found him.

Sy-Fi frowned, his bugged eyes spinning. He shared a silent moment with the dreadlocked one, whose gum-ridden smile stretched beyond the borders of the surgical mask that he wore.

Pinpoints of light fixed on de Mira from beneath slick shades. Sy-Fi held an exaggerated gun in its right hand. Only now that it was aimed at him did de Mira notice the mouth at the end of the barrel.

Strangely, de Mira could still hear the Zeppelin song in the distance. The instrumental interlude managed to fight its way through the mental mayhem to reach him.

"Don't waste your time tryin' to figure it out, mama's boy. There ain't no logical explanation for this shit." The gun spoke in a jive tone that suggested the '70s.

Realizing the width of the tiny street, de Mira yielded to a wave of claustrophobia. As he stood, straightening himself, readying to remove himself from the situation, a gust of hot air from behind lifted the hairs at the nape of his neck.

Fame Eats the Living

6:55 PM

They took her son Gary in '82. The crank calls and the low-rent thugs urged her to give herself up, but Joan wasn't easily frightened, thanks to her estranged father and his twisted XXX-rated morality. His late-night visits were like clockwork, usually during the late teens of every month, around the time her mother was on the rag. He liked to tie Joan down first to nurse her fear.

Joan was on the run. She had been wanted for murder for the last year and a half. As of this month, her motel-to-backseat-to-campground-to-stranger's-bed tour was nine cities strong.

She was running in part from the thing that looked back at her in the mirror when the pills and the booze wore off. It looked like a non-surgically altered, forty-two-year-old woman, which, by Hollywood standards, was damn near elderly.

Joan's was the same old story. She used to be a star. At the height of her fame, she pulled in ten million dollars per film—a first for a leading lady.

As a pre-teen, Joan was awkward. Her long face and wide mouth had yet to find a home on the rest of her underdeveloped body. She didn't know at the time that women spent an arm and a leg to get features like hers, but the fake versions never even came close.

In college, Joan wore her psuedo-feminist ideology on her sleeve. She wasn't above using her sexuality to get what she wanted, though. And she made no apologies for it.

In her prime, the long face made her a "unique beauty"; the wide mouth suggested something mischievous and titillating.

Now that mouth had deep creases in the corners. The long face had begun to droop. She was still able to make it work when she was up to trying. Most of the time, the pills and the booze kept her sedated, though.

You probably know Joan as Jacquelyn Marina. An old boyfriend picked the name from a romance novel. He said it sounded regal, like that of an old-fashioned screen siren. He even tried to sue her fifteen years later—some bullshit about copyright and ownership and intellectual property. *Imagine that,* she thought. *He thinks of me as property.*

Her films ran the gamut from Oscar-caliber tearjerkers to schlocked-out horror, although she shunned her early missteps once her career got going. Her biggest mistake was when she turned down one of the leads in some indie flick called *Dead Bitch Army.* It was one of those weird little films that somehow managed to gain a substantial cult following. According to her agent, it was strictly straight-to-video fare and would do nothing but mark her official induction into has-beendom. She would've fired him for it, but who else would have her at this point? To add insult to injury, they gave the role (of news reporter Linda Ludlow) to Joan's archrival.

Now Jacquelyn Marina went by Joan Smith for security purposes and peace of mind. She had been living under aliases for so long that she had forgotten her real name.

Leaving Jacquelyn Marina behind was the hardest thing she had ever done. It was harder than Gary's complicated birth—even harder than accepting his untimely death.

Ever since she was a child, Joan wanted nothing more than to be a star. She used to dream of the day when she would fight off the adoring fans. No waiting in line for a table or toiling at some insignificant job for minimum wage. She could finally tell her family to fuck off. They were always harping about practicality.

"Why don't you just grow up and get a real job?" her mother would say.

But her mother was the first person Joan called when she landed her first role in a big-budget studio flick. It was hardly the lead (she only had ten lines), but at least she could say that she had finally "made it."

"You hear what they're saying about my movie, mom?" Joan asked. "They're calling me a 'scene stealer,' and I've just been offered $100,000 for my next role. Now, how's *that* for a real job?"

Then she hung up the phone.

Seven years later, Joan was just about washed up. She hadn't had a good role in two years, so she was relegated to TV movies about single mothers in peril and failed sitcom pilots.

"Your problem is that you're still alive," her agent told her, more than half seriously. "Don't get me wrong, but people like you are better off dying young. You were a goddess, Jacquelyn.... Look at Marilyn, or Elvis.... You think they'd be where they are today if they stayed alive? I don't think so. Dying young is where the money's at. It's actually not too late, you know. I'd consider it if I were you."

Joan received the first brochure on a Saturday afternoon—a glossy foldout for the Post-Hollywood Retirement Community (PHRC). She remembered that it was a Saturday because Gary's father had just dropped him off for his visit. The arrangement was every first and third weekend.

It was a mysterious place, the PHRC. The brochures painted it as some kind of seaside resort, but it was all a front for Hollywood's top-secret relocation program.

According to the rumors, it was located somewhere in the Philippines—a maximum-security compound surrounded by razor-wire fences and guard towers. Certain celebrities were sent there after the studios faked their deaths. Even with its ominous reputation, the PHRC wasn't without its own level of prestige, as only a select few celebrities were considered for the program or even knew about it.

Joan had seen the list. It was full of familiar names like Elvis Presley, Jimi Hendrix, James Dean, Marilyn Monroe, Bruce Lee, and John Fitzgerald Kennedy.

There was a rumor that Liz Taylor was once targeted. Supposedly she won her freedom during a late-night poker game between Hollywood heavyweights.

Joan began to fear for her safety. The studio was trying to pressure her into signing the PHRC contract. Running seemed like her only option. It was only a matter of time before they'd resort to smear campaigns or try to take her by force.

Most people don't realize just how the studio system works. Fact is, they own you once you've signed on the dotted line. It was more obvious in the golden age, when people were less cynical and easier to dazzle with technical sleight of hand.

Once they had you in their database, they could use your image however they saw fit. Some people equated it to having one's soul stolen. Currently, the procedure was disguised as CGI motion-capture sessions. They already had Joan's image on file from the sessions she did for *Lady Terminators* a few years back.

Joan was a mess. She hadn't washed in two days and hadn't eaten in more than a week. She was down to her high-school weight, which her agent would call a plus.

"Maybe you haven't been keeping up with the buzz, honey, but you could stand to lose a few pounds," he told her whenever he caught her eating. At her heaviest, she weighed one hundred and twenty-seven pounds. She was 5'8".

"Maybe you haven't been keeping up with the buzz, but you're an ASSHOLE!" Joan would reply. She always wanted to call him a faggot, but she was afraid he'd run to the press and have her labeled a homophobe. That, or being pegged as an anti-Semite, was the kiss of death in Hollywood.

What was it about October that always had Joan feeling down in the dumps? Maybe it was the heavy orange mood that the dying leaves and the naked wooden giants by the roadside bestowed on the mind. Even the lower mammals, to whom daylight seemed an aphrodisiac, lost their voracious appetites. A few stumbled about lethargically, full bellies adding a waddle to their step as instinct guided them to bed for the approaching winter.

Joan pulled the shades closed and plopped down on the stiff bed. Either too firm or too soft: there was never a middle ground with motel beds. She laid back, hands behind her head, and stared at the stucco ceiling. Two years ago, she would have begged for a moment like this, but now the moments passed so slowly that even a half hour seemed like an eternity. And all she could do was dwell on her situation.

She thought about Kevin, the photographer she met in Philly while she was there shooting a movie about a government agent on the run from an unseen antagonist.

Joan laughed at the irony. In the movie, the antagonist turned out to be the Mafia.

She could tell that Kevin was starting to believe all the hype about her, or at least he suspected that some of it was true. The studio was trying to tarnish Joan's image by depicting her as an out-of-control heroin addict, when she had never even tried the stuff.

It was in all the tabloids, though. You could usually find it next to a photo of her that was edited and retouched to plant suspicion. Tabloid TV shows called her a fallen star who'd do anything for attention. They ran docudramas and exposés that exaggerated her drug use and her dysfunctional relationship with her family. They aired fake surveillance footage of Joan storming out of rehab and shooting a pharmacist point-blank when he refused to give her what she wanted. They did all they could to ruin her.

7:20 PM

Kevin was supposed to arrive no later than 7:00.

It was just like him to keep her waiting. Joan pictured his boyish smile and those biceps that never failed to get her going. Maybe he had given up on her. There was something about the way he reacted when she told him the truth about the business and about the PHRC. She could see that his eyes wanted to roll in disappointment, but instead they darted around the room as if he had simply lost interest.

Joan reached for the remote and turned on the TV. She half-expected to see some distorted photo of herself plastered across the screen. Instead, it was Desirée Chang, the Asian reporter who was in fact the whitest-acting bitch on TV.

"In case you have just tuned in, I am standing outside of the Hello Motel in Valley Forge, Pennsylvania, where the body of Gary Rowen was found propped up in front of a television set while a VCR played a continuous loop of his infamous mother's films. Gary Rowen, as you know, is the son of Jacquelyn Marina, who is currently wanted for questioning in two unrelated murders."

Joan switched the channel and threw the remote across the room.

"GODDAMN YOU!" she yelled.

When she finally settled down, Joan heard…

"*Is it true that Joan molested her own son as well?*"

She looked up in time to see the pudgy woman in the studio audience sit down as the talk-show host turned to the panel of gossip columnists onstage for a response.

In a rage, Joan sprung up and kicked the TV from its stand. It landed with a BANG and tumbled into the wall. A low hissing sound indicated that it was still functioning.

Whoa, Joan! Calm down, she told herself. *We weren't going to let them get to us, remember? It's probably just another one of their tricks.*

Joan sat down on the bed and massaged her throbbing foot.

The phone rang. She jumped, startled.

Probably Kevin calling to say he can't make it. He was the only person who knew the phone number there.

She took a deep breath. "Hello?"

"Hello, Jackie." The prim-and-proper tone reminded Joan of her Aunt Madeline and those dreaded finishing lessons. "You know, you're only making things more difficult for yourself."

Joan lowered the phone, closed her eyes, and nodded to escape the surge of raw emotion that she knew would affect her speech.

Her tired eyes rolled over to the clock radio as it blared to life. She hadn't changed the alarm since yesterday, when the rain sang her to sleep early in the afternoon.

The radio played some old-school hip-hop tune: not the soulless, chorus-to-chorus commercials for base sensibilities and knuckle-dragging mental machinations that infected the airwaves all too often, but something born of passion and real talent. It was moody, with dense bass, deep like rolling thunder; it seemed at first to be an instrumental piece until she heard a voice creeping. It reminded Joan of an old John Carpenter score vomited from a mind mired in deep, dark urbania.

"What are we going to do with you, Jackie?"

"I'll tell you what you can do. You can go FUCK yourself! That's what you can do." Joan was careful not to spit it all out at once.

"Sounds to me like you're at the end of your rope. How much longer can you live like this, Jackie? You've got no money, no friends, no place to call home. It's such a shame to see talent like yours wasted. Maybe you weren't aware that you would receive a healthy percentage of whatever your image brings in. Better to just come back and let us take care of your problem."

"How? By sending me to the PHRC? No thanks. It's time the public saw you people for what you really are. Even if it takes me 'til my last breath, I'm gonna be the one to bring you murderers down. And you can keep your money. I've been letting that rule my life for far too long."

A smart-assed snicker from the other end found its way beneath Joan's thick skin.

"And exactly how do you plan to pull that one off, Jackie? You think that tape you stole from research is going to convince anyone? They'll laugh you out of the studio faster than you can say alien autopsy."

"I'll find a way. You hear me? And when I do, we'll see who's laughing."

Joan slammed down the phone down and backed away. She hurried over to her duffel bag and checked for the tape: an orientation video for PHRC employees. Thank God it was still where she left it.

The phone rang again.

Joan slapped the receiver from its place and watched it bounce on the stained, paisley comforter.

"Now, Jackie, that wasn't very nice, hanging up on us like that." The condescending tone spilled out of the phone and snatched away what was left of Joan's resolve. "You aren't going to make us come looking for you, I hope?"

The four walls seemed closer than ever before when Joan looked up. She scanned the small room as if she expected a good response to suddenly materialize from thin air. The phone was still lying on the bed, facing up.

"Jaaaackieeeee.... I know you're still there. I can hear you breathing."

Usually, Joan found it therapeutic to bear down on her bottom lip and move her teeth from side to side, but now she was drawing blood.

Joan cupped her hand over her mouth and cursed the pain quietly.

The sound of keys jingling on the other side of the door gave Joan a rush of adrenaline. She waited, but as usual, the sound faded down the hall and took her enthusiasm with it.

Joan grabbed the phone, hurled it against the floor, and stomped it to pieces.

If there was one thing Joan despised, it was men who lie... especially when they do it with smiling pseudo-sincerity. When Kevin would lie to her, his drooping, vulnerable eyes made her buckle every time, to her own disgust.

Maybe *they* had gotten to him? Maybe they convinced him that she really was a murderer... or maybe they just killed him and made it look like she did it.

Joan struggled to stay awake, but she found herself dozing. She wanted desperately to fall asleep in Kevin's arms and not alone in this hellhole. He was always telling her how sexy she looked when she slept.

CLICK! SSSSHHHHHHHH....

From the floor, the television roused Joan from her catnap. It lay on its side, propped against the far wall.

She checked to see if maybe she had rolled onto the remote. Then she remembered that she had thrown it against the wall earlier.

Joan watched as a static-ridden picture materialized on the cracked screen.

It was a parking lot. Four vaguely recognizable figures approached a pastel-colored staircase. Three of them wore paramilitary gear and gas masks. The leader was a tall, thin woman who looked like a corpse. Behind them, a sign reached up into the purple sky: **Harlequin Motor Lodge.**

Joan glanced knowingly and with great trepidation at the end-table. Her room key rested on top of it. The bright red tag on the keychain seemed to laugh in her face: **Harlequin Motor Lodge, Room 38.**

12:15 AM

Muffled voices leaked through the thin wooden door to Room 38. The "38" reminded Kevin of Joan's tits, which were 38Ds, and he smiled.

The room was empty as far as he could tell. He noticed the television lying broken on the floor.

What the hell? Though it initially raised suspicion, Kevin knew Joan's temper well. She was a spitfire.

Kevin placed the television back onto its wobbly stand and headed for the bathroom door.

"Joan," he called out. "Are you in there, babe?"

He waited a few seconds and then opened the door.

Nothing.

It was just like Joan to leave him hanging. Maybe she was trying to get back at him for not showing up when he said he would.

Touché, I guess. Kevin shrugged. He tossed his jacket on

the bed and took a moment to drink in the room.

He winced at the paisley design, then at the wallpaper, and, finally, at the raggedy, orange shag carpet.

"Could you have possibly picked a seedier place, babe?" he commented to himself.

At least there would be no explaining to do until she returned. Maybe he'd have enough time to come up with a good excuse. Kevin had been mulling over whether or not he should just level with Joan about how he really felt. He was afraid it would be too much for her right now, but enough was enough. Of course she'd accuse him of being a coward, like her father, who abandoned her when she was old enough to realize what he'd done and too big to pin down so easily.

Kevin checked his watch—12:35—and sat down on the corner of the bed. He looked for the remote, hoping to catch the last quarter of the Bulls game. He watched the first half in a bar two miles down the interstate. He decided he needed a scotch before heading over to see Joan.

That damned Jordan, he thought with a boyish grin. *I could watch him all day.*

"What's the world coming to when a guy has to get up to turn on the TV?" Kevin remarked, half-jokingly.

He pulled the knob and was greeted by a screen full of snow and a lightning-bolt crack right down the middle.

"Aw, c'mon. Don't tell me…."

Kevin spun the knob until it popped off in his hand. As far as he could tell, there was snow on every channel.

"Goddammit Joan!" He tossed the knob over his shoulder and pouted. "No TV, no Bulls game...." Then he glanced at the empty bed. "No pussy."

Guilt kept him from pursuing the barmaid that he traded stares and innuendos with all night at the bar. His erection threatened to explode from his jeans when she invited him to her place to watch the stars... and the sunrise at dawn. If Joan found out, it would crush her. He knew that he was all she had.

Kevin considered masturbating, but there was no telling when Joan would return. What if she caught him in the act? That's just what he needed.

He grabbed a pack of Salem Lights from his jacket pocket and started for the front door when he heard a voice break through the interference on the TV.

"Thank God," he grumbled, as the snow gave way to a clear picture. *Hopefully the game is still on.*

Kevin searched for the knob as Desirée Chang babbled something about a murder. It went in one ear and out the other. He flipped through the channels carefully: 3... 5... 6... 7... 9... 11. Desirée Chang's chubby face greeted him from each channel.

"You gotta be kiddin' me," Kevin whined, backing away to make sense of it.

"To recap our top story, actress Jacquelyn Marina and her photographer boyfriend Kevin Reynolds were found dead in her room at the Harlequin Motor Lodge earlier this evening. As of this moment, police are calling the mysterious deaths a murder-suicide, but they aren't yet ruling out foul play on the part of an unknown third party."

Kevin felt the warmth drain from his body. A familiar feeling crept up his spine and pressed his shoulders. It was the same feeling that kept him from screaming when he was held up at gunpoint last summer. He still hadn't recovered completely from it. Only now, he wished it was something as tangible as a man with a gun.

A crime-scene photograph of the two of them, dead, laying side by side and naked from the waist up, was plastered across the TV screen. The rest was hidden beneath the stained, paisley comforter. Their faces and genitals were pixelated, but Kevin could still see the blood that pooled around both of their heads... and he saw the gun that dangled from Joan's dead fingers.

Kevin peered slowly over his shoulder at the bed. He yanked the comforter back and recoiled at the dried blood on the pillows. It was darker (almost black) at the spots where their heads had rested in the photograph.

"OH MY GOD!" He lurched and bolted for the front door.

He yanked it open and stopped short as he was met by a tall, thin woman slathered in hastily applied latex foam. He immediately recognized her from the *Dead Bitch Army* series. This incarnation of the title character appeared to be from one of the sequels, as her look lacked the impact it had in the original. Part three was considered the low point of the franchise. That was the one where they ruined everything by making Mary speak.

"You must be Kevin," she said in a dry, hoarse tone that was only slightly louder than a whisper.

Before he could answer her, she casually unholstered a shotgun that was strapped across her back and squeezed off a shot at Kevin's face.

Gone was the gunshot's metallic ring from the original. The signature sound harkened back to the old spaghetti westerns. Instead, the gunshot sounded flat, without vision, more like an explosion.

Even Kevin could tell the difference.

A Good Ol' Fashioned MindPhuck

Laughter played on a continuous loop in Duncan's mind as he crouched stiff and ready outside the abandoned church. According to the informant, it was where Kagen came to work on his "art."

While his head rang with laughter, Duncan's eyes saw beyond the here and now to a stock memory of his wife Tina's radiant smile, the subtle purse of her lips, and her flowing brown hair. It was the only way to circumvent the cerebral slideshow of Kagen having his way with her before he finally ended her life. The images had been haunting him since Tina disappeared.

Duncan talked himself calm.

"This is for you, Tina," he whispered to the sky and skulked around the building to a boarded-up window on the left side. He had decided that it was the easiest way to gain access to the place when he surveilled the old church last night.

He got down on his knees and used a hunting knife to work the first board loose. It was easier than he thought. As a result, Duncan applied too much strength and flung the board at himself. The board hit him in the face and landed noisily at his feet. He took a moment to focus the pain away. Blocking out physical pain was relatively easy.

The board didn't just hit the ground and stop, either. Because he was trying to be quiet, it flipped and bounced before coming to a stop. Things always seemed to work out that way.

Duncan worried that he had given away his position. He was counting on the element of surprise to give him an advantage. Kagen was a crafty bastard. There was no telling what he'd have waiting in store if he knew that Duncan was coming.

Duncan froze and waited for something to happen. He had his hand on his gun.

Nothing.

He crawled closer to the window and worked a second board

loose, then a third. He could see inside now.

There was an altar buried beneath layers of dust and cobwebs. A large stained-glass window loomed over the altar from behind. There were no denominational insignia or religious fixtures. The pews were much the same. The homeless people who called the abandoned church home before Kagen came along had used some of them as beds. There were various articles of clothing, sheets, blankets, and strange keepsakes to remind them of the lives they once had. Trash-picked food containers, empty cigarette packs, and bottles of booze decorated the floor beneath the converted pews.

This would be Duncan's last chance to avenge Tina. He was taken off the case last week and suspended from the police force just yesterday when he refused to obey repeated orders prohibiting him from following the case. At the station, there was a man in custody who had done time with Kagen in Holmesburg Prison. Before he left, Duncan forced the man to tell him what he knew. That was how he found out about the abandoned church. Duncan broke the man's arm and jaw in the process of getting him to talk. They later found him unconscious in his cell. When he woke up hours later, the man told Duncan's colleagues what had happened.

Duncan knew that he didn't have long before his partner (former partner) came looking for him. The rest of his colleagues wouldn't be too far behind. Duncan felt that he had a moral obligation to keep the promise he made to his wife. It was magnified by the guilt he harbored for allowing her to be kidnapped in the first place.

*   *   *

There was a sudden jolting sensation. The sleeping hand left the warmth of its resting place, unwillingly, a victim of reflexes. The humid air turned cold against its sweaty palm. Searching for comfort, the five-headed thing moved clumsily, without sight and sound, knowing only touch.

*   *   *

So far, Third Eye established two names—Duncan and Tina. As usual with her visions, Third Eye's point of view was bordered by a heavy blur that occasionally bled into the frame and distorted the already fractured images even further. She was used to that kind of thing at this point. She was also used to the abrupt leaps in time and the shifting environments. One minute, she was outside in an open field with the sun smiling down on her, and the next, she was in a dank, abandoned church.

A sudden ripple distorted her view. It was as if a channel had been changed in the fabric of reality.

Third Eye was inside the church. She could see Duncan standing in the center aisle. He was facing a second man who stood up on the altar with his arms outstretched and his legs crossed in a mock-crucifixion pose. As he was positioned in front of a large stained-glass window at the back of the altar, the harsh sunlight kept Third Eye from distinguishing the second man's features.

The second man's right arm twitched and coughed a small gun up from the cuff of his sleeve. He swung his aim and stopped on Duncan.

Duncan snatched his gun from the holster and aimed back. Now they were locked in a stand-off.

It struck Third Eye that she had seen this church before— possibly in another vision. A second later, she forgot about it. This was fast becoming a vicious cycle, and even the realization of that was no more than a fragmented hint snatched away as quickly as it had revealed itself.

A curious heap called Third Eye's attention to the floor at the left of the second man's feet. It was a large burlap sack, like a heavy-duty laundry bag. Something was stuffed inside. She wasn't sure if it belonged to the second man or one of the church's former occupants.

A waterlogged voice came out of nowhere. It belonged to the second man, only his mouth didn't synch with the words. It was clear that he had spoken them, but there was a lag.

"If it's your wife you want, pig, you're too late," the second man said in a too-low tone to Duncan.

Third Eye caught a quick glimpse of the second man's face as he stepped briefly out of and back into the light. He was a big, burly man with a red beard and red hair pulled into a ponytail. His eyes looked like they hurt when he had to keep them open all the way, so he squinted.

Third Eye switched her focus to the filthy, sweat-soaked hair that clung to the back of Duncan's neck like some fibrous cephalopod embracing a victim much larger that itself. The pattern looked interesting to her. She moved down to the burlap sack on the floor. She had completely forgotten about it until she saw it again.

These visions... they had a way of changing the rules on the fly. Third Eye never knew what was coming next. She kept thinking of the word "pig," but she didn't know why until...

Blazing white letters sliced like noisy slivers of light through the dusty layer of her vision and spelled out the word **POLICE**. The letters materialized on the back of the navy-blue jacket that hung from Duncan's broad shoulders. Most likely, they had been there the entire time. That was just how the visions worked. They seemed to have a mind of their own sometimes.

"Where is she, Kagen? Where's Tina?" Duncan said. His voice was affected by the same tone-lowering qualities as the second man's. Third Eye assumed that the second man's name was Kagen.

"She was a good fuck, you know," Kagen replied, "right up 'til the end."

Duncan struggled to maintain some sense of composure. His hands were trembling. Tears welled in his eyes. Large beads of sweat raced side by side down his face. Salty trails marked their paths.

"You've got ten seconds to tell me where she is, you son of a bitch, or, God help me, I'm gonna put yer fucking brain all over that window!"

"You kill me and you'll never find her... *officer*."

Kagen's flippant tone cut deep. Duncan wanted to curl into a tiny ball and cry until the pain went away. He kept coming back to the promise he made to Tina. It didn't matter that he never actually said it to her.

"Just tell me she's alive," he cried.

"Would that make you feel better, pig? Would it comfort you to know that she's still hanging on after all the nasty little things that we did together? I don't know, we got pretty down and dirty. I'm not sure I'd want her back if I were in your shoes."

"STOP PLAYING GAMES AND TELL ME WHERE SHE IS!!!" Duncan roared, taking a few steps forward.

Kagen met his forward motion by equal steps backward.

"Unh-uh…. Don't you come any closer," he warned. He kept his gun trained on Duncan as he crouched and grabbed the wrinkled lip of the burlap sack. "I'll take my bag here and go, and you'll never find out what happened to your pretty little wife."

The bag…. Suddenly, Duncan needed to know what was inside it.

The suspense devoured Third Eye.

"Wait! Stop!" Duncan barked. "What's in the bag?"

Kagen's features melted into coyness.

"That's a good question. Let's see."

Kagen stuck his arm inside. He had to tug at whatever it was before he was able to pull it out of the burlap sack. It was a human head: a female's, with brown hair that appeared to have been carelessly hacked off on one side when her head was severed from her shoulders.

Judging from the way that Duncan crumbled to the floor, the head must have belonged to Tina. She was pretty in a wholesome way. Her eyes stared straight ahead through half-closed eyelids. Her mouth was closed and twisted into a painful grimace. Drying blood decorated the rims of her nostrils. A dried trail of red-black ran from her ear down to the frayed edges of her mangled neck. There were sections of the woman's hair where dried, matted blood began to crack and fall like deep red dandruff.

Tina looked familiar. Somehow, Third Eye knew her when

she was alive. Her mind shuffled through images of corpses in poses: some familiar, some totally alien to her. She was beginning to see a pattern, maybe even a reason....

But then it was all snatched away.

Third Eye had never experienced a vision like this before. It was so vivid, so collectively palpable to all the senses. They were usually more fragmented, not like this fleshed-out scenario. It played out like a story on television.

Clutching her hair in his fist, Kagen held Tina's head out in front of him.

Duncan was completely overcome. His mouth hung open, but no sound was coming out. His eyes were almost equally wide. He was on his knees, bouncing at the mercy of raw emotion, and trying to catch his breath. His arms were too heavy to hold the gun anymore, so it lay on the ground between his knees. He didn't even care that Kagen was still aiming a gun at him.

He looked up slowly and landed face to face with his wife. In Duncan's eyes, she was alive again. Her skin was supple and plump. Her complexion was beaming. She looked like she did when they first met. That was when he loved her most, before the resentment, sarcasm, whining kids, extra pounds, boring sex, and the pointless arguments that lasted for days took over.

First she smiled, then she frowned at him. It was a confused frown that pained him to see. It was the kind of look that compelled a guy like Duncan to do everything in his power to make it all better.

Duncan saw the head speak to him. "What did I do wrong, honey? Wasn't I good enough for you? How could you let this happen to me?"

Kagen hid his face behind Tina's hair and mimicked her voice. His impersonation was laughable, but Duncan was so distraught that he bought it without question. Anything was better than accepting that his wife was dead.

"You told me that you would never let anything happen to me, honey. You told me that you would always protect me."

Duncan's mouth bobbed open and closed. He had the most horrible look on his face. He was shaking his head "no" to Tina's questions.

"I'm s… so sorry, baby," Duncan mumbled through the saliva and tears. "I… I never shoulda left you alone. My God, I'm so, so sorry."

Duncan sank to his ass. His shoulders drooped. He let his head slump forward. There was nothing else to do but cry like a baby, so that's what he did.

"What's-a-matter, honey? Is it too much for you too handle? WELL WHY DON'T YOU TRY LIVING IN MY SHOES! YOU HAVE ANY IDEA WHAT IT'S LIKE TO HAVE YOUR HEAD CUT OFF WHILE YOU'RE STILL ALIVE? NOT JUST ALIVE, BUT COMPLETELY AWARE OF WHAT'S HAPPENING? WELL? DO YOU?"

Duncan put his hands up over his head, as if to defend himself from Tina's" aggression.

"You've got time for everything when it comes to your fuckin' job. But far be it for you to fit your wife into that tight schedule of yours. Hell, I might as well have recited my vows to my fuckin' vibrator. Do you remember what that marriage counselor said, Duncan? He said you were going to have to make a choice between your job and your family. Do you remember that?"

Duncan began to reply.

"Well, I guess you made your choice, didn't you, Duncan? But don't worry yourself about me, hon. Now I got a man who understands how to treat a woman." She half-turned toward Kagen. "Isn't that right, babycakes?"

Kagen leaned in and planted a long kiss on Tina's chapped and cracked lips.

Duncan snapped. He was watching through his arms as the image of a healthy

Tina withered in layers before his eyes. Her alabaster hue turned brown and desiccated. The light in her aquamarine eyes dimmed and took all moisture with it.

Duncan felt his body go numb. He looked down and saw the floor rising toward his face. Or maybe he was falling. Everything went black.

He woke up to the sound of his own heavy breathing and nothing else. He looked toward the altar and saw Kagen dancing around with Tina's face held against the crotch of his pants. When he was done, he tossed it to the floor like it was refuse.

Duncan wasn't looking for it when his eyes spotted his gun on the floor, just out of his reach. He extended his arm and reached forward with his fingernails. He slid his fingers around the handle of the gun and yanked his arm straight. Kagen was rifling through the burlap sack when Duncan locked him in his sights. But then he saw Tina. Her head lay on its side. Her eyes were open and looking right at him.

Duncan blurted out a loud whimper. He looked down and appeared to share a prolonged intimate moment with his gun before turning it on himself.

He squeezed his eyes shut and pulled the trigger.

*   *   *

Third Eye awoke in a stupor. She lay momentarily frozen, her sweaty palms clutching her nightgown, which too had been dampened. The shock of being jarred awake was amplified by the intensity of the vision. Together, they left her loopy, like when she had jet lag.

Who the hell am *I?*

Third Eye sat perfectly still on the edge of the bed and searched the room for clues. The room was white, with concrete walls and no windows or doors. A plush robe was draped over the back of a chair in the corner. A starched business suit was laid out neatly across the arms of the chair. There was a dresser on the other side of the room with a mirror built into the top of it.

She lifted herself from the bed and crept, stupefied, over to the mirror. The sight of her reflection would do the trick.

Third Eye gasped at the woman in the reflection. It was Tina, that man Duncan's wife from the vision. A jagged line began to materialize on the left side of her throat. It traveled across the front and around back until the two ends met. Blood began to pour from the jagged line like a faucet had been turned on full blast. Her head bobbled, then tumbled forward.

Just then, a brilliant explosion of colors snatched away the ghastly sight and replaced it with infinite black.

Muffled voices from somewhere above spoke a familiar name.

"Heavenly Father, please accept the soul of Tina Gordon, beloved wife and mother, as we return her body to the earth from whence it came."

Tina tried to scream, but she had no voice. Her Third Eye closed forever.

Andre Duza lives in Philadelphia with his wife and three sons. He is currently at work on his second novel, "JESUS FREAKS (jç'zes frçks), n. see Zombie," an apocalyptic zombie epic, and a graphic novel, "Euphoriac," with artist, Silverfish.

Visit Andre's Website

www.houseofduza.com

ABOUT THE ARTISTS

Bill Balzer: A New York based digital illustrator, conceptual, storyboard, texture, and trained comic book artist. Bill illustrated cards and various characters for a developing boardgame tentatively titled "Zombie, The Board Game."

Visit him online at: *www.billbalzer.com*

John Dunivant: A Michigan based commercial artist (who also illustrated the cover).

Visit him online at: *www.theatrebizarre.com*

Brenda Wilkinson: "Been drawing and painting for as long as I can remember, but nothing professional. I enjoying giving life (or death) to the images in my husband's head."

Rich Larson: Minneapolis-based Rich Larson draws babes and monsters for fun and profit. Ten collections of his work with airbrush artist Steve Fastner have been published, including the three-volume "Haunted House of Lingerie."

Silverfish: "Born and raised in the Houston, Texas area. Visited Florida a couple of times. Not very comfortable outside during the day. Not fond of Texas summers. Worked in the food service. Drawing since I was 7, when I received a sketchpad for Christmas. No formal art training. Started reading about art history recreationally at age 17. Most influenced by painters Theodore Gericault and Rene Magritte, illustrators Stephen Gammel and Edward Gorey, comic book artists, and the sculptures of ancient Greece."

Visit her online at: *www.angelfire.com/scary/silverfish370/*

Bizarro books

CATALOGUE – SPRING 2006

Bizarro Books publishes under the following imprints:

www.rawdogscreamingpress.com

www.eraserheadpress.com

www.afterbirthbooks.com

www.swallowdownpress.com

For all your Bizarro needs visit:

www.bizarrogenre.org

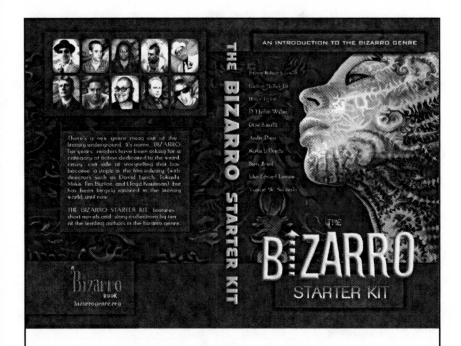

BB-0X1 "The Bizarro Starter Kit"
An introduction to the Bizarro genre

There's a new genre rising out of the underground. Its name: BIZARRO. For years, readers have been asking for a category of fiction dedicated to the weird, crazy, cult side of storytelling that has become a staple in the film industry (with directors such as David Lynch, Takashi Miike, Tim Burton, and Lloyd Kaufman) but has been largely ignored in the literary world, until now.

THE BIZARRO STARTER KIT features short novels and story collections by ten of the leading authors in the genre: D. Harlan Wilson, Carlton Mellick III, Jeremy Robert Johnson, Kevin L Donihe, Gina Ranalli, Andre Duza, Vincent W. Sakowski, Steve Beard, John Edward Lawson, and Bruce Taylor. Get the perfect sampling of Bizarro for only five dollars plus shipping.

236 pages $5

BB-001 "The Kafka Effekt" D. Harlan Wilson - A collection of forty-four irreal short stories loosely written in the vein of Franz Kafka, with more than a pinch of William S. Burroughs sprinkled on top. **211 pages $14**

BB-002 "Satan Burger" Carlton Mellick III - The cult novel that put Carlton Mellick III on the map ... Six punks get jobs at a fast food restaurant owned by the devil in a city violently overpopulated by surreal alien cultures. **236 pages $14**

BB-003 "Some Things Are Better Left Unplugged" Vincent Sakwoski - Join The Man and his Nemesis, the obese tabby, for a nightmare roller coaster ride into this postmodern fantasy. **152 pages $10**

BB-004 "Shall We Gather At the Garden?" Kevin L Donihe - Donihe's Debut novel. Midgets take over the world, The Church of Lionel Richie vs. The Church of the Byrds, plant porn and more! **244 pages $14**

BB-005 "Razor Wire Pubic Hair" Carlton Mellick III - A genderless humandildo is purchased by a razor dominatrix and brought into her nightmarish world of bizarre sex and mutilation. **176 pages $11**

BB-006 "Stranger on the Loose" D. Harlan Wilson - The fiction of Wilson's 2nd collection is planted in the soil of normalcy, but what grows out of that soil is a dark, witty, otherworldly jungle... **228 pages $14**

BB-007 "The Baby Jesus Butt Plug" Carlton Mellick III - Using clones of the Baby Jesus for anal sex will be the hip sex fetish of the future. **92 pages $10**

BB-008 "Fishyfleshed" Carlton Mellick III - The world of the past is an illogical flatland lacking in dimension and color, a sick-scape of crispy squid people wandering the desert for no apparent reason. **260 pages $14**

BB-009 **"Dead Bitch Army"** Andre Duza - Step into a world filled with racist teenagers, cannibals, 100 warped Uncle Sams, automobiles with razor-sharp teeth, living graffiti, and a pissed-off zombie bitch out for revenge. **344 pages $16**

BB-010 **"The Menstruating Mall"** Carlton Mellick III *"The Breakfast Club* meets *Chopping Mall* as directed by David Lynch."* - Brian Keene **212 pages $12**

BB-011 **"Angel Dust Apocalypse"** Jeremy Robert Johnson - Meth-heads, manmade monsters, and murderous Neo-Nazis. "Seriously amazing short stories..." - Chuck Palahniuk, author of *Fight Club* **184 pages $11**

BB-012 **"Ocean of Lard"** Kevin L Donihe / Carlton Mellick III - A parody of those old Choose Your Own Adventure kid's books about some very odd pirates sailing on a sea made of animal fat. **176 pages $12**

   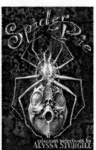

BB-013 **"Last Burn in Hell"** John Edward Lawson - From his lurid angst-affair with a lesbian music diva to his ascendance as unlikely pop icon the one constant for Kenrick Brimley, official state prison gigolo, is he's got no clue what he's doing. **172 pages $14**

BB-014 **"Tangerinephant"** Kevin Dole 2 - TV-obsessed aliens have abducted Michael Tangerinephant in this bizarre combination of science fiction, satire, and surrealism. **164 pages $11**

BB-015 **"Foop!"** Chris Genoa - Strange happenings are going on at Dactyl, Inc, the world's first and only time travel tourism company. "A surreal pie in the face!" - Christopher Moore **300 pages $14**

BB-016 **"Spider Pie"** Alyssa Sturgill - A one-way trip down a rabbit hole inhabited by sexual deviants and friendly monsters, fairytale beginnings and hideous endings. **104 pages $11**

BB-017 "**The Unauthorized Woman**" **Efrem Emerson** - Enter the world of the inner freak, a landscape populated by the pre-dead and morticioners, by cockroaches and 300-lb robots. **104 pages $11**

BB-018 "**Fugue XXIX**" **Forrest Aguirre** - Tales from the fringe of speculative literary fiction where innovative minds dream up the future's uncharted territories while mining forgotten treasures of the past. **220 pages $16**

BB-019 "**Pocket Full of Loose Razorblades**" **John Edward Lawson** - A collection of dark bizarro stories. From a giant rectum to a foot-fungus factory to a girl with a biforked tongue. **190 pages $13**

BB-020 "**Punk Land**"   **Carlton Mellick III** - In the punk version of Heaven, the anarchist utopia is threatened by corporate fascism and only Goblin, Mortician's sperm, and a blue-mohawked female assassin named Shark Girl can stop them. **284 pages $15**

   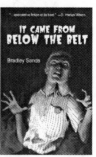

BB-021 "**Pseudo-City**" **D. Harlan Wilson** - Pseudo-City exposes what waits in the bathroom stall, under the manhole cover and in the corporate boardroom, all in a way that can only be described as mind-bogglingly irreal. **220 pages $16**

BB-022 "**Kafka's Uncle and Other Strange Tales**" **Bruce Taylor** - Anslenot and his giant tarantula (tormentor? fri-end?) wander a desecrated world in this novel and collection of stories from Mr. Magic Realism Himself.   **348 pages $17**

BB-023 "**Sex and Death In Television Town**" **Carlton Mellick III** - In the old west, a gang of hermaphrodite gunslingers take refuge from a demon plague in Telos: a town where its citizens have televisions instead of heads.   **184 pages $12**

BB-024 "**It Came From Below The Belt**"   **Bradley Sands** - What can Grover Goldstein do when his severed, sentient penis forces him to return to high school and help it win the presidential election? **204 pages $13**

BB-025 "Sick: An Anthology of Illness" John Lawson, editor - These Sick stories are horrendous and hilarious dissections of creative minds on the scalpel's edge. **296 pages $16**

BB-026 "Tempting Disaster" John Lawson, editor - A shocking and alluring anthology from the fringe that examines our culture's obsession with taboos. **260 pages $16**

BB-027 "Siren Promised" Jeremy Robert Johnson - Nominated for the Bram Stoker Award. A potent mix of bad drugs, bad dreams, brutal bad guys, and surreal/incredible art by Alan M. Clark. **190 pages $13**

BB-028 "Chemical Gardens" Gina Ranalli - Ro and punk band *Green is the Enemy* find Kreepkins, a surfer-dude warlock, a vengeful demon, and a Metal Priestess in their way as they try to escape an underground nightmare. **188 pages $13**

BB-029 "Jesus Freaks" Andre Duza For God so loved the world that he gave his only two begotten sons... and a few million zombies. **400 pages $16**

BB-030 "Grape City" Kevin L. Donihe - More Donihe-style comedic bizarro about a demon named Charles who is forced to work a minimum wage job on Earth after Hell goes out of business. **108 pages $10**

BB-031 "Sea of the Patchwork Cats" Carlton Mellick III - A quiet dreamlike tale set in the ashes of the human race. For Mellick enthusiasts who also adore *The Twilight Zone*. **112 pages $10**

BB-032 "Extinction Journals" Jeremy Robert Johnson **104 pages** - An uncanny voyage across a newly nuclear America where one man must confront the problems associated with loneliness, insane dieties, radiation, love, and an ever-evolving cockroach suit with a mind of its own. **104 pages $10**

   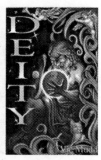

BB-033 "Meat Puppet Cabaret" Steve Beard At last! The secret connection between Jack the Ripper and Princess Diana's death revealed! **240 pages $16 / $30**

BB-034 "The Greatest Fucking Moment in Sports" Kevin L. Donihe - In the tradition of the surreal anti-sitcom *Get A Life* comes a tale of triumph and agape love from the master of comedic bizarro. **108 pages $10**

BB-035 "The Troublesome Amputee" John Edward Lawson - Disturbing verse from a man who truly believes nothing is sacred and intends to prove it. **104 pages $9**

BB-036 "Deity" Vic Mudd God (who doesn't like to be called "God") comes down to a typical, suburban, Ohio family for a little vacation—but it doesn't turn out to be as relaxing as He had hoped it would be... **168 pages $12**

BB-037 "The Haunted Vagina" Carlton Mellick III - It's difficult to love a woman whose vagina is a gateway to the world of the dead. **132 pages $10**

BB-038 "Tales from the Vinegar Wasteland" Ray Fracalossy - Witness: a man is slowly losing his face, a neighbor who periodically screams out for no apparent reason, and a house with a room that doesn't actually exist. **240 pages $14**

BB-039 "Suicide Girls in the Afterlife" Gina Ranalli - After Pogue commits suicide, she unexpectedly finds herself an unwilling "guest" at a hotel in the Afterlife, where she meets a group of bizarre characters, including a goth Satan, a hippie Jesus, and an alien-human hybrid. **100 pages $9**

BB-040 "And Your Point Is?" Steve Aylett - In this follow-up to LINT multiple authors provide critical commentary and essays about Jeff Lint's mind-bending literature. **104 pages $11**

BB-041 "Not Quite One of the Boys" Vincent Sakowski -While drug-dealer Maxi drinks with Dante in purgatory, God and Satan play a little tri-level chess and do a little bargaining over his business partner, Vinnie, who is still left on earth. **220 pages $14**

COMING SOON:

"Misadventures in a Thumbnail Universe" by Vincent Sakowski

"House of Houses" by Kevin Donihe

ORDER FORM

TITLES	QTY	PRICE	TOTAL
Shipping costs (see below)			
TOTAL			

Please make checks and moneyorders payable to ROSE O'KEEFE / BIZARRO BOOKS in U.S. funds only. Please don't send bad checks! Allow 2-6 weeks for delivery. International orders may take longer. If you'd like to pay online via PAYPAL.COM, send payments to publisher@eraserheadpress.com.

SHIPPING: US ORDERS - $2 for the first book, $1 for each additional book. For priority shipping, add an additional $4. INT'L ORDERS - $5 for the first book, $3 for each additional book. Add an additional $5 per book for global priority shipping.

Send payment to:

BIZARRO BOOKS
C/O Rose O'Keefe
205 NE Bryant
Portland, OR 97211

Address

City   State   Zip

Email   Phone

Printed in the United States
146780LV00004BC/1/A